BETWEEN MOONS

CLAIRE ANDERS

A CIP catalogue record for this book is available from the British Library.

Published by TLC Publications Ltd

Cover Design by MiblArt

ISBN 978-1-8381777-4-4

For Irene, who shares my love of books,
and Evie, who loves a good story.

"Dort, wo man Bucher verbrennt, verbrennt man am Ende auch Menschen."

"Where they burn books, they will, in the end, also burn people."

Written by Heinrich Heine in 1821

1

AUGUST 1943 - FRANCE

"*Go.*"

Her eyes closed, Marlene had been blocking out the red light in front of her. She had not wanted to see it turn green. She had been waiting for the signal; one tiny word that would change everything for her. This time, there would be nothing to cushion her landing, no instructor with encouraging words; just the opened canopy above and the reception team below.

The roar of the plane's engine silenced and she leapt out of the plane into the dark skies above France.

The buffeting wind whistled in her ears, and an invisible force slammed into her stomach, knocking the breath from her body. Grabbing with both hands, she searched for the straps of her parachute, and fought to steady her breathing.

Her eyes adjusted to the darkness. The river beneath her was inky black, separated from the night sky by a silver strip of light cast by the full moon. To the east of the river, lights flashed indicating her landing zone. A gust of wind caught her parachute and dragged her out of the path of the light.

The flashing lights became smaller as the glistening water below was replaced by dark, rough shadows.

Marlene pushed down her nausea and focused on steadying her flailing legs. She glided for only a few seconds before trees rushed towards her and branches attacked her body. A thick branch scraped along her arm. Her hand instinctively flew towards the searing pain, and the warmth of her blood seeped between her fingers.

Her feet smacked the ground and forced her forwards onto her elbows. Her parachute hung above her, tangled amongst the trees, and Marlene battled frantically to free herself. With one arm loose and voices now approaching, Marlene froze.

Her heart in her mouth, Marlene's eyes darted around her. The voices were French and they were close. Foliage to her left rustled and two men stepped towards her. The taller of the two was broad and sturdy and led the way. His shirt hung below his sweater and thick braces held his trousers in place. One trouser leg was tucked into his boot; the other was loose and long.

"Welcome to France," he said as he set about untying her from her parachute. "I'm Etienne."

Marlene simply smiled, unsure of what to say or do.

The shorter man, still tall to Marlene's five foot four frame, stood in front of her. He was equally broad, but his sturdiness came from excess weight. His dark, slicked-back hair emphasised the roundness of his face.

"I am Henri. I am your field contact. How was your landing?" He looked at the blood that now covered her arm and hands.

Marlene smiled, trying to make the best of it. "Oh, it was rather undignified, I'm afraid. I drifted off course."

"Yes. Parachuting at night is difficult, even for trained

agents. It's not something journalists should be doing. Are you injured?" asked Henri.

"No. Nothing more than a cut," she replied, choosing not to react to his obvious criticism.

"Good. In that case, let's keep moving. The others will be ready to go now," he said, glancing at Etienne, who was still pulling at her parachute in an attempt to dislodge it from the tree.

Marlene sensed Henri's further criticism. *The other passenger had obviously landed where he was supposed to.*

"There isn't time, Etienne," Henri warned. "We'll have to leave it."

"We can't. If the Germans find it, they'll tear this area apart looking for her. It's snagged on the branches. I'll get it."

Etienne climbed a few feet up into the tree. He tugged the parachute and dragged it nearer to them, then pulled out a pocketknife and began hacking. He climbed further up, cutting at the silk as he went until he was finally able to release it, leaving only thin shreds of orange behind.

"It will have to do," Etienne said, and closing his knife, he shuffled clumsily back down.

Etienne balled up the parachute, and they hurried through the trees. As they traversed the dense woodland, Marlene concentrated on matching her steps with the two men ahead of her, stepping into the areas their boots had already flattened.

They had not walked far when her foot clipped Henri's and she crashed into his back. Henri and Etienne had stopped. Henri turned and, with his finger to his lips, told her to be quiet. Marlene stared into the clearing ahead at the outline of vehicles and people.

Then she heard it.

The harsh, guttural sound of the German accent.

Henri motioned for her to turn and go back the way they'd come. Marlene's senses heightened. Her ragged breath echoed like drumbeats and each careful step crunched the vegetation underfoot. *Surely the Germans must hear that.* She wanted to scream and run.

Henri pulled lightly on her shoulder, telling her to stop. Listening intently, they were met only by silence. Etienne stepped around them both and whispered for them to follow him, leading them into even heavier woodland. After a while, his hand came up, and they stopped. All Marlene could hear was a rustling, like dry autumnal leaves interrupting the path of the night wind.

The others obviously thought differently. They removed handguns from their belts.

Seconds later, the German voices reached her. They had to be looking for them.

With another change of direction, the Frenchmen set off again, Marlene close on their heels, before pausing again to listen. A voice boomed nearby and they took off again. This time they ran, the forest thrashing around them. Henri came up beside Marlene and seized her arm, pulling her along.

The muscles in her legs ached, and her frenzied breathing stung her throat. They were still following Etienne when Henri hauled her off to the side. Etienne ran straight ahead and disappeared into the darkness.

When they finally stopped, Henri pulled her down behind an enormous oak tree. The earth to one side of the tree had fallen away, leaving exposed roots with space enough for them to hide.

Etienne reappeared soon after and crouched down beside them. "I've cleared another path," he said between short, gulping breaths. "Hopefully they will take the bait and follow it."

They sat, their backs pressed against the great oak's roots, and fought to control their wheezing. A twig snapped in the gloom and Marlene's gut twisted. Henri's grip tightened on his gun.

A beam of light shone overhead, lighting up the darkness in front of them.

Marlene pulled her knees closer to her chest, took a deep breath and waited.

2

SIX MONTHS EARLIER - FEBRUARY 1943, LONDON

JOLTED AWAKE BY AN INCESSANT THUMPING ON HER FRONT door, Marlene pulled the blanket she had been wrapped in for days further over her head.

"Go away," she whispered, squeezing her eyes shut.

It worked. The banging stopped and silence returned— but only momentarily.

"*Marlene!*" came a thundering voice from the other side of the door. "I know you're in there! I won't leave until I see you."

"Go away!" said Marlene, loud enough this time for her uninvited guest to hear.

"I will not!"

She smiled, untangled herself from her blanket and padded to the front door in stockinged feet. She hesitated, then resigned herself to the fact that she would have to let him in.

"Fletcher," she said, stepping aside to allow her boss into her flat.

Fletcher burst in with the same confidence he applied to

every situation. If Marlene had not allowed him in, she knew he would have found a way in anyway.

Fletcher had worked for *The Post* as a journalist for many years before he became the editor. Marlene could easily see he'd once made a talented journalist. He had a natural charisma that could disarm even the frostiest of people, causing them to reveal far more than they probably wanted to. His once black hair was now a dark grey with white flecks like cigarette ash. Despite his slackening jaw and widening waist, traces of the handsome man he used to be were still visible, which Marlene did not doubt had helped him to get a story or two in the past.

Fletcher looked her up and down with obvious distaste. "I don't pay you to lounge around here feeling sorry for yourself," he said. "Sure, you've had a shock—it's a tragedy, really —but you're young. You can't let this be the end of you."

Marlene sat and wriggled back under her blanket, her thumb pressing against her wedding ring. "Really, Fletcher? I buried my husband two weeks ago and you're telling me *not* to feel sorry for myself."

Fletcher wasn't listening, which suited Marlene because it meant he had also stopped talking. He picked up a glass vase of purple crocuses that her next-door neighbour had given her. The woman somehow kept colour in her garden all year round and frequently dropped not-so-subtle hints that Marlene should get some gardening gloves and plant a few bulbs to break up the bleak shrubbery that adorned her own front garden. The crocuses had withered a week ago, and the browning petals dropped onto the carpet as Fletcher touched the glass.

He strolled around her room, collecting coffee-stained mugs as he went. With five mugs dangling from his fingers,

Fletcher headed to the kitchen. Marlene closed her eyes and tried to drown out the clanging of dishes.

When Fletcher returned, he pulled a crumpled light blue shirt from the back of her chair, tugging it out from under her shoulder. "Not your usual style."

Marlene didn't tell him she had tried on all of Peter's clothes to try to find ones that still smelled like him.

"He's not attached to those shirts, you know."

Perhaps she hadn't needed to tell him. Marlene wondered if he had done the same thing when his wife had died.

"You need light," Fletcher announced. He marched over to the window, yanked back the heavy curtains and pushed open the small top window.

The light stung her eyes, and she tucked her blanket under her chin. The air wasn't fresh; it was just cold. The cold air tickled the inside of her nose and the scent of her neighbour's coal fire, like stale cigar smoke, caught in her throat.

"So, how are things?" he asked.

Marlene frowned. "I don't feel him around. Not here. Not at the cemetery. He's just *gone*. How can that be?"

"It was just his time." Fletcher's tone softened as he sat down opposite her. "You have to understand that. Have you been eating?"

"A little."

"A little is not enough. Why don't we go out and get some lunch?"

"I'm fine here, thanks."

"Clearly," said Fletcher, sarcasm evident by the word itself rather than the tone. "Haven't your friends been able to drag you out, at least?"

"What friends? Turns out they were all Peter's friends. I've seen none of them since the funeral."

"Any word from your brother?"

Marlene shook her head.

"Does he know?"

"I expect not. I don't know where he is to tell him." Marlene sighed, picked up a tin box from the floor in front of her and flicked through the envelopes inside. She'd received a letter every other month from Benjamin. He wrote with updates about their grandparents' farm until he'd announced he'd sold it. After that, months had gone by between letters. Nothing was dated, so she could not be sure when he had written it, and the postmark was different on each one; various parts of France, mostly, and a couple of letters from Spain. On the rare occasion he'd included a return address, Marlene had written back, but she had no idea if they had reached him before he'd moved on again. None of his letters mentioned anything specific in her letters, so she suspected not.

Marlene pulled an envelope out. "September last year was the last letter."

"He'll get in touch soon." Fletcher smiled. "We miss you at work."

Marlene couldn't bring herself to look at him in case his eyes displayed the same pity as his voice. She knew that would make her angry or make her cry, and she didn't want either.

"I doubt that very much," she said cynically.

"That's true. You are the misjudgement of my career."

Marlene looked at him and tried to feign shock, but only ended up laughing.

"That's better," Fletcher said. "Now, what's a man got to do around here to get offered a cup of tea?"

"I can give you coffee, but I have no milk left," Marlene said, making no attempt to go and make it.

"Is that because you've run out or because you haven't been to collect your rations?"

Fletcher pulled Marlene to her feet and pushed her towards the kitchen. As she busied herself with the coffee, he tidied around her. He ran water to wash the cups he had brought through earlier and the plates that had been sitting beside her sink for days. He wiped the surfaces under each dish he moved into the sink.

"You've done that before," Marlene said.

"Have to now."

She winced. Of course he had, given that he now lived alone. Her colleagues had told her he'd come into the office in the months following his wife's death looking like he'd slept in his clothes. Fletcher himself had even made jokes about not yet being used to the iron. Now, she was sure he was sleeping in his clothes.

Marlene laid two cups of coffee and a tin with a few spoons of leftover sugar on the table and sank into a chair. "When does it get easier?" she asked.

"In time. It just sneaks up on you."

She sighed, sipped her coffee and allowed its heat to travel through her for a few moments of warmth. "Peter was my whole reason for being here. What do I do now?"

Fletcher joined her at the table, tipped some sugar into his cup and stirred. "He might have been the reason why you're in London, but that's all. The only thing you can do now is get on with things."

"With what? We had plans before, but everything just feels wrong now. I don't know what I'm supposed to do."

"Give yourself time to heal. Then, if you don't feel you're on the right path, find a new one."

"Being with Peter *was* my path."

"Well, you're not on that one anymore. You followed Peter here and slotted into his life. Now you need to find the courage to decide what it is that *you* want to do with *your* life."

Marlene contemplated this for a few moments and shook her head. She wasn't ready for this yet.

"How's Peter's mother coping with all this?" Fletcher asked.

"I ... I don't really know, to be honest. Better than me, I expect."

"You haven't seen her?"

Marlene flinched, and her cheeks burned. "Not since the funeral."

She and Mary had never been close, but the woman had been her strength in the days leading up to the funeral. She'd thought Mary had been interfering at first, as she was prone to doing, but with a couple of weeks of perspective, she'd realised that Mary, like herself, had needed to keep busy. Without Mary checking on her, Marlene doubted she would have coped by herself.

But she had yet to return the favour for her mother-in-law.

The house on Durie Lane where Mary lived looked tired and each of the four windows had the curtains drawn. Before Peter's death, Mary had visited Marlene and Peter's flat almost every day, whether or not Peter had been home. As a result, Marlene couldn't remember the last time she had been at Mary's house.

Marlene knocked hard on the front door to make sure

Mary heard her, since the living room was at the back of the house. She knocked again and pressed her ear against the door, listening for movement inside.

"You won't find her in on a Thursday, love," said Mary's neighbour, locking his front door. "She goes down to Cameron Hall on Thursdays. It's where all the womenfolk gather to complain about us men," he said, chuckling to himself.

"Of course," said Marlene. "I forgot it was Thursday."

"Young lass like you shouldn't be forgetting the days of the week. That's for oldies like me," he replied.

"Tough week," she said to his back as he sauntered away up the street.

Marlene perched on the wall opposite Cameron Hall, her long coat stopping her from feeling the freezing concrete beneath her. She watched her breath fogging in front of her face for half an hour. She couldn't bring herself to go into Mary's social club, so she waited outside until the doors of the social club were finally flung open and women streamed out in small groups, chatting and laughing. Ignoring the curious glances in her direction, Marlene kept her head down and watched for Mary. She was eager to avoid conversation, particularly the well-meaning but patronising conversation she'd seemed to have with everyone at Peter's funeral.

Mrs Hopeton, the self-appointed club leader, came out last and locked up the hall. Marlene scanned the chatting women again, thinking she must have missed Mary leaving.

"Hello, dear. How are you?" said Mrs Hopeton, who was now only a few paces away. "It's nice to see you out and about. You're a little late for today if you were thinking about coming back to join us."

Mary had insisted upon Marlene joining her social club. She'd told Peter that it would be good for Marlene to meet some new people. Marlene had indulged Mary for a few months so as not to cause any problems for her husband. She tolerated her mother-in-law showing her off, exaggerating everything she knew about her and talking about her as though she wasn't there.

Peter had known Marlene wasn't happy and that she'd found it awkward. She was the youngest person in the hall by quite a few decades, and that was before they'd conscripted all the younger women to join the war effort. He eventually told her to stop going if she wanted to. Mary had taken it well; so well, in fact, that Marlene could tell Peter had done some groundwork with her.

"No, I wasn't coming back. Well, not today. I was hoping to catch Mary," Marlene said awkwardly.

"Oh? Well, we haven't seen Mary here for the past couple of weeks. Joyce went to see her, but she seems to have taken it really hard, her only son being gone. Of course, you know that, dear. We haven't been able to get her out yet—or even get in, for that matter," Mrs Hopeton said.

The club leader rambled on about how upsetting Peter's death had been for Mary. Another group of women headed towards them. Marlene gave her apologies and slipped away before she was forced to speak with anyone else. She could do without people prying for the sake of gossip.

Marlene rifled through the drawers in the kitchen, searching for Peter's key to his mother's house.

After what had felt like an impossibly long journey back to her mother-in-law's home, Mary still hadn't answered, not even after a second battering at the door and Marlene yelling through the letterbox.

Unsuccessful but undeterred, Marlene had returned home in search of the key. Only one further obstacle remained: they had never had to use his key, so she didn't know where Peter had kept it.

Her heart was racing in her chest. Something was wrong.

Mary would surely answer the door, especially when she knew it was Marlene calling.

Moving to the bedroom, she set about throwing things out of their dresser and onto the floor. In the bottom drawer, her eyes caught a flash of metal glistening through the chipped blue and white paint of a boat-shaped key ring. A quick flick through the half-dozen keys on the ring confirmed she recognised none of them.

Pocketing them, Marlene ran out of the door and raced back to Mary's house.

Trying the keys one by one, she had success on the fifth. The lock turned, her heart rate slowed, and she pushed open the door. Stale air caught in the back of her throat. The hallway was ominously dark, and the house was silent save for the ticking of the grandfather clock towering above her from the top of the stairs.

"Mary, it's Marlene," she called out. Heading towards the living room, Marlene continued to gently call Mary's name, not wanting to startle her. Marlene paused at the living room door and laid her hand on the cool handle. She stepped into the room and swallowed hard.

Mary was sitting in her armchair with a blanket tucked over her legs. Her usually curled hair was messy and matted, and her clothes were wrinkled. The woman who was once always so immaculately groomed was now a frail old woman who looked as though she had no one to care for her. Her face was grey and old, her skin empty as it hung down from her jaw like an orange that had lost its juice. She stared at Marlene as she entered but said nothing.

"Are you all right?" Marlene asked.

Nothing.

She pulled back the curtains to let in some light and sat on the sofa. "How have you been?" she asked Mary.

Nothing.

"I'm sorry I haven't been round. I've been struggling, truth be told, but I don't need to tell you that."

Again, nothing. Marlene was unsure what she should or could say to get a reaction.

Mary sat staring straight ahead, her gaze intense but focused on nothing. Marlene stared at the deep lines around the old woman's eyes as they squinted in the light. Her skin prickled as she recalled the light stinging her own eyes earlier.

The light did nothing for the room except highlight the disarray. Marlene ignored the fact it was a mirror image of her own living room. It was what Fletcher had walked into earlier that day, and it was uncomfortable. Pitiful, even.

"I just miss him so much," Marlene whispered. This got a flicker of acknowledgement from Mary. "I went to the social club, but Mrs Hopeton said they hadn't seen you for a while. They were very concerned about you."

"They were just being nosy." Mary glanced at Marlene before returning her gaze to the space in front of her.

Marlene had told Peter herself that the women from the social club were nosy and judgemental. He'd responded that they were all friends who were only concerned for each other. He'd thought it would do Marlene good to make new friends, but she'd dismissed his comments at the time, thinking he was just trying to keep the peace with his mother. Now, though, she had to admit that Mrs Hopeton had sounded truly concerned about Mary.

"They are your friends. It's only natural they're worried about you," said Marlene.

"I don't think so. You were right," Mary said flatly.

"I wasn't right, Mary. They're not all like that. Mrs Hopeton wasn't gossiping; she was concerned about you. She told me that Joyce had been to see you once, but you wouldn't let her in—and they haven't seen you since."

There was no reaction from Mary. Marlene stared at her, hoping for a flash of inspiration to help her pull Mary out of her gloom. Mary blinked so infrequently it made her look haunted, like there was someone inside but not the person who was normally there.

It was exactly how Marlene felt.

Marlene pressed her ear against the back of her front door. One voice belonged to her upstairs neighbour, but she didn't recognise the other. She waited until the street was quiet and she heard the door to the flat above creak open. She slipped outside and made her way, head down, to the shop on the corner.

Marlene had been living on coffee and tinned pears for much of the last few weeks, and she hated to think what Mary had been surviving on. Marlene didn't drink tea, but she always bought tea alongside her other rations to give to Mary.

She hadn't given her any since Peter had died.

After filling a bag with tea for Mary, her sugar, butter and cheese rations, and a few parsnips and potatoes and bread, Marlene filled a second bag with some ingredients to make soup for herself, then headed to Mary's.

Marlene had the key in her hand this time, and she knocked and waited a minute before letting herself in. She scooped up a wrapped bunch of daffodils that had been propped against the door and went inside. Darkness greeted her again despite the afternoon sun splitting the sky.

"Mary, it's Marlene." She moved towards the living room slowly, giving Mary a chance to register her presence.

Mary was sitting in her nightdress with a newspaper open on her lap. Marlene pulled open the curtains, letting the natural light in. She switched off the lamp beside Mary and sat opposite her.

"How are you?" she asked.

Mary lifted the newspaper from her lap, folded it and tossed it onto the table in front of her.

"Have you been out?" Marlene asked, noticing that day's date on the newspaper.

Mary shook her head. "Joyce came round. She left it."

"That's great. How is Joyce?" Marlene asked, although she couldn't remember which of the ladies was Joyce.

"I didn't see her."

"She must have left these, too." Marlene placed the daffodils on top of the newspaper. "It was good of her to come round. They're all missing you."

Marlene fumbled around in one of the bags she had brought in and pulled out a glass dish. "My neighbour brought me this beef stew. I thought we could have some lunch together. Might be nice to eat something warm. It even has onions in it. I haven't seen an onion in a long time.

She grew them—and the carrots—herself, in her little allotment."

"I'm not hungry," Mary said sullenly, looking at Marlene for the first time since she'd sat down.

"Me neither," Marlene said. She slumped back in the chair. "But I am cold. Even though it's sunny outside and really quite warm, I'm still cold. It doesn't matter what I wear or how many blankets I wrap myself in I'm just cold. All the time."

Something resonated with Mary. She stood up and headed towards the living room door.

"You can start warming the stew," Mary said before disappearing up the stairs.

The stew was bubbling away on the cooker when Mary returned. She'd put on her dressing gown, but otherwise she was exactly the same. She silently laid forks, knives and glasses on the table in the kitchen. Marlene had already taken bowls from the cupboard and had them ready and waiting beside the cooker.

While she had been waiting for the stew to warm through, Marlene had taken a vase from the windowsill. She'd cleared out the long dead flowers, poured away the murky green water and left it steeping in the sink. After a quick rinse, she'd refilled it with fresh clear water and dropped the daffodils in.

She put the vase in the centre of Mary's table and served the stew.

The two women sat eating in silence. Marlene couldn't remember the last time she'd had a proper meal, and her stomach gurgled as it expanded. She watched Mary picking at tiny bites of her stew. She still looked so frail.

"I need to go back to work next week," Marlene said,

talking to ignore the guilt she felt while watching Mary eating.

"Life goes on," said Mary, with something other than conviction in her voice.

"That's what Fletcher said." Marlene sighed. "It scares me. I just want to stay at home, missing Peter. Work will be a distraction, which I know is supposed to be good, but I worry it will make me forget."

Mary looked at Marlene now. Her eyes stared deep into Marlene's soul, making her feel uncomfortable and exposed.

"You will never forget," Mary said. "You loved him. I know you did. And I know he loved you, with all his heart. His love for you is now eternal."

Marlene could not stop herself. Tears came, and she sobbed hysterically. She knew Peter had loved her, but there was something about hearing it confirmed by Mary that devastated her so much in that moment.

His love was eternal, as was hers. They would only ever love each other. They could not grow apart, argue or leave. It was forever.

Mary pulled her chair towards Marlene's and enveloped her in her arms. She shushed her and gently rocked her back and forth as if she were comforting a baby.

"You'll be fine, love. You really will be."

"I'm sorry, Mary." Marlene wiped away her tears and straightened herself up.

"Don't you apologise, dear. That's been inside you for a long time, just waiting to come out. It's out now. It's gone. You can let it go."

Marlene's cheeks burned. "I don't want to go back to work. I don't want to see people feeling sorry for me. Or would it be worse to see that no one really cares anyway?"

"You don't need them to care for you. They're just people you work with. You have friends and family and they're more important."

Marlene couldn't help but think of Benjamin, the only blood relative she knew for sure was out there somewhere. She didn't know if her mother was alive or dead, but Marlene had accepted that she would never see her again.

Although Marlene didn't know where Benjamin was, *he* knew where she was—and he would come back for her one day.

She knew that for sure.

3

MONDAY MORNING'S HEAVY RAIN BATTERED THE STREETS, cascading straight down from the sky and flooding any dips in the roads within minutes.

The worst kind of rain, Peter used to say, but he'd hated any kind of water. Bathing had been a mere necessity for him, rather than something to be savoured. He had been unable to find calm sinking into a deep, steaming bath. He had helped Marlene's grandfather on the farm washing out the animal stalls and topping up the troughs during the few times they had visited, but he hadn't found calm in that either, telling Marlene he hated to be damp and dirty. He'd much preferred the hustle and bustle of city life, as long as it wasn't raining. He'd said he liked the feel of cities compared with country living; something Marlene could not under-stand each time she stepped outside and breathed in the tight, smoky London air. It took her mind back to France, reigniting a longing for air that smelled of nothing but cut grass and flowers or her grandfather burning old crops. She wondered if she had lost those smells forever when she had lost her grandfather.

Marlene sat in her kitchen, trying to wake herself up by having some breakfast. She rubbed her swollen eyes and stared at the toast in front of her.

She tried to forget the comfortable warmth of her bed. When she had finally forced herself out of bed, she had made it immediately to avoid the temptation to throw herself back in.

Wasting what little butter she had left, she smeared a thick layer on a slice of toasted bread, but after two bites, she discarded the rest. She couldn't eat, and she couldn't stay in the flat or she would not leave. She pulled on her heavy overcoat, pushed up her umbrella and threw herself back into the happenings of the outside world.

A short time later, Marlene approached her office building. The heels of her shoes sunk into the soft earth exposed by a section of missing cobbles. The ragged edge of the building suggested the missing cobbles were a consequence of German bombing. It was recent, too, given the building had been intact when she had last been here.

The entry to her office was the fifth door along. Her stomach churning, Marlene pulled up the collar of her coat and headed for the door.

She had arrived early, and for that she was instantly glad. Once on the floor that housed most of the paper's staff, the few people that were already in turned to stare at her. Marlene felt their eyes not so subtly following her as she weaved her way to her desk. She scanned the office before sitting down and was at once annoyed by the uncomfortable, sympathetic gazes cast in her direction.

"Glad to have you back," said Fletcher as he approached her with two steaming mugs of coffee. He perched on the edge of her desk, pushed one coffee in her direction and quietly asked if she was okay.

"I'll have to be," she said. "I couldn't bear another week of you pounding on my front door."

"Ah, it worked!"

"Hi, Marlene. Welcome back," yelled George, the cocky new junior reporter, as he passed the end of her desk and splashed water everywhere as he took off his coat.

"You'll be old news by tomorrow," said Fletcher, reading the disdain on her face. "How's Peter's mother holding up now?"

"Better, I think. Although I still haven't been able to get her out and about. And, yes, I realise the irony in that."

"I never said a word," said Fletcher with a smile, holding his hands up defensively. "You're out and about again now, too. I'll leave you to sort through your things. Staff meeting at ten o'clock, remember?"

Marlene watched Fletcher return to his office. She had not remembered about their meeting, and a quick look over her desk confirmed she had forgotten about much of what she was currently working on.

She picked up the frame from her desk and looked at the newspaper cutting it held inside. Her first front-page story. Fletcher had once told her he had hired her because she seemed so very lost when he'd first met her. She had no journalistic skills, and 'farmhand' didn't exactly give her relevant work experience. She had completed a secretarial course in France, so she knew her way around shorthand and the keys of a typewriter, but other than that, she had nothing else to give to Fletcher.

In the time that she had worked for *The Post*, she had written story after story. In the beginning, they were all heavily edited by Fletcher, and none had made it near the front page. Yet this hadn't bothered her. It was a journalist's dream, she now understood, to have their work on the front page.

Things changed when she was assigned a story about a group of women that had swapped working at home for working on the land. Fletcher had given it to her because of her own farming experience. Most of her colleagues were city people, and stereotypical ones at that. She doubted many of them owned footwear suitable for traipsing around a farm.

Marlene had been enthusiastic about the story from the outset, although that came from her joy at being outdoors again and squelching across muddy fields whilst avoiding inquisitive livestock. But when Marlene had met the women, she knew their story should not be on page nine or ten; it *had* to be on the front page. Their story was both unique and inspirational. More stories had been published since of women doing men's work, with posters printed encouraging the nation to follow their example, but Marlene's story had been one of the first to appear front and centre for the masses to read.

That first front page had changed Marlene. She had wanted the job at the paper as a distraction from her husband's absence, or abandonment as she often thought on days when her conscience allowed her to.

With that one story, Marlene had found that writing about people doing extraordinary things meant so much more to her than merely a distraction.

As her colleagues filtered into the office, a few of them mumbled good morning to her. Most of them continued with their day as if it was much the same as any other. She caught the occasional person scrutinising her each time she looked up and longed for it to be ten o'clock already, so that Fletcher could give them all something else to focus on. Only cocky George had acknowledged the fact that she had not been at work at all for a few weeks. She wondered how it was possible that she saw these people every day but had not built up a relationship deep enough with anyone for them to ask how she was doing.

As a child, Marlene had moved around with her mother every few months until she was five years old and her mother had finally done the decent thing and left her with her grandparents. She had stayed nowhere long enough to make friends until she lived on her grandparents' farm. There, her closest companion was Benjamin, her brother, the first child to be abandoned by their mother.

Benjamin grabbed five-year-old Marlene's hand and pulled her along. The five years between them meant he was so much taller than she was, with a stride so much longer that Marlene struggled to keep up.

"Come on!" he yelled, trying to get her to move quicker.

"Slow down, Benjamin! Slow down."

When he eventually stopped, Marlene's breathing was fierce and her clothing clung to her body, soaked with sweat.

"I don't like this. I want to go back," she said.

"But we're here," Benjamin said. He took a hold of Marlene's shoulders and carefully spun her round.

Her eyes narrowed as she peered through gaps in the bushes. "What is it?" she asked.

Benjamin crawled through one of the gaps and disappeared.

"Benjamin?" Marlene waited, but her elder brother didn't respond. She could hear the rustling of leaves in front of her and scanned the gaps in the bushes for him.

"Come on," said Benjamin insistently, from inside the bushes.

Marlene sighed and got down on her hands and knees. She crawled through a gap, her head down so she didn't scratch her face on the branches poking out. Once behind the bush, she looked up. She could just about make out the path Benjamin must have taken and inched her way along. She squealed as she put her hand through a spider's web and reached back to wipe her hand down her leg.

"Benjamin, where are you?" she whispered. There was something about the confined space and the secrecy of it that made shouting seem inappropriate.

"Over here." Benjamin's face appeared through some bushes further along the path and she quickly scuttled towards him. Following him around a bend in the path led to a small clearing deep inside the bushes.

"Pretty cool, isn't it?"

Benjamin was kneeling in the middle of the clearing. Marlene looked above her head. Willow branches had been pulled taut above her. Following the neat curves, she could see someone had tied them at one end to hold them in place.

"Did you do this?" she asked.

Benjamin nodded, pride on his face.

It was cool in the clearing. The leaves all around them kept out any warmth, but also stopped anyone passing by from seeing in.

She peered again through the gaps.

"It's completely private," Benjamin said. "I've tried

looking out from every angle, but you can't see much. Which is brilliant because no one can see in."

Marlene crawled around the space.

"So this is where you hide all day?" she said, looking around at Benjamin's supplies. There was a water canister, a neatly folded blanket, a crumpled paper bag and one of Benjamin's jackets, all sitting on top of one of the hessian sacks they kept the animal feed in.

Benjamin opened the paper bag and offered the contents to Marlene. Peering inside, she reached in and pulled out a chunk of bread.

"What is all of this?" she asked.

Benjamin shrugged. "Just somewhere to go." Then he got more serious. He held her still by her upper arms and lowered his voice. "You and I are going to have to learn to take care of ourselves. No one else is going to."

"What do you mean?"

"Grandma and Grandpa are getting old. You know what happens to people when they get old."

Marlene wasn't sure if it was a question or a statement, but she nodded anyway.

"We've only got each other, Marlene. You need to toughen up a bit and learn how to take care of yourself. You'll be on your own one day."

Tears threatened to roll down her cheeks.

"Benjamin, don't!" she said, shaking his hands off her. "We won't be on our own. We've got Grandma and Grandpa. You've got me and I've got you."

"You don't need to be scared," he said. "You'll be all right. I'll help you."

"I want to go home."

They trudged back to the farmhouse in silence. When

the house was in sight, Marlene ran towards the door and went inside.

But over the years, she began to realise that Benjamin was right. They did only have each other.

"Right," said Fletcher as he started the meeting. "What's happening in the world today?"

Marlene concentrated on the notebook in her lap. An unexplained heat rose within her and she touched her fingertips to her cheeks. She glanced up without raising her head. She noticed everyone else was also staring at their notepads. If she hadn't known Fletcher better, she would have thought everyone was too scared to be the first to speak to the boss and were looking down, praying they didn't get picked on to start. She looked at George, sure that he would have something to say, but even he was looking down.

"Nothing, apparently," said Fletcher. "Am I going to have to come up with all the stories for you?"

"I've got one," said George. "It's another war story, of course, since that's all we print these days, but it's got a bit of a happy slant this time."

"How so?" asked Fletcher.

"Well, I was in the Lion's Den at the weekend and met up with these boys on leave. They were telling me about this girl who worked with them. She's an undercover agent; gets flown in and out of various places to gather information and blow up a few things while she's at it."

"Huh," came a noise from Terrence, the longest serving reporter, who was squashed into the corner. Despite being squashed, he always put his seat in that position, regardless of how much spare floor space there was. Terrence was also the paper's war correspondent; he'd flown with the RAF and had spent the early months of the war following troop movements in Europe. He liked to remind people of this often and slipped in mention of it in his articles whenever he could get away with it.

"No, seriously," said George.

"A woman? I find that *very* hard to believe, young man."

"Times are changing, Terrence," George insisted. "I interviewed a group of land girls, and they're working on a farm alongside German POWs. They're doing everything the men are doing."

"It's one thing working on the land, but you cannot put a woman undercover in occupied territory," said Terrence.

"And why ever not?" asked Isobel sharply, causing Marlene and a few others to look up. Normally, Isobel was silent in meetings; in fact, she was silent most of the time. At twenty-seven, she was only a year older than Marlene, but already a mother of three and dressed in clothing that looked as though it had come from her own mother. Not that there was much variety in fashion these days. Some of the other reporters questioned why Isobel needed to work; her husband was supposedly rather well off and chosen for her by her parents.

"Come on," said George. "It's a perfect cover. Women must be able to move around far more freely in occupied territory, and who would suspect a woman of blowing up a bridge? It makes perfect sense."

"It does *not* make perfect sense at all! You can't allow this sensationalist rubbish to be printed," said Terrence, turning now to Fletcher. "We'll be a laughing stock."

"I agree with one thing," said Fletcher. "We cannot print this."

"But it's such a new angle," said George. "It's better than

the usual here's what the politicians are saying this week, here's how many people died this week, here's what ..." His voice trailed off to nothing. He caught Marlene's eye briefly before returning his gaze to his notepad.

Everyone else had their eyes fixed on her.

"What?" she asked, although she wasn't expecting an answer. The room was quiet again, and the flush returned to her cheeks. "My husband died. So what?" Her voice had risen to just short of shouting. "There's no need to tiptoe around me. It's a war; people die. And it's our job to report it. We can't not talk about it for fear of upsetting me. And I'm fine, by the way. I guess you were all too uncomfortable to ask, although I'm sure you were all wondering."

Marlene was out of her chair, although she couldn't now remember when she had stood up.

"In fact, I know exactly how I can make this less awkward for everyone," she said, before storming to the door and slamming it shut behind her.

She wiped at her eyes, but there were no tears. She wasn't upset. She was angry.

Marlene sat in the café down the street from the paper's offices. She rested her elbows on the table in front of her, keeping to the edges to avoid the crumbs and sticky marks left over by its previous occupant. There were clean tables, but Marlene had chosen the one farthest away from the café's other customers.

The steam rising from her cup warned her the coffee was too hot to drink, but she choked it down anyway. The liquid was strong, bitter, and seared the inside of her mouth. Coffee was normally a comfort for her, but not today. This cup was a punishment, and she welcomed the pain with every mouthful.

"I thought I might find you here."

She turned, expecting to see Fletcher. George took a seat opposite her. He smiled. Not the pitying smile she had become so used to seeing, but the smug smile that only George seemed to have these days. Marlene had spent little time with George, but each time she had seen him around the office, he was overtly happy. She knew he made several girls in the office overtly happy, as well. She had witnessed them turn pink and giggly whenever he spoke to them. Marlene could see the attraction; George was not her version of handsome, but he was young, with thick blonde hair, much like her own, only shorter, and a constant smile.

"Hi," she said. "Why would you think to find me here?"

"You caught me," he said, holding out a small paper bag. "I was out grabbing an early lunch and saw you over here."

"You gave in a little too easily. I thought you might have been able to think on your feet and get me to believe you really came looking for me."

"You're right. I should have been able to come up with something." George looked flustered, his usual confidence slipping momentarily. "You stormed out at the best bit, you know. Isobel and Terror—sorry, *Terrence*—had an argument about whether a woman could kill a man if necessary. I think, in the end, Terror was the only person in the room without the slightest clue she was pretending it was *him* in front of her as she made stabbing gestures with her pen. She can be quite frightening, our Isobel."

"Good to know."

"Isn't it? And everyone had her pegged as a quiet girl: a wife and mother who cooks and cleans and does as she's told."

"We never thought that," Marlene said dismissively.

"*You* may not have, but everyone else did. They told me. They gave me the guided tour of the personalities in the office within my first couple of weeks."

"Seriously?"

"Yeah. You didn't get the same?"

"No," she said, wondering if they had excluded her for a reason. "Who told you all that?"

"Oh, you know, everyone has their own bit to add."

"And what did they tell you about me?" Marlene asked, hesitantly, knowing that George was likely to give her complete honesty. Given her lack of social connections with her colleagues, she was not sure she really wanted to know.

"Ah! You, Marlene, were an enigma to them all. Some thought you were the moody French girl. Others thought you were the darling of the office."

"Guess they know which now," Marlene said dismissively. "Moody French girl. I can live with that,"

In truth, she was both surprised and relieved that her colleagues' perceptions of her were not worse.

"Me, I prefer to think of you as the girl who's prone to outbursts," George said. "But I have to admit, I feel responsible for your latest little outburst."

"It wasn't an 'outburst'," Marlene said defensively.

"How else would you describe it?"

"A difference of opinion." She smiled involuntarily. It *was* an outburst, she supposed, but Marlene wasn't going to allow George to get the better of her. Keen to move the conversation on, she asked, "So, how long have you been with the paper now?"

George looked disappointed that Marlene had had enough of his game and was changing the subject. "Five months," he said. "Long enough to know when something's wrong. How are you really doing?"

"I'm okay," she lied. "Thanks for asking."

"I wasn't asking because you accused us all of not caring in your outburst."

"It wasn't an *outburst*." Marlene had to smile at his tenacity. Despite his confidence, there was also a humbleness about him which Marlene thought stopped his confidence being mistaken for arrogance. She could see why Fletcher had liked George enough to hire him.

"I was asking because I care. It's awkward for people. I know it's more awkward for you, but it'll get easier. Coffee, please," he said to a waitress clearing up a few tables away.

"Would you like another?" the waitress asked Marlene as she expertly balanced an array of different dishes along her arm.

"Yes, she would," said George, as if sensing Marlene was about to decline.

"My grandmother would have coffee ready for my grandfather every morning," Marlene said, abandoning her plans to leave. "She made it so strong that its scent permeated every room in the house. When I was about twelve years old, my brother dared me to take a sip. Just as I did, we heard footsteps on the stairs. I gulped the coffee down, much more than I had intended to take, and it burned the back of my throat, leaving me in pain and spluttering. I couldn't drink it after that. Then I met Peter, and he asked if he could take me for coffee. It tasted so much better drinking it with him."

"So Peter wasn't French? No one really said anything about your husband. I assumed he was French."

"No, English, London born and bred. He'd spent the

year before meeting me travelling the world. Paris was his last stop before returning home."

Their coffee arrived, giving Marlene a moment to reflect as the waitress set the cups down on the table. Marlene cradled this second cup, cherishing the warmth between her fingers, surprised by how comfortable she was in George's company.

"Nice," said George, nodding. Marlene assumed he was referring to the travelling the world, rather than the sip of coffee he had just taken. She imagined travelling would appeal to him and, as such, she couldn't see why he wasn't in active service. He seemed fit and healthy, and his adventurous persona would probably have made him an excellent soldier. But it would have been rude to ask since the information wasn't volunteered.

"He and a friend were due to leave Paris after two weeks," Marlene continued. "I met Peter when he had only four days left. His friend returned without him, and Peter and I left France together. We were married three months later."

"Three months!"

Marlene nodded. "We just knew."

"And then you started at the paper?"

"Not at first. We married just before we left France. I stayed at home to look after the house. Peter's mother Mary got me involved in her social clubs and lunches and other events, but it wasn't for me. Peter had qualified in medicine and started his first job in the hospital, but when the war broke out, he signed up. Mary wasn't happy, although not as annoyed as she was when she'd found out he'd married me. I wasn't happy either, of course."

Marlene vividly remembered Peter's face when he'd walked through the door that evening. His eyes had been lined with tension and his lips pursed, making them straight and narrow. Marlene had been laying the table, although dinner was not even close to being ready. He'd kissed her lightly on the neck and wrapped his arm around her waist. He'd sat on one of the mismatched chairs that circled their dining table, pulling at her hand until she'd joined him.

"I've signed up," he'd blurted out. Pain had rushed into Marlene's stomach and the ache had stayed with her every day since.

"What?" She'd been confused for a few seconds before she'd understood what he meant. "But you can't."

"Someone has to, and they're allowing me to go."

"But why you? You're a doctor. That's a reserved occupation. You're needed *here*. For the survival of the country. That's what they say, isn't it?"

"Doctors are also needed for the survival of the *soldiers*. We might all have to go anyway, the way things are going." He had held both her hands in his and kissed her forehead. "It's the right thing to do."

"And is that why you're doing it? Because it's the right thing to do?"

Marlene knew her husband wasn't the type to do something selflessly. His family were wealthy, and Peter had led a privileged and protected life so far. He had been well educated and raised with impeccable manners, but he had also been given everything he wanted, including, luckily for her, financial support for his travels across the world. This had inadvertently created a selfishness in him which did not support his protestations that signing up to go to war was 'the right thing to do'.

"Yes, I am," he'd replied emphatically.

"What about your job? What about me?"

He'd leaned closer to her. "I'm not leaving you, Marlene. I'm not your mother."

"This isn't about my mother! This is about *you* choosing to leave your new wife all alone in a strange country where she has no family and no friends—and possibly, heaven forbid, not coming home again. Don't you listen to the news?"

"You have me dead before I've even gone." He had stood up and paced the room angrily. "This is the right thing to do for everyone! This is about *duty*, Marlene. Don't you understand? I'm not doing this to get away from you or because I'm unhappy with our life."

"Yes, you are," she'd screamed, tears in full flow. "You're not doing this out of a sense of duty! I can see you're not happy. You were happiest being on the move all the time. I'm not happy with this, either. We can go away together; leave all of this behind, just like we've talked about. We can do that now. You don't have to do this, Peter. You don't have to put yourself in danger like this."

She had reached out to him, and he had wrapped his arms around her like he always did. It had always made her feel safe before.

Except that time, it didn't.

"Peter was such a free spirit," she now said to George. "He was so happy in France, but returning to London could never compete. Routine smothered him. We often spoke of travelling again, picking up jobs here and there, and Peter had a bit of inheritance from when his father died. He was first deployed to North Africa and I was going crazy with an intense combination of worry and boredom. I was looking for a job, and I found Fletcher. A few reporters had been called up or had moved out of the city. I think that's why Fletcher put up with me in the beginning."

"So *that's* how you got into journalism," said George. "Different. Most journalists I know would tell you it's because they have a passion for digging up the truth. They revel in seeing their work in print, frothing at the mouth when they think they've found an exclusive angle after many, many hours of searching through absolute rubbish."

His passion turned to disappointment, and Marlene felt it was directed at her. She looked at him apologetically.

"Hey, it's not a bad thing," he said. "Makes you one less person trying to get one over on me. We're a ruthless breed, you know. But you're too nice for that, I've always thought. You and Isobel—although she showed another side to herself today."

"Journalism seemed as good a choice as any. I can't drive, and I don't know that I could have worked in the munitions factories. With my farming background, I could have become a Land Girl, but Fletcher saw something in me. I might not have got into journalism for the same reasons as you, but I love it—or I did. I loved telling stories of everyday people doing extraordinary things in the hope of inspiring others. It's just that, recently, the news has a habit of finding me, and that's all I've written about."

"Journalism is needed now more than ever. People need to find out what's going on, but we also have to give them hope to keep going. Words have the power to divide, but also the power to unite. The sooner we can unify the world, the sooner we can rise up and end this."

Marlene looked down at her coffee, now cold in her hands. George's cup was empty. "You're right," she said. "I like that. And it's nice to know spending time with me hasn't left you depressed?"

"Oh, I am depressed," he said, with a loud sigh.

"I'm sorry. I shouldn't have gone on like that," said Marlene, feeling guilty for offloading onto George.

"No, no. It's not you. After your ... *difference of opinion*, Fletcher said I couldn't write my exclusive on the women agents."

"Did he say why?"

"Something about the story not being substantiated. And if there are female agents, we'd never get it through censorship, in case it tipped off the Germans and exposed the women."

"That make sense," she said, trying to offer him a bit of comfort.

"Like hell it does! Well, maybe it does a bit, but if it's not us writing it, another paper will surely pick it up and we'll lose the exclusive." George allowed his head to fall and touch the table. "This could have been it. The story I've been waiting for. And it found me."

"That's the way to look at it, George. It found you, so another one is bound to find you, too."

"Yeah, yeah. I tried that line on myself earlier. It didn't make me feel better then, and it hasn't made me feel better now. I also asked Fletcher about the rumours going round, you know, that we're going to send someone to France. He denied it, but I could tell from Terror's face it was true. He's got the gig. It's so unfair," said George petulantly.

Marlene hadn't heard the rumours. George must have forgotten she'd not been in work for a while, although, had she been in work, she still might not have heard, given that she rarely conversed with her colleagues.

"France. Why would we send someone there?" Marlene pondered out loud.

"To get to the heart of the story, Marlene. Where better to learn the truth about the war than on the battlefields where it's being fought? France is going to be pivotal, and kicking the Germans out of Paris will signal the end of this war."

He was right. Paris under occupation had seemed unimaginable, but then the photographs had emerged and shocked the world. The Allies re-taking the city would show the Germans in retreat. Until that day, though, what was there to report on that hadn't been written already?

"Fletcher's being all secretive about it," George continued. "He said he's sending someone to Scotland and someone to Wales. We all think that's just a cover story, though. But maybe it means two people can go to France. Would you want to go?"

Marlene shook her head. "Not right now, no."

A heavy silence settled between them before George grabbed Marlene's hand and dragged her towards the door. "Come on. Let's get back to the office before it gets any harder for you."

Marlene started to object, but George's persistence was inescapable. She wasn't sure what she had intended to come out of her mouth, but George had taken her so much by surprise that the only thing she could think of to say was that they hadn't paid for their coffees.

"On the account, darling!" he yelled to the waitress who had served them earlier. She smiled in return and immediately started fidgeting with her hair. *George apparently has as many admirers out of the office as he does in it.*

They ambled back towards the office with George chatting incessantly. Marlene had stopped listening, instead fretting about having to walk into the office for the second time that day. She heard George moaning on, still upset about the missed opportunity for an exclusive.

Lost in her own thoughts, Marlene didn't hear the roar

of the bomb until something hard and heavy struck her in the stomach and threw her backwards. She crashed into something or someone before hitting the concrete with a deadened *thump*. A scream rose in her throat, but it wouldn't come out.

Her eyes were drawn to the fire in front of her. She found herself consumed by its brightness, until the orange flames could no longer penetrate the darkness that washed over her.

4

MARLENE SHIVERED AS HER EYES SLOWLY ADJUSTED TO THE dull room, the white walls covered by dark shadows from the sky outside the window. Above hung a single light bulb, uncovered but not switched on. She lay beneath rough white sheets tucked tightly around her body in the way only a nurse could achieve. She remembered an explosion, but not much else.

She was not alone, but she took another minute to properly wake up before turning over onto her other side to see who sat beside her. Fletcher's face was pale and scrunched, his eyes full of concern. It was the same concern Marlene had detected each time she'd seen him these past few weeks.

"George?" she asked, her voice hoarse.

"Yeah?" came the reply from the other side of the room. She turned and saw George coming through the doorway.

"I wasn't sure if you were ..." She looked at Fletcher again, who was now smiling, his face less drawn but with the same look in his eyes.

"Dead?" George said.

"Well, yes," she replied, glad that he was his usual self. There was a dark stain on his shirt collar, which she took to be blood, but other than that, there didn't seem to be a mark on him.

"I'm not dead. Good as always. You, on the other hand," he said, looking her up and down as she lay in the bed, "were lucky to survive. Your first day back at work after burying your husband and you manage to get yourself blown up. To use your words, the news does indeed have a way of finding you."

At first, she stared at him in disbelief, her reaction supported by an intake of breath from Fletcher as he fidgeted in his seat. Then Marlene laughed, leaving only Fletcher to stare in disbelief as George came and perched himself on the end of her bed. She looked at Fletcher but couldn't stop laughing. It eventually caught him, too, and he laughed.

Most likely on account of the noise now coming from the ward, they were joined by an aging doctor with glasses perched on the tip of his nose. "Welcome back," he said jovially. "You gave us quite a fright for a while. How are you feeling?"

"I'm okay," she said, pressing her lips together to stifle her laughter.

"Don't stop on my account," he said. "It's good to see you awake—and laughing, no less."

He pushed back her head and shone a light in her eyes, one at a time. He listened to her breathing and made her push and pull with her arms.

George got up from the bed and strode to the window. Fletcher remained seated and leaned forward, as if he didn't want to miss a secret the doctor was about to tell. "How do you feel?" the physician asked.

"I feel fine," Marlene said.

"That's good. Everything looks good. And do you remember what happened to you?"

"If she doesn't, she'll read about it on the front page tomorrow," George said, turning back to them now. "It'll be an exclusive report called '*Inside the Blast*' by George Thomas."

"I hope you realise how lucky you were, Mr Thomas," said the doctor reprovingly.

"Oh, I do. It's a gift I have, really. Being in the right place at the right time." George was lost in his own world, no doubt already writing the piece in his head.

"That's not exactly the luck I meant. It could have been a lot worse for both of you," the doctor said, scolding George more openly this time.

"I know, Doctor," Marlene said to stop George from saying anything else. "Don't worry. I remember everything, or enough at least to correct his version of events for the paper."

George smiled, taking the hint to shut up.

"So, she's fine, Doctor?" asked Fletcher.

"Seems to be. Like I said, lucky. Not everyone was, unfortunately."

It hadn't occurred to Marlene before that although she and George were fine, there were other people in the street that might not have been. "Did people die?"

"Five so far," said the doctor. "And a few gravely injured."

"Do we know what happened?" Marlene had so many questions swirling around her mind. She couldn't believe she hadn't thought to ask earlier if anyone had been seriously injured. Five people had died, with a likelihood of further fatalities, and she hadn't given them so much as a second thought.

"You don't need to be worrying about that, Marlene," Fletcher said, sitting beside her now on the bed. He smoothed her hair around her face. "The important thing is that you're both all right."

"You should rest," said the doctor. "You've had quite an ordeal. You are one of the lucky ones, but that doesn't mean to say you have to take on responsibility for the death of anyone else. Be glad you're still here to tell the story"

The doctor made some notes on the chart at the end of her bed and continued with his rounds. The silence hung heavily in the air around them. It was George, of course, who broke it first.

"I really should get going to work on the piece," he said.

"Yeah," said Fletcher. "I'll catch up with you later."

"We really have to *do* something," Marlene said, more to herself than to either Fletcher or George.

"We *are* doing something, Marlene," George insisted. "By telling the story, we're hanging up the bad guys for everyone to see."

"It doesn't seem enough. It doesn't seem like it will make a difference."

"What else do you want to do?" said Fletcher. "Everyone has their own part to play in this war, and this is ours. We don't have bombs or guns or whatever else. Words are our weapons. We have to make each edition count because it's all we've got."

George said nothing but nodded in agreement. "I'm going to walk George out, then I'll be back. You need to take the doctor's advice, Marlene. Get some rest, otherwise you're no good to anyone."

Marlene simply nodded and watched the two men leave.

She couldn't rest, though. She couldn't stop thinking about the five people who had lost their lives. Her skin flushed as she relived the heat of the flames on her face and the coolness of the concrete beneath her body.

The concrete where she'd lay, unaware that others all around her were dead.

5

___

It was Thursday, and Marlene planned to visit the social club. At least she *hoped* she would visit the social club. She headed to Mary's house with a script in mind for persuading Mary to go with her.

Marlene had been discharged from hospital the day before, having spent one night under observation. She and George had escaped the blast with little more than a few cuts and bruises. Thinking of the five people who hadn't been so lucky had forced her out of the door that morning. To distract herself, she concentrated on listening to everything she heard on the walk: traffic; two women chatting as they passed her on the opposite side of the street; a dish smashing somewhere nearby; birds singing, their tune uplifting and cheerful. Clearly no one had told them there was a war on.

Up ahead, the branches of an apple tree hung over the pavement. There were still a few apples on the tree, tiny red globes punctured by birds. Marlene reached up and stroked one as she passed. She couldn't believe that the apples hadn't been picked, especially given that they were so accessible to anyone passing by. A bird squawked as her hand touched the apple.

Marlene dropped her hand immediately. "I wasn't going to take it."

Reaching Mary's street, Marlene squinted in the sunlight, trying to see if Mary's house showed any signs of life. She rang the bell before letting herself in with Peter's key.

The curtains were open in every room and daylight flooded the hallway. Mary sat in her chair in the back room. She was dressed, which was a good sign, but her hair lay flat on her head and her usually made-up face was bare.

"Morning," Marlene said.

"Hello," Mary said, turning away as if making clear she wasn't interested in making conversation.

"I was hoping you might come to the social club with me today. It's Thursday."

"I don't think so, dear. I don't want to go there."

"It's somewhat of an experiment for me; almost a practice run for when I have to go back to work next week. *Again*. I really don't want to go on my own."

Mary looked at Marlene now, her eyebrows raised and her expression unconvinced.

"You're only saying that to convince me to go," Mary said.

"No one fools you," Marlene said. "I've been telling myself it's to get you out again, but I honestly think it would be good for me. My last return to work didn't exactly go smoothly. I'm almost more worried about going back this time."

"Well, let's get you over that, dear. I'll get ready." Mary stood up, determination set upon her face, and headed upstairs.

When Mary returned, her skin glowed in the soft light. The new colour on her cheeks, a pale pink lipstick and freshly tousled hair gave Marlene a welcome glimpse of the old Mary. In days past, her mother-in-law wouldn't go to the social club looking anything less than perfect.

"I've got you something," Marlene said, pulling a silk scarf from her bag. It was a gift she had bought Mary before Peter had left. She and Peter had travelled to Oxford for a weekend, and she'd seen the scarf. After Peter's departure, there had never seemed the right moment to give it to Mary.

Marlene tied the scarf loosely around Mary's neck. The light purple silk with a bright fuchsia print stood out against Mary's dark grey top.

"This is a typical French look. Not everyone can pull something like this off, but you can." She turned Mary around to show her in the mirror above her fireplace.

Mary smiled.

They locked up the house and headed to the social club.

When they arrived, Mary took Marlene by the arm.

"You'll be fine, dear," she said, reassuringly, although Marlene was certain she was talking to herself rather than to Marlene.

Mrs Hopeton was on them as soon as they walked through the door.

"Mary!" she said. With warmth radiating from her body, she hugged Mary delicately. "It's so good to see you. We've really missed you. And you too, Marlene."

Mary didn't respond, instead she scanned the room. Marlene stood awkwardly, staring back at the eyes on them. There were about fifteen women in the room, all of a certain age, and most of them were staring in their direction.

"Will you help me make the tea, Mary? Joyce, bless her,

tries her best, but it's awful. She just can't get it right. We're going to have to start again."

"Well, it's hard to judge when you're using these big pots," Mary said, finally engaging. "I'll sort it."

The two women headed over towards the table in the corner that housed the teapots, cups and saucers and the bounty of homemade cakes the women all brought with them. Marlene followed behind them.

Mary poured some tea into a cup. "Oh no, this won't do. It's far too weak." She picked up the two large teapots and carried them back to the kitchen.

With the tea fixed and the chatter in full swing, Marlene observed Mary. It was good to see her out, of course, but she couldn't help but feel that taking care of Mary had been a useful distraction. Marlene had felt her mother-in-law's nerves as they'd entered the building arm in arm, but Mary's friends had involved her straight away in the goings-on. They'd missed her.

Marlene began to wonder why she hadn't made more of an effort to make friends at the paper. Fletcher had more or less adopted her from her first day, but no one else had bothered to get to know her. She knew now she was to blame. She hadn't tried to get to know any of them, to get involved in their work, their lives. She'd go back to work on Monday and no one would rally around her.

"How's Adam?" Marlene heard Mary asking Mrs Hopeton.

"He's fine. To tell you the truth, it feels like such a long time since I've heard from him. I know he's all right, of course, otherwise I would have..." Mrs Hopeton suddenly stopped talking.

Mary reached out and laid her hand across Mrs

Hopeton's. "I may have lost my son, but I wish nothing but a safe return for yours," she said sincerely.

Watching the scene play out before her, Marlene wondered why she'd never seen this side of Mary before. Peter had so hoped they would get along, but Marlene had considered her cold and distant.

It was impossible that Peter's death had humanised Mary. This side of her must have been there the whole time.

Did he have to die for her to open her eyes?

6

DESPITE FLETCHER'S INSISTENCE THAT SHE NEEDED TIME TO recuperate from the blast, Marlene had returned to work on Monday. Her first day back in the office had gone smoother than her last attempt; some of her colleagues had even stopped to talk with her. Asking her how she was following the explosion was apparently easier than asking how she was when she had just been widowed. And George's involvement had made it much more of a talking point, of course. He'd made sure of that.

She heard Fletcher call her name. Grateful for the interruption, she headed to his office.

"What's wrong?" he asked as soon as she sat down.

"I don't know. Everything and nothing."

"You're so dramatic," Fletcher said with a glint in his eye.

"Shut up."

"I've got something that will cheer you up." He tossed an envelope across the desk to her.

At once she recognised the handwriting as Benjamin's. "At last! Why did he send it here?"

She tore the envelope open, pulled the neatly folded

paper out and read aloud. "*Dear Marlene, how are you? I'm well. Keeping out of trouble. B. A man of few words.*"

"Few but powerful, given the glow on your face," Fletcher said. "Where is he this time?"

Marlene flipped the envelope over. "I'm not sure. The postmark's too smudged." She tucked the letter carefully back inside the envelope.

"At least you know he's safe."

Marlene went back to her desk in a better mood. She was glad to receive Benjamin's letter, but it told her nothing about where he was and it didn't reassure her he was safe. She knew her brother; when there was trouble, he found it hard to stay away from it.

Later that evening, Fletcher insisted on escorting Marlene home despite her protestations. Marlene often wondered, if her own father had been aware of her existence, would he have looked after her the way Fletcher did? She had only once asked about her father.

'*He didn't love me, so he wouldn't love you,*' had been her mother's response. Even at five years old, mere months before her mother had left her, Marlene had instinctively known that her mother was a hard person to love. This had been the first—and last—piece of information Marlene had heard about her father, and she held no hope of ever meeting him. She had once overheard her grandparents deliberating who her father could be, so she'd never bothered asking them about him, either.

"So, how is it?" Fletcher asked, interrupting her thoughts. Marlene stared at him blankly, torn from the world inside her own head but not yet back in the present.

"Judging by your silence, I presume not well. Being back at work, I mean."

"Oh," said Marlene. "It's okay."

"It gets easier. Honestly, it does."

"It's not that, Fletch. It was fine. Everyone was fine. I just feel so out of it—detached from everyone and everything. Without Peter, I see how unimportant my life is here. Everything I do feels like it's filling time until I get home. Then I get home and there's nothing there either. Just me."

"You feel that way now because it's still raw. It will all make sense again soon."

"I'm not sure it *ever* made sense. Not really. At first, I suppose I thought it was because Peter was away. I'd convinced myself it was good to keep busy; to stop myself from missing him and imagining the worse. But it's not that. It's just not right."

"Give yourself some time, then we'll have this conversation again. If it's still not right, you can change it, and, of course, I'll do what I can to help. But promise me you'll wait. Now is not the time to be making big changes."

Fletcher put his arm around her shoulders, squeezing her close as they walked.

"Are the rumours true?" she asked.

"What rumours?" Fletcher asked with genuine confusion.

"About Terror being given the opportunity to go back to France?"

"What do people think is going on?"

"That Terror might go back to France and maybe there's an opportunity for someone else to go, too."

"Well, it's true we're being offered an opportunity, if you could call it that. I haven't decided if *Terence* will be the one to go yet. It makes sense. He's keen, and he's been there before. His French isn't great, though, and it's a bit more complicated than it seems. But keep that to yourself."

"Am I a candidate?"

Fletcher laughed. Marlene stopped and glared at him.

"You are absolutely *not* going."

When George had first mentioned it, she'd briefly allowed herself to imagine what it would be like to return to France. In truth, she hadn't considered it too seriously, but Fletcher's absolute refusal to consider her was infuriating.

"Why ever not? It makes perfect sense. Who better to send to France than a Frenchwoman?"

"Marlene, be serious."

"I *am* being serious."

They resumed their journey, which took them past the blast site. Marlene looked up at the building's shell. It had been incinerated. The fire had left nothing but wreckage.

Piles of rubble still smouldered, even days later, and her nose itched from invisible particles in the air. The personal belongings of the building's inhabitants were strewn around, mixed with charred bricks and blackened beams.

She couldn't believe that flames had gutted an entire building and she had escaped with just a sore head and cuts to her knees.

People were meticulously searching through the debris, looking for anything to salvage. A woman not much older than Marlene crouched in the debris, filling a red metal sand bucket with whatever singed scraps she could find among her scorched possessions.

Grit crackled under her shoes from the shattered brickwork. Surrounded by the devastation of war, she wasn't sure if she wanted the courtesy of a second thought by Fletcher when he considered candidates for France, after all.

7

JANUARY 1943

MARLENE HAD KNOWN INSTANTLY THAT THE BOY ON HER doorstep was bringing her news of Peter's death.

He held his bicycle upright in one hand and a telegram in the other. His neatly pressed navy blue uniform outlined with bright red and his black tie could not disguise the fact he was still a child.

He handed her the telegram and said nothing. Marlene was transfixed by his eyes. They were such a pale shade of blue, near lifeless, perhaps hardened from having made this same trip so many times before. She stared at him for longer than was polite, and he shuffled nervously. She wouldn't allow herself to read the name on the envelope she now held. Doing so would be life-changing, and she wasn't ready for that.

"No reply?" the boy asked after a minute of silence. Marlene shook her head, suddenly understanding why he still stood in front of her. The shake of her head was all he needed in order to permit himself to walk away. He pushed his bicycle for a few steps, got on and rode away.

Two women stood on the street directly across from

Marlene's house. Both were staring at her. One had the good grace to hold her hand to her heart whilst the other moved in line with Marlene closing the door to see as much of the spectacle as she could. No doubt she would tell her friends later about the poor girl across the street being given the news of her husband's death.

The hallway closed in on her. Marlene had nothing. No boy on her doorstep, no nosy neighbours across the street. Nothing but the envelope in her hand with her name—Mrs Marlene Edwards—typed across its front.

She couldn't open it. She needed to feel close to Peter again before the words she had yet to read put a full stop at the end of their marriage.

In the bedroom, she opened her wardrobe and pulled out everything she could see that belonged to Peter. She slid items of clothing from the shelves one by one, gently at first, then the intensity of her search grew until she began tossing as many items as her delicate hands would allow her to grab.

With the wardrobe virtually empty, even of her own belongings, she pulled a sweater of Peter's from the heap on the floor and slipped it on. Despite Peter not having worn it for months, she could still smell him on the fabric. It was city air and the sickly combination of aftershave and tobacco. She could pass any man in the street and smell these things, but in her bedroom, it wasn't any man; it was Peter. Her soft cry soon turned to loud, hard sobs that took her breath away each time. She lay amongst the bundle of clothes on the floor, burying her damp face in Peter's jumper.

An hour had passed before Marlene forced herself to get up from the floor. She thought of Mary, knowing she would have to be the one to tell her. Still wearing Peter's sweater and holding the unopened envelope, Marlene left the house.

With no real recollection of the route she'd taken, Marlene stood on the doorstep, staring at the painted red door, willing herself to knock. Several failed attempts later, she heard the wailing of the iron gate behind her at the end of the path.

"What are you doing here? What's wrong?"

Marlene held out the unopened envelope and said nothing.

"What is it?"

"It's a telegram telling me my husband's dead," she whispered.

"Oh, Marlene, come in." Fletcher put his arm around her shoulders and guided her indoors.

Fletcher took the envelope from her hands and opened it. She allowed herself to hope for a second that she was wrong about its contents, but Fletcher's face told her she wasn't.

With all hope fading, she crumpled once more and wept uncontrollably.

8

FEBRUARY 1943

MARLENE AND GEORGE SAT OPPOSITE A SWEATING FLETCHER. Fletcher's office was large, but it felt claustrophobic on account of the newspaper cuttings, scraps of paper, photographs and maps that covered its walls. His desk, twice the size of Marlene's own, was just as cluttered. Piles of books and back issues had spread onto the floor.

Fletcher shifted uncomfortably in his seat and was yet to look at them.

Marlene glanced at George, who was busy staring at Fletcher. "All right there, boss?" the junior journalist asked.

"Yes, all good. But I have a little ask of both of you. Actually, it's quite a big ask, and I can't believe I'm about to say this."

Marlene wasn't used to seeing Fletcher so flustered. His usual style was calm and in control, the ideal skills for a newspaper editor.

He took a deep breath. "It's done. Decided." He wasn't talking to either of them at this point. He took another deep breath and, his composure returned, looked from one to the other.

"I need you both to leave for a month, perhaps two. On an assignment. George, you will go to Wales, and Marlene, you will go to Scotland."

"For a *month*?" It was George who spoke first. "What kind of assignment?"

"Something that's not London. We're a national newspaper and it's time we covered first-hand what's going on in the rest of the country. Long overdue, really." Fletcher picked up a handful of papers. "I've drawn up a basic itinerary for each of you, but you're free to find your own stories and contacts where you can. We have children separated from their parents for four years now; families that have taken some of them in, boarding houses for others. There's a Prisoner of War camp near where you'll be staying, George."

"When do we go?" Marlene asked, tension twisting in her stomach. *Is he really talking about Scotland?* She was desperate to ask what was happening with the posting to France but knew this was not the time.

"There are some things to organise first, so it might be two or three months yet."

"Anything we can do to expedite the process?" George asked. "I really don't fancy winter in Wales."

Fletcher shook his head. "And there's some people I need you both to meet first before we can confirm anything."

Marlene felt George's eyes on her for the first time since they'd entered Fletcher's office. She didn't look back.

"Now, I'm sure you have questions, so I'll deal with them individually. George, we'll start with you. Marlene, could you leave us for a minute or two?"

As she stood to leave, Marlene looked at George. He looked giddy. He understood as well as she did that Fletcher wasn't talking about Wales or Scotland. It was France.

She reached for the door handle and paused. France was her country, but it was also a country overrun with Germans, the people that had caused Peter to draw his last breath. Was it really somewhere she wanted to be right now?

9

MARLENE THREW DOWN HER PENCIL AND CRUMPLED UP THE piece of paper she had been scribbling away on for the past hour.

"*Rubbish,*" she mumbled. She stared at the blank, discoloured back wall of the office, above the heads of the journalists working alongside her. Two days ago, Marlene had interviewed a group of women in the WAAF and had been working to turn her notes into something coherent ever since. There was no way she was going to do that until she had spoken to Fletcher again.

She glared at Fletcher's office door, willing George to come out.

When the door finally opened, Fletcher didn't bother calling her name. He could see she was looking right at him. George came out with a grin that was impossible to hide on his face. *There's no way he's grinning like that about going to Wales.*

Marlene jumped up and marched into Fletcher's office. He closed the door behind her. Pushing a pile of papers back, he sat on the corner of his desk. Something from the other end of his desk tumbled off and clattered on the floor. "Damn it! I need to clean up in here."

Marlene wanted to tell him to get on with it, but he was sweating again and she thought it best to let him talk in his own time.

"Are you sure you want to go back to France?" Fletcher asked. Despite their friendship, his tone was business-like, sharp and to the point.

Her shoulders sank and a smile spread across her face. "Are you serious?"

He nodded.

She knew she should have been thinking about the paper and the war effort and her chance of contributing something huge to each. Instead, she was happy for herself; this was good news for her. It was a turning point; something to focus on besides her current misery.

"Why did you pick me?" she asked, curious, given his earlier fierce refusal.

"I know. I must be mad," he said.

Marlene's face fell.

"Not like that," Fletcher corrected himself at once. "I know you can do this, but it's like sending my own flesh and blood into a war zone. But I have to do what's best for the paper. You're French. All of my journalists are good, but you're the only one who's French. Against my better judgement, it seems like the most sensible decision."

"I don't expect an answer tonight," Fletcher continued. "Go home and think about it. It's a big decision. You'll be in occupied territory for a month, maybe two, and you know the risks associated with that."

She did know the risks. Her husband had paid the price for taking on those risks. She should have been surprised at Fletcher, of all people, asking her to take those risks herself, but she wasn't. The decision felt right, even if she couldn't articulate why.

"What was that story about Wales and Scotland? You know neither of us believed that right?" Marlene asked.

"I need to work on my acting skills, especially as that's what we'll be telling everyone else. But for them to believe it, one of you will actually have to go to Wales."

Marlene furrowed her brow in confusion.

"Look, this is so much more than an exclusive for the paper," Fletcher said. "This is a matter of national security. We have the support from very, very high up to do this. But it's confidential."

"Why?"

"Journalists get one view of war. Citizens get another. And for your safety, I can't have people talking about this. "

She nodded.

"If you get into trouble, we won't be able to help," Fletcher said. "You'll be on your own. So, before you commit, I just want to make clear that at any point, you can tell me you don't want the job."

Marlene looked down. This wasn't just about Peter. It wasn't just a chance to escape her story. This was about telling the story of her people. The world had a right to know the truth about life in Occupied France. That's what she loved about working at the paper; it was a way of telling stories that needed to be heard.

"I'm going," she said.

"Then there will be things to do over the next few months," Fletcher said. "You need to treat it as a bit of an interview. Only one of you will go and they'll meet and assess each of you."

"Who are *they*?" Marlene asked.

"There's some people to meet and things to sign before I

can tell you that. They'll want to be convinced you're the right person for the job." He cupped her hand in his. "They'll also need to be convinced this is the right time for you to do something like this."

It had taken her only minutes to decide to leave France when Peter had asked her. Despite her initial hesitation, it took her only minutes once again to decide to go back.

If only one of them could go to France, Marlene was going to make sure it was her.

10

MARLENE SAT SIPPING HER COFFEE AND REPLAYING THE morning's meetings in her mind. Her first meeting was in the office of a rather friendly man in Whitehall who seemed completely disorganised and spent five full minutes looking for his glasses. After the first minute of his painfully slow search, she wondered if it was some kind of test, although she couldn't fathom what the appropriate response was supposed to be.

When the man eventually found his glasses, in his jacket pocket of all places, she was certain it was a test. The point of it, and how her inaction had been received, remained a mystery. He had put on his glasses and spoke to her about where she was from and why she had moved to London. Their conversation had taken only another five minutes before he had escorted her along the hall and had left her sitting in a room on her own.

A few minutes later, her next two interviewers had appeared. One carried a thick file, which he made a show of opening and flicking through each time she answered a question. The other had looked completely uninterested, as though he had dismissed her as a candidate on sight.

Marlene had expected the interview to be challenging and had worked hard to calm her nerves before entering the building. As the interview progressed, she relaxed, having anticipated and had an answer prepared for every question they put to her. The hardest part so far had been that second five minutes when she had had to talk about why she'd moved to London. Apart from telling her they were representatives from the Special Operations Executive, she still knew little more than what Fletcher had told her.

As she finished her coffee, instead of feeling as though her preparation had paid off, Marlene felt as though she had missed something. It was all too easy, and there could be no way the rest of the process was going to be this straightforward.

She flinched as a voice whispered in her ear, lips touching her hair. "Had your first interview?"

She spun around and came face to face with George.

"What are you doing here?" Marlene glanced behind him to check he was alone. He lowered himself into the chair opposite hers.

"Same thing you are, I think. Replaying it over in my mind, looking for where I went wrong."

"George..." she started.

"I know. We're not supposed to discuss it. Our ability to keep our mouths shut is no doubt part of the assessment."

"So why are you opening yours?"

It was George's turn to look around him. He leaned across the table and again spoke in a whisper.

"Look, there's no way I'm going to France. I'm young and fit and can handle myself in a fight." He raised his hand to silence her before she interrupted him. "But I don't speak the language, so what can I really do there? You'll be going. Assuming they can get over ... you know." He moved his outstretched hand up and down her.

"What?" Marlene asked, although she was sure she knew what he meant.

"That you're a woman. My first impressions are that there are quite a few Terrence's there who'll struggle with that."

"Just because I'm a woman ..."

"You don't need to convince *me*," George interrupted. "My point is, as long as they're only speaking to our paper—and I don't know that they are—you've got the job. This will be one of the most adventurous but terrifying things you'll ever do. Despite the need for secrecy, you'll also need people you can trust. I just want you to know you can trust me."

Marlene took his hands and nodded. "I appreciate the support, George. Really, I do."

She was growing to like George. He was eager to impress, but he was good at making people like him too. He was also probably right. The only woman she had seen in the building had been sat at the Reception desk.

A waitress appeared and George ordered a coffee and a carrot scone plus a refill for Marlene. He chatted about his neighbour, a self-appointed fire marshal, who liked to sit on the roof of his building for an hour each night with a pair of binoculars and a bucket of sand. Marlene only half-listened. It had been quite a week. She had even enjoyed some of it, although she immediately felt guilty whenever the thought entered her mind.

George's scone arrived. He flipped it upside down and spread butter on the bottom. The waitress topped up Marlene's coffee, and George waited for her to leave before he took a bite. He held his hand up as if he was going to say something, so Marlene waited as he devoured his scone in four bites.

"Sorry, I was starved," George said as he wiped his hands. He glanced around them again. "I might have some insight into the next phase of the interview process, if you can call it that."

"How? And why would you share it with me?"

"I know someone. A girl." He shrugged his shoulders and smiled. "I need you to do well here, and I can help."

"Why would you do that?" Marlene asked.

"Firstly, so you come back alive. Secondly, if you do well, there might be another opportunity like this one. And when there is, I'm taking it."

Marlene couldn't help but laugh. "Thank you for putting my safety as your first point."

"Of course," he said. "Which brings me on to my next point. French lessons. The next assignment that comes up will be mine. The only thing standing in my way is that I don't speak French."

"One has to admire your tenacity and self-belief."

"One must first believe it's possible in order to make it happen. And I believe with all my heart that I'll get there. There's a story I need to tell. I'm not sure what it is, but I know it's a big one. Will you help me and teach me French? I'm already taking classes. Well, I will be; they start on Friday. With your help, I know I can master the lingo faster. And besides, I'll be forced to spend the winter in Wales as part of your cover story, so you owe me. Please."

Marlene detected a slight wobble in his confidence. His face was radiating hope as he waited for an answer.

She sighed. "I can already tell you're going to be a difficult student."

George jumped up and kissed Marlene on each cheek.

"See, I'm a natural. You done?" he asked, looking at her empty coffee cup. "We've got interview preparation to do."

He pulled money out of his back pocket, dropped it onto the table and picked up Marlene's coat from the back of her chair.

She slipped her arms into her coat. A lot had happened since returning to work.

11

MARLENE SAT IN BROWN'S COFFEE SHOP JUST A FEW STREETS away from the address she'd been given on Baker Street. Receiving the date and time of another meeting was the only confirmation that she had passed the initial interview process. George had also been invited back, although he remained unconvinced that he was a genuine contender for the role.

She took a sip of her coffee and looked up as the door to the coffee shop chimed. A young woman strutted in with the brightest smile on her face. Clutching an oversized handbag, the woman made her way to the counter to order. Marlene looked around at the other patrons; an elderly man reading a newspaper in one corner and a younger man, two tables away from Marlene, probably in his mid-thirties, who was staring out of the window, lost in his own thoughts. If she hadn't been on her way to a meeting, she would have struck up a conversation with the young woman to find out the good news she had clearly just received to cause such a reaction. Fletcher had told her that a curiosity about people was an essential skill for a journalist, and she had since found that most people were quite happy to talk about themselves when invited to do so.

Her stomach gurgled, and her attention shifted from the young woman to thoughts of what would happen at the meeting. Marlene didn't know what to expect. Her preparation had included going over the answers she had given in her previous interview, plus coming up with answers to additional questions George had fired at her. There was little else she could do. The only insight George had received from his contact was that they would attempt to break her to see if she was SOE material.

Checking her watch, Marlene took a last gulp of her coffee and headed directly to 64 Baker Street.

Marlene found the address with ease. She lingered on the opposite side of the street as pedestrians stalked by the sand-coloured building. There were no outward signs that it was home to a clandestine organisation. A woman with chestnut hair and a long royal blue coat opened the door and entered the building. Marlene caught a break in the traffic and dashed across the road to follow her in.

Once inside, a receptionist greeted Marlene and escorted her up two flights of stairs to an office at the end of the corridor. Alone in the room for a few minutes, Marlene looked around her, but the plain office with its bare walls and empty table gave her no clues about what was to come.

When the door opened and a dark-haired man walked in, Marlene recognised him instantly as the man who had been staring out of the coffee shop's window only ten minutes earlier. He wore a tailored pinstripe suit, having apparently added the jacket on his return; Marlene recalled he had been wearing a dark blue jumper in the café.

"Good morning," he said, extending his hand. "I'm Marcus Mayer." He spoke with an accent that suggested he came from a wealthy family and had an expensive education.

Marlene stood and shook his hand. "It's good to meet you, Mr Mayer," she said. She wondered if she should mention noticing him earlier. Deciding that her trustworthiness was part of the assessment process, she added, "I believe we've just come from the same place. Brown's Coffee Shop."

He smiled, and placed a paper file on the desk in front of him, its edges curled and a coffee stain on one corner. The file looked out of place considering Mr Mayer's sharp suit and the equally sharp pencil he'd lined up next to it. "Please, have a seat. I understand you've been briefed on the role of the SOE? The Special Operations Executive."

"As much as they could tell me."

"Quite. You'll understand the need for absolute discretion. And for the details of this meeting to remain strictly confidential."

Marlene nodded. "Of course."

"On paper, you meet our needs. The next stage in the process is to ensure you're clear on what you would be volunteering for. If you decide to work with us, we'll be sending you to Paris. I need you to know there's a high chance you will not come home again. The Gestapo in Paris are particularly brutal, and they give no one the benefit of the doubt. If you fall under suspicion, you will be tortured and killed."

Marlene gulped. She understood the risks. But she also understood why she was here. A Frenchwoman who had previously lived in Paris was surely better able to navigate those risks than many others the SOE might look to recruit.

"What will the work entail?" she asked. No one had yet clarified what was expected of her once she got over there.

"Keeping your eyes and ears open. The training of our operatives includes things you *must* do and things you *cannot* do in France. Our information is only as accurate and up-to-date as the intelligence coming out of France. Upon your return, you'll be debriefed and asked to write reports on everyday life."

"To keep the training of your operatives relevant?"

"Yes. Our mission is sabotage and subversion. To do that, our agents have to be able to walk around without anyone giving them a second glance. One of our recruits was captured after walking out in front of a car, having forgotten that the French drive on the other side of the road. Another attempted to purchase alcohol on a day when French cafés were not permitted to sell it. Those sorts of mistakes cost lives."

Mr Mayer opened the paper file and scribbled something beneath Marlene's photograph. There were over twenty sheets of paper in the file and she couldn't imagine how details of her life could take up that much space.

"We'll take any opportunity to strengthen our knowledge of everyday life," Mr Mayer continued. "Nothing is too insignificant: café protocol; changes in how rationing works; the availability of common items; standards of dress. Anything that might help someone blend in and be mistaken for an average French citizen going about their day."

Marlene now understood why this arrangement had been sanctioned. The owner of *The Post* received an exclusive, and SOE gained another source of intelligence to help their agents operate covertly. They were hiding in plain sight of the Gestapo and needed local knowledge to avoid standing out in the crowd.

"Will I be allowed to write about my time in Paris for *The*

Post?" Given the secrecy surrounding her interviews to get to this point, she wasn't entirely convinced that she would.

"Yes. Although the timing of publication is a question for another day."

Marlene stared at the wall behind Mr Mayer. He'd made it clear that this assignment could be her last. Now she realised she might not be permitted to publish any of her work associated with it. "Assuming I pass your tests here, what's next?"

"This is just the beginning. You will be subjected to psychological assessments and receive training including self-defence and avoiding detection. If that goes well, you'll receive parachute training."

Mr Mayer paused, as if giving her time to ask questions. She pressed her fingers to her temples as she tried to untangle the thoughts whizzing through her mind. It took her a few seconds to realise the tapping she heard was her shoe jerking against the table leg. She uncrossed her legs and planted both feet on the floor.

"Your cover story is that you have moved back to Paris from the countryside to stay in your uncle's apartment. If you are arrested, your best protection is to reveal that you're a journalist, although there's no guarantee it'll help. Let me say again, if you are arrested, there's little chance you'll make it back home. If that's not a risk you're willing to take, I'd insist you do not board the flight."

Marlene bit her lower lip to stop it from trembling. The decision to return to France was no longer straightforward.

"Take some time to think it over," said Mr Mayer, standing up to show their meeting was over. "Meet me here at the same time on Friday. If you confirm you still want to go, I'll make the arrangements for your training to begin."

He shook her hand once again, and she gripped him

tight. Along with her personal reasons for returning to France, Marlene was also being presented with an opportunity to contribute something far bigger than she could ever have imagined to the war effort.

The only question which remained was whether she was brave enough to accept the risks.

12

MARLENE ARRIVED AT WINTERFOLD HOUSE EXPECTING TO SIT in a classroom for a few weeks. Mr Mayer hadn't given her any further details about what her time at the SOE training school would involve. Deep in the Surrey countryside, the house didn't offer many clues, either. The windows were obscured by net curtains and overgrown hedges. Given the grandeur of the building, she presumed it had, at one time, employed a staff of gardeners to keep the grounds as stately as the building. No longer, though.

There were two men outside the house, casually dressed, and Marlene wasn't sure if they were instructors or other potential recruits. One of them smoked a cigarette and pointedly exhaled the noxious vapour in her direction.

"Just go in," said the other man with his thumb pointing towards the building's grand façade. "They're expecting you."

Marlene nodded and approached the front door. She stepped between the concrete pillars and heaved open the door, coming face to face with another man standing on the other side.

"Oh, I'm sorry," she said, moving back to allow the man to come out.

He glared at her and stood still, blocking her entry. "I've been waiting for you," he said. She guessed he was in his mid-fifties. He wore black trousers and a white shirt with crisp creases along the arms. No jacket and no tie. She was just about to extend her hand and introduce herself when he spun around and marched away.

"Follow me," he called without looking back.

Marlene stepped into the building and looked around her. The interior was a shadow of the opulence it must have been in its hey-day, before the British Government had requisitioned it. All of the internal doors were closed, and the air was dusty and stale. The only natural light came through the open front door and was quickly extinguished when she let the door close behind her.

She picked up her pace to catch up with her escort as he strode along the dimly lit corridor straight ahead. He didn't introduce himself and his demeanour made clear he wouldn't be answering any questions she had about what was to come. She gulped hard as a woman came towards her with her hand across her face. Blood seeped through her fingers and Marlene caught the glint of tears in her eyes.

Her escort stopped outside a door and held his hand out, indicating for her to enter. She glanced back along the corridor. They were alone, and the man's silence was unnerving. Her chest tightened as she stepped inside, her companion's footsteps fading behind her.

Marlene squinted as her eyes adjusted to the brightness inside. Other than a small wooden table and two chairs, the room was empty. The burgundy and gold patterned wallpaper gave the room a perception of warmth despite its sparseness, and the open curtains on the large windows gave her a view of the property's extensive gardens.

With no one around, she dropped her bag in a corner of the room and wandered across to the window. A dozen people sprinted back and forth across the lawn, and it dawned on her that her training might be more hands-on than she had expected. SOE were unlikely to allow her to tag along on one of their clandestine operations without first making sure she could handle herself in the field.

She had barely registered the shuffle behind her when her arm was grabbed and she was shoved against the strip of wall between the two windows. She opened her mouth to scream, but no sound came out. Metal scraped along the floor, and her attacker pushed her violently into the nearby chair. Only then did she see him for the first time.

Her breath caught in her throat at the sight of his German uniform.

He bound her wrists to the arms of the chair and tied her ankles together. He yelled in her face in German, spittle spraying across her skin. Her knowledge of the German language wasn't good enough for her to translate it.

The man pulled a knife from a sheath attached to his uniform. Sunshine reflected on the metal and bounced around the room. He dragged the other chair towards him, positioning it directly in front of Marlene's. She flinched as he pressed the flat side of the blade onto the top of her knee.

It's a simulation. She repeated the words over and over in her head. Swallowing down the bile in her throat, she stared at him.

His icy stare challenged her to react.

She gripped the arms of the chair to stem the shaking

that had engulfed her. The hatred in his dark eyes bored into her, and she looked away from him.

He lifted the blade from her knee and pressed the tip into her thigh with just enough pressure to pierce through her trousers without puncturing her skin. She'd never been afraid of knives, having grown up on a farm, but no one had ever threatened to plunge one into her body before.

It's a simulation.

He moved the knife again and leaned towards her, this time pressing the knife to her throat. The smell of stale nicotine from his breath made her stomach lurch. Marlene froze, her breathing shallow as the cool blade pushed against her skin. Her fear intensified as she considered that this was only day one of her training.

"My job here, Mrs Edwards, is to get you to withdraw." He spat the words at her, and his lips curled up in a sneer.

Mrs Edwards.

If his job was to get her to withdraw, he had just made her more determined than ever. Someone wearing that same German uniform had taken the life of her husband. Now, she had the chance to play a small part in the plan to halt the Germans in their tracks and force their retreat. She smiled at the man in front of her as he withdrew the knife. "Then let's get started," she said.

She braced herself as the back of his hand came thundering towards her cheek. The simulation was becoming very real, but her resolve to get through it only grew stronger.

So far.

As abruptly as he had arrived, the man stood and marched from the room. Marlene exhaled and raised her eyes to the ceiling. She understood now why Mr Mayer had repeatedly warned her she might not make it back from

France. Whatever happened to her at Winterfold House would be nothing compared to what the Germans might do if she were caught.

Her skin prickled as the man returned with a brown leather case. He put it on the table to her left and snapped open the brass catches. He ran his hand along the inside of the case. "I'm going to take you through each of these until I get what I want."

All Marlene could see was metal.

"And what is it you want?" Her cheek throbbed from where he had struck her and her voice sounded shakier than she would have liked.

"I want to send you to the cooler."

Marlene hesitated, unsure if she wanted to know. "What is the cooler?"

"It's where we send those that fail their training."

He picked up a small metal clamp and sat before her again. She winced at his touch as his rough hand peeled her fingers away from the arm of the chair and he positioned the clamp on the tip of her thumbnail.

"I will use this one for tearing off your fingernails," he said. "It looks very similar to the instrument I will use to extract your teeth if you don't tell me what I want to know."

She recoiled, pressing her back hard against the chair. He pressed down on the top of her hand and squeezed the clamp. The tip of Marlene's fingernail dropped to the floor, her shoulders sagged, and a tear ran down her cheek.

The man untied her hands and legs while Marlene fought the urge to sob. Her middle finger found the jagged edges of her thumbnail. She took a deep breath and stood, pulling at her clothes to stop them from clinging to her damp body.

He picked up her bag from the corner of the room. His

grisly expression had given way to a softer smile. "Shall I show you out or show you to your room?"

Marlene's mouth went dry. Within just a few minutes, this man had caused her to question almost every thought she'd had in the last few weeks. She gazed down at the rest of the metal instruments in the leather case: knives; spikes; lengths of chain. Their purpose was too horrifying to imagine.

George's contact had been right. SOE's training instructors were going to try to break her. The threat was no longer theoretical. She could choose to go home now, or face the prospect of life never being the same again.

She licked her lips and swallowed. "My room, please," she said.

13

HER COLLEAGUES AT *THE POST* HAD ORGANISED CAKE, alcohol and music for her and George's last day. Marlene wasn't sure how many of her colleagues believed that she was going to Scotland and George was going to Wales, but that was the cover story they'd been told and she and George were sticking to it. Fletcher had denied the rumour about them being bound for France, and no one had spoken publicly about it since. They had either kept their secret or everyone was keeping up the pretence for Fletcher's sake. Marlene suspected it was the latter, given no one had asked him to elaborate on her whereabouts when she'd disappeared for her training with SOE.

She watched George basking in the attention. She admired his spirit, so happy and optimistic; the type of character she wished she could be. She knew she had a habit of looking for the negatives rather than just enjoying the positives. But she frequently told herself that being abandoned by their mother as a child would undoubtedly make a person cynical. Other times she would force herself to say out loud all the things in her life she was grateful for. Her list ultimately consisted of Peter, her grandparents, and Benjamin. When she'd started working at the paper, she had quickly added Fletcher to the list.

These days, Marlene did not consider herself cynical. She mostly considered herself justified. Her grandmother had died, and only a few months later, her grandfather had followed. She missed them terribly. Peter had put himself in danger when he didn't have to and lost his life in the process. And Benjamin had all but abandoned her, too. Although he would keep in touch with her infrequently, it was always on his terms. She had no way of contacting him if she needed to.

She was completely isolated. Fletcher was her one constant, and now she was about to leave him.

Terrence had been skulking around the office all morning. Each time Marlene glanced up from her desk, she caught his eye and he looked away. It was quite apparent that he had something to say and would not rest until he'd said it.

"Terrence," Marlene called out. When he turned in her direction, she waved him over to her. She had to put the poor man out of his misery. "I expect Fletcher has told you about me going to Scotland."

"Yes, he did," said Terrence. "Best of luck to you."

Marlene scoured his tone for sarcasm but found none. He was well known for not thinking much of female journalists. She could only imagine what he thought of her for taking the opportunity that he surely believed was his away.

"I'll be leaving next week," she told him; a fact that she was aware he already knew. However, she did not believe he had been dancing around all morning just to wish her luck, so she wanted to give him a chance to air whatever was on his mind.

"You can't underestimate the danger you'll be in," he said. *This was it. He'll be on a roll now.* "I've been on the edge of battlefields. The troops just leave you to get on with it on your own. They had far more important things to be doing than making sure I was all right."

Bragging yet again. She thought about interrupting him to say that rural Scotland wouldn't exactly be a battlefield, but he clearly knew what was really going on, and so she couldn't see the point.

"What you're about to do is infinitely more dangerous. If something had happened to me, human nature would have made those boys help me out, I'm sure of it. But you'll be on your own, surrounded by enemy soldiers, some of whom I'm sure have no humanity in them at all."

She had, of course, considered the danger she was putting herself in, and SOE had reminded her of it often throughout her training. Fletcher had insisted that the danger was his reason for initially discounting her, as opposed to believing he didn't think she could do it. France was her home. She had told Fletcher that she had to be in less danger than either Terrence or George because who would be suspicious of a Frenchwoman living in Paris?

Although Fletcher had agreed with her, he still didn't want her to go. She didn't know what had changed his mind, but she was grateful for it. This was her chance to do some-thing important and to get back home for a while; to get away from London and everything that reminded her of Peter and the life she had planned to have and yet never would. She had told herself that the only danger was getting into France. Once there, she was just another Frenchwoman trying to navigate life in an occupied territory.

"If you're careful and do a good job, this could be a

career-defining opportunity for you," Terrence said, pulling her back to their conversation.

Marlene had never seen this side of Terrence before. She hadn't even known it existed. He was not being pompous or critical of Fletcher's decision to give the assignment to a woman; he was giving her advice. She had never thought of it as a 'career-defining opportunity' and felt momentarily guilty about taking that opportunity away from someone else, but she needed to go back to France for so many reasons.

"What was that about?" George said, coming over to her once Terrence had left her to her thoughts.

"Some friendly advice, believe it or not. When do you go?"

"I'm on the train tomorrow morning. You?"

"The day after, hopefully."

"You scared?" George asked.

"I don't know. I think I should be terrified, but I'm not. Not yet, anyway. Without Peter, I've felt like an outsider in London, so I feel like I'm going home. But I know I'm going to a very different place to the one I left."

14

PUSHING OPEN THE HEAVY BLACK IRON GATES, MARLENE
entered St Mark's Cemetery. She carried a single red rose as
she made her way through the narrow dirt paths.

"Morning," said an older man out for a wander with his
wife and dog. The little terrier was tugging on his lead,
trying to rush ahead, sniffing everything he came across.
The woman smiled at Marlene, offering the uneasy smile of
strangers in uncomfortable situations. They were both in
the same place, but their reasons for being there were different; Marlene, carrying a flower, walking at a pace indicative
of going somewhere; the other woman, perusing the head-
stones, ambling wherever the notion took her, or at least
following wherever the terrier took her husband.

Marlene wondered why death fascinated people. What
does a person get from reading the snapshot of a stranger's
life that decorates their headstone?

When the time had come to compose Peter's headstone,
despite words now being her profession, they'd deserted
her. She'd had to rely on the funeral director to suggest
something fitting. Peter's mother thought it irresponsible

that she and Peter had not discussed their funeral wishes. She told Marlene that when Peter's father had died, she knew not only the inscription to be carved on the headstone but the hymns to be sung at the funeral, and even the suit she would bury him in. She was frustrated by Marlene's lack of preparedness and Marlene had overheard her telling the funeral director it was ' ... most likely because she's French'.

Marlene had thought it more to do with Peter being twenty-six years old when he died. Planning funeral arrangements was not something people thought about in their twenties. Even though their courtship and first year of marriage had been interrupted by war and death was all around, death was still something that happened to other people.

The couple and their dog were out of sight as Marlene approached Peter's headstone. She knelt down on the grass, the morning dew soaking through to her skin. She had followed Peter to England out of love, but although they had never discussed it, she knew she'd always intended to return to France at some point. It was her home, and she had always seen her life in Britain as temporary.

She had been visiting Peter's grave every week for almost three months. The once or twice she had allowed herself to think about returning to France she had been racked with guilt for days for even contemplating leaving. Now she was doing exactly that, and she wasn't sure why. It was more than a desire to return home to familiarity. Something was pulling her, like she was being given an opportunity that, if she did not grab it, would pass her by and would not return.

She laid the rose at the foot of Peter's headstone and silently said her goodbyes.

～

Fletcher had insisted on making her dinner before she left. As Marlene mashed the potatoes to be served alongside the sausages and carrots Fletcher had already plated up, her host paced around the kitchen. She had only seen Fletcher pace around that way twice in all the time she had known him. The first time had been when the owner of the paper made a planned trip to the offices. Fletcher rarely saw him and had told Marlene that whenever he had come in the past, he had brought bad news. The second time was when his mother-in-law had been coming to stay with him for a weekend.

Fletcher had confided in Marlene that he had only seen her a few times since his wife's funeral. She had been openly critical of him while his wife was still alive, passing frequent non-complimentary comments about everything, from the state of the house to the state of his suits. Fletcher's wife had been the buffer between the two, and although the old woman had always been upfront with her disappointment about her daughter's choice of husband, his wife had always got him through the day or the occasional weekend unscathed. Marlene had told him to say she could not come to stay with him. A man should not be ridiculed in his own house, Marlene had said. She had only known Fletcher for three months by this time, but their bond had formed so quickly that she knew Fletcher would never agree. He would have the old woman in his house, put up with her abuse and return to work the following week upbeat, celebrating her departure rather than dwelling on her verbalised disappointments.

Fletcher had told Marlene that he had employed her because he felt she was a lost soul and that he saw his own image reflected in her. His wife had been gone a matter of weeks when they'd met, and Peter had left two months prior to go to battle. Fletcher soon became the person who kept her going when she would otherwise have given up.

As she spooned the potatoes onto the plates, she said, "I can't believe I'm about to return to France."

"You don't have to go, you know," Fletcher replied.

"Don't worry about me. I need to do this."

"I'm not sure about this anymore, Marlene. I thought I was and, believe me, I fretted about this decision for weeks. I somehow convinced myself it would be good for you to go, but now, I just don't know."

"Stop it, Fletch," she said, taking him by the shoulders. "This *will* be good for me. Try to remember why you're sending me in the first place."

"I wish I hadn't mentioned your name."

"What do you mean?" she asked. It only took a second before his meaning became clear. "This wasn't your decision, was it?"

He shook his head. "But that doesn't mean I don't think you can do it. I just can't make peace with sending you into something I know is so dangerous. Being French makes everything easier. You were immediately the preferred choice."

"Being French also makes it less risky. The inescapable risks are getting in and getting out. The rest of the time, I'm just another citizen going about their business. Who is going to bother me?"

"I know, Marlene, but it's different thinking about it and then knowing it's really happening. It's ... frightening. I'm sending you into a war zone. You could get killed over there."

"Fletcher," she said, still holding him, shaking him lightly to get him to focus. "Have you forgotten I was almost blown up here a couple of months ago? We are at war. It's dangerous everywhere."

"I know, but that's different."

"It's not different. Do you remember what you told me about Peter? You told me you believed everyone had a time to die, and back then was Peter's time. Wasn't that what you told yourself when you lost your wife?"

"I still believe that. I *have* to. But that doesn't mean to say you can put yourself in harm's way and expect it not to interfere with the process."

"Actually Fletcher, that is *exactly* what it means," she said, smiling at him. "When Peter died, I blamed myself for not doing more to convince him not to go. I tried to talk him out of it. I screamed about it, cried about it for days, but ultimately I accepted he was going. After the news, the worst possible news, I spent many hours trying to figure out other things I should have done to stop him from leaving. You told me—quite forcefully, if you recall—his death had nothing to do with me. Nothing, in fact, to do with Peter and his decision either. It was simply Peter's time to go."

"You remember everything, don't you?" he said, seemingly placated for now. He wrapped his arm around her shoulders. "If you want to go—if you're really sure you want to go—you have my support. But if you have any doubts, any doubts at all, don't go. Never mind about the paper; we can do something else. Do what's best for you."

She buried her face in his shoulder. "You are on my list, Fletch, and I love you for that. I'm going."

"What list?" His face was still tense with worry, but he was no longer panicking.

"The list of good things in my life." She reached her arms behind him and hugged him back.

She needed to get away from London. The life she had

built with Peter no longer existed. She needed to find her own life now, since there was now no one else's life for her to ride along with.

"You've made up your mind, haven't you?"

"I have. It will help me get over everything that has happened, and, of course, I get to help you at the paper. I'm sure you're secretly glad to be rid of me, anyway." They were sitting now, and she took his hands over the table. "Thank you for everything you've done for me. For taking a chance on me and giving me the job."

"There's no need, Marlene. You've proven yourself many times over."

"Do you tell yourself that as you're correcting my copy each week?" she said, laughing. "You always have such faith in me. I wish I had it in myself."

"Are you kidding? You are about to walk into Occupied France—and you actually *want* to do it. If that isn't faith, what is?"

The reality of leaving him now hit her. Fletcher had become her closest friend over the past year; her anchor to London in Peter's absence.

"I don't have the words to tell you how much I'm going to miss you," she said. He squeezed her tighter. "Now, can we eat our food? I'm starved, and who knows how long it will be before I get a good meal again?"

Marlene didn't linger at Fletcher's once they had finished their dinner. She had to get out of there; Fletcher had given her too many chances to change her mind, and she was worried spending more time with him would make her want to take one of them.

A car was arriving early in the morning to pick her up. She hadn't been told exactly where she was heading, only that the weather looked good and they expected her flight to go ahead.

Standing in her bedroom in front of her wardrobe, she ran her hand along the clothes hanging inside and wondered if she should pack them. She would take nothing to France. She would be there for at least a month, but there was, of course, a chance she might not make it back.

She slipped her hand inside the cuff of one of Peter's shirts, still hanging neatly on the right-hand side of their wardrobe. She brought the sleeve up to her face and stroked her cheek with it.

"Will I feel you over there?"

She straightened the shirt and closed both of her wardrobe doors. A jewellery box sat on top of her dresser, and she opened it. She slipped off her wedding ring and placed it in one of the two small compartments on the top layer of the box. The other compartment held a tiny gold-plated horse with a loop to attach a necklace. It was the only thing she owned that had belonged to her mother. She had tried many times to give the horse away, but she'd never been able to part with it.

Her mother hadn't given it to her. On the day she had dropped Marlene off at her grandparents' farm, she had left nothing behind except Marlene. Marlene had found the horse in her grandmother's bedroom, and when she'd found out it had belonged to her mother, she had asked to keep it.

Marlene ran her finger along the outline of the horse and closed her jewellery box.

As she did, the air-raid siren started wailing. With a sigh, she headed to her front door, put on her coat and shoes and flicked the light off in her hallway. With her hand on the lock, she could hear her neighbours outside; heels clicking, shoes shuffling, hushed voices and someone crying. Marlene stood still until the noise outside had quieted. The siren still wailed and she could hear the distant rumbling of an aeroplane, but no other noise.

She silently unlocked her door and stepped outside. Everyone was gone, having already made their way to the public shelter. Marlene strolled into the middle of the road outside her house and stared up into the clear night sky. The full moon shone down on her, confirming it was almost time to leave. A distant explosion lit up the sky above her. She stretched out her arms, closed her eyes and bid London a farewell.

15

THE AIRFIELD WAS NOTHING LIKE WHAT MARLENE HAD imagined. She had expected it to be bustling with activity, but it was eerily quiet. There were a few men in uniform roaming around, looking intense and worried, which was a little daunting, but otherwise it was empty. It was late, of course, with only one scheduled flight, as far as she was aware.

Captain Milligan, a steely looking man with broad shoulders and a thick moustache, had escorted her from her house to the cottage near Tempsford military base where she had spent the night. Fletcher had arrived just as she was leaving, to give her one final chance to change her mind. When Captain Milligan had introduced himself, she'd wondered whether he was Fletcher's contact, but no glimmer of recognition passed between the two men. She still hadn't figured out how Fletcher came to be involved in this, and she knew better than to ask him again. The man was like a stone wall when he wanted to be.

Two other men in uniform stood with Captain Milligan,

huddled over a map. Marlene could hear them talking but couldn't make out their words.

When the group disbanded, Milligan came over to her with another man. "Approximately thirty minutes until we go," he said. "Do you need anything?"

She shook her head. He looked down at her hands, which she could feel were trembling. "It's just nerves, you know. Being here is so ..."

"Real," Captain Milligan said, sympathising. "It's to be expected. Most people suffer from an attack of nerves before take-off. The flight will be fine. Your pilot is one of our most experienced and has flown many moon flights. Officer Simpkin here will help you get ready?" Captain Milligan pointed to the man beside him, a friendly-faced man with short brown hair and ruddy cheeks.

"Good to meet you," said Officer Simpkin, extending his hand as Captain Milligan marched away.

"Good to meet you, too," she said, shaking hands. His handshake was much softer than she had expected; in fact, she feared she had shaken his hand too hard in anticipation of what his would have been like. The darkness beyond the aeroplane hanger was now lit with the outline of a plane and a row of lights along the ground. "Is that the plane?"

"Yes," Simpkin said. "Nervous?"

Marlene nodded and allowed Simpkin to strap a parachute to her back. *How long do two broken legs take to heal?*

"Tell me, Officer, do many people injure themselves parachuting from planes?" It was a question that had never occurred to her during her training.

"A few cuts, bruises and strains, but nothing to worry about, really. The biggest concern is not the jump; it's the Germans. They know what we've been up to, dropping people into France to support the Resistance. They're actively patrolling any fields they have identified as offering good drop zones and landing strips."

Her heart beat faster and she felt overwhelmingly naïve and unprepared for what she was about to do.

"Don't worry, we have secure communications with the reception committee on the ground. The pilot will only signal for you to go when he knows it's safe. You'll be travelling with another person, so that should make it easier for you."

"Oh?" She waited expectantly for further details.

"It's best you know as little as possible about our operation," Captain Milligan said as he reappeared. "You can't share what you don't know. Until you reach your eventual destination, keep the questions to essentials only. This is the beginning of a particularly challenging time, Ms Villeret."

Ms Villeret. Better get used to my French name again. Avoidance was a familiar path for her, and if she could avoid seeing and saying Peter's name every day, it could only be a good thing. She was not sure, however, that she was truly ready to let go of his name.

She said nothing about the particularly challenging time she felt she'd already experienced. Instead, she would follow the captain's orders and ask only what was necessary. Besides, the more questions she asked, the less she wanted to go. Her aim now was just to get to France, causing the least amount of damage to herself along the way.

"Ready?" Milligan asked.

Without looking back, Marlene strode out into the darkness to the waiting plane.

Entering the undercarriage of the plane, she was nothing short of terrified. She made eye contact with the only other passenger and wondered if he felt the same.

"Hello. I'm Marlene Villeret." She took her seat, thinking

handshakes probably weren't appropriate under the circumstances. Her companion simply nodded. Seemingly, names were also not appropriate.

The man looked supremely confident as he double-checked the containers that were stowed away with them before taking his own seat. His confidence conveyed that he had done this before, which should have been reassuring to her.

It wasn't.

She could not think about what awaited her in France, or why she was leaving England. All she could think of was that she was about to jump out of a plane. She felt fear, but it wasn't fear of death. The way Marlene looked at it, if she killed herself, she would have lost nothing, since she had nothing left to lose.

Acceptance of that fact was more terrifying to her than death.

16

AUGUST 1943 - FRANCE

MARLENE OPENED HER EYES. SHE FELT AS THOUGH SHE'D closed them only moments before, but the surrounding forest was now aglow with the rays of sunshine that had burst through the gaps in the trees.

"Sleep well?" asked Etienne.

"How could she? Her story was almost over before it began," said Henri. Marlene sensed something in Henri's voice. Resentment, perhaps.

He's right, though. She was here to report on life in Occupied France, and the Germans were on her as soon as she stepped foot on French soil.

She shivered. None of them had prepared for sleeping outdoors, and the already low temperature had plummeted during the night.

Etienne had spread the silk of Marlene's parachute on the ground as a barrier between their bodies and the crunchy, frozen earth. Marlene had been the last of the trio to wake, although she couldn't remember if Etienne or Henri had managed to get any sleep. She folded the parachute into a manageable-sized square.

"We don't want to be caught carrying that around," said Etienne, taking the folded parachute from her and placing it in a hole in the ground, along with the jump suit she had just removed. The hole must have already been there because Etienne did not attempt to prise any dirt free from the frozen forest floor. Instead he gathered branches and clumps of loose moss to hide the evidence.

They set off towards the road, taking their time as they moved through the trees. Etienne and Henri were still on high alert and said nothing. Marlene's steps were heavy with exhaustion. She fell further and further behind the two Frenchmen, neither of whom noticed. A burning sensation in her body intensified with every step as she tried to catch up. She didn't doubt that the pain she felt now was nothing compared with what she might have experienced at the hands of the Germans had she not drifted off course.

It took an hour of trekking through woodland before they reached the road. "Stay back within the trees and follow the road. It will lead you into town," Henri said.

"You're not coming with me?" Marlene asked, panicking that they were leaving her out here alone.

"Yes, we are," Etienne said, giving Henri a look. "We will take you to the safe house. We'll get your tickets and papers to get you to Paris."

Marlene so looked forward to arriving in Paris, where the streets would be busy with people for her to blend into and concrete to walk on, rather than the uneven ground currently underfoot. She briefly allowed herself to imagine being locked away in her temporary apartment, soaking in a bathtub. She used the image of safety as a motivator as they trundled on.

∾

Marlene and Henri lingered in the trees opposite the office building Etienne had disappeared into minutes before.

It was still early, but the village of Mer was already flooded with people. The white buildings with grey roofs and the requisite church steeple in the centre reminded her of her grandparent's farm and the town that it bordered. Its familiarity helped her to relax a little.

"It's safe," Etienne said when he returned and the trio continued their march. "We're going to a safe house near here. Not the one we planned but, given we are on foot, this one is best."

"We will have to send someone to the other house to collect your things," Henri said, his tone once again betraying his dissatisfaction about the inconvenience Marlene was to them.

They approached the front steps to the safe house; a charming, two-storey cottage with a bright red door. A woman who must have been well in to her seventies greeted them. She introduced herself to Marlene as Madame Amireau and moved with ease despite her age as she led them to a sitting room at the front of the house. Marlene glanced around the dark hallway at the pictures on the walls; paintings, landscapes mostly, and the occasional photograph. A staircase ran off the hallway, the top landing of which was Marlene could see was bathed in bright sunshine, vividly contrasting with the lack of natural lighting downstairs. Marlene supposed the curtains upstairs were not as heavy as the ones downstairs.

"Take a seat," the elderly woman said whilst gathering up a collection of newspapers spread out over the sofa. "Would you like something to eat? Tessa, my granddaughter, is making breakfast. Etienne, will you tell her you're here?"

Madame Amireau gently pushed Marlene onto the sofa

and motioned for Henri to sit. He said nothing and simply strolled out of the room after Etienne.

"My name is Marlene." Marlene took the woman's hand and shook it lightly.

"It's nice to have you here. How was your landing?"

"Bumpy. It didn't quite go to plan." Marlene hoped Madame Amireau would not take her lack of further explanation as rudeness. Marlene knew acutely that she was now in occupied territory and was unsure of who to trust, particularly as she had been briefed not to trust anyone.

"They never do." Madame Amireau smiled at her. "Let me check on Tessa."

Marlene sat alone in the sitting room for a few minutes. More photographs adorned the comfortable room. Frames of varying sizes covered the wall above the fireplace, and Madame Amireau featured in most of them. She was younger in many of the photos, but it was unmistakably her. The biggest frame held a photo of her wedding, and there was another, presumably, of her children and her grandchildren. Marlene wondered which one was Tessa.

A green vase bursting with bright multi-coloured flowers sat on the table near the fireplace. *This is Madame Amireau's family home, although it currently had a different use.* She supposed houses such as this were invaluable to help the Resistance move both people and supplies around the country. What possible reasons could the Germans have for suspecting an ageing grandmother of conspiring against them?

Marlene breathed deeply and allowed herself to sink further into the sofa. As the large cushions hugged her shoulders and neck, she found herself becoming a little drowsy. After a long uncomfortable night in the forest and the journey to get here, which must have easily been five or six miles, Marlene was extremely grateful to not be on the move. Even more so when Madame Amireau returned to announce that breakfast was ready.

"It smells wonderful." Marlene sat down at the kitchen table. "I hadn't realised how hungry I was until now."

"Lucky you," Etienne said, appearing in the doorway, with Henri trailing behind him once again. "I've been famished all night."

Tessa—Marlene presumed, since no one had introduced them—poured Marlene a cup of coffee and told everyone to help themselves to the food. She had prepared nothing short of a feast, given the scarcity of food these days; the table was packed with bread, sliced meat, cheese, baked tomatoes and stewed apples, their sweet smell filling the room. Etienne and Henri tucked in straight away, loading their plates with masses of everything. Marlene took a gulp of coffee, at first enjoying the heat it provided before the flavour eventually came through. Her face twisted at the intense bitterness.

"It's ground acorns or something," Tessa said. "We haven't had real coffee for a long time now. You get used to it." She passed Marlene a bowl with a bit of sugar in the bottom.

Marlene guessed Tessa was around the same age as her, although they had sharply contrasting looks, Marlene with her shoulder-length blonde hair and Tessa with her long dark hair. Tessa's skin was so pale, it was verging on grey. Marlene wondered if it was a symptom of the strains of living under German rule or if there was another reason as to why she looked almost ill.

Etienne, between mouthfuls of food, gave Madame Amireau and Tessa a full account of the events of the previous night. Marlene was rather surprised by his openness and wondered if their roles in the Resistance extended beyond providing a safe place to stay. Henri sat quietly, concentrating only on his breakfast.

"Quite an ordeal for your first night," Madame Amireau said to Marlene.

"Yes, but we got her through it," Etienne said, flashing Marlene a reassuring smile. "But, unfortunately, there's no news of the others."

"Caught, and who knows where they'll be now," Henri said bluntly, looking at Marlene for the first time since he'd come into the kitchen.

"Then it's just as well Marlene drifted off course or you would all have been caught," said Madame Amireau, her sharp tone reminiscent of a strict schoolmistress.

Henri, suitably chastised, remained quiet for the rest of breakfast before leaving the room under the pretence of needing a cigarette.

"I'll run some water," Tessa said once Marlene had finished eating. "No doubt you could do with a bath."

Marlene self-consciously ran her fingers through her knotted hair.

After a scrub and a change of clothes, courtesy of Tessa, Marlene found Henri waiting for her in the kitchen. He had also cleaned himself up and now sat with his eyes closed, leaning back on one of the kitchen chairs. His breathing was slow and heavy, and he looked relaxed. A map was laid out on the table in front of him.

She knocked lightly on the wooden doorframe. Henri opened his eyes and the now familiar scowl returned to his face. He gestured for her to sit in the chair opposite him.

"Memorise this street," Henri said, pointing to a spot on the map. "There's a café called Alain's. If you run into any trouble, go to the café. Alain will be there serving. Short and bearded; you'll see him straightaway. Ask him if Lucile has been in today. He'll tell you no and that you should come back tomorrow. I'll meet you in the café the following morning. If it's urgent, tell him it can't wait. I know where you'll be staying, so I'll contact you. Only say it's urgent if it actually is. It's too risky to chance it for anything else."

"I understand. But I don't expect I'll need you for anything," she said to reassure him she would not get in his way.

"The plan is for you to be gone within a month, but moon flights are tricky. I'll be in touch nearer the time to confirm if it's going ahead."

"Okay. My handler already told me my return is weather dependent."

"And we likely lost one of our best landing fields last night, so I'll have to find somewhere else for the plane to land."

"Do you know how the Germans knew we were there?" Marlene asked.

For the first time since her arrival, Henri smiled, but Marlene was certain it was more out of amusement than friendliness. "I understand your job is to ask questions," he said. "But just so you know, I won't be answering any of them."

With that, Henri pushed back his chair, stood up and left the kitchen, and, once again, Marlene was alone; something she decided she ought to get used to. After all, her field contact had made it quite clear he wanted nothing more to do with her until the time came for her to leave.

17

MARLENE'S FALSE IDENTIFICATION PAPERS AND HER TRAIN tickets to Paris arrived the following morning. She'd been given the address of her apartment in Paris before she'd left London. She had been told to memorise the route from the train station so as not to be seen consulting maps, and if anyone on her journey asked, she was to say she had been visiting her cousin for a few weeks and was now returning home to Paris.

She'd slept only marginally better than she had the previous night in the forest, despite the marked difference in both safety and comfort. She had spent much of the early hours quietly reciting the directions to the apartment. Once she left the safe house, she would be on her own for the next month.

Etienne and Henri had left the day before, wishing her well, Etienne more so than Henri. Marlene had decided that Henri's problem with her stemmed from her being a journalist. He had been curt with her from the second they'd met, even before the Germans had closed in on them, so his disdain for her couldn't have been because of that. All she could do was shrug off his attitude towards her, which was easy given that she wasn't anticipating seeing him again until it was time for her to leave.

She thanked Madame Amireau as she and Tessa went upstairs to get ready to leave the safe house.

Tessa opened the small suitcase she had packed for Marlene, which she had stocked with clothing. Her original supplies had been dropped from the plane. Etienne had returned to the drop site later the previous day and reported back that it had been cleared of everything: the signal lights, the dropped packages and the vehicles the reception team had arrived in.

"It's not much, I'm afraid, but you have all the essentials," Tessa said. "And I got the notebook you asked for. I've popped your food coupons inside. It's all I had. I hope it's all right."

"It's perfect, thank you," Marlene said. She picked up her new shoes and ran her thumb across one of the rubber pads on the sole.

"They stop your soles from wearing too quickly. Shoes are hard to find. They also help you get around silently when you need to," Tessa said, raising her eyebrows. "One more thing," she continued, rummaging in a drawer. "If you find yourself in trouble, wear lipstick. The Germans can't see past a pretty face and red lips."

Marlene took the tube of lipstick Tessa held out for her. She removed the lid and twisted the base until a bright red stick appeared.

"My mother wears this colour," Marlene said. She could see her mother's face; her big smile, glossy red lips surrounding perfectly straight white teeth that were always on show in public but rarely shown when there wasn't an audience. The memory now was as vivid as it was then.

The two young women descended the stairs shortly after, and Madame Amireau hugged Tessa for a long time before opening the front door. Marlene wondered if Tessa would not be returning there for a while or if their proximity to the war, more so because of their underground activities, meant there were no casual goodbyes anymore.

The deaths of the people in London from the bomb blast Marlene had been caught up in made her thankful for the last few weeks she had spent with Peter. She could not help but feel deep sorrow at the thought of those people leaving their homes in the morning and not returning in the evening, not returning ever again. She and Peter had known he was leaving for months, with the distinct possibility he might not return. Despite still not being happy with Peter's decision to go to the front, Marlene had buried those feelings and savoured her time with him. They had regressed to the early days of their relationship. They went to dinner and to the movies. Enjoying each other's company, they had stayed up all night talking, marvelling at their luck at finding each other. And they had cried as Peter left and darkness engulfed Marlene. It was only recently that Marlene could think of those last weeks with fondness. It did not make her any less angry that Peter had been taken from her at such a young age, but it made her see that other people had it a lot worse than she did.

"Is it awful here now?" Marlene asked as Tessa accompanied her to the train station. Tessa's presence was a relief; Marlene was grateful for not having to navigate her way to the station on her own.

"You mean with the occupation?"

Marlene nodded.

"Only if you think about it. Distraction is really the only way to deal with it." Tessa dug her hands into her coat pockets. "Oh, I forgot to give you this," she said, pulling a small folded map from her pocket and tucking it into Marlene's. "It might come in handy."

Marlene pushed the map deep into her pocket. "I was sort of hoping being here would be distraction enough," she said, thoughts of Peter creeping up on her again.

"Unfortunately, it can be very quiet these days. Still, there are things you can do to liven it up a bit and make an impact," she said, winking at Marlene. Marlene took this to be a small symbol of the secret the two now shared. "Good luck," she said, giving Marlene a quick hug.

Marlene's hands tingled as she entered the station. She had been warned in London that the Germans used the railway system extensively. She flinched at the clanging of metal nearby, and stifled a cough so as not to draw attention to herself. There was no sign of the Germans, but a row of wooden crates ready for boarding indicated they were likely close by.

When the train arrived, Marlene kept her head down, stepped off the platform and on to the train. She was now going it alone.

18

ADRIENNE

ADRIENNE STOOD AT THE FOOT OF THE CONCRETE STEPS, HER eyes fixed on the stone cross that pulled her in every day in the hope that her silent words would end her torment. She climbed the steps and walked through the imposing doorway, allowing her hand to run along the smooth wood of the door. Her finger caught a tear in the wood, and a splinter pierced her skin.

"It seems nothing will get through this war untouched," she muttered to herself, looking at the bullet wound in the door. She pulled the sliver of wood from her skin and wiped the droplet of blood it produced away with a handkerchief.

Inside, the musty smell peculiar to churches, even before the war, hit her. She walked up the aisle, conscious of her shoes shuffling on the dusty tiled flooring. It had been a long time since she had worn nice shoes. She stopped at the front of the church and lit a candle. The wick caught fire, and when the flame settled, she took a seat in the first row beside another woman. There were only a few people in the church, but the warm glow from the number of candles burning told her that there had already been many visitors that morning.

Adrienne glanced at the woman. A black scarf was wrapped around her neck, and a black hat and coat lay beside her on the bench. She had her eyes closed and held a little red book—a prayer book, Adrienne assumed—her bony hands red with open chilblains, a common sight since the outbreak of war. Her tiny frame was frail, and her shoulders protruded through her blouse. She turned and looked at Adrienne.

"My son," the woman said, returning her gaze to the candles.

"My husband," said Adrienne in reply.

"May they return home safely," the woman said, before closing her eyes again.

Adrienne watched the candle she had lit. It burned brightly compared to its neighbours, their low flames showing they were near the end. She prayed for Tomas, to give him enough strength to get through his ordeal and return home to her, and she prayed for the woman who sat alongside her and her son.

As she got up to leave, the scent of extinguished flames came upon her and followed her out of the church. Adrienne pushed any thoughts of meaning away and simply took it for what it was.

19

AFTER STANDING FOR THE FIRST HALF OF HER JOURNEY, Marlene caught sight of a woman folding her newspaper and pulling her bag onto her knee. She inched her way through a crowd of people, and, perfectly placed, she slipped right into the vacant seat when the woman stood up to leave at the last station before Paris.

Her seat was beside a woman with two small boys. The older of the two boys looked at Marlene as she sat down. She smiled, and he looked away quickly, first to his mother, then back to the toy car he had been playing with. The wooden car was painted red and blue and had a white number seven painted on its roof. *The colours of the French and British flags.*

"Luc and I got told off again in school," the younger boy said to his mother.

"Uh-huh," she replied.

"Well, remember I told you about 'three throw'? Well, that's what I call it, but Luc wants to call it 'slide and throw'. Anyway, we were playing it in class and the teacher said we must wait until lunch before playing it. It wasn't our fault, though. Sabine said it was not our game and that her brother had been playing it before us. I was telling her that 'three throw' was mine and Luc's, and the teacher told us off. Don't you think my name is better?"

"Uh-huh," his mother said again, her stare fixed on the countryside speeding past the window. Marlene suspected the woman's mind was elsewhere, and it was fortuitous that her 'uh-huh' sounds were rather well placed.

"I called it that because each player gets three chances," said the boy as he continued to explain the game to his distant mother with such passion.

"*Smmmassshh!*" said the older boy loudly as he crashed his car into Tessa's handbag, which Marlene had now claimed as her own. It was sitting on the table between them. Crashing noises followed his screeching as he flipped the car in slow motion and placed it upside down in front of Marlene.

The train slowed until it came to a stop. As she looked out of the window onto the platform, Marlene could see groups of German soldiers waiting, their hands either gripping their rifles or otherwise occupied by cigarettes. She fidgeted in her seat, feeling for the papers stowed inside her coat pocket. Her stomach tightened, and she had to concentrate to slow her breathing.

The doors to the carriage opened, and two of the soldiers entered. They stood in the aisle close to Marlene, and her body tensed at their presence. She turned her head sideways, feeling as though her secret was written on her forehead.

The younger boy stopped talking and sat perfectly still, his head bowed. His mother, now alert, placed a protective arm around him and he snuggled in. The older boy gripped his wooden car, and he, too, sat with his head bowed. He would occasionally glance at the soldiers from the corner of his eyes, still not lifting his head.

The train picked up speed again and was now non-stop to Paris. As the German soldiers scanned the carriage and spoke quietly between themselves, Marlene was struck by the feeling of having nowhere to go.

The thick edges of the map Tessa had given her pressed into Marlene's thigh. She ran over the route to the apartment again in her mind, comfortable that she would not have to refer to the map. She was familiar with the district, so she only had to remember the directions to the particular street the apartment was on. Standing in the middle of Paris studying a map was one way of telling everyone that you didn't belong. *As is having a map of Paris in your coat pocket when Paris is supposed to be your home.*

For the forty-five minutes the remainder of the journey took, the carriage was eerily quiet, interrupted only by infrequent murmurings and the moaning of metal from the train. The two boys jumped up as soon as the train pulled in and made their way to the door, followed by their mother. Marlene sat pondering whether to wait until the soldiers had disembarked before moving. In London, she would always be one of the first to get off the train, especially when on her way home. If she were acting normally, she would be on her feet by now, impatiently waiting for the doors to open.

Deciding she was thinking too much into it, Marlene stood up. Just as she did, one of the soldiers moved and blocked her path in the aisle, but he quickly stepped backwards and motioned for her to pass. Keeping her head down, like the boys before her, she moved by him. She could not look him in the eye for fear her own eyes would betray her.

Gripping the handle of the small suitcase she had stowed at the end of the carriage, she tried to pull it free of the other cases stacked on top of it. Noticing her struggling, the soldier she had encountered only moments before moved closer towards her and lifted the other cases, which allowed her to release her own.

She quietly thanked him, but before she could turn away, his hand clasped hers and he took the case from her. This time, she looked into his eyes. His face was relaxed, his mouth a gentle smile, not fierce as she had expected. She stepped onto the platform and waited to see if this was it. Was she going to be arrested? She had done nothing wrong, she told herself; nothing except parachute into an occupied country, cavort with members of the Resistance and carry counterfeit papers. Looking around the station, all she could see were German soldiers and the occasional glint of gunmetal, their steely stares scrutinised both passengers and papers, and everyone tried their best to walk as far away from the soldiers as they could.

The soldier holding her case carried it down onto the platform, placing it on the ground beside her. With nothing more than an easy smile, he strode on ahead. Marlene stared after him.

When he turned back to her and smiled as he reached the front of the train, without thinking, she smiled back.

Marlene knew the streets of Paris well enough, and the more she walked, the more familiar they began to feel. She had walked *Rue de Rivoli* many times. But what she saw on this journey was very different.

One side of the street had trees growing above iron railings, its branches poking through the gaps, which was reminiscent of London and one of its gated gardens. The other side was dull concrete with a decorative strip of stone and narrow windows marking each floor. It, too, might have looked like a building in Central London had it not been for the giant swastika flags fluttering above the heads of the passers-by. Evenly spaced along the entire length of the building, the deep red of the fabric in sharp contrast to the grey concrete, the flags were no doubt designed to be as imposing as they felt.

There were fewer Germans than there had been in the train station, but Marlene travelled with her head down regardless, avoiding all eye contact, unsure how to publicly react to any Germans she encountered.

Glad she had meticulously committed the route to her apartment to memory, Marlene knew every turn to take and made it to her street with no issues. Scanning the door numbers, she looked for her building. The blue door of Number 22 stood out bright against the building's stone walls, dark with dampness from an earlier rain shower that Marlene had been fortunate enough to miss.

The smart thing, she knew, would be to take her suitcase to the apartment and then go back out for some essential supplies. She also knew, however, that once safely indoors, she would not want to come out again. She'd spent twenty-three years of her life in France, five of which in Paris itself, but now she felt abandoned in a foreign land where she no longer knew the rules.

She walked straight past her building. From the map she had studied at the safe house, she was certain she would find a few shops only a street away.

Marlene entered the grocery shop, grateful that there were no other customers. Despite the reports on the lack of food across France and experiencing rationing first-hand back in England, the offerings on the shelves surprised her. The selection was limited but the quantities plentiful, and she used the coupons Tessa had given her to purchase her meagre meat and cheese rations and as many vegetables as she could carry. She looked at the queue outside of the *boulangerie* and decided that bread would have to wait until another day.

Her arms ached under the weight of her shopping bag and her suitcase, and she was glad to be back at Number 22. She stepped inside and onto a grey tiled floor leading to concrete steps. The handrail accompanying the steps was a mix of black iron and wood and looked immaculately maintained.

She moved clear of the door and allowed it to swing shut.

One of the handles of her shopping bag slipped from her fingers and her carrots rolled out onto the floor. She sighed and put down her suitcase to retrieve the escaped produce.

"Can I help you with something?"

Marlene jumped at the voice of a man now standing behind her in the doorway. He towered over her, and she was still comparatively miniscule even when she had straightened up. His thick dark hair made him appear, at first glance, younger than he was, but the lines in the skin of his face, however, were deep-set and many.

"Oh, no, I'm fine, thank you," she said.

"Are you visiting?" he asked.

"Yes. My uncle keeps an apartment in this building, so I've come to stay for a while," she said, unconvincingly repeating the cover story SOE had given her before she left London.

"Your uncle?" The man lowered his eyebrows, as thick and dark as his hair, and scarcely hidden by his thin-rimmed spectacles.

Fletcher had thought her delivery of the cover story was unconvincing, and he had insisted on her repeating it to him over and over again until she was sick of it. She had argued that she didn't need a cover story because she wasn't doing anything wrong; she was just writing articles. Nevertheless, SOE had insisted on a cover story for her own safety, which she now understood. How could she have possibly told anyone she was a journalist? But with this one conversation, she feared her cover had already been blown and she stood anxiously looking at the frowning man in front of her.

With no words feeling adequate enough to diffuse her spiralling self-doubt, Marlene simply nodded.

"Let me help you," he said, picking up her suitcase and heading up the stairs.

She followed him nervously up to the next floor. Apartment D was the second apartment on the right. Passing her new neighbour's door, the smell of boiled cabbage overwhelmed her and had the immediate effect of evaporating the hunger that had followed her from the train station. The man kept on walking, past Apartment D, and began to climb the stairs up to the last floor.

"Apartment D. This is me."

"Oh," the man said, returning with her suitcase. "My apologies."

Marlene noticed his tone was now lighter. His eyebrows had smoothed out, and she suspected that so, too, would his frown lines, had they not been so deep-set. She put the key in the lock and thanked the man for his help. She went to take the case from him, but despite her protestations, he insisted on bringing it inside for her.

Marlene tentatively opened the door, unsure of what would meet them inside. The first thing of note was the strong, stale smell of trapped air. Beyond that, the entire apartment was in darkness from the drawn curtains.

Marlene dropped her shopping by the door and went to the windows to pull back the curtains. The room had two long but narrow windows with an ornate black railing beyond, and, for a second, she hoped it might have been a small terrace that she could sit on, but it wasn't.

The man brought her suitcase into the middle of the room and looked around as the light spilled in. There was one main room, which contained the stove, a wooden table and two chairs, a single bed and a well-worn armchair by the window. Marlene looked into the tiny bathroom with its small single window and decided its size was based more around function than comfort. She couldn't see any storage throughout the apartment, but looking at her little suitcase, she decided it probably wouldn't cause her a problem.

"The place has been empty for some time now," the man said flatly.

"Yes. This happens now, I suppose." Marlene wondered if the disappointment she felt looking around her new home was evident on her face.

"I'm sure it will feel like home in no time," said the man. She smiled at him, trying to appear a little more upbeat. The apartment was small but adequate.

"Thank you for your help," she said, moving towards the door. She didn't want to seem rude, but Marlene was desperate to be alone so she could wallow without feeling guilty her behaviour was being witnessed by someone else.

"Well, welcome to the building," he said as he followed her lead. He stopped just outside, pushed his hair away from his forehead and bowed his head. "I am Michel Coreil."

"Marlene Villeret," she said, extending her hand. He held her fingers lightly, kissed them and made his way back downstairs. Marlene heard someone open the door to the apartment next to hers. She quickly closed her door, not wishing to have any more encounters that day. She clicked the lock into place and fell against the door.

"Home sweet home," she muttered to herself despondently. Being in the apartment brought back memories of her early childhood and the many cold and unwelcoming apartments she had stayed in with her mother.

The chilly night air seemed to penetrate the window and dampen five-year-old Marlene's forehead, which was resting against the glass. The train's vibration pulsed through her, adding to her drowsiness. Her mother had shaken her awake at five o'clock and had told her that they were going on a trip and she needed to get dressed. Marlene had snuggled herself further under her blanket, not really registering her mother's words.

Seconds later, her eyes snapped open as the cosy cocoon she had made was broken. Her mother had pulled her blanket into a heap at the foot of the bed, and the cold night air surrounded her. Her mother was dressed and already wearing her coat. A set of clothes had been laid out for her. It was the Sunday dress.

Marlene loved the Sunday dress, as her mother called it. It had blue and white flowers on it, accompanied by a lace trim around the neck, sleeves and along the hem. Her mother always tied a silky blue ribbon around her waist, tying it again and again until satisfied she had formed the perfect bow. Then she would comb Marlene's hair and secure it with more blue ribbon that stood out radiantly against her blonde hair.

"Mama, why can't I wear the Sunday dress every Sunday?" Marlene had once asked.

"Do you remember when we first came to live here?"

Little Marlene had nodded.

"Well, do you remember eating cabbage and potatoes every day?"

Little Marlene had scrunched up her face. Six months on, and she still got nauseous whenever she smelled boiled cabbage. The smell seeped into every room and lingered for days.

"That's what would happen if you wore the Sunday dress every Sunday. It would stop being special for you."

Little Marlene couldn't imagine ever feeling about her Sunday dress the way she felt about boiled cabbage, but she knew her mother was right. She was always right. Rather than wishing she could wear it every week, Marlene instead cherished the occasions she did wear it and the uninterrupted time she got to spend with her mother as she added the finishing touches to the outfit.

Little Marlene had climbed out of bed and pulled on the Sunday dress as her mother stood waiting in the doorway. She smoothed down her dress, looked around for the blue ribbon, and smiled when her mother dropped to her knees and held out the sliver of fabric. Marlene watched the concentration in her mother's eyes as she set about tying the ribbon around her waist. Years later, she would picture those eyes again and again, searching for some sign of sorrow, any hint of regret, for what was to come.

"Mama, I don't like being outside at night," said little

Marlene, rubbing her eyes sleepily as they hurried to the train station.

"It's not night, darling. It's just very early. Do you remember what I told you the last time?"

"The sun likes to sleep late during the winter."

"That's right. It gets up very early for us all summer long, so it deserves a rest in winter, don't you think?"

Neither the thought of a trip, nor, in that moment, wearing her Sunday dress excited her. Marlene had to fight to keep her eyes open as they walked. When they finally boarded the train, she allowed her eyes to close again. Her mother said nothing throughout the journey, so Marlene sat quiet also, drifting in and out of sleep.

The next time she woke, the darkness had given way to daylight and, although the sun hadn't yet come out, the sky was bright.

"We're going to see your grandparents," said Marlene's mother, finally breaking the silence that had loomed been between them since they had left the house.

Marlene looked up at her mother. Her mother looked at her as if waiting for her to say something. Marlene had known that she had grandparents, of course, but she'd never met them and knew nothing about them, except that they lived very far away.

"It will be nice to see them, won't it?" her mother asked.

"And we're staying there?" Marlene asked.

"For a little while, yes."

Marlene was used to moving around. In her five short years, they had moved every few months.

This last six months was the longest Marlene could remember staying in one place. She remembered on one train journey hearing a girl sitting in the seats behind chatting away excitedly about being on a train for the first time.

Marlene stole a glance and thought it odd that this girl, who was so much older than she was, had never been on a train before. Marlene was now well used to trains, having travelled many kilometres on them each time her mother decided a change of view was required to solve all of their problems.

She had once asked her mother what problems she had because Marlene didn't have any. She never found out, but she knew they were big problems because it was the first time she had seen her mother cry.

Marlene's hopes crumbled as soon as they pushed open the door to each new apartment. They were always the same. A dark corridor awaited them and taunted Marlene as the air that escaped chilled her more than the darkness under which they had arrived. She would always step in behind her mother, who fumbled for a light switch, and the resultant yellow light that flickered intermittently did nothing to alter Marlene's initial feelings. Each cramped, damp apartment mirrored the one they had just left.

Only their last apartment had been different. It was, without doubt, the nicest apartment they had lived in. Marlene had been sure within minutes of arriving that this one would be the one to fix all of her mother's problems. Marlene had her own bedroom and a table upon which she could put her collection of dolls, if four qualified as a collection. Her mother said she couldn't get any more, or she'd be forced to choose who would be left behind the next time they moved.

Marlene looked at the small bag her mother had brought, glad this journey was just a trip and not another move.

The damp morning air turned warmer with the dawn as they walked from the train station. Stopping at the end of a dirt track road, Marlene looked up at the house ahead of them.

It was a small farmhouse with smoke already billowing out of the chimney, despite the early hour. A collection of barns sat to the side of the house, and cows and a handful of sheep dotted the fields in front. Marlene wondered if this had been the place her mother had lived when she was a girl. Her mother had spoken little about her childhood, but Marlene thought this must have been the place from the little she knew. A single tree stood tall in the yard.

The farm looked a friendly place, but Marlene had pangs in her stomach as they made their way up the track. But whether they were hunger or nerves, she couldn't decide.

Now, twenty-one years, a train journey and another new apartment later, Marlene had those same pangs in her stomach. Except this time, Marlene was certain hunger had nothing to do with it.

20

IT WAS THREE DAYS BEFORE MARLENE EMERGED FROM THE apartment again. Telling herself she hadn't been in hiding, she quietly closed her door and crept downstairs. Reaching for the handle of the entrance door, her stomach lurched at the thought of what might await her outside. She heaved it open and stepped out onto the street.

She took a deep breath. The only fresh air she'd had in three days had come from the window she'd opened just a crack. Glancing in both directions, she looked at her old watch, not really registering the time. Its face was scuffed and scratched from her days in the countryside and had probably received another scratch or two from her crash landing in the woods. It was the only item SOE had allowed her to bring. Everything else, even her underwear, had been provided for her, to make sure it was French.

Marlene looked at her watch again, set to Berlin time as she'd been instructed to do before leaving London. It was still early, but she had expected to see more people going about their business. Until she met Peter, she had often felt lonely in Paris, but she had never felt alone. In the Paris she had lived in, she could not recall ever being on an empty street.

When Marlene had first arrived in Paris, eight years ago now, the volume of people she saw every day had amazed her. Living on a farm with her grandparents and her brother, she had been used to seeing only those same faces for days at a time. When she'd ventured down into the town, the dozen people she would come across knew her by name and usually what she had been sent for.

Paris was so different. For a long time, she'd felt as though she was standing on the wrong side of the window and was looking in. Benjamin didn't seem to have much time for her, and within a week, she had run back to the farm. Her grandfather had persuaded her to give it more time before deciding whether or not to stay. He'd said the city was glamorous, prosperous and full of culture; that she only saw it through homesick eyes and needed to get out and explore it. Previously, she had one farm that was hers; now, she had an entire city.

Marlene had taken his advice and had made an effort to explore the city whenever she could. She had never learned to love it, not in the way she loved the farm, but touring around helped her to see a Paris she could at least appreciate. To some Parisians, not loving Paris was the ultimate sin, so she had kept this view to herself. Now, being back in Paris, she felt once more on the wrong side of the window.

Marlene walked for a few bleak minutes before she began to see signs of life; people in windows opening blackout curtains to let the new day in; people en route to work. No children. No Germans. She needed people to blend in with, and she needed a story for Fletcher. That, after all, was why she was here.

Marlene had told her interviewers in Baker Street that

she wanted to give the people of France a voice outside of their homeland, that it would be her contribution to the war effort, but she didn't really believe it. The women she had interviewed for the WAAF were actively helping the war effort. The soldiers who had so willingly abandoned their families were helping the war effort. She saw the value in providing details of life in France to SOE, but how could writing about life in everyday Paris help? Would it help defeat the Germans? Would it free France? Would it keep the Germans away from Britain?

It was too late to question if she was doing the right thing. Marlene had made her choice and would have to get on with it. Besides, there was no way to leave until the plane returned for her at the next full moon. More people were coming and going now, getting on with their lives. Keeping society functioning has value. This is what she had told Peter when he'd wanted to leave her.

As she wandered around her new neighbourhood, Marlene encountered her first group of uniformed soldiers. They paid her no attention as they passed, chatting amongst themselves. The men didn't unnerve her as much as they had on the train, but her journey, she supposed, was the most unsettling bit. Here, roaming around the streets of Paris, she blended in with the hundreds of other people the soldiers saw every day. She put it down to her nerves being on high alert after her unusual entry into France and the events in the woods. The few days she had spent indoors had helped little; they had surely only added to her anxiety.

Marlene arrived at what she concluded was the centre of her neighbourhood. There were long, wide streets with a variety of cafés, restaurants and shops on either side, and each street led to a square named *Place Grenat* that seemed to be a meeting point for friends and market traders. A flower-seller had set up on one side of the square, a news-paper stand on the other, and a man was selling an assort-ment of wooden chairs and stools from a cart near to where she stood. It was like a separate little town within the city. Each café and restaurant had outdoor seating, but few patrons despite the mild weather. Almost every person was either on the move or huddled in small groups in the square.

Marlene took a seat on one of the iron benches dotted around the area. A large clock tower sat to her right; also set to Berlin time. Observing the morning rituals of everyone that worked and gathered here made her relax a bit. When she had first started working for Fletcher, he had given her writing materials to carry with her everywhere. He habitu-ally said you never knew when an idea or a story might present itself. Fearing writing in public would only invite questions and suspicion here, she'd left her notebook at home and planned instead to just watch. She had a good memory for detail, and would hold everything in her head until she returned to her apartment. Marlene had decided she would keep diary entries of anything interesting or useful, which would serve as her notes for SOE when she returned to London. Those diary entries would also be the basis for the articles she would write for *The Post*.

She scanned the restaurants. She had loved eating out with Peter and, when he had first left, she had continued to eat out on her own every week. The routine helped. But she had not dined out since his death and wasn't sure she would have the courage to sit alone in a restaurant here.

"Morning, *mademoiselle*," said an old man as he lowered himself slowly onto the bench beside her. "This cold weather is not good for the hips. Not good at all."

She smiled at him and returned his greeting. Old age

had the effect of messing with the body's temperature gauge. Her grandparents had been the same in their later years; had the fire burning all year round, even in the highest temperatures of the summer.

"I've not seen you around here before," he said.

Startled, her eyes narrowed as she stared at him. The man shifted awkwardly until he found a seated position he was happy with. Deciding her imagination was running away with itself and the poor man was just making polite conversation, Marlene told him she had only recently returned to Paris to live in her uncle's apartment while he was away. She had been trained to stick to the same story, no matter how chance and insignificant the meeting appeared to be.

The old man leaned over and picked something up. "Would you look at that? Shame to let it go to waste." He showed her the cigarette stub he'd scooped up and dropped it in his pocket. "I come here every day. Just to sit. It might be cold, but it's just as cold in my house, thanks to those blasted Germans." He didn't even attempt to keep his voice low.

Marlene stiffened and glanced around her to see if anyone had heard.

"Oh, don't worry about it, sweetheart; they're not afraid of me. I've said it to their faces, but they don't care. There was a time when I would have done more than just say it to them, if you know what I mean, but the old shell can't manage it anymore. It's barely able for my stairs," he said, knocking on his knees like he might a door. "Still, I expect I'd better keep my voice down. I wouldn't want to be causing any trouble for you."

Marlene let out her breath. She didn't want to be attracting any trouble to herself, either. For a moment, she wondered if the old man really had said such things to the Germans. She expected not, or he might not have still been here.

"Is Paris how you remember it?" he asked.

"More or less," Marlene said, grateful for the change of subject.

"Shameful, isn't it? If I'd been gone for ... How long did you say you'd been gone?"

"Oh, not too long."

"Still, if I'd been gone for any length of time and came back to find it overrun with Germans, I would have expected it to have been blown to pieces, barely a building left standing. But no, look at it, unbelievably normal. We just handed it over to them. We gave them the heart of our country, and for what? I don't have a radio anymore, so I can only imagine what they are saying about this on the news, but it can't be favourable, I'm sure. The most distressing part was not seeing the Germans walking in; it was watching the French walking out. Friends. Family. Neighbours. They left in their thousands before the Germans arrived. How could life possibly be the same again?"

Marlene wondered how many times he had repeated this rant. The old man was right, though. She had expected mass destruction, but Paris was in a better state than London. Physically, at least. Perhaps even the Germans saw the beauty that most of the world saw in Paris.

Doubtful. More likely they hadn't needed to destroy it because it was just handed to them.

Marlene wondered what repercussions that decision would ultimately have. Her grandfather used to say to her, '*Making decisions is like throwing pebbles in water. The bigger the decision, the bigger the potential ripples, so make sure you always think about the ripples*'. He had said it so often that when she had told him she was marrying Peter and moving to London, all he needed to say was, 'Have you thought about the ripples?'.

She watched the cafés fill up and only half-tuned in to the old man's continued ranting. Marlene couldn't decide if there was a story to be told about him or not. Fletcher had told her once that a journalist could make a story out of a white wall; it was how the story was constructed that made it interesting. She had stared for many hours at many white walls, and they had yet to present her with a story.

"How long have you lived around here?" she asked him, hoping he hadn't already given her the answer while she hadn't been listening.

"Me? Oh, well, it must be coming on for forty years. I never wanted to come, but Madame Fortin insisted. That was my wife. She's gone now."

"I'm sorry," Marlene said.

"Don't be. I'm glad she's not here to see this. It wasn't easy for us, you know. You young ones don't really know what hardship is. Sure, you feel it now, but it's still easier than we had it. You complain that there's no fuel for your cars, but we never had cars; couldn't afford them. Every time the power is out, you can't cope. I have a neighbour—young woman, your age, I expect—got a couple of kids running around that she doesn't know how to look after, and every time the power is out, one of those kids gets sent to knock on my door for candles. You'd never find someone my age getting caught short like that. And you certainly wouldn't find them getting caught short twice."

Marlene laughed, which was not the reaction the man was hoping for, judging by the look he gave her, but his little rants amused her. She liked him, and was glad that with everything else going on, a neighbour with a candle shortage was what was upsetting him the most.

"I was sitting right here the day everyone left. They walked down this very street. I saw a woman fall down, right over there where that bicycle is sitting. And do you know what happened?" he asked, not pausing for an answer. "*Nothing.* Everyone around her kept going. By the time I reached her, she was gone. Dead. Shameful, it was."

Marlene shook her head. Looking directly at the scene made it even more horrific. SOE wanted surface level details. Fletcher wanted something deeper. He wanted to know how the occupation has changed people. And it has changed them. No one in the Paris she knew would have walked on as a woman lay dying in the street. That was what she would have to convey in her articles.

"Can I buy you a coffee?" she asked him, hoping he wouldn't continue his anti-German rants in a public place. A story about residents fleeing their homes, focusing on the need to still stand up for those that aren't able to stand up for themselves, was forming in her mind.

"No, thanks," he said.

Marlene stood, a little relieved he didn't accept her invitation.

"I never drink the muck now. It's not real coffee, you know. The Germans have snagged all the good stuff. That's how they keep us under control, you know. They control the heat, the light and the food. Even the coffee. You come back here one day though, sweetheart. It's been nice chatting with you," he said.

"You too," she said, not looking forward to her coffee as much now.

The coffee *was* muck. She'd forgotten all about her first sample at the safe house until he'd said, but it would have to do. She'd found that if you filled it with sugar, if there was any, it wasn't half as bad.

She left the old man sitting on his bench. At least she knew where to find him if she needed any more detail to flesh out her story.

21

ADRIENNE

ADRIENNE STOOD IN THE HEAD TEACHER'S DOORWAY, watching Monsieur Mayotte sitting at his desk. Despite it having been his desk and his office for ten years, Adrienne knew he no longer considered it so. Having retired two years before the occupation, he'd returned to the post when his successor had fled Paris. She had tried to talk him out of it, but he had insisted it was his duty to return while he was still able to.

"Ah, Adrienne! Morning," bellowed Monsieur Mayotte, noticing her in the doorway. "Have you heard Antoine Steunou will not be returning?"

"No, I hadn't. Is he all right?" she asked. Having been away for two years, the man had returned as sharp as ever. He always knew what was going on before she did.

"It seems the family packed up and left in the night. No one knows where they've gone or why. Strange, isn't it? One would have thought that those of us who had stuck around would do so now for the duration. In any case, please remove him from the attendance register."

"I will. How peculiar."

The school had been used to seeing students disappear in the early days of the war as people took off to escape the occupation. The children that remained were more or less constant.

Adrienne hung up her coat and quickly set to work completing her early morning duties. After she had amended and handed out the class registers, she took the morning's post and papers into Monsieur Mayotte. As she entered his office, he slammed the cabinet door closed and locked the door, pocketing the keys.

"Everything okay?" she asked, putting the post on Monsieur Mayotte's desk.

"Yes," he replied. He returned to his seat and began to rifle through the mail Adrienne had brought to him.

"What have you got in there?" Adrienne asked, staring behind him at the locked cabinet.

"Everything needed to run this place when I'm not here."

Adrienne tilted her head and frowned.

"Don't worry, I'm not going anywhere yet," said Monsieur Mayotte without looking at her. "But the war will soon be over and then the children will come back in their droves. When that happens, I won't be staying around."

Adrienne took a deep breath. "Do you really think it will be over soon?"

"Weapons will not win this war; people will. The people of France have had enough. They will soon be ready to rise up, and when we do, it will be over."

Monsieur Mayotte had a certainty etched across his face that Adrienne wished she shared. She smiled and moved away from the desk, closing the door on her way out. Adrienne had only worked with Monsieur Mayotte for four years before he had retired, but they had become close friends and had remained so once he had gone. She and Tomas, before the war, had regularly visited him and his wife. Adrienne enjoyed her work, but she much preferred it when she was providing secretarial support to Monsieur Mayotte. Despite her initial reservations, she had been glad to see him every day again.

In the last year, Adrienne sensed that his full attention was not on the school, not that she blamed him. He seemed to have distanced himself. She thought at first he was adjusting to no longer being retired and the routine of once again having things to do every day. But he had not settled down much at all. She, of all people, knew what it was like to have things going on that you didn't need a constant reminder of, so she left him alone.

Back at her desk, Adrienne organised her remaining workload for the day and straightened her typewriter. Once she had finished, she opened her cabinet and removed a tiny trinket box decorated with blue and white flowers. She placed it on the far corner of her desk beside a red flower made from a delicate silk and a framed photo of Tomas. His sleek black hair was neatly combed to one side, and his smile was so big that it whisked her away to happier times whenever she looked at it.

She took her handkerchief and dusted the photo before adjusting it several times until it was in just the right position.

22

THE PLAIN, BLANK NOTEBOOK SAT ON THE TINY WOODEN TABLE, open at the third page. Marlene never wrote on the first two pages of any notebook she kept so the ink couldn't transfer to the front cover. It wasn't the pretty notebook she had tried to bring with her, but it would do its job.

When she had been told how little luggage she could take with her to France, Marlene had gone out and bought a new notebook. She had chosen one with green butterflies on the cover and a deep red ribbon placeholder running along its length. When her luggage had been inspected prior to the flight, the notebook had simply been tossed aside. If it wasn't available to buy in France, it couldn't go, and so they had replaced it with a nondescript book of plain paper with a dull grey cover.

Marlene was disappointed not to have the fancy one, but she was grateful it had been replaced at all. Who knew where that notebook was now? The Germans had surely gone through the contents of her original suitcase. *Was someone writing in it, or had it been used to keep a fire going for a few more minutes?*

Marlene recorded the date and scribbled down her observations so far, including how she had been able to stroll through the neighbourhood, unchallenged from street to street and café to café, and the old man she had happened across who had vehemently expressed his negative opinion of the occupation. He, too, went unchallenged. She included false details of her train ride from the countryside and noted her disappointment that her uncle hadn't been able to meet her in person when she'd first arrived.

The candle beside her flickered, its glow not bright enough to illuminate the full room. She lay down her pen and stared into the dark corners of the apartment. On the plane, she had felt as though she was going home; now, she recognised she had romanticised the absence of France in her life. She was still alone, locked inside an apartment with nothing but her own thoughts and an occasional rumble in the distance, which definitely didn't sound like thunder.

She turned her notebook to the back page and began doodling. The alternative was going to bed and lying awake in the darkness with dark thoughts as her only companion. That was one thing that hadn't gone away despite the miles she had travelled.

What *was* different was her ability to do something about it. In France, she was no longer powerless to act against the Germans who had taken Peter away from her. She knew how to get in touch with Henri and, therefore, she had the contacts, the geographical opportunity and the desire. Skulking amongst them, that desire was stronger than ever before.

So, what's stopping you?

A knock on the door interrupted Marlene's thoughts. The main door downstairs made such a terrible bang when it closed that it sent tremors around the internal walls.

Certain no one had come in, she expected to see Monsieur Coreil, but she still opened her door cautiously nonetheless.

"Evening, dear," said the old woman now standing in the hallway. Her dark grey hair was long, twisted into a bun and clipped on top of her head. She smiled warmly enough, but she had the look of a woman who could very much take charge when necessary. "I'm Madame Cloutier from Apartment C."

"Oh. Well, nice to meet you, Madame Cloutier. My name is Marlene Villeret."

"I thought I'd stop by and introduce myself. We seem to have been missing each other over the past few days. And I've been meaning to give you this, to welcome you to our building," said the old woman, holding out a jar to Marlene. "It's jam. I made it in the summer when I visited my son. He lives in the countryside, so he grows all sorts of berries on his land. He doesn't know what to do with them, mind you, and neither does that wife of his. I preserved the lot, and I've been eating it ever since."

"Thank you," Marlene said, reaching out to take the jar. The old woman didn't move from the doorway; she just smiled expectantly at Marlene. Marlene suspected that the woman would be the type who, once inside, would not easily leave. "Well, it was nice to meet you."

"And you, dear. I'm just next door if you need anything. We've got to look out for each other these days, if you know what I mean."

"Quite," Marlene said, closing her door.

The old woman's hand shot up and pushed against the door to stop it from closing. "I remember him, you know," she said. "Nice fellow, but very quiet. A bit like yourself."

"Sorry. Who do you remember?"

"Your uncle." The old woman must have spoken to

Monsieur Coreil, who had obviously repeated the story Marlene had told him. "You don't look much like him, but I suppose you wouldn't. He left a while back. I was surprised to hear he still owned the apartment because no one has come here in a long time. He was just like you; stayed home a lot. He didn't work ... well, he said he was a writer and therefore worked from the apartment, but I had never heard of him. Can't have made that much money with his writing. Now, what was his book called again? *After the Hills*, or *Before the Hills* or something like that. Anyway, I've never come across it."

Marlene was desperate not to become snared in conversation. The old woman had already caught her off guard simply by mentioning her uncle. She didn't want to be asked questions about a fictitious uncle, but neither did she want to simply agree or disagree with anything said, through fear of offering something that could be easily challenged. She suspected the apartment belonged to the Resistance, and she wondered whether the man Madame Cloutier remembered had been a part of it. Marlene told herself again that she wasn't doing anything wrong.

"I didn't know he had any family, either," the old woman continued. "But I'm not surprised, really. He kept himself to himself. One thing I do know is that he liked my jam."

"And I'm sure I will, too," said Marlene. "I look forward to trying it."

The old woman finally made her way back to her own apartment, and Marlene slumped against her now closed door. Her stomach growled, but she couldn't face soup again. She'd thought soup would stretch her meat rations out, but almost a week of the same dinner was getting to her. Day old bread sat on her countertop, now calling out for a slick of jam.

Marlene wondered who the man, her 'uncle', was. He might have been a struggling writer who had given up the apartment when he had gone. It was possible that someone from the Resistance had taken it over with the intention of it becoming a safe house, where it had lain empty and on standby. She thought it more likely that the man was connected to the Resistance.

She would have to watch out for Madame Cloutier. Nosy neighbours were one thing, but nosy neighbours when you had a secret to keep were entirely different.

23

A WEEK HAD GONE BY, AND MARLENE WAS FEELING MORE comfortable going to and from her apartment, taking different routes as much as possible as she had been trained to do. Varying her routine would help her get to know her neighbourhood, and make it harder for someone to track her movements, her training instructor had said.

Madame Cloutier stuck her head out of her door to say hello almost every time Marlene passed by, but she rarely saw anyone else. She had become accustomed to the occasional footsteps passing her door and shuffling on the floor above her, but she had otherwise avoided any further conversations with her neighbours.

She still felt tense travelling through the streets of Paris, but she thought all of its citizens probably shared that tension, given the ever-present reminders of the German occupation.

As her confidence grew, Marlene found herself making more of an effort to go for a stroll. She wouldn't find snippets of information or a story stuck inside, she reasoned, and so she began to take herself off to comb the streets whenever she could.

Up ahead, a group of older women were perched on the edge of a fountain, its water spewing above their heads. Their animated chitchat reminded Marlene of Mary and her group of friends from the social club.

She wandered over to them and plonked herself on the steps in front of them.

"*Bonjour*," she said simply. She had no desire to join their conversation, but listening to the chatter of the locals was why she was here. She could put their words in print on her return to London. Marlene also knew that this age group was more attuned to the day-to-day realities of wartime living. Mary had told her soap would be the next item to be rationed months before it had happened.

"*Bonjour*," one of the five replied politely, although they carried on chatting, not really registering her presence.

"My cousin has a *German* living in her house, so you're not even safer in the countryside," one of the women shrilled. "I'm probably safer here, since no one is interested in living in my tiny apartment."

"Oh, I *cannot* imagine that! Living near you is bad enough, but in your own home? Is nowhere off limits?"

"Seemingly not. They've no respect for anyone's borders, do they? My cousin came home one day, and she swears she could tell he'd been in her bedroom. He'd been searching for something. No idea what, but she could smell his tobacco lingering in the air."

"There they go now," yelled one woman. "Dirty Germans!"

Marlene couldn't help but admire their willingness to voice their views. She'd seen so many people, herself included, clam up and go in the opposite direction whenever there were Germans in sight. But she'd found that older Parisians, like her neighbour Madame Cloutier, had strong opinions and were not afraid to share them.

Marlene eyed the group of German soldiers whose mere presence had provoked the woman. They had obviously heard. There were three of them, and one had stopped and turned to face the women and Marlene. Their eyes cast to the ground, the other two waited to see what was going to happen next.

The German sauntered towards the women. His comrades looked at him, but stayed where they were.

"What did you call me?" the German asked in surprisingly good French.

"Not specifically you, *boy*," the woman spat. "It's *all* of you."

"I think you should be on your way before you get yourself into trouble," the soldier said.

Marlene remained seated in front of the group. The German towered over her. She really wanted to stand and move away, but she dared not attract his attention.

"We will not," the woman said. "This is *our* city, not yours. We have a right to be here. You don't."

"This is not your city. Your leader gave it to *us*. And I'm ordering you to disperse." His French was not perfect, but it was good. The aggression was obvious in his tone, and Marlene feared the worst. The women simply stood from the edge of the fountain and folded their arms in defiance.

Marlene stood up, unsure of what she could do, but inaction felt like the wrong response. With the added height given to her by the steps, she looked the German right in the eyes, but he stared straight through her. The women had wound him up so much, he now only had one focus.

"You will disperse immediately or you will be arrested."

The German pushed past Marlene and grabbed the woman he'd spoken to by the upper arm, forcing her down the steps.

The other four women began shouting over the top of one another. The German hadn't seemed to notice the audience as passersby slowed to see what would happen next. His sole focus was on the old woman he held in his grip.

Marlene eyed his friends, still standing back, watching and saying nothing. Her heart thudded in her chest.

One of the women barged her way past Marlene to reach her friend. "Get your hands off her!" the woman yelled.

One of the two onlookers finally spoke. He said something in German, which Marlene didn't understand. The atmosphere calmed a little, and the German dropped the old woman's arm.

He turned to the other four women. "I will not tell you again. *Disperse*."

The German glowered, and Marlene caught his eye. Quickly looking away, she followed behind the group of women. One of them had put their arm around the shaken old woman and pulled her firmly to one side. The tension from the brief standoff remained as the other women followed their friends.

The sound of German voices and heavy boot steps eventually fell silent as they, too, marched away.

"Are you all right?" one of the women asked their friend when they finally spoke again. "How dare he grab you like that!"

"I'm fine. I can't believe the audacity of those Germans," she said with as much vehemence as that which had got her into trouble in the first place.

Marlene tailed the women, unnoticed, for a short time.

Their brush with the occupiers had seemingly done nothing to change the topic of their conversation, and she slipped away at the end of the street.

Marlene had been in Paris for a week now, and that small display was the first sign of aggression from the Germans she had witnessed, albeit they hadn't instigated it. To find something she could write about, she would have to seek out more opportunities to witness interactions between French citizens and German soldiers.

She turned towards her apartment. The German had looked her right in the eyes. The callousness behind his stare sent a shiver down her body.

24

THE THUD ON MARLENE'S BACK CAME OUT OF NOWHERE. Something hit her right between the shoulder blades, and for a few seconds, she struggled to take a breath. Turning slowly, her eyes dropped to the ground. A football rested against her left shoe and a group of children stood nearby, staring in her direction.

The children turned their gazes to each other, eyes flickering backwards and forwards, as if silently working out which of them would be brave enough to collect the ball.

With the decision seemingly made, a boy stepped forwards and came towards her. Interestingly, Marlene noticed that he was the smallest of the group. His black hair was slicked back and he looked grubby, and his trousers had holes in each knee.

"I'm sorry," the boy said. "We weren't paying attention. But we promise we'll take more care in the future. Can I please take our ball back?"

Marlene smiled at his sweet apology. She could imagine another person might have roared at the boys for playing football in the street. She was more likely to tell them to pay closer attention, so the boy was doing well in answering her complaint before she had even voiced it.

Marlene nodded, and the boy quickly grabbed the ball.

"Thank you," he said, before dropping the ball onto his foot and launching it over to the other boys. Marlene laughed and shook her head. The boy was once again oblivious to who else might have been in his path.

As Marlene turned away from the boys, a crowd of people had gathered on the street ahead, spilling out onto the road. Marlene slipped among them and manoeuvred herself near the front. Two German soldiers stood in the street beside two small black cars. One soldier held a car door ajar, watching the open door to an apartment building. The other soldier surveyed the crowd.

"What's going on?" Marlene whispered to one of her fellow onlookers.

"A Jew, apparently," someone from elsewhere in the crowd whispered back.

A man was brought out of the building, flanked by another two Germans. One soldier prodded him in the back and he squared his shoulders, raised his head, and walked steadily towards the waiting car.

"But that's Louis. He's not a Jew," a woman to Marlene's left insisted.

"But he's been *hiding* a Jew," another voice replied.

Two women appeared in the doorway. The younger of the two sobbed and only kept moving because of the German soldier pushing her from behind. A tiny, frail older woman accompanied her, her hair covered by a floral headscarf. The lines on her face gave nothing away, and her gaze was firmly fixed ahead of her. She rubbed the sobbing woman's arm soothingly as they stumbled along.

"That'll be the Jew, then," another voice called.

Marlene couldn't believe what she was seeing. She wanted to intervene and help the distraught woman, but she knew there was nothing that could be done.

"Papa! Papa!" someone yelled from behind her. She jerked forwards as a young boy propelled himself through the swarm of people.

The German soldier that had been surveying the crowd grabbed the boy by one arm as soon as he'd reached the clearing.

"Papa!" the boy called again.

The man being arrested froze, his eyes wide and staring. The distraught woman sobbed louder and spun around. She lashed out at the soldier that had been pushing her along. Her arms flailed in all directions as she struck out at him and dodged his attempts to grab her.

"I'm here! I'm here! Don't panic," said a voice in the crowd, and a man stepped forwards. "He's my boy," the man said, grabbing at the boy's jumper and pulling him free from the soldier's grip.

Marlene's eyes darted back to the man being arrested. His eyes glazed over as he stared at the other man and water came rushing into them. There was no nod, no gesture of any kind, but Marlene knew exactly what was happening.

The soldier flanking the man yelled and gestured in the boy's direction. He knew what was happening, too.

The German turned to go after the boy and Marlene stepped into the space left by the crowd and collided with him. Mumbling an apology, she stepped to the side, leaving a gap too small for the soldier to get through. After making another attempt to pass her, he lost his temper.

"Out of the way!" he commanded in perfect French, with fury in his eyes. He pushed her sideways and stormed past.

Craning her neck to see beyond the crowd, Marlene

thought she caught a glimpse of the man and the boy with the slicked black hair turning into a side street.

The arrested man was shoved down into the rear of the car. The distraught woman had now gone limp and was being helped to another car by the older woman and an impatient-looking soldier.

The German who had pushed her out of his way returned empty-handed. Marlene shrank back as he, too, started yelling. She turned and weaved herself through the crowd, resisting the urge to run and avoiding eye contact with everyone she passed.

She'd put herself at risk. Marlene didn't know what might have happened if the furious soldier had spotted her again, but the alternative—what might have happened had he caught up to the boy—was too frightening to wonder.

Thirty or so people stood by and watched. Friends and neighbours stared on as a family was torn from their home, and only one man had stepped forward to help.

Despite the attention she had brought to herself by stepping into the soldier's path, taking action was the right thing to do.

25

AFTER LEAVING WORD AT ALAIN'S THAT SHE NEEDED TO SEE Henri, Marlene arrived at the café the following day, expecting to find Henri waiting for her. Instead, Alain offered her nothing more than a scrap of paper with directions written on it and an emotionless nod.

After a ten-minute journey on foot, the note led Marlene to a tree on the edge of the woods by the river. It was the same type of tree as that which had ensnared her on her first night in France, only there were little leaves left now, as autumn already seemed to be turning to winter. It stood tall and, despite being surrounded by other trees, looked lonely in its skeletal state. Tentatively, Marlene approached the dark figure stood beneath it.

Henri had seen her. He lit a cigarette and strode towards her.

"Has something gone wrong?" he asked. He kept walking, heading back towards the edge of the river.

"No, nothing's wrong. Thank you for coming. I wanted to discuss my role here with you," said Marlene.

"Your role? You're ready to return to London already? Paris is not what you thought it was going to be, huh?"

"No, no. It's not that. I don't want to go back. Since I'm here anyway, I hoped I might be of more use to you. Be a little more ... *active*."

Marlene watched him to gauge his reaction. His face gave nothing away, but Henri stopped and turned towards her.

"Being active can be dangerous."

She felt like a child whose teacher had just told her off. "I realise that, Henri. I understand it means greater risk."

"A greater risk for whom? The people that I work with are highly trained operatives, prepared to give their lives if necessary. If one person makes a mistake, it risks exposing so many others. You're a journalist, apparently, not an operative. You could too easily be the one to make a mistake."

Marlene wasn't sure how much Henri and Etienne had known about her when she'd first encountered them. Henri had previously said that he knew it was her job to ask questions, but they had discussed nothing else about why she was in France.

"Everyone has their part to play, Marlene, and you are already playing yours," he said.

"Two days ago, I saw a family being taken from their home while thirty people did nothing but watch. That's not right," she said.

"Why were they taken?"

"Apparently, they were sheltering a Jew. She was the tiniest old woman, Henri. How could she possibly be a harm to anyone? But everyone just stood there."

"What is it you expected them to do?" Henri asked. "They've all heard the rumours, if they haven't already witnessed it themselves. People who stand up to the

Germans die. Those that help Jews—and sometimes even those that merely live nearby—die, too."

"I can't walk around Paris, surrounded by German soldiers, and feel as though I'm letting them away with it." The pitch in her voice was rising, and tears formed at the corners of her eyes. "They need to pay for what they've done."

Henri scanned the area. Marlene wasn't sure whether it was to see if anyone was around to hear her or if it was because he was uncomfortable with her display of emotion.

"What is it you want them to pay for, Marlene?"

A sudden wind surrounded her, and she shuddered at the chill emanating from Henri as he waited for her response. His eyes bored into her as though urging her to confess.

"What do you want them to pay for?" he asked again.

"For this. For being here," she said, her arm gesturing vaguely all around her.

"Why did you come to France?" Henri asked.

"France is my home. I cannot stand back and observe her unwanted occupation," she said in a voice that didn't even convince her.

"You're leaving in two weeks. That's useless to me," he said.

"I can stay. I was already told that my time here might be longer than a month."

He shook his head and sighed. "Everyone has their own reasons for involvement; their own motivations. No one is involved for the greater good. Revenge is personal. And from the look in your eyes, your motivation is too personal for you to get in any deeper," he said.

"I can do this," she said. "Please."

Marlene might have had other motivations, but she

couldn't believe what Henri was saying. Of course there were others putting themselves at risk for the greater good. She wondered whether it was living a lie, like he had to, that had made him so cynical.

"Have you ever killed a man?" he asked, quite matter-of-factly.

Marlene shook her head. Every emotion possible was bubbling away under her surface, fighting amongst themselves, all trying to emerge the victor. She was somewhere else, observing from a distance, willing herself to speak. But to say what? She had wanted to convince Henri to let her do more, but now she had vocalised it, her request sounded dangerously naïve, even to her ears.

Henri rubbed the back of his neck and moved to a mound of rubble that had once been a part of the wall leading down to the river. He sat down and motioned for Marlene to join him.

"I am trained to kill a man," he said as Marlene settled beside him.

Marlene pulled her coat tighter around her slight frame. Henri's tone might have warmed—as much as was possible for him, anyway—but the air around them was bitter.

"What they don't teach you is how to deal with the emotions involved. They can't, I suppose. Sometimes I set explosives and see death as an orange flame. Sometimes I see death as an anonymous uniform falling to the ground in the distance. It's the death of Germans by my hand. I still go to sleep at night. But sometimes, I see death consuming a man right in front of me. I see the life drain from his eyes and seep from the wound I have just made in his flesh. I don't know this man. He's someone's son; someone's husband. I don't sleep that night."

Henri stared at Marlene, waiting for a response. All she

could do was nod as if in agreement, although she wasn't sure what she was agreeing to.

"Think about that, Marlene. How many sleepless nights could *you* endure?" His eyes burned into hers. "Once you know the answer, we'll talk again."

Henri stood and headed off towards the trees. He offered no goodbye, but then he didn't need to; he'd made his point.

Returning to her feet, Marlene walked back along the river. A tear finally made its way down her cheek, closely followed by another, then another. As her tears became heavier, the energy that her meeting with Henri had sucked from her returned, and she ran.

When she reached the busy streets again, Marlene forced herself to slow down. Running would bring attention to her she didn't need. She wiped the sweat from her forehead with the back of her hand and took a deep breath. As she did, her eyes locked onto a German army uniform striding towards her. She lifted her eyes.

His intense gaze was fixed on her.

26

Sweat returned to Marlene's forehead as the German reached out and grabbed her arm, stopping her in her tracks. Her gaze fixed on the uniform, her only focus being what that uniform represented; what it was capable of. She stood motionless for a few seconds, unsure of what to do. The man released his grip and lowered his hand.

"Are you all right, *mademoiselle*? You were going pretty fast there." He spoke French with an accent that would have betrayed his origins even if his uniform hadn't.

"I am."

"Where were you running to?" he asked.

"Nowhere. Home."

He stepped forwards to look around the corner she had flown around seconds before. "Why the hurry?"

"It's cold and it's getting late," she replied. Until now, she had never seen a German soldier walking alone. As a minimum, they usually patrolled in pairs.

She stared at his face for the first time, waiting for his next move. He smiled; not the smug, satisfied smile she had so often noticed on the faces of German soldiers, just a smile.

"Did I hurt you?" He moved back towards her and touched the arm he had grabbed.

She shook her head and stepped away from his touch.

"You don't like me much, do you?" he asked.

His question took her off guard. This was not the first time that she'd had to speak to a German soldier, but it was the first time she had been stuck for something to say. She had been told to answer questions as truthfully as she could. The truth was easier to keep track of, making it less likely that she would slip up and reveal too much but, on this occasion, a truthful answer would cause nothing but trouble for her.

"No, I don't," she said, not caring about the consequences in the moment.

The soldier did not react. His smile faded fast, and he stood staring at her with dark brown eyes. She wanted to run away from him, but fiery emotions from her meeting with Henri simmered inside her and she could not help herself.

"I don't like you at all, actually," she continued, the words seeming to explode out of her. "In fact, I despise you and what you're doing to France; to the world! Spreading your poison everywhere. For what? To serve the ambitions of one man. And at what cost? Do you ever think of the people who have died at your hand?"

The soldier removed his hat and held it in front of him, revealing thick dark hair that matched his eyes. "I do. I often think of them."

Breathing hard now, the anger she had bottled up since Peter's death exploded, and Marlene could no longer contain all the feelings that had been strangling her from the inside for the last nine months. The soldier in front of her could have been the one who took her husband's life. And if it wasn't him, it was a soldier *like* him, who wore the same uniform, and fought for the same cause.

She thumped on his chest, her tears flowing, hot and heavy. "It's your fault. It's your fault!" She continued to repeat the words until her energy subsided.

The man held her wrists. His grip was light, and the wool of his cap pressed against her hand. She could have pulled away any time she wanted to, but she didn't. Standing there, her head bowed and her wrists being held by this German, Marlene was drained, as if he had taken her life force from her, leaving nothing but a shell behind.

She braced herself for the consequences of her actions, waiting to be arrested, searched, questioned and God only knows what else; waiting for him to get his retribution.

"I think of their families, too, and the loss they'll be experiencing." His voice was quiet, and he lowered her arms and let go of her wrists. "But know this; some of the people I have killed, if I hadn't, would surely have killed me. Loss would be my family's burden to bear once again. I can't expect you to understand, for I do not understand it myself, but it is the only explanation I have. One day, this war will be over, and those who are left will return home. Will they return home murderers? Even your men?"

"Our men have no choice." The anger was now gone from her voice; all that remained was solemnity.

"*I* have no choice." His voice was now as quiet as hers. He no longer watched her, instead picking imaginary fluff from the sleeve of his military issue coat. "Germany is my country, and it, too, is being ravaged by war. Food is in poor supply and bombers have destroyed buildings. I've lost loved ones, including my wife, and those that are left live in the same conditions as yours. If I do not fight here, I am dead, and so is my remaining family. I have a daughter. She turned five last month. I missed her birthday. Fighting a war I didn't ask for, to make sure she gets to see her next."

Marlene stared up at him now, words failing her. Without another word, the German stepped out of her way and gestured for her to pass him. She felt an urge to talk more with him, but she didn't dare. She simply walked away from him and didn't look back.

27

MARLENE TOSSED AND TURNED THROUGHOUT THE NIGHT, thinking of the German soldier. Fear had consumed her as soon as she had seen him walking towards her, but her anger had rapidly taken over. And he had allowed her to vent that anger. He had allowed her to direct it towards him without consequence.

She forced herself out of bed and spent the first part of the morning writing, but her mind kept dragging her back to thoughts of the German. He'd said he had a daughter. *He's someone's father. Does it matter?*

She needed a distraction and thought that the impact of the occupation on French children would be a feature worth writing.

It was late-morning when Marlene found a café opposite a school. She ordered some food and chose a table outside. Eating alone was easier than she expected when she reminded herself she was working.

The dull start to the day had given way to bright sunshine, but there was a definite chill in the air that confirmed winter was near. Fortunately Marlene had wrapped up well before leaving her apartment, expecting to sit outdoors to observe the children.

From where Marlene sat, she could see the school's play area. The school itself was small and the building run down, typical of that area of the city. She liked it because it reminded her much more of home; smaller, although still a part of the city. She had never been one with a desire to live in the most fashionable area and, from her experiences with Peter's mother and her friends, knew that she didn't fit in with the people who lived there.

Marlene's choice of marital home had dismayed Mary. Although only a ten-minute walk away from her own house, it wasn't considered to be a good area, and certainly wasn't good enough for her son.

A figure paced back and forth in front of a window in the school building. A teacher, Marlene presumed. From the number of children running around the playground, she guessed that there must only have been a handful of teachers now left at the school.

"I expect that's the quietest the playground has ever been," Marlene said to the waiter as he brought over the water she'd asked for.

"Yes. Not much noise these days," he said. He sat down on a seat at the table in front of hers. "It's funny—or rather sad, I suppose. I used to get such terrible headaches when the children ran around screaming at lunchtimes. I never could understand why anyone would sit outside for lunch and put up with the noise. Now that so many of the children are away, it unfortunately reminds you that things are not normal."

The waiter looked quite comfortable, sitting and chatting to Marlene, and he appeared to have no plans to resume work. But with only one customer, Marlene didn't imagine he had much to do.

She nodded in agreement. "It is funny how the state of a nation is so easily identified by looking at its children. When they're gone, what does that say about what's going on in the place?"

"Exactly my point," the waiter agreed, now getting agitated. "The Germans have the city so terrified that people no longer feel it is a safe place for their children to be. Mothers and fathers would rather send their child away to the countryside or non-occupied zones, rather than risk bringing them up here. Sometimes they're sent to live with family, but others are left in the care of strangers because their parents fear for their safety in their own home. It's not right."

"Sadly, that's not unique to France. It happens in other countries too. Children are sent away from cities to avoid the bombing." Aware of the waiter's eyes on her, she stopped talking in case she said too much.

As the last few days had proved, despite the fear almost everyone spoke of, there were still people who were not afraid to voice their opinion in public. Marlene's expectations of what it would be like to live in an occupied city did not match the reality. She could go wherever she liked, and sometimes days would pass and she would not see any Germans if she avoided some key locations. There were noticeably fewer people than in the Paris she remembered, particularly children, but what else had changed? She wondered to what extent this perception was a veneer. How far beneath the surface would she have to scrape to see the oppression and domination?

"I'll get your lunch," the waiter said now, straightening the seat he had taken as he left. Marlene had not heard a bell or anyone call, but his waiter's instincts had been right, as he returned within seconds with her food.

As she ate, she watched the children in the playground. One boy in particular caught her attention. He sat on the steps leading towards the entrance while the other children had split off into one bigger group and two smaller groups. He sat outside all three. With his chin resting on his hand, he looked bored. Marlene remembered the feeling well, or rather she remembered sitting on the outside of the groups.

Marlene had been to four schools in her first year of schooling, so she was always the new girl. She hated those initial few days in a new school. There was none of the excitement she had felt when she'd started school for the first time; the joyful anticipation of the unknown, before she'd learned to fear it, and the possibility of new experiences and friendships. Starting a new school was not like that. The other children were always curious about the new girl, especially when considering each of the schools she went to were quite small. New pupils were rare. They would ask where she was from, what it was like there, why she had moved, and the occasional child would ask why she had no father. Marlene hated the attention anyway, but she hated it even more so because her mother had told her each time they left a town that they were not to talk about that town again.

After the first new school, Marlene had told her mother that the children had been asking where she had come from, and she'd asked if it was okay to talk about the town just to tell them that. Her mother had snapped that other children should mind their manners and, clearly, their own parents hadn't taught them to be as polite as she had taught Marlene. Marlene didn't really understand how asking where someone was from constituted bad manners, but didn't question it any further.

Occasionally, she'd told people she couldn't remember where she was from. The playground was the worst, not knowing if anyone was going to ask her to play, so she would sit on the steps, as the little boy did now, lonely and unhappy.

A woman came out of the door, triggering the children to run past her and head inside. The little boy remained seated, and the woman—the teacher from the window—sat beside him. She spoke with him for a few seconds before placing the back of her hand on his forehead. He hadn't joined in with the other children, not because he wasn't invited, but because he wasn't feeling well. The teacher led him inside, leaving the playground empty and muted.

Marlene began writing in her head. The children of Paris were not unlike the children of London. There were noticeably fewer children in the city; all packed off to friends and family in the countryside like their British counterparts. Many of them, like the British, must be missing a parent; fathers who had gone off to war and had been expected back when the Germans had taken over but had so far not arrived.

She wondered how many teachers had fled the city, although with fewer children to teach, perhaps it wasn't too much of a problem. There weren't any children in her apartment building that she had come across. There were six apartments: Marlene's own, Madame Cloutier's, the nosy neighbour from next door, Monsieur Coreil, whom she had met when she first arrived, his neighbour, whom she had yet to meet, and two others on the top floor. Marlene occasionally heard creaking floorboards from the apartment above hers, and footsteps passing her door, but no voices.

"Finished, *mademoiselle*?" asked the waiter, appearing at her side. She nodded, and he picked up her plate. "How was everything for you?"

"Perfect, thank you."

"Can I get you anything else? Some more food? Some coffee?"

About to decline, Marlene noticed the teacher from the school slipping into the seat the waiter had occupied earlier. She faced Marlene but watched the waiter, no doubt waiting for him to be free. *Odd time of day for a teacher to be visiting a café, just as the children had returned to lessons from their lunch break.*

"*Mademoiselle*?" the waiter prompted.

"Ah, sorry. Yes—coffee, please," Marlene replied.

"Of course," he said and headed back into the restaurant without even acknowledging the woman at the other table.

Marlene watched the other woman. Being discreet wasn't an option considering there were no other customers, but the woman seemed oblivious to Marlene's attention. Her petite frame mirrored Marlene's own. She ran a pale hand along the side of her head, smoothing her black hair, which was already neatly pinned back. Her eyes, rimmed with dark circles, appeared sunken into her face, and her forehead was creased with worry rather than age.

The waiter returned with two coffees on a scratched silver tray. He deposited one in front of Marlene with a simple smile and took the other to the teacher. She thanked him, and he nodded in response before disappearing back inside the café.

Marlene was surprised by the lack of exchange between the woman and the waiter. Clearly, she was a regular enough customer for him to know her order without asking, but there was no familiarity, no conversation at all, which Marlene found odd, considering the waiter's personality.

The woman cupped her coffee in both hands and bunched up her shoulders as if freezing, despite her long coat. The café was still empty, so she could have had her pick of indoor tables. If Marlene thought she would have been able to get a sense of the atmosphere in the playground from inside, that is where she would have sat.

The woman sipped her coffee, staring absentmindedly into the street. Marlene wondered what was going on in her life to make her dark eyes so lacklustre and lifeless.

Moments later, the woman deposited money on the table and left. Marlene hadn't yet touched her coffee but got up anyway, went inside and paid her bill.

"Do you know that woman?" she asked the waiter. "The teacher."

"Oh, she's not a teacher. She comes a lot—only for coffee. Is there a problem?"

"No, no problem. I just wondered." Marlene thought she ought to offer some poor excuse to dissuade any suspicions and said, "I wanted to ask her where she bought her coat."

"She doesn't say much. I think she likes me because I don't make her talk." Given Marlene's experience with him, she would have found this difficult to believe if she had not witnessed it for herself. "She came in a few times and I tried to get some conversation going, but she didn't respond. So, I thought it best to leave her to drink her coffee. I always try to chat with the customers; creates a better atmosphere, don't you think?" He'd asked a question but didn't take a breath, let alone wait for an answer. "I expect you noticed we're not exactly busy these days. With everyone so short of money, it makes for a slower trade."

"Are there any days you are busy?" she asked. She had

passed a lot of cafés around the city and most had been busy, or certainly steady, at least.

"Sometimes, but it's by accident, I think. We don't have passing trade down here, not like the cafés on the main streets, so we only really serve locals. Are you local?"

"A few streets away," Marlene said. "Do you ever get any Germans in?"

"No!" the waiter said forcefully. "I wouldn't hear of it! I wouldn't serve them, even if they came with pockets full of cash. Although I expect their style is more to barge in, order what they want, devour it and then leave without paying. That's what they've done to France, except the leaving part, but that will come, I'm sure of it. Anyway, they stick to their own places."

"Their own places?" asked Marlene. She'd been told this during her training and she had seen German signs across the city but hadn't lingered too long to see what was going on.

"They have their own cafés and restaurants. They even have their own cinema. It's a better one than ours."

Marlene hoped for his sake that Germans did not enter the café. If the waiter was true to his word and did indeed refuse to serve them, she suspected he would come off worst. His chatter, however, had helped her to decide what to write about next. There might be no useful information for Baker Street, but painting a picture of German-only venues for *The Post* would help to show the risk of losing this war.

Which meant she was going to have to find some.

28

MARLENE WOKE UP GASPING FOR AIR. HER NIGHTDRESS CLUNG to her body and a bead of sweat ran down her forehead, stopping at her eyebrow. It was the same dream; always the same dream. Peter was standing, his face serious, everything else around him a blur. The sight of him made warmth spread throughout Marlene's body, but then his face contorted, bullets pierced holes in his flesh, and a bright red stain leaked across his uniform. She dragged herself out of bed and into her tiny bathroom.

Once dressed, she couldn't stomach breakfast. Looking around the dreary walls of the apartment, Marlene realised she had nothing left in Paris. Nothing left in France. Her grandparents were both gone, as was the farm. Benjamin had sold it despite promising them he would look after it, and now she had no idea where he was.

Pulling on her coat, she headed out. She needed a different view and some fresh air.

As Marlene opened the door to her apartment, something fell inside and scraped its way down her shins. She sighed. It didn't hurt, but it snagged her stockings in a couple of places. She didn't exactly have an abundance of stockings with her. She tugged at the snags before checking to see what had been resting against her door.

She picked up the object, gripped the wooden frame with both hands and marvelled at the intense colours that seemed to radiate heat from the canvas. The burnt orange skyline with streaks of fiery red like flames. The people in varying shades of grey, small and only identifiable as people by their generic frames. The Eiffel Tower, tiny in the distance and black against the bright colours of the sky.

Marlene flipped the painting. A slip of paper was tucked between the canvas and the frame.

To bring light indoors. Michel Coreil.

The signature on the paper matched the signature on the painting itself. She smiled. Her downstairs neighbour had obviously been as disappointed as she had by the inside of the apartment.

She put the painting aside. She would pick a place to hang it when she returned.

As so often happened to her in London, a combination of the fresh air and her distracted state of mind meant Marlene had walked a lot further than she had intended to. She looked around to orientate herself. There was a gate on her right-hand side that was ajar, and beyond it, a tunnel of overgrown hedges and tall trees. Intrigued, she went through the gate and followed the path.

The path was longer than she expected, and it led to a garden with a strip of water that was too big to be called a pond and only just big enough, perhaps, to be called a lake. It was beautiful. The towering trees blocked any view of the surrounding buildings. It was a wall of green, interrupted only by the occasional patch of wild flowers and a statue of a woman lying on her side on top of a moss-covered plinth that overlooked the water.

The expanse of water itself was a perfect rectangle. It sat within a clearing that was as wild and unkempt as the rest of the garden appeared to be, where the grass was long and stood straight. It was clearly not grass that was walked on often.

She looked around the perimeter of the garden for any signs that might say who owned it. She could see nothing.

Marlene fell in love with the garden straight away. It was an unexpected sanctuary within the city. It was peaceful, the foliage lessening the noise of passing traffic, and so green despite the season.

When her nosy neighbour from next door had mentioned she didn't go out much, Marlene had realised this was true. Once she saw something or had an idea sparked by a conversation with a local, Marlene would usually head back home to write up her diary notes and wouldn't go out again. She had forgotten to go outdoors to do something for herself.

Completely encapsulated in her surroundings, she could forget all about the daily commotion of the city beyond. It was the most perfect piece of Paris she had ever come across.

Marlene wandered around the edge of the water for a time as the sun dulled in the sky. She picked a handful of wild flowers on her way out, agreeing with her artistic neighbour that the apartment really could do with a bit of colour.

29

MARLENE STROLLED THROUGH THE STREETS, HEADING FOR *Place Grenat*, the square in her neighbourhood. As she approached the corner, she stared at the giant swastika on its white and crimson background billowing in the breeze. There were so many of them across the city, but Marlene could never get used to seeing them.

She knew the occupying soldiers usually congregated on this side of the square. To avoid them, Marlene would ordinarily take one of the other roads which bypassed it. It hadn't occurred to her that the square would be home to a German-only restaurant, just a few minutes away from her apartment.

The dark clouds overhead threatening rain and the artificial lighting inside the restaurant made it easy to see the clientele in great detail. Inside was a sea of German uniforms, broken up only by the occasional waiter or waitress. The sign above the door was written in German, presumably replacing what had once been written in French.

One diner came out, cigarette in hand, and leaned back

against the wall to finish his smoke. As the door fell shut behind him, a quick burst of music and laughter escaped from inside the restaurant.

Two German soldiers headed in her direction. They were no doubt on their way to relax and fill their bellies. Her neck stiffened, and she crossed her arms. One of the soldiers caught her eye and nodded in greeting. She looked away and stepped into the nearest café so she would not have to pass them. The café was warm, and the accompanying scent of coffee was so strong that it almost smelled real. She lingered at the door, willing the soldiers to keep going. They did.

"*Mademoiselle*," the man behind the counter said, acknowledging her entrance.

His gentle smile helped Marlene to relax and she ordered a coffee. Scanning the small room for a place to sit, a familiar figure sat at a table by the window; the woman from the school. Her eyes focused on the book she read, her forehead still furrowed deeply and her fingers entwined in a lock of black hair that had fallen loose. Although Marlene was not keen to sit by the window, talking with the woman might give her the substance she needed for her article and the chance to enjoy a coffee with company instead of being alone yet again.

She picked up the chipped cup placed before her and walked across the room. The woman looked up as Marlene approached, as though she sensed eyes on her. With a shy smile, she raised her hand to the chair opposite, inviting Marlene to sit.

"Thank you," said Marlene politely. "It's so busy in here."

She took a seat and stared anxiously into the darkness outside. The dull lighting in the café obscured everything on the other side of the window, something which unnerved

Marlene, since she had just seen how clearly people on the outside could see in.

"Yes, Philippe's is a busy place," the woman said.

"Philippe's?" asked Marlene, confused.

"Yes. Here. It's called Philippe's."

"Oh ... of course," said Marlene. She had been so focused on getting out of the path of the German soldiers that she had not noticed the name of the café in which she sought refuge. Marlene placed her cup in front of her face, pretending to be cooling its contents, and pulled her hair out from behind her ears. "Thank you for letting me sit. It's nice to have some company."

The woman nodded. "You're welcome," she said.

"I think I saw you the other day, actually. In the café opposite the school."

"Oh yes," the woman said. Marlene could tell that the woman was being polite but insincere. She had clearly been distracted at the time, but even more so than Marlene had realised, given that the woman had not noticed the only other person in the café that day. "I go there in the afternoons. Goodness, you must think I spend all day and all night in cafés."

Marlene laughed. "We all need something to help us pass the time. I'm Marlene."

"Adrienne. Pleased to meet you."

For the next hour, their conversation was light, mostly around foods they missed and how long it might be before they tasted good food again. Marlene was careful not to give too much away, and she sensed Adrienne was being just as guarded.

They settled their bill and left together. Dusk had now turned to dark as they ambled away from Philippe's.

"*Halt!*" someone cried out from behind them. Adrienne

and Marlene glanced at each other and quickened their pace.

"*Halt!*" The voice was closer this time, and a hand grabbed Marlene's shoulder. She stopped, as did Adrienne alongside her. Turning, they came face to face with two Germans. They were out of uniform, but there was no mistaking them for soldiers.

The man who had grabbed Marlene's shoulder spoke in German while the other stood smirking. Marlene didn't understand what he had said, but she could smell alcohol on his breath.

"We party?" he said, in French this time.

They weren't in trouble yet, but a quick glance at Adrienne confirmed she was equally as unnerved as Marlene.

"We have to go home." Marlene pronounced each word slowly and clearly, although she doubted it would help either of them to understand her. What she really wanted to tell them was that they were drunk and should sleep it off somewhere, but she didn't want to provoke them. Drunken strangers were worryingly unpredictable, who knew how drunken *Germans* were likely to react.

The more vocal of the two said nothing in response but bowed in front of them, his friend still smirking. Marlene took this as a sign he would not push it any further. She stepped backwards a few paces, pulling Adrienne with her before they turned to walk away. As Adrienne linked her arm in Marlene's, Marlene gave a sharp intake of breath as an arm reached across her stomach and hauled her backwards.

The drunk German spun her around to face him, his fist pressing hard into her side.

"Stop it! Get off!" she cried, pushing at his shoulders to escape his grip.

He only held on tighter.

His breath skimmed her cheek as he spoke more German, his voice getting louder and more aggressive as he fought to maintain his hold on her.

"Do something!" Adrienne yelled to the other German, who just stood by and watched.

Adrienne tried to help Marlene push the German off, but his grip around her waist was strong and he didn't budge.

"Ready to run?" Marlene said, speaking to Adrienne and hoping neither of the Germans would understand.

"Yes," Adrienne said.

As soon as Marlene registered Adrienne's acknowledgement, she kicked her foot out as hard as she could. Grateful that his boots did not extend up past his ankle, Marlene's kick collided with the German's shin, causing him to call out. His grip immediately loosened, and she seized the opportunity to push him hard. As he stumbled backwards, Marlene and Adrienne turned and ran.

Marlene didn't dare look behind her in case it slowed her down. The yelling and the heavy pounding on the streets was enough to confirm the drunken Germans had given chase; she only hoped they were too drunk to maintain their pace.

She reached out and pushed Adrienne in the direction of an alleyway.

"There's no way out," Adrienne said.

"There is. Keep going."

They emerged from the alley onto a cobbled street with narrow, steep steps.

They climbed the steps, taking them two at a time.

"This way," Marlene whispered, turning into another alleyway that led them back to a main street.

When Marlene felt sure they weren't being followed, she slowed to a walk. Adrienne followed her lead, both women now risking a glance to make sure there was no sign of the Germans. The only noise was the sound of their heavy breathing.

Marlene was more grateful than ever before for her training in London. Using different routes to and from her apartment as she had been instructed to do meant she knew which alleys linked with others and which were dead ends.

"Are you all right?" Adrienne asked, panting. "That was ..."

"Pretty terrifying," Marlene said, completing the other woman's sentence. "Has that ever happened to you before?"

"Not to me, thankfully, but it's not the first time I've seen them hassle French women."

"I think we've lost them," Marlene said, looking behind them again. "Hopefully that's the last we've seen of them."

"For tonight, maybe. They seem to be everywhere these days. Hopefully they're too drunk to recognise us again."

"Yes," Marlene agreed. "My apartment is this way. Yours?"

"Two streets over," Adrienne said, pointing in the opposite direction. "Will you be all right from here?"

"I'll be fine," Marlene said, more to reassure herself as her pulse continued to race. "Thank you for the company. Until the end there, I was finally feeling relaxed."

Adrienne smiled and nodded. "Same here. I'll be in Philippe's again on Friday at six, if you're in the area."

"In that case, I'll make sure I am."

30

ON FRIDAY, MARLENE HEADED TO PHILIPPE'S TO MEET Adrienne. She had passed Alain's café on the way to see if Henri had left word for her. Three morning visits and now an evening visit, and Henri had still not appeared. With only a week left until the next full moon, Marlene was determined to make contact. Her journal was brimming with details she could write up for Fletcher and, she hoped, details that would be useful to SOE. There were lots of words, but she wasn't ready for her time in France to come to an end. There was more she could do here to make a difference.

Marlene scanned Philippe's. Adrienne hadn't arrived yet.

"I've kept a table by the window for you," Philippe said as he poured her coffee. "Adrienne told me you were coming in."

"Thank you."

Philippe, holding on to her coffee, came out from behind the counter, walked over to a table right in the middle of the café's large window and put down her cup. "I've not seen you in here before. Before the other day, I mean."

"That's right. That was my first visit."

"Am I late?" Adrienne said as she removed her coat and gloves and headed in their direction. Marlene was grateful her arrival had stopped Philippe from asking what appeared to be on his mind.

"Coffee, please," Adrienne said. "I need something to warm me up."

"Of course. Any news?" Philippe pulled the chair back for Adrienne to sit.

She shook her head, and he squeezed her shoulder as he walked away to get her order.

"Everything okay?"

Adrienne nodded. "My husband never cared for coffee. I often wonder what he would think of the stuff we pretend is coffee these days. A Frenchman who doesn't like coffee. Have you ever heard such a thing?"

"I was a late bloomer with coffee, too."

Adrienne found this inexplicably funny. Her laughter was catching, and Marlene laughed along with her. She forgot about the danger all around her and allowed herself to laugh and to relax.

"I'm sorry, Philippe," Adrienne said as Philippe returned with her coffee.

"Don't apologise. It's so rare to find something to laugh at because of the war. If you do, make it last as long as possible." Philippe put a cup down in front of Adrienne and topped up Marlene's before moving on to another table.

Marlene stared into the darkness outside. All she could see was her own reflection. The nerves she had felt during her last visit to the café had gone. This time, she wasn't looking for a story. Tonight, she was just a woman having coffee with a friend, and she savoured that feeling.

Adrienne stopped laughing and stared intensely into her cup. "My husband is a prisoner of war."

"I'm sorry," Marlene said, unable to think of any other suitable response.

Adrienne picked up her coffee and cradled it in her hands. Marlene noticed that Adrienne's cup was in much better condition than her own. There were no cracks or chips. Adrienne shivered, and Marlene caught the slight tremble in her hands. "Some people say that Tomas would be better off dead than to be a prisoner. Perhaps it's selfish of me, but at least while Tomas is a prisoner, I know he is alive."

"I understand. It gives you hope," Marlene said. "As long as he's a prisoner, there's a chance he will come home."

"Exactly," said Adrienne.

"My husband was killed at the beginning of the year," said Marlene.

"I'm so sorry. You must think that my complaining is for nothing."

"No, of course not. We all have a right to complain at the moment."

"Do you have children?" Adrienne asked.

"No. It was just the two of us. The two of us and our plans for the future." Marlene blinked hard as tears formed.

"You can still have your plans. You just need to adjust them a bit," Adrienne said. "That's what Tomas always said to me. I didn't like to talk about it, but he made me. He said that I needed to have a plan for what I would do if he didn't come home again. He said I had to know what to do so I wouldn't crumble and die along with him."

"Tomas sounds like a sensible man."

"Oh, I'm sorry. I didn't mean to imply *you're* crumbling." Adrienne shifted uncomfortably in her seat.

"No need to apologise. You're right. I *am* crumbling. Or at least I was. I'm not so sure now I'm back here."

"Back here?"

"Excuse me?"

"You said you weren't sure if you were still crumbling now that you're *back here*."

"Oh," said Marlene. "In Paris. I only moved back to Paris a short time ago. I lived in the countryside with ... Pierre."

She needed to stop speaking, or at least pay more attention to her words. Perhaps it was the lack of people around her to talk to recently or not having Fletcher, her usual confidant, but she felt as though she needed to offload. It was a dangerous game. The more she said, the more likely it was her cover could be blown, but if she skirted all detail for fear of undermining her backstory, she worried Adrienne would focus more on the mystery. "I lived in Paris when we met. When he died, I felt it would be better if I returned home."

"It doesn't feel like home at the moment, though, does it?"

Marlene recognised the sadness in Adrienne's voice. She lowered her own. "What was it like when the Germans first arrived?"

"Honestly, it was quiet. I think we all expected the worst, but then it didn't happen. Not at first, anyway. They were on their best behaviour. Only now do we see the brutality that lies beneath."

Marlene couldn't imagine how it must have felt to see the enemy parade into your city knowing the horrors experienced by other nations in the same situation. She shook her head, hoping to clear the image from her mind. "My husband didn't like coffee either. He liked tea," said Marlene.

"Tea?"

This wasn't so funny given that Peter was British, but telling anyone that was unnecessary and would lead to questions Marlene didn't want to answer. Yet it still made Marlene laugh. She closed her eyes and saw Peter's face. For the first time in many months, she pictured him smiling. As Adrienne laughed along with her, the ache inside of Marlene uncurled and released.

Once the women had regained their composure, they got up to leave. Marlene noticed Philippe behind the counter. His eyes were locked onto her, and when he saw her take notice, he quickly looked away. Adrienne waved over to him and he smiled the same gentle smile he had given Marlene on her first visit.

But when he returned his gaze to Marlene, his smile was gone.

31

MARLENE UNFOLDED THE BLANKET WHICH NORMALLY LAY across the bottom of her bed and smoothed it down onto the grass beside the lake. The water was so still, and the long grass underneath her was like sitting on fluffy cushions. She'd been to the garden now half a dozen times since she'd discovered it and had yet to see anyone else. She liked that. The garden was somewhere that was just hers, where she could hide herself away from the rest of the city without having to be cooped up in her apartment.

She inhaled deeply, filling her lungs with fresh air and her nose with the scent of grass. She couldn't ever remember breathing such fresh air in Paris. But she also didn't remember ever visiting a garden when she had lived in Paris, which might have explained it. In this place, she could lose track of time. She experienced a tranquillity here that she hadn't felt for a long time.

A blackbird rustled in the bushes to her left, busy pecking at the ground. He treated her to a few seconds of song before flying off. Marlene wasn't sure she had ever heard birdsong in Paris. The bustling city she remembered had changed, and the tension of life in an occupied city melted away whenever she stepped into the garden.

She unpacked her lunch—the usual bread and tiny amount of cold meat—and wolfed it down. She normally took time over her meals these days, savouring every bite, regardless of how unappetising it might be, to make it last longer. But today she just needed food in her stomach. She blamed autumn. When the leaves fell from the trees, she became ravenous. As a child, she had spent long summers outdoors on the farm, eating her way through more than her fair share of the fruits she was supposed to pick. When the weather turned colder and the fruit was picked, she ate only at mealtimes and, as a result, always felt hungry during the day for the following few weeks until her system adjusted. Her grandfather, of course, told her it was her imagination, and that she didn't know what hunger was. She was glad he was no longer here to see rationing again.

Her daydreaming was interrupted by the noisy coughing of a figure on the other side of the lake. He had not been sitting there when she had first entered the garden, yet she had not noticed him arrive. He, too, was alone.

He got up, and she watched him stride in her direction. She thought for a moment he might have been the owner, wondering why she was here.

"Hello again," the man said. He continued his approach until he stood near the edge of her blanket.

"Hello," she said in return, examining his face for a hint of recognition but unable to place him. His dark brown eyes bored into hers, lingering for longer than felt comfortable.

"You don't recognise me, do you?" he said.

The polite thing to do would be to lie and say that of course she did, but her face had already given it away. "I'm afraid I don't, sorry."

He smiled. "I look different out of uniform, then?"

"Uniform?" Then it hit her: the soldier she had run into following her rendezvous with Henri. "Oh, of course. I'm ... Yes, you look different out of uniform."

"I'm glad."

"Why?" Marlene asked.

The moment the word left her mouth, she regretted it. He took her question as an invitation and sat next to her on the grass. She bit her lip and looked over to the water. Her hand twisted the corner of the blanket, but the anger she'd experienced the last time they met had gone. Perhaps it was his lack of uniform.

"Your accent ..." she said, her words trailing off. He had a hint of an accent, but it wasn't as strong as she remembered. Was it possible that his lack of uniform made him sound different too? "Your French is good."

"I spent a year in France before the war," he said. "I love Paris. I love most cities, actually; the anonymity of them, the history and the architecture. Don't you think?"

"Not really," she said, reluctantly disagreeing with him. "I prefer the countryside."

"So you are not Parisian?" he asked. "You look so at home here, I would never have guessed that you are a country girl."

Marlene stiffened. It seemed an innocent enough question, but wasn't that how all interrogations started? His lack of uniform might have initially comforted her, but that reassurance had quickly dissolved. She feared she had already provoked suspicion and raised her guard further.

As if sensing her reluctance to chat with him, the German spoke again, and he continued to talk for quite some time. He spoke about what he loved about the city, the buildings he had visited for their design features and their

significance in history. Architecture had never been a particular interest of hers, so he could have been making it all up,
but his passion, however, seemed real.

"When I wear my uniform, I don't get to observe as
much as I'd like. I can't take it all in because I'm too
conscious of everyone else observing *me*. Have you ever felt
like that?"

Marlene hesitated. She'd felt exactly like that on her first
day back at work after Peter's death. "You have to expect
people to be like that, though. It's not every day they see
soldiers walking amongst them. Although that's not strictly
true anymore."

The hairs on her arms prickled as he watched her. She
knew she would have to be the one to make excuses and
leave. "Well, I should go," she said.

"Of course," he said, jumping to his feet. He put out his
hand to help her up, and, hesitantly, she took it. He either
didn't notice or pretended not to. "I am Niklas, by the way.
Pleased to meet you," he said, still holding her hand.

"Marlene."

He folded her blanket and passed it to her. "Well,
Marlene, perhaps I will see you here again and we can
continue our conversation when you have some more time."

He accompanied her out of the garden and she turned
left, despite the quickest route to her apartment being to the
right. He turned left with her.

After a few minutes of walking in silence, Niklas stopped
and pulled Marlene across the street with him. His grip was
so light that it did not alarm her.

"Look up. Isn't it incredible?" he said.

"What?" she asked, not sure what she was being asked to
look at.

"This building. It was built in 1602. Do you see the date

carved in the stone? Spend a day wandering around Paris and you will come across all of the major architectural styles. Each style tells a story about the people of that period; their affluence, their values and their aspirations. I love how each building is ornamental, in its own way. My guesthouse is hundreds of years old, too, and I go to sleep at night imagining the lives of those who lived in it before me. Do you see this one here?" Marlene's gaze followed his arm. "Do you see how the roof shimmers in the light? If you have an interest in architecture, this city has examples of it all."

She looked at the building again and tried to see whatever it was that Niklas had seen to cause such a reaction in him. Architecture was definitely a love of his. His eyes darted around, picking up minute details that were hidden from her eye.

"You are underwhelmed by this building. You don't see its beauty?" Niklas asked.

"I don't look at buildings the way you do. For me, buildings are just places where people go to live, to work, to eat."

"The beauty of a building is to see the unseen. Yes, to see the now, but also to see the past; the soul of the building and the legacy of its creator. I love history, so architecture and history combined is like ... Tell me something you really like. Something which is a favourite of yours."

She stuttered and stumbled for a few seconds. "I don't think I share the same passion for anything," she said, the truth in her statement wounding her.

"Ah, but you do. What is it you do?"

Stick to your story. "I'm a writer," she replied.

"And do you love it?" he asked.

She thought for a minute. "I did. But I feel like I've lost my way with it a little."

Niklas nodded and looked thoughtful. "That's a

common feeling, especially now. Something will happen soon to reignite your passion for writing. If it doesn't, perhaps it's time to find a new one. Life moves on. This is what I tell all of my students. For those that are not interested in history, this is okay, for it is not their passion. But they must continue to try because only by trying new things will we discover new things we are passionate about."

Marlene looked at him. She sensed nothing sinister there. For the first time in a long time, she felt understood, like it was okay to feel lost and be searching for a way back. Her shoulders dropped and released a tension that had been there for far too long.

"You said you tell this to your students. Which students?" she asked.

"In Germany," he said. He appeared cooler now, as if her question had doused the flames of his passion. "I am a teacher of history."

"But you are a soldier," she said, immediately feeling foolish. He wasn't though. He was like Peter. Peter was a doctor with a wife and a mother and friends. This soldier was a man with a job and a daughter who signed up to serve his country. *Everyone has a life outside of their uniform.*

"Well, goodbye, Marlene. I hope to see you again," he said.

Marlene watched him stroll away. In that moment, reality was so far away that they could have been a man and a woman on any street at any time.

As Marlene headed towards her apartment, someone knocked her sideways. The man grabbed her to stop her from falling into the road and pulled her towards him. He quickly apologised and let go of her arm. Before she had a chance to respond, he had moved away and continued down the street.

The brief second was all it took, however, to see that the man was Henri and that their collision was no accident.

Hesitating, she wondered if he expected her to follow him. Deciding against it, she dug her hands into her pockets and stayed on course. Her right hand touched a slip of paper that had not been there seconds before and her heart pounded. It took all her willpower not to pull it out and read it in the street.

Once inside her apartment building, Marlene ran up the stairs as quickly as she could, almost bowling Madame Cloutier over in the process.

"What's got into you?" yelled Madame Cloutier.

"Sorry," said Marlene, unlocking her door and slipping inside. This was not the day to be trapped in conversation with her neighbour.

Marlene scanned her apartment and dropped her keys onto the table. Caught up in the secrecy of it all, she closed the curtains and pulled the slip of paper free from her pocket.

The only words written on it were: *Tree. Five o'clock.*

Marlene looked at her watch. It was a quarter past four. Grabbing her keys, she paused at the door. She retrieved her notebook and stashed it in the waistband of her trousers. If she were being sent back to London, she would at least have her notes, if nothing else.

She headed out, relieved that an indignant Madame Cloutier had already gone.

32

MARLENE WAITED BY THE TREE WHERE SHE HAD LAST MET Henri. It was a thirty-minute walk from her apartment, and she had arrived early. She fiddled with the notebook in her waistband.

Time ticked by, but there was no sign of Henri. She thought of their last conversation. He hadn't mentioned trees. This tree was the only location that made any sense to her. She waited for another twenty minutes before heading back to the path by the river, unsure of what to do next. She kept looking around her, but she saw no one except for the occasional fisherman dotted along the wall.

Had he meant a different day? She tried to visualise the slip of paper, but it didn't help. Was there something else on the note that she hadn't seen?

With no sign of Henri, Marlene headed back towards her apartment. She considered going to Alain's and leaving a message for him, but decided against it. Henri had made contact with her first this time, she would wait until he was ready to do so again.

As she walked, she couldn't shake the feeling that

someone was following her. She glanced over her shoulder but no one looked in her direction. Reluctant now to return to her apartment, she turned right at the bottom of the street instead of the usual left and kept going.

Startled by a hand on her elbow, she sighed with relief to see Henri now striding by her side. Silently, they walked together, Henri touching her arm with his to show her which direction he wanted her to go in and linking arms with her when they arrived at their destination so he could guide her up the steps and into the apartment building he had stopped in front of.

Only when they were in an apartment on the third floor did Henri speak.

"The best way to spot a tail is to look in a window, not to turn around."

Marlene nodded, annoyed with herself. She knew that. Her training instructor at SOE had told her.

"But you did the right thing by changing direction and leading me away from your apartment."

Marlene looked around the room. It had one window on the wall to the front of the building and a door set into the back wall which she presumed led to the rest of the apartment; a bedroom and bathroom, perhaps.

"Where are we?" she asked, moving closer to the back wall. There were no furnishings in the room; instead, only maps of the city that were taped to the wall. Five maps, all identical.

"Do you still want in on the action?" Henri asked.

Marlene pretended to be studying one of the maps before speaking. Henri had rejected her. What had changed his mind? And did she really believe she could handle the pressure?

"What would I need to do?" she asked, sensing Henri's impatience with her.

"Deliveries. It's just documents. I'll tell you where to pick up and where to drop off."

"Why?"

"It's better you don't know. You can't tell anyone what you don't know."

"No I mean, why now? Last time, you were pretty clear that ..."

"Things change," he said, cutting her off. "Are you up for this or not?"

She nodded.

"And you realise the danger this puts you in?"

She nodded again.

"Good. Then I need you to meet me somewhere." He joined her beside the maps.

Marlene knew what she was getting herself into; she just hoped she could do it without anyone, including herself, getting hurt.

33

"Coffee, please, Philippe," Adrienne said to the café owner.

"Coming up," he replied, already pouring.

"How's trade?" She glanced around the café. All the small metal tables were empty, except for an old man in the far corner who looked asleep.

"Comes and goes. Can't really expect much more with a war on. Are you okay?"

"Yes," she said, now cradling her coffee. "You know how it is."

"Any word from Tomas?"

She shook her head.

"I'm sure he's fine. I feel it."

Three years earlier, Adrienne had learned that her husband Tomas had been captured by the Germans and sent to a work camp. Driving herself mad at home, she'd needed to get out, and Philippe's, being close to her apartment, was the first place she'd come to. It had been full of people and an opportunity to drown out the deafening silence of home. She had told no one of the news of Tomas that day. Talking about it would have meant acknowledging it, and she wasn't ready then to do that.

Within ten minutes of her arrival, however, Philippe made it clear he was the type of café owner who knew everything about everyone. He came to her table and immediately introduced himself. He knew all of his customers and knew she hadn't been in before. She'd given her name only, successfully dodging his other questions with banal answers.

She'd declined his offer of a refill and left, fully intending not to return. She hadn't wanted to talk; she had just wanted to not be alone.

She'd passed the café every day on the way to work after that, although she had never noticed it before. She'd never even been to it with Tomas when he had been around, despite finding out from Philippe later that he and his café had been open for business for many years. However, after that first visit, she'd avoided the café, and thus the questions, often crossing to walk on the opposite side of the square as she passed.

One night, when heading home from work, she'd turned onto the square while Philippe was outside clearing tables, and she'd caught his eye. He'd recognised her and stopped what he was doing until she got closer to him.

"Hello again," he'd said happily. "Can I get you another coffee?"

Perhaps because he'd caught her off guard, or perhaps because she was ready to talk, she'd agreed and gone inside. She'd sat on a stool at the counter for almost two hours and, barring the odd interruption from other customers, she'd talked. She'd told him about Tomas, her work in the school, and her wish to leave the city, even though she could not. Tomas had to know where to come home to, after all.

Even now, after all this time, Philippe still asked Adrienne every time he saw her if she'd heard from Tomas. Each
time she said no, he would reply by saying, "I'm sure he's
fine. I feel it." It was silly, she supposed; Philippe couldn't
possibly feel if someone he'd never met was fine or not.
Regardless, she appreciated someone else thinking about
Tomas besides her.

No one else really asked her about him. They either had
their own stuff going on or they didn't want to upset her.
Philippe gave her the opportunity to talk about Tomas if she
wanted to, but he was happy to leave it at that if she didn't.

"School okay?" he asked, as if sensing today wasn't a day
for talking, and moving on to something more neutral.

"The usual, really. Monsieur Mayotte is sure the war will
end soon, and we should prepare for the children to return,"
Adrienne said.

"You're not convinced?"

"Even if it ended tomorrow, I'd expect it to be some time
before things returned to normal, wouldn't you?"

"Either way, the war is not yet over, nor will it be for
some time, I fear," Philippe said gloomily.

"What makes you think that?" she asked.

"Just a feeling," he replied.

Another of his feelings.

"In any case," she said, "I suspect what's actually going
on is he's tiring of it all again. He's ready to get back to his
retirement."

"Who can blame him?"

Adrienne wondered silently how long it would take for
Tomas to come home if the war ended tomorrow. Would the
gates to the work camps be opened as soon as the war was
declared over? She suspected not. The Germans had already
agreed to send their men home but hadn't done so. *If* the

Allies were victorious ... She stopped herself. The implications of the Allies being defeated were too frightening to consider.

A group of German soldiers interrupted her thoughts, clattering their way into the café. Their conversation and obnoxious laughter grated on her, yet the old man in the corner remained sound asleep. She wondered if he, too, was here to avoid the loneliness of home.

One of the soldiers approached Philippe at the counter and asked for four coffees.

"Evening," the solider said to Adrienne in French as he paid Philippe.

She nodded politely in response. *Does anyone ever get used to this?*

The soldier went back to his noisy friends. Two of them were engaged in a pretend fight that resulted in a chair being knocked over. The soldier who had ordered the coffee snapped at them in German and picked up the chair. Philippe delivered their coffees and returned to Adrienne.

"Regulars," he mumbled.

"Really? I've never seen them," she said, staring over at them.

"Maybe not those ones. The soldiers, though—they've been coming in a lot. It's not good for business."

The door chimed again and three girls pranced in. Each girl was a mirror image of the one before, with curled hair and make-up on their cheeks that clashed with their bright red lips. They didn't order anything, instead choosing to sit at the table nearest the soldiers. Immediately, the soldiers took interest in them and started chatting amongst themselves with lots of prominent nods towards the girls.

"I'm not yet thirty, and they make me feel old," Adrienne whispered to Philippe.

One of the soldiers turned his chair around to face the girls.

Adrienne jumped up. "Time for me to go," she said, shaking her head disapprovingly.

She was not sure which group frustrated her more; the soldiers who had invaded her country and were now invading her sanctuary or the girls who should have been angry with these men for even being here, but instead flirted openly with them.

Adrienne left Philippe alone to watch the rest of the show.

34

Marlene woke to darkness, as usual, although she still couldn't get used to it. Even in the height of summer, the requirement for blackout curtains meant she had been waking to darkness for years. If only the dense fabric could be removed. Marlene believed that the morning darkness was, in part, responsible for the dark mood that consistently consumed her.

Henri had given her another set of directions to memorise. She had repeated them so many times whilst lying in bed last night that she didn't think she'd actually be able to drop off. She had, and she had woken up later than usual, which she was glad of because it now gave her less time to think. As she dressed, Marlene distracted herself with thoughts of the egg she had managed to get her hands on for breakfast; her first egg in months.

Marlene lowered her egg into the pan of bubbling water and cursed when it cracked a little and a trail of egg white leached out into the water. Listening to the egg rattling against the pan brought back memories of the farm; the only house in France that she had truly called home.

"Happy birthday, beautiful," said Marlene's grandmother as she smoothed thick clumps of damp hair away from little Marlene's forehead. She was soaked through from sweat but couldn't remember if she'd been dreaming or if it was just time to lose her winter blankets.

Her grandfather was stood in the doorway, holding a breakfast tray. His dark eyes were beaming at her. Marlene always said his eyes were back to front. They were so shiny, you should have been able to see your own reflection in them. All you could see was the reflection of her grandpa's own thoughts, whether happy or sad or angry. Marlene's mother had the same eyes, and she had been sad a lot.

"Gracie laid these eggs especially for you today, knowing it was your special day," he said, placing the tray which held orange juice, two boiled eggs, buttered toast, and a blue envelope beside her on the bed.

"Don't be silly, Grandpa," said Benjamin as he bounded into the room. "Gracie doesn't have thoughts of her own, and if she did, she'd hardly be thinking about Marlene. She'd be plotting her escape from that coup, away from all the squawking of the others."

"Is that so?" said Grandpa. "How cynical you are becoming in your old age."

"I'm only eleven. You make me sound like I'm twenty-five or something."

"I'll remind you of that one day. See if you still feel the same way," said Grandma.

Marlene tore open her birthday card. She wanted to eat her eggs whilst they were still hot. Breakfast was normally milky porridge. Eggs, being the top seller at the farm shop, were a rare treat. Tracing the brightly coloured six on the birthday card with her finger, Marlene looked out of the window to the side of her bed. Her bedroom was to the front of the house and had a view right up the farm track, all the way to the main road. She had yet to close the curtains since her arrival. If her mother one day came walking back up that path, Marlene wanted to be the first to see her.

Marlene drained the pan and peeled the shell from her egg. Her stomach still lurched whenever she saw Germans, but she had not feared for her life. Today might change that.

There would be trouble if anyone discovered she was a journalist working for a British newspaper. She took precautions and kept her diary notes factual, omitting anything that might be construed as a direct criticism of the occupiers. Before she'd arrived, she had laughed at the irony. A journalist sneaking around Paris so the Germans didn't censor her, only to have to hand over all of her articles to the Ministry of Information in Britain before anything could be published.

It was easy to detach from her role with SOE. All she had to do in France was keep her eyes and ears open. The work for them would begin once her feet were safely back on London soil.

But today was a different scenario altogether. Working for the Resistance *in France* could get her killed. Henri had made that quite clear.

An image of a furious Fletcher flashed in her mind. Minutes after he'd offered her the opportunity, she'd known he was not comfortable with the decision. But he was convinced that the articles she would write on her return to London had value; that an authentic account of life under occupation would help bolster Britain to keep going. She'd been more sceptical.

Working for Henri was something bigger. Something that, without question, would help Paris; help France. Tessa from the safe house had told her there were many ways to make an impact. Marlene wanted to make an impact. Henri might have been right when he'd said her motives for returning to France were personal, but her choice wasn't about revenge.

It's just the right thing to do. Isn't it?

Marlene found the apartment block where she would get a crash course in avoiding detection with ease. Thinking it best to let Henri feel in control, she hadn't told him she had received the same training in London. Following the instructions he had previously given her, she had collected her newly acquired bicycle from Alain's on the way and now stowed it in the back of the building. She rang the bell for Apartment 3E and went up. Henri was waiting for her at the top of the stairs.

He led her into a small apartment, the walls of which had been roughly knocked through to create one large room. There was an enormous map of the city covering one wall, twice the size of the maps she had seen on the walls of the other apartment, and this one had lots of scribbled writing and arrows and crosses drawn onto it. On the other wall were various pictures of buildings, none of which she recognised. A large table with half a dozen chairs surrounding it dominated the middle of the room. A closed trunk sat in the corner nearest the window, and the journalist in Marlene wanted to open it. She imagined this room had been privy to some key plans of the Resistance and wondered whether any of the neighbours suspected what was on the opposite side of their walls. She suspected not, or it wouldn't be considered a safe place to keep all this stuff.

"I'd expected you to be in the basement," she joked, laughing nervously.

"You still want to do this?" Henri's tone was stony, as she had come to expect.

The now familiar image of Peter's face as bullets pierced his body and claimed his life flashed in her mind. "Yes, I do," Marlene said, feeling more committed than ever.

"Okay. I've cleared it with London."

Marlene wondered if someone had told Fletcher and just how livid he was.

"You'll be a courier," continued Henri. "Nothing more, nothing less. We will continue to call you Lucile. I will give you an address where you'll collect packages. You will not know what you are carrying, and you will not know the significance of them. This way, if you are arrested, you can't reveal that which you don't know. You also won't be able to tell anyone."

"I would *never* tell anyone," Marlene said, resenting the suggestion. Henri clearly hadn't trusted her since their very first meeting, although she had never fathomed why. She would show him now, though.

"That's what everyone says before they tell someone. Trust no one, Marlene. You think no one will know you are working for the Resistance. They think that as well."

"Who?" she asked, not sure what he was suggesting.

"People working for the Resistance. Collaborators working with the Germans. They all think they are doing it undetected, but you never know who might be watching, what they think you're up to, or who they think you're working for. You might become known to someone in the Resistance, and because we are all trained not to trust, they will presume you could be working for the other side, or have your own agenda. You'd do well to presume this, too."

Marlene thought about his statement—*your own agenda*—and wondered if he was referring again to the personal agenda he'd suggested she had. She didn't suppose it mattered. Despite Henri sounding as though he wanted to scare her, for now, the excitement of it all was carrying her away. If everyone was so mistrusting of everyone else, it wouldn't matter what they thought her reasons were. She'd rather the Resistance thought her motivation was seeking revenge for Peter than believing she would ever work for the Germans.

35

ADRIENNE

THE ARTWORK STUCK TO THE WALLS BROUGHT LIFE TO THE otherwise dingy classroom. The misshapen animals, colourful apartment buildings with giant trees overhanging them and the little sailboats bobbing on a bright blue ocean reminded Adrienne that this situation was only temporary. She often forgot that there had been life before occupation, just as there would be life after. One child's painting caught her eye. It was of an aeroplane, painted a dark grey with the Nazi swastika in a deep red emblazoned on its side. In the five years since their marriage, she and Tomas had yet to be blessed with a child. She traced the red symbol with her finger, hopeful that no child of hers would ever have such a picture in their young mind.

"Ah, there you are," said Monsieur Mayotte, as she returned to her office. "I was about to come and look for you. Everything all right through there?"

"Yes, it's all fine," she said.

"Good. Let me lock up in here and I'll walk out with you," he said, returning to his office. "I expect we could both do with getting home after today."

"Yes," she murmured.

She picked up her coat and put it on. Wandering over to Monsieur Mayotte's office, she tied the belt of her coat. As she reached the doorway, Monsieur Mayotte locked his wall cabinet. He pushed the door to his large walk-in cupboard closed and dropped the keys into his jacket pocket, leaving the door unlocked.

"Ready?" he said. They left together, and Adrienne used her keys to lock the main door to the building. She locked it, unlocked it, then relocked it again. Monsieur Mayotte smiled at her habit.

"Are you going out tonight, dear?" Monsieur Mayotte asked. She shook her head and linked arms with him as they walked. "You really should try to get out some more. It's not good for you, a young girl like you, to be home alone every night."

"Oh, I get by just fine. There's no need to worry about me."

"I know," he said, patting her hand. "I can't help it, though. Will you be all right from here?"

He stopped and let go of her arm.

"Of course. Where are you going?"

"I have a couple of errands to run before I go home."

"Can I help?" Adrienne asked, more just to see what he would say. She couldn't remember a time in the last year that Monsieur Mayotte hadn't walked her at least part of the way home.

"I'll be fine on my own." He turned and strode away before she could say anything further.

As their journeys now took them in opposite directions, she watched Monsieur Mayotte for a few seconds as he continued up the street, heading away from her. His stride was purposeful but not speedy. *Like his character*. The man was up to something, she was sure of that.

Curiosity nibbled away at her. She just hoped he knew what he was doing.

36

Every Saturday morning, *Place Grenat* filled with makeshift stalls as the farmers came to town to sell what produce they had. The stalls were not as plentiful as they once might have been, mainly relying on whatever remained after their supplies had been requisitioned by the Germans. Marlene sauntered amongst them as they set up. The sun was only just rising, but Marlene had woken in the early hours to the thundering noises of a country at war and hadn't been able to get back to sleep.

Marlene had struggled with how grey everything was when she had previously lived in the city. The apartment she had lived in at the time had a view only of other apartments. Coming from the countryside, she had missed wide-open spaces, green land, flowers and trees. Paris was claustrophobic and dull by comparison, only springing to life in the evening when lamps were switched on everywhere and the city was aglow with light.

Now, the daytime dullness was brightened by red, white and black flags, and she would give anything for it just to be grey again.

Being in the market as soon as it opened, she had a precious few minutes of fewer people. The neatly arranged cabbages, leeks, artichokes and carrots seemed to bring hope to the surroundings.

When the traders were open for business, Marlene was third in the queue for bread. Something brushed against her ankle, and she looked down to see a Resistance-run newspaper had blown against her shoe. She bent down to remove it, taking her time so she could scan the headlines. From the corner of her eye, Marlene could see the woman behind her stepping backwards, as if trying to disassociate herself from Marlene. Marlene flicked the paper to the side and stood up.

When she had collected her bread, she loaded her basket up with hearty vegetables from the limited selection on offer. The number of people in the square swelled, and she noticed what she thought was a disproportionate number of men in uniform. Elbows and shoulders attacked Marlene as shoppers scrambled about to get the best goods.

She breathed deeply once she emerged from it all. Looking back at the wall of bodies, she couldn't remember if the market had always been this chaotic or if those luxurious few minutes of calm while the traders had still been setting up now made it feel worse than it actually was.

"Get out of there!" yelled a woman at a little girl who had jumped off the pavement into the puddles on the road, left by the previous day's wet weather. The mucky water splashed up the girl's legs and sprayed in all directions, soaking Marlene's stockings. The woman grabbed the girl by the arm and pulled her out of the puddle and back onto the pavement.

"Are you okay?" she asked, looking at the marks on

Marlene's stockings. The water had left dark stains as the dirt clung to the nylon.

"Yes. Don't worry about it." Marlene smiled at the little girl, who now looked sheepish, her head bowed and her sharp blue eyes staring up.

"Do you have something to say to the lady?"

Before the girl's lips had moved, a car came racing down the street, driving straight through the offending pools of water and drenching them all. The little girl screamed as, given her height, she came off the worst.

"Damn Germans!" yelled the woman after the car.

"Shhh!" Marlene looked over to the market. "It's full of them."

The woman wiped the dirty water from the girl's face with the sleeve of her coat. The girl sobbed as her blonde ringlets now hung wet and straightened, sticking to her face.

When the women parted and Marlene reached the corner of the street, she could see where the Germans in the car had been going in such a hurry. A man wearing only his trousers and vest—no shirt, socks or shoes—was being escorted into the vehicle that had soaked her only a minute before. Two German soldiers were man-handling him, his hands behind his back, and shoved him into the back seat of the vehicle.

Another soldier appeared at the door of the house carrying a suitcase with a coiled wire trailing from a corner. He hurried to the back doors of a grey van parked in front of the car. It looked like a laundry van. The door was open just a crack, but it was enough for Marlene to see that there was no laundry inside. Whatever the barefooted man had been up to, he had been caught out by a laundry van.

She watched the vehicles speed off again with a

nauseous feeling in her stomach. Of course she knew there were risks in actively working against the Germans, but now, seeing it right in front of her, she cursed herself. She wiped her damp hands down the front of her coat. *What are you doing, Marlene?*

Marlene made a mental note of the building number and street name so she could tell Henri.

"Marlene," someone yelled from behind her and she turned. Niklas ran from the market towards her. "How are you?"

"Fine," she said, glancing around her.

"You have no colour. Are you sick?"

"No, I'm okay. I just saw a man being thrown into a car by some of your friends."

"Whoever they were, they are not friends of mine."

"What will happen to him?"

Niklas looked up the street, but the car had gone. "I don't know. It depends what he was doing, and ..." He looked down and kicked the kerb. "If he's prepared to talk."

Marlene reached for the wall to steady herself. She'd seen the man's bare feet scraping along the concrete as the German soldiers had shoved him towards the car, but something told her his feet would be the least of his concerns when he arrived at wherever they were taking him.

"How can you do this to people?" Her voice was quiet as she reached out and pushed him, her eyes avoiding his and focusing, once again, only on his uniform; a pistol clipped to one side of his body, a sheathed knife on the other. The last time she had seen such a knife, it had been pressed against her throat.

"War is not as simple as good and bad; right and wrong. Much of the suffering of your people has been at the hands of those in *French* uniforms, not German."

"A French uniform, perhaps, but it's a German pistol at their head."

"They are not Germans. They are Nazis. There's a difference," Niklas said.

"Is there?"

"Is it possible for a whole nation to be evil?"

Marlene sighed. She was being unfair, but the man frustrated her. Niklas wasn't argumentative, but he had a way of saying something simple, just one thing, that then tugged at something she thought she knew for sure and caused her to question more than a few of her beliefs.

He stepped forwards and lifted her chin with his hand. Marlene had expected to flinch, but the warmth of his touch soothed her. She had no option now but to look into his eyes. "Good people will have to do some unspeakable things to end this war. The opportunity for talking has long since ended. It's no longer as simple as the uniform they wear."

He removed his hand from her face. "Can I walk with you?"

"I'm almost home," she said. "Maybe another day."

"Of course," he said, already backing away, his hands out and by his sides. "Let's meet tomorrow. By the clock tower at twelve."

She knew that her increasing involvement with the Resistance dictated that she should get as far away from Niklas as she could, but there was something about him. He was away from home for politics he could not understand and seemingly did not share. Her head, of course, told her he was German and she shouldn't trust him; that he was the enemy. But her instincts told her he was different.

"I can't. I'm sorry," she said.

Marlene watched Niklas disappear into the crowd. She blew out a shaky breath and her chest tightened. She wasn't sure if the sensation was residual after watching the half-dressed man being thrown into the back of the car, or if it was because she had desperately wanted to say yes to Niklas.

37

MARLENE APPLIED A SECOND COAT OF BRIGHT RED LIPSTICK. She had not considered herself particularly beautiful before, but with her blonde hair now delicately curled and a little makeup giving her pale, tired skin a healthier glow, even she had to admit she looked good. It gave her a confidence she had not yet experienced since returning to Paris. It gave her a mask to hide behind. She thought of her mother, always heavily made-up, touched the lipstick with her finger and dabbed more colour onto her cheeks.

Tessa had said lipstick would make the Germans immediately less suspicious of her. They would be more inclined to gawp or whistle approval than they would be to stop and question or search her. If she were stopped, Marlene's papers would likely be examined with less scrutiny, and some soldiers might even flirt with her. After all, what harm could a beautiful woman do to them? She hoped Tessa was right.

Henri had instructed her to go to the newspaper shop on *Place Grenat* and ask for the collection for Lucile, the name she had only ever used to contact Henri. He had made her practice the exchange with him repeatedly until he was comfortable she could do it without drawing attention to herself. What she hadn't been able to practice was collecting a package for the Resistance from a shop that was directly opposite a German-only restaurant.

Her confidence from moments before now deserted her as she made her way through the narrow streets on foot. She welcomed the coolness of the breeze that flowed through her hair as she moved. Her skin tingled, and she remembered Henri's words, "If in doubt, smile."

Turning into *Place Grenat*, Marlene could see a group of German soldiers sitting in her path. They had gathered outside a café, but from their demeanour, they were relaxed rather than on alert. One chased after another for some reason, but she could sense the rest of them had their eyes on her. She tucked her hair behind her ear, wiping away a bead of sweat that had trickled down the side of her face. Walking at a comfortable pace, her toes clenched in her shoes, a glance upwards confirmed the look on their faces was approval rather than suspicion. The whistle as she reached the end of the square was further confirmation.

She turned and smiled, as Henri had told her to, her heavy red lipstick helping her to play a character, one that was unafraid of the occupiers. A passerby glowered at her like she was a traitor.

Marlene stepped inside the shop. The man behind the counter watched her walking towards him.

"*Bonjour*," Marlene said. Her voice cracked, and she coughed to clear her throat. "I'm here for the collection for Lucile."

The shopkeeper's face was stony, and he turned away. She scanned the headlines on the newspapers in front of her as she waited. Each one contained lies or, at best, misinformation. The man turned around again and handed Marlene a newspaper. She thanked him and left the shop, aware of his eyes boring into the back of her head.

She gripped the folded newspaper under her arm. Somewhere within its pages, it held a coded message. Instructed by Henri never to look inside, Marlene was oblivious to what, and where, the message was. She scanned the passing windows as she walked, to make sure no one was following her, and she fought every part of herself not to look inside the paper as she headed to her drop point.

You can't reveal that which you don't know.

Although Marlene had heeded Henri's warning, it was the tight folds in the newspaper that really stopped her from sneaking a glance. She feared that if she unfolded the paper, she would never get the edges to line up as sharply as they did again, and someone would know she had looked. The concern, she expected, would not be that she had looked, but perhaps a suspicion that she had passed something on. For now, her inquisitiveness remained unsatisfied.

Nearing her destination, her gaze settled on a man up ahead waiting for someone. He held a folded newspaper that he bounced back and forth in his hands.

The man scanned the streets around him, looked at his watch and strode huffily in Marlene's direction. Once close enough to hear him mumble under his breath, she braced herself for impact.

They collided and the man clutched Marlene's forearm to steady her. "I'm sorry, *mademoiselle*," he said. "I wasn't looking where I was going. Are you all right?"

Marlene detected a slight twang in his accent, which told her French was his second language. She supposed it would probably pass unnoticed by a French-speaking German. It could even be a regional variation that she herself did not recognise.

"Yes, fine," she said, giving him a polite smile.

He bent down and picked up the newspapers they had dropped simultaneously and handed one to Marlene.

"Thank you," she said, taking the paper.

"Sorry again." He returned her smile and stepped aside to allow her to pass.

Exchange complete, she continued on her journey without looking back.

38

MARLENE PAID FOR HER CINEMA TICKET AND HEADED INSIDE. The events of her day seemed unbelievable to her now. It had only been a few hours since she had carried out the courier drop, and she'd spent the time since writing her diary notes on her observations of life in Occupied Paris. It had taken her all of twenty minutes to collect and swap the newspaper, but those twenty minutes had changed everything. Now, she was actively carrying out work that undermined the Germans, and dread hung in her stomach at the possible consequences.

She thought about Fletcher again. Her expanding involvement with the Resistance was specifically what he'd said he did not want to know when he had given her the brief. He wanted her to gather information about everyday French people and how the war was affecting their lives. He wanted the individual perspective from teachers, housewives, children, shopkeepers, market traders. Everything else, he'd said, should be left to the official war correspondents.

The apartment had begun to suffocate her, and she'd

had to get out. The cinema, she'd decided, would be a welcome distraction, and there would be safety in its darkness in case her guilt was written across her face.

She entered the cinema quietly, purposefully going in late so the lights were down and everyone else was already seated. Quickly scanning the crowd, she slipped into an empty seat near the back.

Seconds later, someone slipped into the seat right beside her.

"I thought it was you."

She turned around, stunned. "Niklas. What are you doing here?"

"Are you here alone?"

"Yes," she whispered, noticing that he hadn't answered her question. Heat rose in her throat, and she dabbed sweat away from her top lip, even though it wasn't warm in the cinema.

"I have one piece left." Niklas handed her a small square of chocolate wrapped tightly in its paper.

She took it from him, hoping he hadn't felt her hand tremble. He smiled and slumped down in the seat, preparing to sit still for the next hour or so. She stared at his outline for a long time. Tonight was a night she really needed him not to be with her.

The screen flickered in his eyes. He looked like he was still smiling, presumably just at being here, away from the reality that was his life.

Snapped out of her thoughts by the sound of an explosion somewhere in the distance, she jumped, but no one else acknowledged the noise. She wondered how many Germans had been killed.

Still staring at Niklas, tears burned behind her eyes. *Is a British soldier killing a German soldier any less murder because a*

British politician had said it was the right thing to do? She might not have been pulling a trigger, but she wondered if what she had done today was contributing to those murders.

Niklas turned to look at her, and she spun towards the screen. She didn't want him to see her tearful eyes in case he questioned her and she blurted out everything. He squeezed her hand and whispered for her to eat her chocolate.

Marlene had never imagined she would come to Paris and befriend a German, and she was certain that if she told anyone about him, it would spell trouble for both of them. But Niklas was just a person; a good person forced to be a long way from home, doing things he didn't wish to be doing, nor that he felt was right, to protect his family. Who would not have done the same thing? She couldn't believe that she had run into the only German soldier to find himself in this predicament. There had to be more. To believe in the good qualities of humanity was to believe that most of the soldiers were like Niklas, and the war was being driven by one man and his select group of evil cronies. The percentage of people that were truly rotten to the core had found each other and were perpetuating this path to death and destruction.

"I should go," Niklas whispered as soon as the movie ended.

"Me too," said Marlene.

He grabbed her hand, and they slipped out of the cinema as the credits rolled and the lights came on. Once outside, Niklas dropped her hand and put his hands in his pockets.

"How did you know I was here?" Marlene said, asking the question that had been on her mind throughout the film.

"Just my lucky day," he said. "Can I take you to lunch tomorrow?"

She shook her head. "I can't."

"Then meet me at the clock tower on *Place Grenat* at four. I want to show you something."

Her head was screaming for her to dismiss him, but she nodded.

Niklas smiled, and she lost sight of him as she allowed herself to be carried away by the crowd leaving the cinema. As she was jostled by the throng of cinemagoers surrounding her, Marlene couldn't shake thoughts of Niklas and how convenient it was that he had spotted her in the darkness.

Each time she saw Niklas, he changed her view of what was right and what was wrong. But each time she saw him, a tingle spread across her skin that she knew she *must* ignore.

39

Niklas was waiting for Marlene beside the clock tower. Seeing him stood there in uniform, with people bustling by in all directions, the reality of what she had agreed to had suddenly become very clear. He had not seen her yet, and she contemplated slipping down the alley. The time they'd spent together in the cinema had been in silence, and that had been uncomfortable enough. Her breathing quickened at the thought of being openly in the company of a German soldier for all to see. While their other meetings appeared incidental, she knew she couldn't, and shouldn't, trust him. Just being here was a bad idea, and it was especially foolish for a journalist working undercover. Yet she still couldn't walk away.

Niklas spotted her and waited for her to approach him. He smiled, and the nerves in Marlene's stomach hopped around in all directions.

"Everything okay?" he asked.

"It's fine. I ... I didn't expect you to be in uniform," she said.

"Oh, I'm sorry. I didn't think," he replied. If he was

offended, he didn't show it. "I only have a couple of hours. I have to get back later. I should have thought."

"No, it's fine. Perhaps this wasn't such a good idea."

"No, it was. Come on, let's go," he insisted, and he marched on. His face had changed, but she couldn't read his expression. She turned and followed him.

They walked by a number of cafés and a handful of market stalls selling flowers, fabric, and trinkets. Niklas wasn't the only German on the street, but more people watched her than him.

They passed a group of traders selling their wares from on top of sacks positioned directly on the pavement. Marlene locked eyes with one of them; an older man, his eyes peeking out from beneath his hat and puffs of smoke escaping out of the side of his mouth where he held a cigarette. She quickly looked away as her stomach churned.

She had known before they had even reached *Rue de Rivoli* where Niklas was taking her, but she had said nothing. And now, in front of her, stood the majestic façade of the Louvre. She stopped. Niklas took a couple of steps before he realised, and he stopped, too.

He motioned with his arm for her to take in the sight before he turned to face her. Her feet planted, she could feel him studying her face, her reaction obviously not what he had expected.

The Louvre where Marlene had first met Peter. A frequent visitor to the galleries, she visited the Louvre more than any of the others. It was home to a painting of a bridge that cut through a night sky. The changing light and the shadows cast by the positioning of the painting's visitors made the stars in the sky dance across the canvas. She loved the painting and wondered what the artist had been thinking when he'd decided that view would be the one he would paint. The painting was not especially well known, but she'd listened to other visitors marvel at the textures and the brush strokes and the light and felt it rather inadequate to say that she just liked the picture.

She sat on a stone bench in front of the bridge painting when two men came over and stood in front of her. One of the men—an art student from the look of the bag he carried and the sketchbook he held—attracted attention with his loud opinions as he made grand sweeping movements with his arms across the painting. The other man stood silent for several seconds before realising they had obscured Marlene's view. He pulled at the arm of his friend to guide him out of the way and gave Marlene a quick smile and nodded his head in her direction. She returned his smile and tried unsuccessfully to drown out the ramblings of his loud friend.

After another few minutes, the quiet man let out an exaggerated yawn, apparently designed to tell his friend it was time to move on. His friend ignored him and pushed him down on the bench beside Marlene, telling him he had to take a few notes before they could go.

"Are you also an art student?" the man asked her in English, almost immediately after he sat down.

She shook her head.

"Do you speak English?" he asked, looking quite uncomfortable.

"Yes. Do you speak French?" Marlene asked in response.

"No. I've never been particularly good with languages. Or art," he said, motioning towards the painting. The louder friend stood right in the middle of the artwork, craning his neck so much that it would not have surprised Marlene if he had tipped himself over.

They spent several minutes chatting, or rather he spent several minutes chatting about himself. She found out his name was Peter and that he had completed his medical studies, and he was now travelling Europe before he started his new hospital job. His mother, of course, was not happy about this because his father had died and Peter was all she had left. However, his view centred around not merely living the life his parents had wanted him to live. He lived in London and had became a doctor because that was what was expected of him. He had stopped off in Paris to visit his friend, the loud one, who was studying art in the city. By the time his friend had completed his notes, Marlene felt she knew all there was to know about Peter Edwards.

"I'm sorry. It seems I have monopolised the conversation. Can I take you for coffee to make it up to you? I promise I'll be quiet—and I won't bring him," he said, nodding playfully in his friend's direction.

"Okay," she said, surprising herself.

It didn't take Marlene long to realise there was more to Peter than she had initially thought. He was on the last week of his European tour and ended up spending it all in Paris with Marlene.

They said goodbye at a café on the morning of Peter's last day, exchanging addresses and promises to write. Her time with Peter had been the best week she had spent since coming to Paris, and she almost couldn't bear it as she watched him walking away. While she intended to keep her promise to write to him, she silently feared he wouldn't and she would become nothing but a fond memory of his travels.

When she arrived back at her apartment, she found a

letter waiting for her. Bile formed in her throat as she recognised the handwriting. It was her grandfather's, and he never wrote to her. She knew immediately that something was wrong and packed her bag and bought her train ticket within the hour.

When she arrived at the farm, her grandfather was at the sink, clearing away plates. The kitchen was her grandmother's domain, and he usually wasn't allowed in except to eat. He smiled as she came in, took her bag, and hugged her. His letter had said that her grandmother wasn't well and Marlene should visit if she could. Now, as they sat down, he explained that her grandmother had come down suddenly with a virus and she hadn't yet been able to shake it off. He was so calm as he spoke that Marlene hoped her concern was an over-reaction.

She headed upstairs and opened the door to her grandparent's bedroom. The curtains were drawn, and a glimmering light in the corner made it look as cosy as it felt. Marlene had rarely been in this room during her years living at the farm. A dresser in the opposite corner was cluttered with photographs and floral trinkets, while the rest of the room was bare in comparison. There were no pictures on the wall, and the only other pieces of furniture were the bed, the small table that housed the light and a chair that had been turned to face the bed.

Marlene moved towards the chair, picking up the book that lay on the seat before settling down. Her grandfather was not normally a reader of books, but the tiny figure in the bed looked too weak to reach over to the chair to retrieve or return the book. She took her grandmother's small hand, the icy coolness sending a shiver up Marlene's arm, and moved her fingers across the tiny bones sitting just beneath loose skin. Marlene thought she was asleep until the miniscule movements of her grandmother's hand gently gripped Marlene's. Marlene squeezed back and kissed the top of the small hand.

Marlene's grandfather had followed her upstairs and now stood in the doorway. "Have you heard from Benjamin?" he asked.

"No. Nothing for a while now. Have you?"

After spending two years in Paris, Benjamin had become a drifter, and they all relied on him to keep in touch, which he rarely did.

"Not yet, but I've sent some letters."

Benjamin finally appeared at the farm a week after Marlene's arrival. Her grandmother died that night.

When Marlene returned to Paris, a letter awaited her. She knew it was from Peter before she opened it. She'd spent a long time studying Peter's address and the tiny letters with which he wrote. The envelope wasn't sealed, and the lack of postage indicated it had been hand-delivered. She slipped the paper out and read the letter.

Peter had decided to stay in Paris for another month and had given her an address where she could find him. The letter was dated the same day she had left for the farm three weeks ago.

After only one more week together, Peter, too, had fallen in love and refused to leave without her. She took him back to the farm to meet her grandfather, but she'd already decided that she was going with him. Surprisingly, her grandfather didn't object. Her grandmother most definitely would have, but she had seen a change in her grandfather since his wife's passing. Marlene described him to Peter as sad.

Her grandfather told her to live her life, but think about

the ripples, his way of saying every decision had repercussions. Three months later, she and Peter were married.

Her grandfather died shortly after. His death notice said 'peacefully in his sleep', but she knew his last days had been anything but peaceful. Benjamin had not made it to her wedding, but thankfully, he did turn up to their grandfather's funeral.

Marlene looked around now at the barren walls of the Louvre. It certainly didn't have the same grandeur she'd seen on her previous visits. She couldn't help but compare the missing artworks to the precious things in her life that were also missing. One day, the art would return to this building, but what she had lost was gone forever.

"It's a beautiful building, isn't it?" asked Niklas.

Marlene could feel him studying her. "It's like it's talking to me," she whispered. "Like it remembers me. It's showing me things I haven't thought of in such a long time."

Niklas reached out to her and enveloped her in his embrace. She forgot about being in public with a German soldier. To bring her here, he could not have known. She now had no doubts about this man. He was exactly who he said he was.

She was the duplicitous one of the two.

40

ADRIENNE

THE COUNTER AT PHILIPPE'S HAD NEVER BEEN SO CLEAN. Adrienne watched Philippe wipe it down for the third time since her arrival only ten minutes ago. He kept glancing at two men who were seated at the opposite end of the counter to her. She didn't recognise them, but that wasn't unusual. Many of the faces in the café had changed since the occupation.

When the men got up to leave, Philippe looked happy to be waving them off, but his shoulders remained hunched and his jaw tight.

"Adrienne," he ventured as soon as the door closed behind the departing customers. "How much do you know about your new friend?"

"Excuse me?" Adrienne asked.

"That girl who comes here with you now. How much do you know about her?"

"Why do you ask?" She had seen him being frosty towards Marlene, although she had denied seeing it when Marlene had mentioned it. She'd reassured her that

Philippe was funny like that and told her not to take it personally.

Philippe lowered himself to equal her seated position. "I saw her. Cavorting with a German."

"So?" Adrienne said, amused by his dramatics.

"So ... She is obviously collaborating with them," he said.

"Now hold on, Philippe," Adrienne snapped. "You can't go around accusing people of being collaborators with nothing to substantiate the claim."

"I saw them," said Philippe, refusing to back down.

"What exactly did you see? Marlene talking to a German? Paris is swarming with them. They're inescapable. You talk to them in here," she reminded him.

"She wasn't just talking to him. She was *with* him. Only him. They were going somewhere. I don't know where, but they were going there together."

"Even so," Adrienne said, "that doesn't mean she's a collaborator."

"What other explanation is there?"

"I don't know, but it's not that."

"I see her sometimes, sitting in the square. She does nothing; she just watches people. Why would someone do that?"

"She's a writer. They get lost in their own heads sometimes, don't they?" said Adrienne. She didn't know why Marlene would go anywhere with a German, but she knew that Germans had killed her husband. *If it had been Tomas ...* Adrienne thought, then stopped herself.

"I'm just telling you what I saw, Adrienne. You'd do well to stay away from her," Philippe warned. "Collaborator or not, the girl's trouble. If you ask me, if she's happy to be seen with them, what else is she happy to do for them? Associating with her will end badly for you."

She shook her head. "No, I don't believe it. There has to be another explanation."

41

MARLENE CHOPPED THE VEGETABLES AND TOSSED THEM INTO A pan. She liked to blame a lack of ingredients for the blandness of the food she cooked. Whilst her grandmother had taught her how to appreciate flavour, she had never quite perfected it with her own cooking.

The door downstairs slammed, and the surrounding walls shook. She hated that door. Tucked away in her tiny apartment with the door locked and the heavy curtains secured, the door on the floor below still made her feel exposed and on edge whenever it slammed. The *click-clack* of Madame Cloutier's wooden-soled shoes on the stairs or the shuffling noises her upstairs neighbour made usually relaxed her again.

After initially thinking the apartment directly above hers was empty, Marlene had become attuned to the light steps of its male occupant. She hadn't met him but had caught a couple of glimpses of him; an older man, but fit enough that he could still take the stairs two at a time.

Another slam and the apartment walls shook again, only this time the slamming had been someone crashing into her door. Standing motionless, she listened. A man's voice was speaking, but it was more grunting than words. Her door shook again as the man rattled at the door handle.

"Who's there?" she called.

"What are you doing there?" came the gruff reply.

She quickly scanned the room for signs of anything that would give away her secret, her guilt.

"Who's there?" she called again. "What do you want?"

The door shook violently. "Let me in!" yelled the man.

Metal clanged against the lock, and Marlene glared at the door. Was it the previous tenant of the apartment? Someone that knew of her Resistance work? Whoever it was, it wasn't good. Marlene clutched her chest, screwed her eyes closed and froze.

"You there! Enough!" The thunder behind the door stopped. "I said *enough*! I've had about enough of you! Coming in here at all times of the day and night, causing upset every time."

Marlene recognised the sharp tones of Madame Cloutier.

"Enough of me? I've had enough of *you*, old woman," the man bellowed in response.

Marlene took from the now heated conversation that the man was her elusive neighbour from upstairs.

"Probably so drunk you thought this was your apartment."

"I know what's going on!" the man slurred. "I know *exactly* what's going on."

"Get going with you. Go on."

Marlene imagined Madame Cloutier shooing him away. She certainly didn't seem the type to be cautious or fearful around an angry drunken man.

After a few seconds of thudding on the stairs, a door upstairs slammed shut.

"Are you all right in there?" Madame Cloutier said, knocking lightly on the door. Her words might have become friendlier, but her tone was still one of chastisement.

Marlene unlocked the door and forced a smile at her elderly neighbour. Her eyes were fixed on the stairs which led to the floor above, towards her neighbour's apartment. The door was closed and all was now quiet, but the commotion had disturbed her greatly.

"Don't you worry about him. He's no doubt sound asleep now. I would normally say that the war does terrible things to people, but that's just him. He's always been a troublemaker."

"Has he lived here for a long time, then?"

"We've been here for many years, the two of us. Seen a lot of folks come and go. I say he's always been a troublemaker, but he didn't start out that way. Not that I saw for the first few months, anyway. He moved here with his wife. Lovely girl, she was. Anyway, she put up with a lot from him, I imagine. But she died."

"Oh no," said Marlene, not really wishing to be involved in gossip so close to home, or, in this case, within the walls of her home, but intrigued nonetheless. "Poor man."

"Poor man indeed. At first. But then you have to choose whether to let it destroy you or whether to come back fighting. You can guess which one he chose. Poor girl. A blessing now, however, that she bore no children because he wouldn't have coped with that. He can't cope with just himself."

"It makes you realise how lucky you are. It's sad," Marlene said, to stop her neighbour from revealing any more details of the poor man's tragedies. "Still, he's home now, so things should be quiet for the night."

"Not necessarily. It's still early. I have seen him go back out again in the night. And in the state he gets himself into, he attracts the wrong folks. He brought some Germans home with him one night. Well, I suppose they brought *him* home and dumped him in his apartment. I can't imagine they were just being nice, though, can you? Between you and me, I think he has a certain sympathy with the Germans, if you know what I mean."

Marlene twisted her face and hoped she looked appropriately disturbed. "It sounds like he might stay put this time. No doubt fallen asleep, as you say, Madame Cloutier. Thank you for your help with him."

Madame Cloutier said goodnight and returned to her apartment. Marlene stood with her door open for a moment longer and stared towards the apartment above. Grief was something she knew too well. Focusing only on the affinity she felt with this, she pushed the image of him being a sympathiser away for another day.

Early the following morning, Marlene went in search of a hiding place. She required somewhere vacant enough for the storage of some basic supplies, yet not so remote that it was too far away from help if needed.

But Marlene had no idea how to find such a place. The altercation with her upstairs neighbour had unsettled her. Whilst it might have been entirely innocent on his part, the actions of a drunken fool, *she* wasn't innocent, and she wanted to find somewhere to go if her apartment was ever compromised.

She knew of plenty of alleyways and churchyards she could shelter in for a time if she had to disappear at night, but there was nowhere really to hide a bag. She briefly considered stashing supplies in the garden she had found but dismissed that quickly; Niklas would know to look for her there.

The more time she spent with him, the more certain she became he would not bring any trouble for her unless he was forced to. But no one could know what their limits would be under questioning from the Germans. *The Nazis.* She prayed she would never have to find out.

Marlene left her apartment, retrieved the bicycle Henri had arranged for her and headed for the outskirts of the city. She knew if she cycled far enough, she would eventually leave the bustling city behind and the countryside would open up. It had to be somewhere she could cycle or, at worst, run to, but not so far away that she would need to take a train.

On a quiet road lined with trees, Marlene spotted the tips of a building above the trees and made her way towards it.

She dismounted her bicycle and wandered up the path that led to the building. Her breath seemed loud in her ears and she cast a glance behind her to check she was still alone. The old ruin reminded her of the outhouses on her grandparents' farm. It was not too far outside the city limits, yet seemed completely deserted.

Crouching behind a burned-out car, the flames long extinguished and plants now growing amongst the twisted metal, Marlene watched for signs of life. Everything was still. She crept further up to the building, pushed open the heavy door and satisfied herself that it was derelict.

The roof, long past repair, did not seem to let much

water inside, which provided decent shelter for a ruin. The windows had been boarded up and kept out the bulk of the draughts, although there was space enough between the planks of wood on one window to allow her to see if anyone was approaching. She breathed a sigh of relief, comforted by the thought she had now somewhere else to go other than her apartment. She left the ruin, intent on returning later with a small stash of supplies.

Marlene's stomach grumbled for breakfast when she arrived back at *Place Grenat*. Her legs were heavy from her cycle and her throat was dry. The encounter with her rowdy neighbour had made her so keen to find somewhere else to go that she'd left that morning as soon as it was light outside.

She crossed the square, heading away from Philippe's, pushing her bicycle alongside her. The café owner didn't seem to like her much, and without Adrienne there to be the buffer between them, the atmosphere was strained. Adrienne had dismissed her concerns when Marlene had raised them with her, but she knew to trust her instincts.

"*Bonjour*," said Niklas, suddenly appearing alongside her.

Marlene stopped and looked around them. "Niklas. What are you doing here?"

Niklas shrugged his shoulders.

"Are you following me?" she asked.

"I come here sometimes." He folded his arms and his eyes dropped to the ground. "Perhaps hoping to run into you."

Marlene didn't know what to say. Her thoughts alternated between trust and suspicion each time she saw him.

"Can we get some coffee?" Niklas asked, breaking the silence between them.

Marlene shook her head, slightly flustered. She wanted to turn around to see if Philippe was watching her through his windows, but she dared not.

"Then come cycling with me tomorrow night."

Marlene laughed, then put her hand to her mouth, hoping she hadn't drawn any attention to them. "Don't be ridiculous."

"Well, if you don't want to be seen with me during the day, night-time fixes that."

Even though his tone was light, she sensed the disappointment in his voice.

"I'll have you back before curfew, and I won't be in uniform."

"I don't know, Niklas ..."

"I'll meet you at the clock tower at seven."

She nodded, and the tension in her stomach evaporated as he left as quickly as he had appeared.

42

Marlene sat watching Adrienne pack up her desk slowly and carefully. Everything had a place in the cupboard behind her or in her desk drawers. She picked up a photo frame from the edge of her desk and turned it to face Marlene.

"This is Tomas."

Marlene took the frame from Adrienne's hands. "He's very handsome. He looks very happy."

"He is. We were."

"You will be again." Marlene handed the photograph back, and Adrienne placed it inside her cupboard and closed the doors.

"Adrienne, are you still here?" Monsieur Mayotte asked with surprise as he came out of his office.

Marlene's arm jerked at Monsieur Mayotte's unexpected presence, and she cracked her elbow on the edge of Adrienne's desk.

"Yes. I'm leaving now," said Adrienne.

"Do you have plans this evening?" he asked.

"No, just home."

Marlene rubbed the sting out of her elbow. She got up from her seat and extended her hand towards Monsieur Mayotte. "I'm Marlene."

"Ah, Marlene," he said, shaking her hand firmly. "Adrienne speaks fondly of you."

"As she does of you, too."

"Well, she has to speak like that about me otherwise I can make her life here miserable." He laughed a deep, hearty laugh at his own joke. "Although I'm sure she will tell you I make her life here miserable, in any case. Is that right?"

"Absolutely," Adrienne said, playing along.

"Adrienne tells me you're new to Paris, Marlene. It's a ... an *interesting* time to move, wouldn't you say?"

His questioning surprised Marlene, and her cheeks flushed. His tone suggested something other than the usual pleasantries, but Adrienne didn't react.

"Strange times, indeed," Marlene said.

"And where was it you moved from?"

He's not letting it drop. "Giverny. That's where my family is from. But I'm not new to Paris. I lived here for many years." It was the truth, and she didn't think the schoolmaster would accept her just saying the countryside, which is what she had told her neighbours and Adrienne when they'd asked.

"It is difficult, I suppose, for people in your situation."

For a moment, she wondered if he was referring to the double life she was now living, but she dismissed her suspicions. If she had not told Adrienne her true purpose for being in Paris, there was no chance Monsieur Mayotte could know.

"Young people, I mean," clarified Monsieur Mayotte. "I'm afraid this most recent turn of events has really limited the young. Being young was such good fun. We would go out to eat, go dancing, have a drink, and stumble home in the early hours. That was just what we did. Like now, we had little money, but the freedom to do such things was something that was taken for granted. It must be difficult for you."

"It's just as difficult for you, I imagine," she said.

"Oh, I'm fine. Madame Mayotte takes good care of me. I really am always amazed at what awaits me at the dinner table at night. What she can do with so little! But you can see that for yourself," he laughed, patting his stomach. He was joking again, but Marlene could see from the looseness of his shirt collar and his ill-fitting jacket that he had once been a much larger man.

"Shall we go?" Adrienne asked.

"I'll see you ladies out." Monsieur Mayotte flicked off all the lights and Adrienne closed the door behind them, locking it, unlocking it, then relocking it.

They walked together in silence, the air between the three of them awkward and heavy.

43

Marlene leaned her bicycle against a low wall and waited for Niklas. Her eyes surveyed the street, looking for familiar faces. She drew her hand up to her stomach. Her nerves were back, although there was a flutter of excitement in there, too.

A bell chimed behind her, and she turned to see Niklas cycling towards her. He wore dark trousers with the collar of a pale blue shirt folded over a dark blue woollen sweater, his unfastened jacket splayed around him by the wind.

"Race you?" he said, cycling in a circle around her, his boyish grin wide.

She accepted his challenge, hopped on her bicycle and pedalled as fast as her legs would allow, back along the street Niklas had come down. It wasn't enough; Niklas sped by her and screeched his bicycle to a stop across her path. The frigid air nipped her ears, her hair billowing behind her, and she heard nothing except her own laughter as she braked and stopped only inches away from him. Her heart pounded in her chest, and her breathing was heavy.

"Faster *and* fitter than you," Niklas teased. Marlene raised her hands and conceded defeat.

They cycled slowly beside each other for a time, getting their breath back.

"Glad I persuaded you to come?" Niklas asked.

"It wasn't so much persuasion, it was more of an order," said Marlene. "But yes."

It was a calm evening when not racing through it. Niklas veered to the left and bumped his bicycle up onto a tiny footbridge. Marlene followed. Her tyres kept slipping between the cobbles, and she gripped the handlebars and concentrated hard to keep going in a straight line.

They dismounted in the centre of the bridge, and Marlene could not resist dangling herself over the wall to see what lay beneath the bridge. Another cobbled street sloped downwards, curving around a bend and out of sight.

"You'll topple over if you're not careful," said Niklas.

"No, I won't. You wouldn't let me."

Her racing heart rate had returned to normal, and she gazed up. The full moon stood out like a lighthouse in the sky, guiding those who took advantage of its benefits. The moon had a significance for her it had never had before. She thought of men and women gliding in the moon's path—the unknown, the excitement, the fear. She should have been looking at the moon from the edge of a field as she climbed aboard a flight back to London.

"Beautiful, isn't it?" Niklas said. "My daughter is a stargazer. She said she liked the blackout because she can see the stars better. She's too young to understand its true meaning.

Marlene shivered. She wrapped her arms around the front of her body and rested her back on the stone wall.

"Are you cold?" Niklas started to remove his jacket.

"No, don't. I quite like it," Marlene said.

He leaned back beside her and his warmth seeped through his jacket and into her as they stood together, his arm touching hers.

"How can such a beautiful evening follow such an ugly day?" Niklas said. "Today, an explosion derailed a train and—"

Marlene cut him off. "Can we not talk about this?"

"Sorry. Bombs are not the best topic of conversation for a night out."

"No, it's not that. It just ... It reminds me you are a soldier and ... I don't know. I don't like to think about what you do during the day."

Niklas looked down and nodded. Marlene suspected his topic of conversation had been to halt any continuing thoughts of his daughter. He must be missing her terribly, and she felt selfish for not allowing him to change the subject. But being out with Niklas the soldier felt a greater betrayal of Peter than being out with Niklas the man; the father. A group of giggling girls interrupted her thoughts as they made their way across the cobles, hindered by their high-heeled shoes and something alcoholic.

Despite Niklas offering to accompany her home, Marlene cycled home alone. She needed the air to clear her head before she locked herself in her apartment for the night. Arriving back at her building, she stowed her bicycle under the stairs and retreated to her own apartment. She closed her curtains and tried very hard not to think about Niklas.

44

AFTER TAKING WHAT WAS NOW HER FOURTH DIFFERENT ROUTE to the newspaper shop, Marlene stepped inside. The shop was empty, besides an older woman hunched over something in the corner and the usual man eyeing her as she walked towards him. She didn't know his name. He hadn't said a single word to her during any of her visits; he had merely handed over the newspaper and watched her leave.

"*Bonjour*. Collection for Lucile," said Marlene.

He took his time, as Marlene had come to expect, watching her for longer than was polite. Instead of turning and picking up one of the folded newspapers from behind him, he bent down and retrieved something from under the counter, his eyes on her the entire time. He held out a note. She reached to take it, but he clutched it tighter and looked down.

Marlene looked at the paper. It said *Café. Ten o'clock*, reminiscent of the note that Henri had slipped in her pocket two weeks ago. The man scrunched up the paper and nodded towards the door. There would be no collection for Lucile today.

Leaving empty-handed, Marlene made her way straight to Alain's and looked around for Henri. She had arrived first, and the café was quiet. Alain, the man behind the serving counter and her only way of contacting Henri, poured her a coffee. Taking a seat in the far corner facing the door, she didn't have to wait long.

"Let's go," Henri said as soon as he reached her table. Marlene abandoned her coffee and dutifully followed Henri out, nodding her thanks to Alain as she went.

"I have something else for you. It's a little different this time," Henri said. As he ambled along the street beside her, he made no mention of the note he had left for her. "I need someone to accompany a man from the train station and deliver him to an address. It's not far, but he's not familiar with the city. Can you do it?"

Marlene glanced around her, uncomfortable that they were having this conversation in the open. "Should we go somewhere?" she asked.

Henri stopped and glowered at her, his eyes narrowing and his nostrils flaring. "Can you do it or not?"

The man was always curt with her, but this interaction felt especially hostile. "Has something happened?" she asked.

"Hush!" He continued walking, and she couldn't help but think he needed to take his own advice and keep his voice down. "His train arrives tomorrow at noon. Will you do it?"

She didn't know the man well, and she'd only had a few interactions with him, but her instincts told her something was wrong.

"Yes," she said, not feeling like she had any other choice.

"In here," Henri said, passing her an envelope, "is a photo of the man you will meet. Study his face so you can recognise him at once. He's been told to leave the train from the third carriage and to expect a blonde woman to meet him. You will deliver him to the address inside. Memorise the address, then burn the envelope and its contents."

"Who is he?" Marlene asked, not expecting Henri to give her an answer.

"It's better you don't know." *His standard response.* "Any other questions?"

She shook her head, tucked the envelope in her pocket and watched Henri stride away from her. Henri still did not trust her. He had picked her up on her first night in France, arranged an alternative safe house when things had gone wrong and organised her safe passage to Paris. Had that been Henri's doing? Or was it Etienne and Tessa?

Had he really given her any reason to trust him?

The next day, Marlene was at the train station at noon sharp, hoping the train wasn't late. The train had arrived, but no one was yet disembarking. She stared at the swastika painted on the side of the carriage and shuddered. She'd known to expect Germans in the station, but there were so many of them in such a confined space. When the day came for her to courier a person rather than papers, there had to be an abundance of them. She pushed her shoulders back, dug her hands into her coat pocket, and took a few deep breaths.

The passengers finally disembarked, and she scanned the faces of those leaving the third carriage. She recognised her package instantly. His face was entirely as expected, but his short stature and thin frame surprised her. When she had envisaged accompanying a man to the address she had memorised, she had not envisaged that she would be the taller of the two. As she allowed the man to kiss her cheeks, she feared their unlikely pairing would only attract attention.

"Thank you for meeting me," the man whispered to her before offering his arm for her to take. His pronunciation was so poor, it made Marlene question how much French the man could speak.

Marlene plastered on a smile and linked arms with the man, adopting an air of being intimately acquainted with him. She turned her head, allowing her hair to fall across her face as they passed the first collection of German guards and glided towards the exit. She did not trust herself to maintain her happy exterior.

Once clear of the station, Marlene brushed her hair off her face. "How was your journey?" she asked, hoping he could understand her. She knew Henri would not approve of her speaking to the man, but the silence made her more anxious.

"Uneventful," the man said in English. She stiffened and scanned the street in front of them. He relaxed his arm into hers, perhaps glad to have left the train station, or thinking the worst part of his journey was over.

The streets of Paris had a way of making you feel safe after you had been in an enclosed space with military uniforms. Marlene had come to dislike walls around her, which contrasted greatly with her feelings when she'd first arrived in Paris and wouldn't leave the confines of her apartment unless she really had to. She now much preferred the openness of the outdoors, the smell of the fresh air and the cool weather on her cheeks. The Parisian side roads had become her haven now, with enough twists and turns that you could quickly be out of sight of anyone you passed by. Something about the speed with which the scenery changed was reassuring.

They travelled the rest of the way in silence. Marlene hoped her companion could not feel the sweat on her hand as she gripped his arm. She longed to unfasten her coat, to allow the crisp air to circulate her body. It had seemed perfectly simple, to find the man at the train station and escort him to an address not too far away. It had not occurred to Marlene that there would be language problems. She had not had time to think of what she would say if they were stopped; how she would explain her fluent French while his was non-existent.

Relieved to be at the address she'd been given, she buzzed Apartment One twice. The door clicked as someone released the lock from the inside and she pushed it open. A man loitered in the doorway with dirty clothes and matted hair that suggested he'd had a tougher route than she had to get here.

"Welcome," he said in English, making not attempt to lower his voice. She hoped the building did not have its very own Madame Cloutier, standing behind her apartment door all day and listening to everyone else's comings and goings.

The two men shook hands, and the agent was ushered inside. The scruffy man moved to block the doorway, making it clear Marlene's job was now done.

"Thank you," her companion said from inside the apartment, just before the other man stepped back inside and closed the door.

As soon as Henri had asked her to do it, Marlene had felt like agreeing was a mistake. For the first time, she felt totally unprepared to operate in Henri's world.

Once back on the main street and heading back to her apartment, Marlene unfastened her coat. Her heart thudded in her chest. She had nothing to hide now—not at this moment, at least—but her rasping breaths struggled to push down the wave of nausea that threatened to overtake her body. When she'd realised he spoke little French, and with a terrible accent, she'd also realised how much danger they were both in. Being directly responsible for someone else's life was too much.

The heat that had been building inside engulfed her, and Marlene gasped for oxygen. Her fist pounded her chest in a futile attempt to slow her racing heart. She reached out with a shaky hand and grasped the railing beside her. As she lowered herself to the ground, she allowed her forehead to slide along the cold metal and a strangled sob escaped her lips.

By the time Marlene arrived back at her apartment, she had stopped shaking. She'd skipped lunch and was planning an early dinner and an early night, but despite feeling physically weak, her appetite was gone.

The door to her apartment building slammed shut behind her as she traipsed up the stairs. She heard the now familiar lock on Madame Cloutier's door turn and knew her neighbour would be waiting for her when she reached the top. Marlene usually tried to make time for a few polite words with her, but she really wasn't in the mood for chatting tonight.

"You've had a visitor today," Madame Cloutier said as Marlene reached her door. The old woman was waiting inside her doorway. "They didn't knock and I couldn't see that anything had been left for you, so I suspect they must have put something underneath your door."

"Thank you, Madame Cloutier. I'll take a look." Marlene had to admire the old woman's spirit. She hadn't asked Marlene why she had moved here, but she wasn't afraid to make it known she was keeping an eye on her. "I can't imagine what it might be," she added, when it looked as though Madame Cloutier was waiting around for an explanation.

Marlene pushed open her door. An envelope sat on the floor inside her apartment. "Only a letter," she called out, then stepped inside and closed her door before Madame Cloutier could say anything else. She heard Madame Cloutier's apartment door closing seconds later.

Marlene's name and the apartment address were written on the envelope, but she didn't recognise the handwriting and there was no postmark. She went over to her window and looked around. The few pedestrians that were on the street were walking. She couldn't see anyone lingering outside, so she presumed whomever had delivered the letter was gone.

The envelope was unsealed. It contained a single sheet of paper. She sat at her table, appreciating the warmth from the late afternoon sunlight that poured in through the window. Unfolding the paper, she read the handwritten message.

I'll be on the 3 o'clock train on Thursday. Meet me at the station. B

Marlene stood still, too many thoughts swimming in her mind. Who had delivered the letter? How could Benjamin possibly know where she was? Was there a chance it wasn't really from Benjamin?

It would be the first time in three years she had seen her brother—if it wasn't a sadistic game by the Gestapo to lure her into harm's way. Would they even know she had a brother? Her heart was pounding, and Marlene wondered if she had the patience to wait two whole days to find out.

45

ADRIENNE

MONSIEUR MAYOTTE STROLLED OUT OF HIS OFFICE AS Adrienne was leafing through the last of her paperwork for the day.

"Are you ready to go?" he asked.

"Almost. I just need to put this away, then check the classrooms," Adrienne replied.

"You finish and I'll walk the floor," Monsieur Mayotte said. He laid his coat on the end of her desk, his keys jangling as they touched the wood, and sauntered off to check the windows and doors in the rest of the building.

Adrienne's eyes followed him. When she heard the heavy door slam shut at the end of the short corridor, she turned her gaze to the coat in front of her. Something inexplicable was drawing her to the keys and the locked cupboard they opened. Perhaps it was just the fact that it was locked. It was calling upon a childlike instinct to look inside.

The temptation was too much, and she quickly grabbed the keys. She glanced through the glass door to check Monsieur Mayotte was not returning and ran into his office.

She knew the key she sought immediately. It was a short fat one that looked out of place on the ring. Her own keys were an exact replica, bar this one single key and those to their respective homes. The lock was stiff but turned after a bit of force.

One side of the cupboard was full of files she recognised; schoolwork. On the other side rested an old, battered brown suitcase standing on its end.

She had not yet heard Monsieur Mayotte return. The door to her office made a noticeable popping sound as it opened, as though the office was a bubble that had been burst, allowing the air inside to escape.

Opening the case a little, she peered inside. It contained a typewriter. She put her hand inside the case to feel around. She had never seen Monsieur Mayotte use it, but there was nothing else in the case or the cupboard except for the typewriter.

She closed the cupboard doors, locked them once more and moved swiftly back to her office.

Monsieur Mayotte appeared just as she returned his keys to his pocket. With his coat in her hand, she picked it up fully and was relieved to find some papers underneath. She snatched up the papers as though they were what she had been looking for all along and placed his coat back down.

"Everything okay?" she asked.

He smiled and nodded as he pulled on his coat.

Adrienne stuffed the papers in her cupboard and picked up her own coat.

"And what does this evening have in store for you?" Monsieur Mayotte asked as they left.

"Just a book and my bed."

"You're not meeting your friend?"

"Marlene?"

"Yes, Marlene. She's an interesting girl."

Adrienne shook her head and locked up, distracted by thoughts of Monsieur Mayotte's strange behaviour. There was nothing in the cupboard that needed to be hidden. She knew he was up to something, and her curiosity was far from satisfied.

46

THE TRAIN STUTTERED ALONGSIDE THE PLATFORM BEFORE finally coming to rest with an audible mechanical sigh. Marlene scanned the windows but couldn't see Benjamin. The brief letter hadn't indicated the purpose of his visit, and her stomach churned at the thought of what he might be here to say, but she also really needed to see a familiar face and be herself for a time, instead of the Marlene who kept secrets from everyone she met.

"Marlene!" She turned in the direction of the call. Her brother clumsily descended the steps from one of the rear carriages. Running to him, she looped her arms around his neck and hugged him. "How are you?" he asked, pulling her arms back down.

"I'm all right. I can't believe you're here. How did you find me?" Thinking about the last time she had been in the station made Marlene nervous, and there were too many people nearby in uniforms. Besides, Benjamin's gaze seared straight through to her guilty conscience. "Let's get out of here."

Marlene glanced down at Benjamin's legs. His right foot scuffed the ground, giving him a slight limp.

"Farming accident. Part of the reason I had to sell up."

The silence between them stretched each minute of the journey back to Marlene's apartment.

Marlene fumbled with her keys before entering the apartment block. Benjamin followed her in and she held onto the door until it clicked closed. He went to speak as he took in the inside of the building, but Marlene shook her head and put her finger to her lips.

"Here," she whispered as they approached her door. It suddenly struck her that Benjamin had already stopped outside her door a moment before she had spoken. *He sent you a letter. Of course he knows your apartment number.* They entered the apartment, and she chided herself for her paranoia as she bolted the door.

"What's going on?" Benjamin asked.

"Oh, nothing. I didn't want my neighbour to hear, that's all. She's rather nosy. I didn't want her asking questions."

"So, that explains why we entered your building in silence, but not why we've been in complete silence since the station. You have nothing to say to your own brother these days? No explanation why you're in Paris during a war?"

"Let me put some water on," she said, busying herself at her tiny stove and wondering how well, or not, her brother was going to take this.

～

Perched on a wall that ran alongside the river, Marlene was glad Benjamin had insisted on filling his flask full of hot tea then leaving the apartment. She had to admire his patience. He listened to her small talk between her apartment and the river without interrupting her once.

"I guess Fletcher told you I was here," Marlene said, desperate now to get the conversation started.

"I was obviously not impressed to find out you'd come back to Paris," he said. "I understand why you did it, though. I'm sorry about Peter."

She wondered if that was her brother's own conclusion or if Fletcher had suggested it. "I'm not running away from events back home, if that's what you mean," she said.

"Home?"

"Hmm. I suppose, yes. London is my home now." She knew she had a decision to make about where she settled when this was all over. She still had time, though, she hoped.

"So, have you made any friends here yet?" Benjamin asked, tearing off a piece of bread from the small lunch they had brought with them and layering it with ham. Benjamin had brought the ham with him; a sizeable piece wrapped neatly in paper.

"Oh yes, a couple. Adrienne works at the local school. We meet up once or twice a week."

"That's good."

"Yes. Her husband is in a work camp. It's good for us to get out. Get some dinner or a trip to the cinema. There's still a lot going on in the city."

"And your other friend?" he asked.

"Sorry?" Marlene said, confused.

"You said you had made a *couple* of friends. You've mentioned Adrienne. Who's the other?"

"Oh, just a few people, really, like my neighbour and the

guy who runs the café where Adrienne and I go." Philippe certainly wouldn't consider her a friend, and even an acquaintance would be pushing it. Had she been a man, she might have thought Philippe saw her as competition for Adrienne's affection.

"Are you lonely here?" Benjamin asked.

"Benjamin, what is wrong with you?" She couldn't help but laugh at the unexpected question.

"I wonder if Fletcher made a mistake by sending you here. Perhaps it wasn't the best time in your life for such a big change."

Her smile disappeared. He watched her now as she shifted uncomfortably. She stuffed a piece of bread into her mouth and refused to look him in the eye.

"We should go," Benjamin said quietly as he stood up. She looked at him now, but he stared over her shoulder. She followed his gaze and immediately flinched. Niklas and another German were heading their way.

Niklas called out her name, and Benjamin's body visibly tightened. The other German accompanying Niklas lifted his cap to Marlene as he got closer, glanced at Benjamin and kept walking. Marlene stood now, her gaze darting between Benjamin and Niklas.

She cleared her throat and tapped Benjamin's arm. "This is Benjamin."

"Your brother," Niklas said with a broad grin. *Did she detect relief in his eye?* "Marlene and I have spoken of you often. Pleased to meet you."

Niklas extended his hand towards Benjamin, but Benjamin turned and scowled at Marlene.

"This is Niklas," she said, loosening the collar of her coat.

"So, what brings you to Paris?" Niklas asked.

"Just checking up on Marlene," Benjamin said.

"Ah. As you can see, she is well."

Benjamin frowned and nodded.

"I have something for you," Niklas said to Marlene. He pulled a bar of chocolate from the pocket of his coat and handed it to Marlene. She took it from him and gave him a fleeting smile. Her eyes lingered on the pistol at his hip.

"I have to go," Niklas said, nodding towards the other soldier, who was now some distance away. "It was nice to meet you, Benjamin. Maybe we will meet again one day."

He didn't try to shake Benjamin's hand again, but patted him on the upper arm and ran off to catch up with his friend.

Benjamin stared at the chocolate, then at Marlene with disbelief.

Marlene inhaled deeply to let the tension escape her body. She looked at Benjamin, who had dropped again to perch on the wall. A bead of sweat ran down the back of her neck as she waited for him to speak. She sat beside him.

"I know what you're thinking ..." she said after less than a minute. She had to get this conversation started so it could end.

"What am I thinking, Marlene?" he asked.

"He's not bad. I know he's German, but he's different. He doesn't want to be doing this any more than we do, but it's how it is."

Benjamin sat quietly and let her ramble on with her defence of Niklas.

"I met him one day in the street, and I've seen him a few times since. Paris can be quite small in that respect; it's easy to come across the same faces time and time again. He's different from the other soldiers. Of course I thought the same as you when I first met him, but honestly he's just a nice man trying to survive, like the rest of us. They threatened his family, you know. They told him that if he didn't join the army, he would be a traitor and his family would die. He has a young daughter waiting for him."

"Have you finished?" Benjamin asked quietly when her impassioned speech had fizzled out. "Why are you so keen to defend him?"

"I'm not. I know you're thinking I'm involved in some kind of trouble with him, but he's not like that."

"And the chocolate?" Benjamin asked.

"What?"

"Him bringing you chocolate suggests he's more than a random acquaintance. What kind of relationship do you have with him?"

Marlene ignored the question. She knew there was nothing she could say that wouldn't sound like she was protesting too much.

"I can't believe you would be so stupid!" Benjamin said, his face reddening. "Have you forgotten why you're here, Marlene? You're *spying* on them. Sure, it's journalism not bombs, but any information you report helps London understand the lay of the land. Why are you drawing attention to yourself in this way? You're not here to get involved with a *German*."

Marlene looked down to the ground, jumped down off the wall, then stared at Benjamin as aggressively as he had her.

"I am not *involved* with a German."

"What would you call it?"

"He's different."

"So you said. But he's not. The army he fights for

invaded our country and now fights to keep you, me and our people under their control. They'll use France as a base for taking over everywhere else. You cannot trust him. He is German."

"Well, I do. I *do* trust him. And it's not the Germans who are the problem; it's the *Nazis*. And, yes, some Germans are doing horrible things, but that's what happens in war. Most of them are as oppressed as we are."

"You're not telling me you have *sympathy* for them? One of them killed your husband! Or have you forgotten about that?"

"How dare you! Peter's death is not something I will *ever* forget."

At least Benjamin had the good grace to appear sorry. Although their conversation had become heated, Marlene controlled the volume of her voice. She spoke quietly but fiercely, hardly moving her lips at all. "It's ... *complicated*," she said.

"It's only complicated if you allow it to be. There are good guys and there are bad guys. It's important to know the difference."

"I'm not a traitor, if that's what you're worrying about. Quite the opposite actually."

"Meaning?"

She knew straight away she should not have said anything. Their argument was now destined to get worse.

"What do you mean you're the 'opposite'?"

"I mean, I'm helping. I'm here to report on what is happening. Would I be doing that if I was a traitor?"

"Marlene ..."

She sighed in resignation. Benjamin wouldn't like what he was about to hear. She had planned to speak to him about it when the time was right. This, she knew, was not the right time, but she had no choice.

"When I arrived here, I was met by a couple of men who set me up in the apartment, with clothing and identification papers. They both work for the French Resistance."

"Marlene, what *are* you involved in?" Benjamin sank further into the wall, waiting for Marlene to continue, but she said nothing. She couldn't look at him. Instead, she sat beside him, allowing tears to roll down her cheeks.

Benjamin put his arms around her and waited. Marlene knew he didn't believe that Niklas was different; he would think Niklas was using her for something that could only lead to trouble. Now, she was about to confirm that she was perfectly capable of finding trouble on her own.

"I thought I wanted to do more," she began again, her voice still shaking. "Once I was here, I saw the German soldiers wandering around like they belonged here. They eat in our restaurants, drink in our cafés and have their photographs taken to no doubt show their families that they have been in Paris. They treat it like a holiday. They don't appreciate the horror they put everyone through. Adrienne lives each day without her husband whilst he does God only knows what for the Germans, and they don't care."

"All the more reason for you to stay out of harm's way. You're risking enough just by *writing* about it."

"That's my point, Benjamin; it doesn't *feel* like enough. How can it? Words on a page after the fact don't change what's happening—but the Resistance might. I met Henri, one of the men who helped me when I arrived, and told him I could do more. He was reluctant, of course, but then he contacted me again and told me I could help by being a courier."

Marlene waited for Benjamin's reaction before she

continued. He ran his hand through his hair and rubbed the back of his neck. She couldn't look at him, but she could see his knee bouncing up and down from the corner of her eye.

"It was easy at first. I just had to swap newspapers with people. But the other day I had to accompany a man from the train station to an apartment. He didn't speak a word of French, and I haven't a clue what I would have done if anyone had stopped us. It was terrifying. And now I wonder if I've made a mistake."

She watched Benjamin, but he did not look up. Her panic seemed pathetic to her now that she had voiced it out loud. She thought of the men, men like Peter, putting themselves at risk on the battlefields every day. They had no choice. Surely she should help them if she could?

"Maybe I should toughen up and get on with it. The cause is worth it, don't you think?"

"Worth what? Your life?" Benjamin asked sharply.

"Better people than me have lost their lives to this cause."

She thought of Peter again and how much she wished he were here, or somewhere other than St Mark's cemetery.

"And what did you say you've been doing?" Benjamin asked.

"Just delivering things," she said. "Coded messages, mostly, so I don't know their meaning. It's better that way. If I end up being questioned by the Gestapo, I can't reveal what I don't know. It's the safest way to do it. Each person only knows their little piece of the chain. That way, if someone gets caught, it's only their piece of the chain that breaks. Everything else is still in place."

"Listen to you," Benjamin said, glaring at her. "You sound like an instruction manual. Did you swallow everything Henri told you?"

"I can't believe you're reacting this way." Marlene was angry now, too. "I know you're worried about me, but this is a good thing I'm doing. If I can help ..."

"Help what?" he said, cutting her off. "Bring Peter back?"

"That's not going to happen," Marlene whispered.

"I'm glad you realise that. I thought for a minute there you'd gone mad. Look," he said, calmer now. "You're supposed to be finding out about everyday life. Isn't that why Fletcher sent you here?"

"He didn't *send* me. I wanted to come."

"You're grieving. You shouldn't be involved in something like this. You're not thinking straight."

Marlene sighed again, frustrated that he could not see her point of view.

"You said yourself you didn't think you're cut out for it. Now's the time to stop."

"I can't."

"Why? Because Henri will be angry with you?"

"No." She stared out across the river, thinking of why she had contacted Henri in the first place. "Because it gives me something to *do* about it. It's not only about Peter. Being here, I have too much time to think. You have to see the Germans wandering around, Benjamin."

"I just did, and you said he was your friend."

Benjamin was pointing out everything that had been pulsing through her mind for weeks now. She had tried to convince herself of the good she could achieve. She steeled herself by believing that her involvement might help to get people like Adrienne's husband home, but then she would see Niklas and think she might be helping to sentence people like him to death.

The only difference now was that Benjamin was saying it

out loud. When the words were spoken, she couldn't ignore them.

"Does this German know everything about you?" Benjamin asked.

Marlene shook her head.

"Then what makes you so sure you know everything about him? Walk away, Marlene. From all of it."

Benjamin busied himself putting everything that was readily edible into the bag he held. He scanned Marlene's tiny apartment as if looking for anywhere else that food might be stored.

"I can see your appetite hasn't changed, then?" Marlene teased him.

"It's a long journey," he said, by way of an explanation.

"To where?" She didn't expect an answer but thought she'd ask anyway.

Benjamin didn't bother looking up from packing his food parcel. "You're the one with secrets here, remember?"

Marlene winced. Not only was she in no rush to be chastised by Henri for wasting his time, but she also felt she should do more to help while she was here and able. She needed to feel like she was doing something that would actually make a difference. Except these feelings were restricted to times when she was not thinking of Niklas or Fletcher. When either man crept into her thoughts, she wavered.

"If you sense trouble, promise me you'll get out," said Benjamin, looking at her again. "Do you remember where my old apartment building is?"

"Yes," she said.

"Go there. The same apartment. You'll be safe. Promise me."

"I promise. Are you sure you won't spend the night?" Marlene asked, already knowing the answer. Benjamin could certainly never be accused of overstaying his welcome.

After telling her simply to take care, Benjamin left her alone in her apartment.

47

ADRIENNE

ADRIENNE WAS ALREADY IN THE OFFICE WHEN MONSIEUR Mayotte arrived to start his day. She was standing by the open window, stifling a yawn and hoping the autumn air blowing in would wake her up.

Monsieur Mayotte placed a package on her desk. It was wrapped in brown paper and tied with string.

"What is it?" Adrienne asked as she crossed the room to return to her desk. She ran her hand along the brown paper holding the soft parcel together.

Monsieur Mayotte glanced behind him before answering, "It's beef."

"*Beef*? This whole thing?"

Monsieur Mayotte nodded.

"Wherever did you get it?" Adrienne asked, astounded. Just holding the parcel gave her a boost of energy.

"A friend has a farm and brought me some. I thought you could use it."

"Well, yes, I certainly could, but shouldn't you take some of it for yourselves?"

"We already did. Enjoy it." Monsieur Mayotte headed to his office.

Adrienne stood for a minute, staring after him before deciding to follow him. She hovered in the doorway, her hand ready to knock, but instead she just watched him. They had known each other for a long time, and she knew he was preoccupied with something.

"Why do you lock that cupboard?" Adrienne blurted out without knocking.

Monsieur Mayotte looked up from behind his desk and paused before answering. "I like my papers to stay organised, that's all."

"Why do you have a typewriter in there?"

Monsieur Mayotte smiled at her. "I should really scold you for snooping, shouldn't I?"

"I'm sorry. I'm just worried about you."

"There's nothing to worry about."

"I know you're up to something. And don't deny it. I know you." In all the years they had known each other, he had never lied to her. But he had also never given her a reason to snoop through his office.

He pressed his lips together and drummed his fingers on the desk. "I'm not up to anything ... wrong."

Adrienne opened her mouth to speak but was quickly silenced by Monsieur Mayotte's raised hand.

"My friend, the one who gave me the beef, told me that the school in his village is being used to house the Germans."

"Oh, goodness, can you imagine?" An image of classrooms being turned into makeshift sleeping quarters flashed through Adrienne's mind.

"Don't worry about me," said Monsieur Mayotte.

Adrienne hesitated at the door, but it was clear to her

their conversation was over. There was no point in attempting to discuss it with him any further. Whatever Monsieur Mayotte was up to, he had no intention of involving her, and, if she was honest, she was a little relieved.

She went back to her desk and smiled as Monsieur Mayotte yelled his parting shot.

"And stay out of my cupboard."

48

ON SATURDAY EVENING, IT TOOK MARLENE JUST TWENTY minutes to walk to Adrienne's apartment. She pushed opened the heavy wooden door and walked through the cobblestone entrance, emerging from the archway into the building's inner courtyard. Adrienne had said her apartment was straight ahead, and her green door was visible from the archway. Daylight was fading fast and the cobbles were damp, making the courtyard look dreary.

Adrienne's apartment, by contrast, was bright and welcoming. Marlene was glad she had stopped to buy flowers. She had chosen a neat bunch of pink chrysanthemums, and the flowerpots bursting with colour on either side of Adrienne's door told her that her friend would appreciate the gift.

The door opened before Marlene reached it.

"I was watching for you," Adrienne said. "Come on in."

Marlene went in and found herself in Adrienne's living room. There was no hallway. Every other area of the apartment seemed to be accessed through an archway at the rear of the living room.

"A proper fire," Marlene said, immediately moving towards it to feel its warmth. She watched the orange flames dancing and crackling in front of her, bringing back memories of her grandparents' farm. "These are for you." Marlene passed Adrienne the flowers. "And let me say, it smells incredible in here. That's not the same cabbage and carrots I have been eating all week."

Adrienne smiled and shook her head. "No, it's not. Can you keep a secret?"

"Of course. I'm intrigued."

"It's beef. A stew with real meat—lots of it—and onions and red wine. I even managed to get some potatoes. It's been cooking for hours. Although, I have to admit, I was a little nervous my neighbours might smell it and report me. So far, so good."

"Oh, I can't wait," Marlene said with a wide grin. "I haven't had a good meal in weeks."

"Weeks? Try *years*."

A pang of guilt rattled in Marlene's stomach as a consequence of lying to her new friend and thoughts of the sausage and mash she had eaten with Fletcher before she'd left London. She had even had cake. Isobel had baked a farewell cake for her and George. Everyone had a slice and was delighted to learn that Isobel had got her hands on real eggs, butter and cream.

There were food shortages and rationing in both countries, but Marlene was hungrier in Paris than she could ever remember feeling in London.

"These are beautiful. Thank you." Adrienne smelled the flowers. "The table's through here."

Marlene followed Adrienne through the archway and into her kitchen. The smell of the stewing beef had her salivating in anticipation. As Adrienne busied herself putting water into a pale green ceramic vase and trimming the stems of the flowers, Marlene snuck a peek inside the casserole dish that lay resting on the top of the stove and breathed in the comforting warm air that escaped when she lifted the lid.

Once they sat down to eat, the two women took their first few bites in silence.

"Oh, it's *delicious*," Marlene said, pausing for only a few seconds before shovelling another forkful into her mouth. The succulent meat fell apart in her mouth, and the rich sauce transported her to another place and time. "It's unbelievable. Where did you find it?"

"Monsieur Mayotte has a friend in the countryside. I'm so glad you could come over. I know a lot of conversations these days are about food, but I can't really go around talking about this meal outside of my house."

"Monsieur Mayotte is an interesting man," Marlene said.

Adrienne's mouth curled. "That's funny. That's exactly what he said about you."

As Marlene headed home, the black clouds she had seen earlier drenched her. The streets were almost empty, and there were no soldiers in sight. *Even soldiers don't like the rain.*

She pushed open the heavy door to her apartment building, and it slammed behind her as she climbed the stairs. She removed her coat and shook the rain from it.

"Don't you put all that water on those steps!" said Marlene's neighbour, her arms tightly folded across her chest. "I slipped on those very steps this morning because someone had done just that."

"Good evening, Madame Cloutier. I hope you're well this

evening," Marlene said, choosing to ignore her grumbles about the rainwater on the stairs.

"You were late home yesterday," said Madame Cloutier.

"It was a busy day."

"It's not good for a young girl to be out on the streets after dark."

"I was home before dark." Marlene unlocked her door. "Don't worry about me."

"Someone has to," Madame Cloutier called before Marlene said goodnight and closed her door.

Inside her apartment, Marlene locked both locks on her door, hung up her damp coat and pulled across the blackout curtains. She cringed for her curtness with Madame Cloutier, but she told herself that the old woman was far too interested in people's comings and goings for Marlene to spend too much time chatting with her.

Her gaze was drawn to the unappetising pot of soup that sat on top of her stove. There was no growling in her stomach tonight. She could still taste Adrienne's stew as she peeled off her clothes and got into bed. Despite the relatively early hour, it didn't take long for exhaustion to consume her, her eyes to close and her subconscious to take over.

49

On Sunday evening, Niklas lay stretched out on the grass, propped up on his elbow as Marlene sat cross-legged alongside him. She couldn't remember the last time she'd felt completely at ease. When she entered the garden, its plants and trees embraced her like a loved one and filled the hollow inside of her.

She reached her hands behind her, planting them on the grass, and sank back. Niklas grinned, and she wished they were in a different time and a different place. But then, they likely wouldn't have met.

And Peter would have still been alive.

Gazing at the ashen sky, Marlene had an uninterrupted view of the crescent moon, its arc like a shy smile when she tilted her head. Without further word from Henri, she would have no reason for extending her stay again. At the next full moon, she would be on her way back to London. So much had happened, yet she still wasn't ready to leave.

"Are you with me?" Niklas asked, cutting through her thoughts.

"Sorry. It's just being here with you," she said.

Niklas raised his eyebrows, but he didn't move. "I'm not sure how to take that."

"I'm not sure how you should take it, either," she said. She could hardly tell him she felt disloyal to her husband. That would mean acknowledging she had feelings for Niklas, and she wasn't ready to admit that to herself, let alone say it out loud.

Each time she left Niklas, she told herself her time in Paris was limited and her focus should be entirely on her work. But each time she saw him, he made plans to meet her again, and, truthfully, she didn't resist anywhere close to enough.

"About Benjamin," Marlene said. "That was the first time I had seen him in a while, so he didn't know that we are ..." *We are what?* She didn't know how to finish that sentence. "He was just surprised to see you."

"Oh, I understand. I seem to recall you didn't much like me either when we first met," said Niklas.

Marlene laughed and lay down. Niklas joined her, taking her hand in his. They lay in silence for a while, listening to the breeze billowing through the trees and the occasional rumble of a vehicle passing beyond the perimeter of their sanctuary.

Niklas yawned. "Excuse me. I had a late night. Do you remember when that used to be a good thing? Here, it's a late night because resources are stretched with so many units leaving for—"

"Can we not talk about the war?" Marlene said, cutting him off. "Let's imagine our reality is different. For a little while, at least."

"My mother still talks about the last war."

"Do you remember it?"

Niklas propped himself up on his elbow again, looking

down at her. "Not really. I was eight or nine when it ended. All I remember is that my father didn't come home. I can't have that be my daughter's experience, too. So I do what I have to do to survive."

"You're going home to her."

"I am. I have to make it. But you're right; let's talk about something else."

She admired Niklas for truly living in the moment. One minute, he spoke of his father not returning from war and his own daughter, and in just a second, he could change the entire atmosphere around him. She pictured him in front of a classroom, controlling it effortlessly. It wasn't just his words; it was his tone. He had the type of personality that influenced those around him. He was unassuming to look at, like Peter, but when he opened his mouth, you listened. "You must be a wonderful teacher."

He closed his eyes and smiled. When he opened them and looked directly into her eyes, Marlene's skin tingled and a rush of warmth engulfed her.

"Why's that?" he asked.

"You have a ... I don't know ... a way about you." She reached out and ran her hand down his arm, her fingers sliding down the wool of his sleeve. When they had first met, she'd felt afraid, but it wasn't of him. It was his uniform that had frightened her. His warm breath moved across her cheek as his face inched closer to hers.

She sprung up and sat cross-legged again, her hair tingling on the back of her neck. "Is there a way to find out where a particular prisoner of war is being held?"

He sat up, too, apparently accepting that the moment they'd shared was over. "Why do you ask?"

"A friend of mine's husband is a prisoner of war, and she has no idea where he's being held. She can't visit him; can't write; can't send him anything. I haven't said this to her, but she really doesn't know if he's even alive."

"Do you know the circumstances of his arrest? Asking questions brings attention. Sometimes these things are best left alone."

Marlene let out a long sigh. She wanted to help Adrienne, but she knew that having someone asking questions about Tomas's whereabouts was unlikely to help anyone. It was a risk she could ill afford to take, but Marlene supposed she'd begun to surround herself with those.

50

MARLENE CYCLED ALONG WITH A SEALED ENVELOPE IN HER pocket, clueless as to its contents. Something clipped her back wheel, and she felt herself losing control. A young boy of four or five years old bounced off the pavement and into her path. She gripped the brakes and whipped the handlebars away from the terrified figure. Losing her balance, she was thrown to the ground, her right leg snared beneath the bicycle's metal frame. The boy gave a yelp and fell into a heap on the road. His little face, pale with fright, crumpled and tears fell.

Marlene dragged herself out from underneath the bicycle and crawled over to the boy. She struggled to get to her feet and pulled the boy onto his, sitting him on the doorstep of the nearest apartment building.

"Are you okay?" she asked, smoothing down his dishevelled hair. The boy's whimpered words were inaudible as his crying continued.

"What did you hurt?" she asked, wiping the tears from his face. His chubby little hands pulled at the leg of his dark shorts to reveal a bloodied knee, and Marlene reached into her pocket for her handkerchief. She dabbed it at the boy's knee and watched the blood soak through, colouring the wings of a butterfly whose outline had been stitched into the fabric. It was the only handkerchief she possessed in France and had been stowed away in a pocket in the small suitcase Tessa had kindly packed for her. She didn't know if Tessa had put it there, intending to gift it to Marlene, or if it had been accidentally left the last time the suitcase had been used. She smiled at the boy, who had stopped crying and instead sniffed loudly, wiping his runny nose on the sleeve of his heavy jacket.

Marlene tied the handkerchief around his little knee, pulled up both of his socks and got him onto his feet again.

"There you go, young man. Next time, make sure you look in the road before running out."

The boy nodded and gave Marlene a big smile, holding no grudges for the wound on his knee nor the tears he had cried.

"Where's your mother?" she asked. The boy pointed down the alleyway and ran off, his bloodied knee not slowing him down at all.

Marlene straightened herself up and brushed her clothes down. The palm of her left hand stung. Dirt and gravel from the road was now mixed with blood that had made its escape through the scuffs on her hand.

"That was quite a fall." An old man who now held her bicycle approached her.

"Thank you," Marlene said, taking her bicycle from him.

"You're welcome, dear. Do you have another handkerchief?" he asked, looking at her hand.

"Oh, it'll be fine," she said, picking some bits of dirt out of her grazed skin as he handed her a folded, pressed handkerchief from inside his coat. "Oh no, it'll be fine, really."

"You have a greater need than I," he said, taking her hand and placing the handkerchief on top of the scratches.

"Thank you," she said. "You're very kind."

"Be safe," he said, and he turned and sauntered down the street.

Marlene wiped the dirt from her hand, the motion stinging her skin. The handkerchief had the initials *W.B.* embroidered in one corner. She watched the old man shuffling slowly down the street; *W.B.*, she presumed.

Funny, back home, handkerchiefs are so scarce they're rationed, and here, two strangers were happy to give theirs away.

It did not escape Marlene's notice that, when in London, France was home; when in Paris, London was home. She so desperately wanted to be happy with what she had; anything else and she risked turning into her mother, jumping from one thing to another in a continuous search for something better.

She stuffed both of her hands into her pockets to store the handkerchief in one and to check that the envelope she carried was still nestled in the other. Instantaneously nauseated, she pulled her pocket inside out.

It was empty.

She frantically searched the other pocket, hoping she had simply put it in her left pocket rather than her right. It, too, was empty, except for her new handkerchief. She carefully unfolded the handkerchief, although she knew, of course, the envelope was too big to have slipped between its folds. Nothing.

She scrunched the handkerchief and thrust it back into her pocket. Her eyes scanned the street, both where she'd stood and where she had lain following the crash. She only hoped the envelope had fallen into one of the small pools of water on the road. Being turned to mulch in water would be better than lying somewhere else between her collection site and here, waiting to be read.

The envelope could not have been in the folds of her own handkerchief because she had unravelled it to tie around the boy's knee. She would have seen it had it been there. Certain that no one had approached her on her journey so far, she was confident that the envelope had been lost and had not been taken by anyone. She hadn't read the message, so she wouldn't be able to verbally pass it on. Her only option was to get word to Henri.

She mounted her bicycle once more and headed towards Alain's café. The collision had delayed her and left a few scratches in the three of them; the boy, herself and her bicycle, which now had ragged strips of silver glistening through the relatively rust-free blue paintwork.

After leaving the café, there was nothing more Marlene could do until she met with Henri the following day. She pedalled toward her apartment, holding her handlebars with only her right hand. Her left hand throbbed and the cuts and scrapes stung. She had washed her hand in the café's bathroom, but she still felt grit beneath her skin and was keen to get a proper look at it.

When she reached her street, Niklas was perched on the front steps of an apartment building a few down from hers. She coasted her bicycle past her own apartment and stopped beside him.

"What are you doing here?" she asked as she dismounted.

"Hoping to see you." His boyish grin fell away as he spotted the handkerchief wrapped around her hand. "What happened to you?" He peeled the handkerchief back and winced at the blood on her hand.

"Honestly, it looks worse than it is."

Niklas held her hand and tapped the scuffed skin. His hands were warm, and she enjoyed the touch of another person. Her gaze lingered on his face. Or perhaps it was *his* touch she enjoyed. She cleared her throat and snatched her hand back, pressing the handkerchief back into place.

"We need to get that cleaned up. Can I come up and help you?" He glanced towards her apartment.

Her eyes widened. "Absolutely not! My neighbour would have a fit if she saw you."

"Then you're coming to my place. Drop off your bicycle and let's go. No debate."

Marlene knew she should have refused, but part of her was curious to see where Niklas lived. Another part of her craved his company.

On the way to his guesthouse, he had promised no one would see them together. She had told him again that it wasn't him she didn't want to be seen with; it was his uniform.

They snuck past the main living area of the guesthouse, their entry drowned out by music and raucous laughter, and entered his room. It was meticulously neat. Each of his few possessions had a distinct home. The only thing not organised in the room was a stack of books beside the bed, each pointing in a slightly different direction from the one below.

"You like books, then?"

Niklas nodded. "The day I saw books being carted out of my school library and set alight was the day I knew my life would soon change forever."

He sat down on the bed and stared at the pile of books.

The bedspread was a bright red floral pattern. Probably not to his taste, but it made the room homely.

A deep crease spread across his forehead and she wanted to comfort him, but she didn't trust herself to reach out and touch him. She knew that there was nowhere good that could lead. "I like it. It's much better than my accommodation," she said.

Niklas looked at her curiously. "What are you doing here?" he asked, standing again.

"Avoiding being seen with you in public," she said, hoping he thought it was a joke.

"In Paris, I mean. Your husband was British, right?"

Marlene looked at him. She didn't remember telling him Peter was British.

"Sometimes you call him Pierre. Sometimes you call him Peter," he said, knowing exactly what she was thinking. "Why did you come back here?"

Marlene contemplated her answer for a long time. Why *did* she come back here? Her grief had driven her to return to Paris, but it had also clouded her judgment. She was here to give ordinary people a voice, but she had begun to distract herself by running around trying to prove something to Henri, a man who would have happily abandoned her on her first day in France if Etienne hadn't insisted they accompany her to the safe house.

She wanted to tell Niklas the truth, but she stayed silent.

He walked over to her and wrapped his hand around the back of her head. His fingers slid smoothly through her hair, and he pulled her towards him. His warm breath melted on her lips, and he paused, giving her the opportunity to pull away. She didn't. Their lips met briefly before she lowered her head, resting her forehead on his chin.

"I'm sorry," he whispered. "I've wanted to do that for so long."

"Don't be sorry. I want to, I really do ... but I can't." She pulled back and looked at him now. "It's too soon for me. I don't want to spend the next fifty years a widow, but I'm not ready to let him go yet."

"I know this is ..." he searched for the right word. "*Unconventional.* But you can trust me, and I trust you. I know you, and I hope you know me, too. You can't always tell the good people from the bad by the colour of their uniform." He kissed her on the forehead, his lips lingering as if reluctant to leave her skin. "Let's get this hand sorted out."

Marlene sat on the only chair in the room, stroking her newly bandaged hand. "What's this?" she asked, picking up a leaflet from the table beside her. It was written in German, but she recognised a map of the city tucked into its pages.

"I suppose it's the German guide to Paris. Useful addresses and places to go that are ... German-friendly." Niklas dug his hands into his pockets as Marlene continued to skim the pages of the leaflet. It reminded her they really were from two very different worlds.

Niklas picked something up from the top of the stack of books and handed it to her. It was a photograph of him, beaming in the centre, with his wife on his left and their daughter on his right. They all looked so happy. His daughter must have only been around two years old at the time it was taken, and she already looked so much like her mother. Marlene hoped that would bring comfort to Niklas rather than pain in the years to come.

With only two weeks left in Paris, Marlene wasn't quite sure how to say goodbye to Niklas.

51

MARLENE ENTERED ALAIN'S CAFÉ. SHE WASN'T SURE WHAT the protocol was for resigning from the Resistance, but with only two weeks left in Paris, she couldn't jeopardise her return. She would tell him she had missed the drop the day before and that she wouldn't do any more. Unless her flight couldn't land, she wouldn't be looking to extend her stay any further.

She took the coffee Alain had made for her and sat down at the only vacant table. The older couple at the table next to hers mustered whatever smiles they could in her direction, and Marlene couldn't help but think of how tired they looked. Her grandparents, being farmers, had never been able to fully retire. They'd hired more help in their later years, but they had still worked the farm for hours each day until they came home weary. She could see that same weariness on the faces of the man and woman next to her. The war had to end and, if showing people what occupation really looked like inspired them to keep pushing ahead, that's what she would do.

Henri was right. She had a personal reason for returning

to France—lots of personal reasons, if she was truly honest with herself—but for the first time since her arrival, she knew exactly what she needed to do next. Children should be with their parents, husbands with their wives. Every single person's story mattered, and she was in the privileged position of being able to share those stories. Her only job now was to get back to London and get writing.

Marlene caught sight of Henri striding past the café. She got up and headed after him.

They walked in silence. Marlene was eager to talk, but she knew enough to know that a conversation like that shouldn't take place in the street, despite Henri's previous lack of discretion.

Henri turned into the lane behind the café and entered through the back door. Marlene followed, and she found herself in what she surmised had to be the café's stockroom.

She told him about her cycling accident and losing the paper she'd been entrusted with, but he seemed unconcerned. For someone whose natural disposition was anger, Marlene expected more of a reaction. Instead, Henri pulled an envelope from inside his coat.

Marlene raised her hand. "I can't," she said. "I'm leaving for home in just two weeks, and I can't jeopardise that."

Henri leaned towards her, his voice low. "Until you're on that plane, this doesn't stop."

Marlene was taken aback. She had expected him to be annoyed, as he had been every time he was in her presence, but she hadn't considered that he would say no; that she had to keep going.

"Look, Henri, I'm sorry. I can't." Her voice cracked a little, and she hoped he hadn't heard it. "You were right about me the first time. We each have a role to play, and this isn't mine. I have work to do at home. It's different from the work you do, but it's important work nevertheless, and I need to get back safely to do it. Something is off. I don't know what or why, but something's not right and I need to lie low until I leave." Marlene's cuts tingled beneath the bandage Niklas had wrapped around her hand.

Henri sighed and looked away from her. She could see him thinking and thought it best to stay quiet until he spoke again.

"I need this delivered to a radio operator. It's important and must go tonight. The address is on the back and the key is inside. Make sure she gets it. Do this, and then you're done."

Marlene's jaw tightened. Although every fibre of her being told her to walk away, she knew Henri wasn't giving her a choice.

She took the envelope and stalked out.

52

IT WAS DARK WHEN MARLENE LEFT HER APARTMENT BUILDING with Henri's envelope tucked inside her coat pocket. Instead of being relieved that it was her last drop, her breath quickened as she noticed someone following her. Only a few streets away from her apartment, going back was not an option. Her pursuer timed his steps to match hers and kept his distance. Marlene stopped to look in the window of the *boulangerie*, pretending to be perusing the scant goods on sale. One figure reflected in the glass stood out, stationary, as everyone else streamed by.

Her long coat hugged her body as it protected her from the bitter winds, but still she shivered. She started again and kept changing direction, grateful that her knowledge of the Parisian streets was once again helping her to avoid dead ends.

As she edged closer to her destination, the streets became quieter. She took a deep breath, then halted and turned, forcing her pursuer to confront her or walk on by. He was only a few feet behind her, his head down and a hat pulled low to obscure much of his face. He glanced in her direction but kept on walking, turning left onto the street she had planned to take.

Marlene also turned left and paused under the golden glow of the street lamp. She scanned the long street, but the man was nowhere in sight. Turning back, she retraced her steps and took a few more random turns. Unsure whether she had lost him, she headed to the address Henri had given her, hoping to arrive before the radio operator, despite her detour.

Marlene glanced at the door numbers as she walked to work out which side of the street her destination would be on. It was on the left; a large terraced building with six floors. She briefly scanned the windows, but there was no sign of life behind the black iron grates that surrounded the windows. Even the street was quiet.

She approached the grey door, slid the key into the lock, slipped inside and firmly closed the door. She tugged at it to make sure it was locked. Like her apartment, the door led directly into the building, with two apartments on the ground floor and a stone staircase leading straight up to the others.

She entered the first apartment. It was unlocked, and once inside, her eyes struggled to adjust to the dim interior. She swallowed the sick feeling rising in her throat and headed straight to the window. There were no lights on in any of the windows in the building opposite. She hoped that meant no one would be looking at her.

No one except whoever had followed her here.

She took a deep breath and scanned the street. It was empty.

A wooden box sat under the window, containing candles and a large box of matches. She struck a match and held it to the already singed wick of a candle that sat in the middle of the window frame. The candle fizzed into action, and she fitted the glass globe over the metal holder. The glass globe was blackened from too much use and too little cleaning, and the flame became a faint glow. Hugging the wall beneath the window, Marlene kept out of what little light the flame generated.

She moved back and forth to get a clearer view of the street beyond the iron grates. A couple, arm in arm, appeared from the corner. As they made their way up the street, she hugged the wall again so as not to be seen. She observed them to see if they were heading for the apartment.

Holding her breath as they halted in front of the building, Marlene heard the murmuring of their voices and strained to make out the words, but couldn't. The woman giggled and threw her arms around the man's neck. He kissed her, a long passionate embrace, and they resumed their stroll, heading away from the apartment.

Marlene found her breath again. She stayed still until their voices disappeared into the distance. The candle still burned, and the street was once again empty.

Crouching on the floor inside the apartment with her back against the wall, her eyes fixed on the door, Marlene thought the door handle moved. The door wasn't locked, but when no one entered, she dismissed it as her imagination. Breathing out, she allowed the air to escape from her body.

The sparseness of the apartment sent a chill through her. The walls were bare, and the only furniture consisted of four small wooden stools. Like her own apartment, the kitchen filled a tiny corner of the main living area, the only other room being a small shower room. The window had one heavy, lined curtain currently pushed against the wall.

If the door did burst open, how could she explain her presence? She stared at the glow from the candle and the shadows the flickering flame cast on the walls. They looked alive. She tried to imagine they were on her side.

It was almost eight. She had waited for over an hour. She had to leave soon so she could travel before the main streets emptied. Darkness now enveloped her as the smell of the exhausted flame drifted towards her. The radio operator had not arrived. She hoped they hadn't had trouble of their own.

Marlene pulled the envelope Henri had given her from her pocket. If someone was still watching her, she couldn't be found with it on her, but could she really leave it behind? She contemplated opening it to see how risky it would be to leave it, but then Henri's words about not being able to reveal what you didn't know drifted back to her.

She moved slowly to the window, putting her hand out to feel for the box of candles. Forcing her hand down the side of the box, wax sliding under her fingernails, she moved as many candles as she could to one side and pushed the envelope to the bottom. Dropping the key in also, she moved her hand away, allowing the candles to fall back into position.

She left the apartment, pausing at the front door, wondering if it was best to stay put. If she hadn't been arrested by now, her own apartment was as safe as anywhere.

Marlene headed home, hoping she would make it.

THE SQUARE WAS QUIET EXCEPT FOR THE GENTLE RUSTLE OF Resistance newspapers that littered the ground as Adrienne walked. In the fading light, she caught the headlines, not daring to pick one up and be seen reading it in public. Sensing someone's eyes following her, she glanced around, seeing only an old man resting on a wall. Unnerved, she quickened her pace towards Philippe's café.

Philippe was outside, as he often was, sweeping the ground in front of the café, and he smiled as she approached.

"Everything okay?" he asked, looking over her shoulder.

"Yes, fine. Just in need of a quick coffee before going home."

"Coming up," he said, following her inside.

Despite the late hour, the café was busier than she had seen it in a long time, and each of the seats at the counter was occupied. The only free tables were those bordering a table of four uniformed German soldiers. They sat talking in low voices, the table in front of them noticeably devoid of any cups or plates. Refreshments were not what brought them to the café. Philippe brought her coffee, and her thanks was drowned out by the noise of the chairs scraping along the hard floor as the four men moved their chairs to fit in a fifth.

"That group—the same men, this time—have been regulars over the past few days," whispered Philippe.

"Do they ever buy anything?" she asked, trying not to look at them.

"No, but I don't think I'll have that conversation with them," he said. "Any news on Tomas?"

She shook her head, and he left her alone.

After finishing her drink and saying goodnight to Philippe, who seemed intent on spending the evening outdoors sweeping the same ground he had already swept, Adrienne headed home. She thought of the Germans inside the café. She'd seen groups of them in before, but this group was agitating Philippe more than any of the others ever had. It wasn't right that ordinary people were no longer comfortable in their own space. From the day the Germans had marched in, the city had been on edge.

Adrienne pushed open her front door and was startled by someone quietly saying her name. The old man she had passed earlier on the square was now standing a few feet away from her.

"I'm a friend of Tomas. I have news of him."

Her brow furrowed. Adrienne scanned the empty courtyard. Despite being deeply uncomfortable with the situation and not convinced by the man in front of her, the pull of possible news was too great. She stepped aside and invited him in.

～

Adrienne led her visitor into her small kitchen, where she motioned for him to sit. The window let in no light. She pulled the blackout curtain into place—well-rehearsed movements, even in the dark—and put on the lights. The man's skin was well weathered, but he couldn't have been much older than thirty. He pulled off his coat and straightened up, stretching out his back as he did so.

"I'm less of a threat if I seem frail. All hunched over, all people see is an old man," he said as he sat down, no doubt having seen the confusion on her face. She sat at the opposite end of the table. "My name is Jean Chapelle. I was in the same regiment as Tomas. We agreed that if something happened to either one of us, he would tell my wife and I would tell you."

Adrienne recognised his name. Her stomach tightened and blood rushed to her head. She brought her hands to her face. Her cheeks were burning and water gathered in her eyes, blurring her vision.

"No, no, he's alive," he said quickly. "Last week, they were going to transfer us to a camp in Germany. During the transfer, some of us escaped. They recaptured some almost straightaway and ... executed others. But some of us made it. I went back to look for Tomas, but he wasn't there. I hoped he would be here."

Adrienne shook her head. "Maybe he's injured somewhere."

"No. I've looked everywhere. They must have taken him."

"How do you know ..." She stopped herself from asking the question. She couldn't bring herself to say it out loud. There must surely have been consequences for those that tried to flee.

"I saw the bodies. He wasn't there," said Jean. "He's strong and fit, so he can work. He's valuable to them."

"Are you saying that for my benefit or yours?" Adrienne recognised the feelings etched on his face; the pain and the guilt. Two feelings she had an abundance of.

"Both," he said. He reached across the table and took her hand. Now, they both sat in silence, lost in their own thoughts, until the sound of an explosion somewhere in the distance brought them back to their realities. "Anyway, I thought you should know what happened."

"Can we get him out?"

"He's probably in Germany now."

Adrienne slumped back in her chair. "How was he?" she asked, not really wanting to know the answer.

"He worries about you, mostly. He spoke of you often."

She wanted to be comforted by this, but the explosion in the distance had been followed by gunfire, which still rattled on.

"It sounds close," she said. She got up and peeked behind the blackout curtain.

"Resistance activity, most like. I should go. It's already dark, and I have quite a distance to go."

"No. It's too late, and there's too much activity tonight. You can stay here until morning."

"I can head in the opposite direction. It'll be safer that way."

"Please stay. I'm sure Tomas would want you to. It'll be safer for you to travel in the morning, when you're one of hundreds in the streets."

Jean twisted in his seat and chewed at his fingernails. He glanced at the door.

"I'll get some blankets. I don't have a spare bed, so it won't be terribly comfortable, I'm afraid," Adrienne said.

"Much better than what I've been used to."

Adrienne smiled and nodded, but his words cut her like a knife as she thought about where Tomas slept at night. With that image in her mind, and an escapee sleeping in her living room, Adrienne expected a long, sleepless night.

54

WHEN MARLENE WOKE, SHE DARTED OUT OF BED, DESPITE having been unable to sleep properly for thinking about the previous night. She had been followed. Someone must now suspect her of being part of the Resistance.

She had been replaying her movements of that week in her head, over and over again, all night. She'd performed two exchanges, and both had gone smoothly. Yet someone had identified her as a person of interest. *Why?*

This was the first time she had been followed. SOE and Henri had told her what to watch out for, and it had been the first instance of her noticing any signs. She wondered if Henri would move her to another apartment or whether she'd have to stay locked inside a safe house until her flight back to London. She couldn't leave Adrienne and Niklas to think she'd just disappeared, but she pushed all thoughts of getting a message to them to the back of her mind. *One step at a time.*

Marlene dressed as normal, then breathed deeply and lay extra clothes out on top of her bed. She slid her notebook into the small handbag Tessa had given her and instinctively touched her watch; the only two items that belonged to her. She dressed again, and again, until she was wearing as many layers as she could fit underneath her coat. To anyone that might be watching, it had to look like a normal day, not as if she was packed up and ready to leave.

Pulling back the heavy curtains, Marlene casually glanced into the street. She fiddled with the curtains for longer than necessary to get a good view. Those first few days in Paris, she had sought refuge in this apartment for three days. Now, it was a cage. A cage with an open door. But whether or not she made it to freedom was entirely down to someone else. Someone who she couldn't see, but she knew was out there.

When Marlene opened the main door, a sharp wind caught her, and she was grateful for the layers, if not the circumstances, especially since she didn't know how long it would take Alain to contact Henri. She would give anything to be complaining of the cold and wishing the added extra layers were a choice, rather than a necessity.

The door slammed behind her, and she headed away from the apartment for the last time. Turning every few streets, she took the least direct route she could think of to the café. She felt alone yet exposed, as if all the passers-by were watching her. It was possible that some of them were. The wind stung her face, and her eyes watered heavily.

As Marlene pushed open the door to the café, Alain smiled at her and nodded to the table in the corner.

Henri was waiting for her. All of the other tables were empty. The lock clicked behind her, and Alain disappeared through the door in the back wall of the café.

"How did you know?" Marlene asked as she rushed towards him and took a seat.

"The operator you were due to meet contacted me last night," said Henri quietly.

"Thank goodness. What happened?" she asked. "Are they safe?"

Henri nodded and poured Marlene some coffee. She held the cup close, feeling the warmth between her hands. Despite her layers, the chill inside of her wouldn't leave. When she'd arrived at her apartment the previous night and closed the door behind her, the sigh of relief she'd wanted to give didn't come. It still hadn't.

"Well, we know one thing," said Henri. "It wasn't the Gestapo following you or they would have arrested you before you even reached the apartment. The Germans are brutal. You would have been tortured for information. Whoever it was, they have their own agenda or they would have told the Germans where to find you."

"Well, whoever it is, I can't understand how they've become suspicious."

"Last night was the first time someone has followed you?"

"I believe so," said Marlene.

"What have you done recently? Have you done anything that might have exposed you? Told anyone who might have betrayed you?"

Marlene thought back to her evening with Niklas at his guesthouse.

"Nothing out of the ordinary." She wasn't sure if Henri believed her.

"Has anyone new entered your life?" he asked. She shook her head. Niklas knew something was going on with her, but he hadn't pressed her for details. Someone had followed her, but it had nothing to do with Niklas. "We'll need to keep a close eye on this situation." He mumbled now, as if talking to himself rather than Marlene.

"*Keep a close eye on it*?" Marlene asked incredulously. "I thought you said that if I was compromised, I would have to leave. I've come prepared to leave."

She pulled open her coat to show the several layers of clothing she wore.

"You think you were followed ..." Henri started before Marlene curtly cut him off.

"I don't *think* I was followed. I *was* followed."

"Okay. So, you were followed to the apartment," he said, although clearly in an attempt to pacify her. "But they didn't follow you here, so they don't know where you live."

"We don't know that," said Marlene. She crossed her arms in front of her chest and stared at Henri.

"You think someone followed you here?" Henri asked.

"I don't think so, but I can't be sure. And he started following me only a few streets from my apartment."

Marlene couldn't believe Henri's response. Dread built up in her stomach as she realised he wasn't going to help her.

"Even if he is still watching you, we don't know it's because he's identified you as helping the Resistance. It could be because of that story you've been writing."

His attitude towards her employment had not improved any.

"If I thought it was Germans, and that you were in danger, I would get you out immediately," he continued. "Whoever this is wants you to lead them somewhere—or to *someone*. There could be an opportunity here to identify those working against the Resistance. We can keep a closer eye on you, and if we think you are in danger, we'll get you out. You said you were up for this. You said you could handle it."

"But this changes everything, surely?" said Marlene, knowing it was futile.

"Until we find out who's behind this, nothing changes. Pick up your package for Lucile as planned, then meet me here at the same time on Wednesday. I'll be watching you, too," said Henri before he got up and left her alone.

He had decided that Marlene was going back to her apartment until the next full moon. And he had reneged on their deal. It wouldn't stop until she was on the plane.

Marlene sat motionless in the café long after Henri had gone and Alain had returned. She took no comfort from his last words.

I'll be watching you, too.

55

MARLENE ENTERED HER APARTMENT BUILDING AND ALLOWED the door to fall behind her. She had considered going to the ruin to hide out there, but with two weeks to go and with Henri her only actual contact, she knew that wasn't an option. Before she reached the first step, she turned suddenly and slipped her hand between the door and the lock. Her knuckles banged into the doorframe, and she cursed softly to herself. She freed her hand and pushed the door closed, allowing the lock to quietly click into place. Climbing the stairs, she made sure her heels didn't touch them and give her away. She couldn't face Madame Clouti-er's questioning today.

Nursing her bruised knuckles, she hoped to sneak past Madame Cloutier's door, but her elderly neighbour was already peering out of the door, waiting for her. Madame Cloutier put her finger to her lips and motioned for Marlene to enter her apartment. Marlene glanced up the corridor towards her own apartment. Her door was open, allowing a thin strip of light into the corridor. She hesitated, not wanting to involve anyone else in her troubles. She shook her head and crept backwards. Madame Cloutier began frantically waving at Marlene to come in.

The strip of light was interrupted as a man in a long dark coat stepped in front of the gap in the door. Staring at the back of his head, Marlene knew she had seconds to decide. She hurried into her neighbour's apartment.

Madame Cloutier bolted the door behind them as silently as she could.

"I have to get out of here," Marlene whispered. Tears welled in her eyes, but she refused to let them fall.

"You can't go; they'll see you. They've been here for nearly an hour. They'll leave soon. You have nothing for them to take," said Madame Cloutier.

"An hour? They must be waiting for me. Someone is probably watching from outside. They will know that I have come into the building. They will search everywhere until they find me. It's too dangerous for you if I stay."

Madame Cloutier nodded in agreement. "We'll have to hide you."

The two women looked around the small apartment. It was identical to Marlene's own, only warmer and more welcoming. With only two rooms, the options for conceal-ment were limited. Marlene pulled back the side of the curtain that veiled the window and looked into the street below. People were going about their business, hurrying home to get out of the cold, unaware of the situation unfolding in the building. She saw nothing suspicious, but she also saw no way out.

She turned to see Madame Cloutier sliding a knife into the side of the wooden fireplace. The space for the fire held three chunky candles, evenly spaced on a rectangular tray.

Marlene moved forwards to help. The panel released its hold on the main fireplace and revealed a treasure chest of colour; three shelves brimming with teapots of various sizes and colours.

"Help me take these out," said Madame Cloutier.

They took the teapots out one by one and placed them on the barren shelves on the opposite wall. Once the space was empty, Marlene slid the shelves out and crouched down in the gap. She pulled her knees in tight to her body and lowered her neck as far as it would go. Madame Cloutier handed her the handbag that held her precious notebook and the shelves, which she was somehow able to find room for in the tiny space, and picked up the panel she had just removed.

"Open up!" bellowed a rough voice from the other side of the door. The words were French, but the accent was unmistakably German.

"Don't make a sound," breathed Madame Cloutier as she replaced the panel and lightly banged it back into place.

Marlene heard the banging on the door and Madame Cloutier's muffled voice. Boots thumped on the floor. An instruction was given in German, then more banging and scraping as the soldiers presumably moved around what little furniture was in the apartment.

"What are you looking for?" asked Madame Cloutier, her voice strong and unflustered.

"Your neighbour," replied a voice.

"Marlene," said Madame Cloutier. "What has she done?"

There was no reply. Marlene was worried for Madame Cloutier's safety. She shouldn't have been in this situation. She should not have come back to the apartment. It had only been a matter of time before they came for her. Annoyed at herself for allowing Henri to talk her back in against her better judgment, she listened to the noise from the room, her eyes shut, praying they wouldn't find her and that Madame Cloutier would suffer no consequences for helping her.

The next scraping sound was followed by a smash. The teapots. Then silence. Another instruction was given in German before the boots retreated.

"Marlene, they've gone," whispered Madame Cloutier. "I will leave you there until we are sure. Are you okay?"

"Yes," said Marlene as she huddled in the darkness. Her back was aching from the unnatural position, and her head hurt from the heat that had built up in the small crevice for the short time she'd been hiding there, exacerbated by her multiple layers of clothing. The man she had seen through the gap in her door was a German soldier, which meant she could no longer return to the building. She would have to go back to Henri. He would have to arrange somewhere else for her to stay whilst she waited for her flight back home.

She heard the knife slip between the panel and the fireplace again, and light from the apartment spilled into her hiding place. Madame Cloutier took the shelves out and helped Marlene to free herself. Struggling to straighten her back fully, she moved over to the mess of broken china littering Madame Cloutier's floor.

"I'm so sorry," said Marlene.

Madame Cloutier picked up a piece of what had been, only a few moments before, one of the finest teapots in her collection. It was white with a gold stripe running down the handle and golden flowers on either side. It was now missing one of those sides. She watched Madame Cloutier sit and cradle the object and thought about how old she suddenly looked. Looking around at the other pieces covering the floor, Marlene spotted one that looked like it had survived the episode. She picked it up and kneeled in front of Madame Cloutier.

"That one is old and stubborn like me," said Madame Cloutier, running her hand along the side of the bright green teapot. "It belonged to my mother, so it has seen its own ups and downs. It was a gift from her cousin, who stayed with us for a while."

"Was the collection your mothers?" Marlene asked.

"No, just this one. It was the only one I had for many years. When I married, my husband gave me one, then, when my son was grown, he bought me another for a birth-day, and another for my next birthday and so on. An acci-dental collection, you might say. When the occupation came, the Germans stormed the houses and took anything of value. Not that my collection has a monetary value, you understand. My son wanted me to leave Paris. He wanted me to stay with relatives in the country, but I figured it would be safe enough here for an old woman. I could do no one any harm, therefore what harm would they do me?"

"Did your son hide the teapots?" Marlene asked.

Madame Cloutier nodded. "He made the shelves and closed off the fireplace. It's been sealed off like that for too long."

"Is the other side the same?"

"Yes. A couple of pictures; my father's timepiece; some of my husband's things. I knew about you, you know. A young girl just appearing next door. No one moves during wartime, and if they do, they move away from occupation, not to the heart of it. You are working for the Resistance?"

"Well, it's not really what you think. I write for a newspa-per. A British one." Marlene stopped short of telling her anything else. She had been enough of a burden to the woman already.

Marlene breathed deeply. This wasn't the time to panic. She'd always known she might get caught. Her superiors in Baker Street had been clear about that before she'd left London. But now she had actively taken part in the Resistance. She could no longer claim to just be a clandestine journalist.

"Stay here until you think they have gone," said Madame Cloutier.

"No, I can wait next door. It will be safer for you if I'm found there. They must know I came into the building, so they will know that I've seen them. My apartment is probably the last place they will expect to find me and, if they come back, they cannot find me with you."

"My apartment has a hiding place," said Madame Cloutier nodding towards the fireplace. "Does yours?"

Marlene was forced to accept her neighbour's logic. As she relented, she only hoped she could one day credit her with saving her life.

56

THE KEY TURNED IN THE LOCK, AND MARLENE EXHALED loudly in relief when Madame Cloutier shuffled in. The Gestapo, of course, wouldn't use a key, but such was Marlene's level of anxiety that she feared every little noise was them returning for her.

"We have a plan. Let's go," Madame Cloutier said, standing in the doorway.

Marlene put her coat back on, grabbed her bag and followed the old woman. She turned to look at her own apartment door.

"Is there anything you need from your apartment?" asked Madame Cloutier.

Marlene's hand reached for her bag where she'd stashed her notebook earlier. She shook her head. "I have everything I need."

Monsieur Coreil waited for them at the foot of the stairs.

Marlene's breath quickened at the sight of the door to the apartment building and the subsequent thoughts of who was waiting on the other side. She clenched her fists to stop her neighbours from seeing her trembling hands.

Monsieur Coreil said nothing, but he motioned for her to follow him. He led her the short distance along the corridor on the ground floor to where she stored her bicycle. Tucked behind the stairwell was a door. She had once checked to see if the building had a back entrance, but she'd missed this door. It was small; much smaller than any of the three people who now stood before it. Although it was painted white, it was just as grubby as the walls. With no frame, and a tiny teardrop-shaped metal handle, Marlene hadn't even realised it was there. Monsieur Coreil pulled on the handle, and the door swung outwards.

"Go in," Monsieur Coreil said, pushing Marlene in first. She reacted just in time to avoid banging her head on the low ceiling. He and Madame Cloutier stooped and followed.

"I will not turn on the light, but I have this," Monsieur Coreil said. He clicked on a torch and shone it around the space.

It was some sort of storage area. The room was small, and the ceiling was low inside. Metal cages stowed boxes, bags, and pieces of old furniture.

Monsieur Coreil shone the torch at a metal grate in the wall. "There's my idea." Marlene saw daylight on the other side and smiled. "It's not a huge space, and it will be a squeeze, if you can get through at all. On the other side, there's nothing but a big wall. I don't know if there'll be anything there to help you climb over it. I don't know how it's accessed, but it's not from this building. On the other side are gardens belonging to the apartments behind ours. You'd have to find a way through them to get back out onto the street."

"I'll take my chances. I don't see any other way," Marlene said.

Monsieur Coreil raked around inside one of the metal

cages and produced a screwdriver. He unscrewed the metal cover over the air vent and stepped back. "I think you'll need to take off your coat and your bag if you want to fit through."

Marlene removed her coat and, to the surprise of her companions, started peeling off the additional layers of clothing she had put on that morning.

"I didn't expect to be coming back," she said by way of an explanation. "I'll have to leave these clothes here, but I need my coat and bag." She slipped her coat back on and pushed her small bag into the opening.

"You might need this," Monsieur Coreil said as he handed her the screwdriver. "Good luck."

"I don't know what to say. I can only say thank you. You've both saved my life." Marlene tilted her head back and blinked away tears. Given the kindness shown by the two people in front of her and the risks they were taking for her, a simple 'thank you' seemed completely insufficient.

"We hope so, dear," Madame Cloutier said, reminding Marlene that there were still massive obstacles for her to overcome if she wanted to make it. Monsieur Coreil helped her into the air vent and pushed on her shoes as she wriggled herself along towards the fresh air on the other side.

Once Marlene had scrambled over the wall and through the gardens behind her apartment building, she headed to Alain's to contact Henri again. But, on the way, she had taken a detour and now stood by the river, watching the flow of the water. She desperately wanted her time in France to be at an end.

If the man that had followed her had been German, why had he waited until the following morning to search her apartment? He could have grabbed her off the street. She had seen that happen to others. If he wasn't German, who was he, and why had the Gestapo been the ones to perform the search?

Her anger at Henri intensified. He must have known he was risking her life when he'd sent her back there. She had known herself it was wrong, yet she had gone along with it, and had been forced to rely on relative strangers to risk themselves to get her out. She could think of no reason for the Gestapo to suspect her neighbours having helped her, but that didn't mean there wouldn't be repercussions.

"The drop," Marlene said aloud, checking her watch. She hadn't picked up Lucile's collection and had neither the time nor the inclination now. She had nothing to exchange, but she hoped she could ask whoever turned up for their help.

Marlene didn't want to draw attention to herself by running, but brisk walking left her panting heavily as she approached the exchange site. The same courier she had met for most of her drops waited up ahead, despite her being almost twenty minutes late. He stood at the side of the newspaper kiosk, scanning the street in front of him. It was almost empty. The cafés had only a handful of old men tucked inside reading newspapers, and the few pedestrians who had braved the bitter cold had their heads down as they strode along the street.

The courier spotted her, and she held her hands out to her sides to show they were empty. He waited.

As she neared, the arms of a man came from behind the courier and ensnared his neck. Marlene halted, then ran to the doorway of the building next to her and shook the door. It didn't open. No one else noticed the commotion the two men were making. The courier's legs kicked, and his hands grabbed at the arm locked around his neck. His face was bright red, his eyes filled with terror.

She pressed her back tight to the door and hid behind the concrete entryway. She couldn't intervene. The other man would too easily overpower her. She needed something she could use as a weapon. She peered around the concrete frame. The courier had stopped fighting and his body slid down to the ground.

The face of the other man had been concealed behind the courier, but it was now visible to Marlene. His lips were pressed together and his eyes were wide as he scowled at the body at his feet.

A blade dripping with blood hung loosely in the man's hand.

He bent down over the body and wiped the blood on the courier's shirt. His other hand went straight for the newspaper that now lay a few feet away and opened it. He apparently knew exactly what he wanted. Hunting around in the courier's coat and trouser pockets, the man discarded everything he pulled out. He turned and shook his head.

Marlene followed his gaze to another man who had appeared on the corner.

Her skin prickled and beads of sweat rushed to its surface. The two men dashed out of sight, but a glimpse was all it had taken for her to recognise the familiar features of Henri. Marlene's legs buckled beneath her and she fell to her knees. Her entire body shook, and despite her sweating, a chill spread throughout her.

The door she had hid in front of opened and an old man emerged. He was speaking to her, but she couldn't hear what he was saying. She clambered to her feet, using the hand he offered as support, then took off, staggering back down the street she had walked up only a few minutes before. She fought for breath and stuck close to the wall, using it to steady herself as she went. At the first break in the buildings she came across, she turned and went down the alleyway.

Stopping halfway in, she violently vomited.

57

ADRIENNE

Putting her finger on the last word she had read, Adrienne stopped and listened. She'd heard someone at her door, but the noise had been so faint that she couldn't be sure. Deciding it was the darkness and the evening quiet playing tricks on her, she went back to her book.

With barely a few words read, she heard it again. It was definitely someone at her front door. She edged towards the door. Visitors had become few and far between and were always pre-planned. She wondered for a second if it might be Jean returning, or someone that had found out about Jean. A voice said her name.

"Adrienne," came the voice again. "It's Marlene."

"Oh my God!" Adrienne gasped as she opened her front door and Marlene stumbled inside. "What's happened?"

Adrienne quickly looked up and down the courtyard to make sure no one had seen Marlene, then closed and bolted the door. Marlene propped herself up against the wall, her breathing heavy and her cheeks stained with tears. Adrienne could see her trying to speak, but no words were coming out. Wrapping her arm around Marlene's waist, she led her further into the small living room and lowered her into a seat beside the lit fire.

"You're freezing," Adrienne said, noting the icy coolness of Marlene's body. She smoothed down Marlene's hair and pulled a blanket off the back of the room's only other chair, wrapping it around Marlene's shoulders. Marlene's hands shook as she took the edges of the blanket and pulled it tighter around herself.

She stared up at Adrienne, her face crumpled and her shoulders shook violently as she sobbed. Adrienne perched on the arm of the chair and held Marlene until her loud, heart-breaking sobs ceased.

Eventually, the two women sat in silence. The hours ticked by and the fire burned out.

Adrienne heard Marlene's breathing deepen as she drifted off to sleep. Leaving her for only a few seconds, she retrieved a blanket from her bedroom and settled herself on the chair opposite Marlene. She, too, eventually drifted off into a fitful sleep, waking every so often to check on Marlene.

"Morning," Marlene said when she finally woke. She stirred in her chair, her eyes still heavy from sleep.

"Not quite," said Adrienne. "It's only two in the morning."

"I'm sorry, Adrienne, I've been trying to figure this out all day, but I should never have come here. I had nowhere else to go. I really shouldn't be here."

"It's okay," said Adrienne in a soothing tone of voice. "Talk to me."

"I can't. I can't tell you what's going on."

"You can."

"I'm in over my head, Adrienne. Everything is happening around me, *terrible* things, and I have no way out. I shouldn't be here," Marlene said, standing up. She looked around for the door but was disorientated and stumbled around as she continued to speak. "I'm putting you in danger. You've been so kind to me, and I don't want to do that to you. I should go."

"Marlene," said Adrienne, her tone sharp but with concern rather than anger. "Sit down. Try to calm down. You said it yourself; you have nowhere else to go."

"My brother has a place. I should go there," said Marlene.

"Tell me where it is. I'll go in the morning, and I'll bring your brother here."

"No, you can't. He's not there. It's just an old place of his. I don't know who's there now, but he said it was safe."

"It's not safe if you don't even know who's there. You're safe here for now. No one knows you're here. I checked when you came in. No one was following you."

"How would you know?" Marlene asked, peering through Adrienne's curtains.

"Are you working with the Germans?" asked Adrienne, taking no offence at Marlene's tone and ignoring her question.

"What?" Marlene asked, bewildered. She sat back down on the chair opposite Adrienne.

"Philippe told me he thought you were involved in something like that."

"How does Philippe know?"

"So you *are* working for the Germans?" Adrienne said, looking down at her hands.

"No, I'm not. I promise. I'm with the Resistance,"

Marlene said, shaking her head. "I thought I was so careful, but even my next door neighbour knew. Why didn't you say?"

"Because I didn't believe it. I don't have your kind of courage."

"I don't have courage. I only couriered information, and I couldn't even keep a secret from the little old lady next door."

Adrienne could see Marlene was on the verge of tears again. "I know what you need," she said, hoping to distract Marlene. She got up and left the room, returning seconds later with two glasses of Port.

"Thanks," Marlene said, taking the glass and gulping down a mouthful. "I saw a man die today. He was a courier, like me, and I was supposed to pass him information, but I saw him get killed because of it. And Henri just stood by and watched."

"Who is Henri?" asked Adrienne, surprised that was her first question.

In the short time Adrienne had known Marlene, she had always believed her to be honest. Occasionally, Marlene would randomly change the subject or provide an answer to a different question than the one that had been asked. Adrienne had never pushed her on these things, mostly because she didn't want to know anything which didn't concern her. She didn't trust her own ability to keep a secret, and she definitely didn't want to unintentionally harm her friend. When Philippe had told her of his suspicions, the accusation had made sense, but Adrienne knew there had to be another explanation. She had simply refused to believe that Marlene was a bad person.

"Henri works for the Resistance. Or at least I thought he did."

"Maybe it's the courier who's not who you think he is," suggested Adrienne, trying to help Marlene make some sort of sense of the situation.

"Maybe, but I don't think so. I don't know what's going on, but I think Henri is behind it."

"Philippe said he saw you with a German. Perhaps it was him."

"That's Niklas. It wasn't him. Is that why Philippe thinks I'm a collaborator?"

"I expect so," Adrienne said. "How can you be so sure it wasn't him?"

"I just know. Niklas is trying to get through this, the same as the rest of us."

"You really believe he has nothing to do with what's happening now?"

"Absolutely," said Marlene without hesitation.

Adrienne was not convinced. With the Germans occupying her country and her husband being held captive at their mercy, she had no faith in anyone who called Germany their home.

"So, you moved here to work with the Resistance?"

"It's complicated. I work for a newspaper in London. They sent me here to report on life under occupation. Members of the Resistance helped to get me here. That was all. Once I was here and saw some of what was going on, I was ... I don't even know what I was. Angry, I suppose. Henri was my contact here. I asked if I could help him in other ways. He refused at first but came back and asked me to make some deliveries for him. I'd only managed a handful of drop offs. The next thing I know, someone followed me and the Gestapo are searching my apartment."

The two women sat staring at each other.

"Thank you for not throwing me out," Marlene finally

said. "I just need to figure out what to do next. I'll leave first thing in the morning."

Although she might not have been working for the Germans, Marlene was still involved in something that attracted a lot of trouble and a heavy penalty if she was caught. And now Adrienne was involved, too.

"I think I know someone who can help," said Adrienne. "For now, let's get some sleep."

58

MONSIEUR MAYOTTE'S STUDY WAS COMPLETELY UNLIKE HIS office at the school. Marlene sat on one of his dark green chairs, the firm cushions barely giving way for her. Two walls were lined floor to ceiling with books which appeared to be organised first by their height and secondly by the colour of their spine. There was a fire burning in the grate, which gave the room its warmth and created an orange glow.

Whereas the school office was stark and impersonal, this was part of Monsieur Mayotte's home. It felt private and safe. The walls were decorated with framed certificates, the occasional photograph of Monsieur Mayotte posing with smartly dressed men, and a wedding photo, directly above his desk. Marlene wondered why his desk faced the wall. It was a grand piece of furniture that one might expect to be the central focus point in the room, but instead, it had been tucked into a corner with its no doubt decorative front obscured by the wall.

The room not only contrasted with the school office, but it was also greatly at odds with what Marlene had expected.

She recalled Madame Cloutier telling her how the Germans had swept through private homes, taking anything of value. She, therefore, expected sparseness and empty shelves. If Monsieur Mayotte had hidden the contents of his study when the invasion had first occurred, he had since reinstated it or, despite first impressions, none of its contents were of any value.

"Adrienne has filled me in on your predicament, Marlene. I expect some people will want to talk to you when you get to London," said Monsieur Mayotte.

Marlene nodded, feeling like a child being chastised. The trouble in France was all too real to her, but she had not considered the consequences that might await her back in London.

"You'll be fine, but I'm sure someone will need to understand what you have done here; who you have met; what you were asked to do, and by whom. It seems there may be troublemakers in our midst that we need to deal with. Adrienne mentioned a man by the name of Henri."

The image of Henri looking out over the courier's dead body sparked in her mind. She clamped her eyes shut and put her head to her knees.

Monsieur Mayotte waited until she straightened before he spoke again. "From what I hear, his actions are certainly not protocol, so I suspect you are right about him." He clasped his hands together, his knuckles turning white.

Adrienne had convinced Marlene to stay in her house the following morning until she'd returned. Monsieur Mayotte, she had told her, was involved in Resistance work himself, or at least had links with people in the Resistance. Either way, he would know how to help Marlene. Marlene had been sceptical that the grandfatherly person she had met had connections with the Resistance, but now, hearing him speak, Marlene was convinced Monsieur Mayotte was directly involved. She also suspected that Henri, or at least the name, was familiar to him.

"I have a friend who was kind to me," she said. Monsieur Mayotte had turned his back on Marlene and was writing something on a piece of paper. "Do you think there's any way to get a message to him, to let him know I'm leaving?"

"Did he work with Henri?"

"No," she said, rubbing her leg with the palm of her hand.

"The German?" Monsieur Mayotte asked.

"Yes," said Marlene. It seemed Adrienne had told Monsieur Mayotte everything they had discussed.

Monsieur Mayotte stopped writing. "There's really no way for us to do that. If he has not already caused trouble for you, he certainly will if he finds out you have been in contact with the Resistance. Even if he could be trusted, he would be obligated to disclose everything he knows. Him not knowing where you are is probably why you are still alive."

The onslaught Marlene had expected from him didn't come. Somehow his gentle reaction made her feel worse than a shower of anger. She felt small, as though Monsieur Mayotte would think of her as a silly little girl who had been so easily manipulated and was now in tow with a German. She understood how it looked and why no one, not even Adrienne, believed her that Niklas was different.

Henri might have fooled her, but she could not believe that Niklas was anything less than genuine.

Monsieur Mayotte had given Marlene a slip of paper with

an address on it and told her she would be safe there until her flight. She would have to get herself there that evening, but she would need to change her appearance to deceive anyone looking for her.

Monsieur Mayotte's wife now stood in front of her. "So, let's see what we can do with you," she said as she brushed back Marlene's blonde hair. "Brunette is less likely to stand out."

Too drained to speak, Marlene allowed Madame Mayotte to guide her to a bathroom and close the door behind them without a further word said.

She sat on a stool, looking at her own tired reflection in the mirror judging her. Her pale skin appeared even paler against the darkness beneath her eyes and the red scratches that had appeared on her cheek. She couldn't remember when she had scratched her face; possibly inside Madame Cloutier's fireplace or on the concrete she had forced herself against to avoid being seen by the courier's murderer.

Madame Mayotte carefully measured liquids from a variety of brown glass bottles. She mixed the pungent concoction and layered it onto Marlene's hair.

When Marlene's new brown hair was rinsed clean, Madame Mayotte combed a new parting in her hair and cut in a fringe with professional precision.

"Were you a hairdresser?"

"Still am, dear."

But with a very different clientele.

Once she returned to the study, Monsieur Mayotte explained to Marlene how to find the address he had given her.

"I'll go with you," Adrienne said. Marlene reached out and squeezed her new friend's hand.

"No, you will not," said Monsieur Mayotte. "It's too dangerous for you. You will say your goodbyes here and leave separately."

Marlene nodded. She didn't want to be outdoors by herself, but she knew that Monsieur Mayotte was right. Adrienne did not argue.

"It's time to go," he said, getting up and walking towards the door. "Come down when you're ready."

He left the two women alone. The atmosphere was heavy. They both knew that this was probably the last time they would see each other. Marlene was lost for words. Adrienne had taken a great personal risk by helping her. It would have been easy for her to avoid becoming involved when Marlene had turned up on her doorstep. Others might have sent her away or, worse, reported her.

"You've been a wonderful friend to me," Marlene said. "You have saved my life; a debt which I can probably never repay."

"You would have done the same for me. I'm glad we got to know each other. These last weeks have been easier having someone to share them with," said Adrienne, as a tear rolled down her cheek. "Make sure you have a safe journey home."

"I will, thanks to you."

They hugged each other, Marlene taking her time to pull away. She would miss Adrienne greatly. She promised she would write to her and would come back to see her once the war was over. Adrienne promised the same.

Marlene left Monsieur Mayotte's study by herself. He waited for her at the door at the foot of the stairs.

"Do you have the paper I gave you?" he asked.

"Yes." She held up the paper and wiped her watery eyes with her other hand.

Monsieur Mayotte took it from her. "What is the address?"

"45b Avenue Borda."

"Good. You won't need this, then." He scrunched up the paper, satisfied that she had committed the address to memory.

Monsieur Mayotte reached for the door handle. She placed her hand over his. "Thank you."

His face was serious, but the kindness she had seen in him was still there. "Good luck."

She smiled to Madame Mayotte, who had now appeared in a doorway off the hall. The woman smiled back.

The door clicked shut only seconds after Marlene had stepped out into the stairwell of the apartment building.

59

ADRIENNE

At eight o'clock that evening, after dinner, Adrienne helped Madame Mayotte to clear the table and wash the plates. Monsieur Mayotte remained seated, smoking one cigarette after the other. He didn't smoke during school hours, so Adrienne thought he must have been catching up.

"I hope your friend will be all right," said Madame Mayotte.

"Me too," Adrienne replied. She wished she could have gone with Marlene and not sent her out into the streets alone. "Do you think we can find out if she made it?"

"We will hear if she did not," said Monsieur Mayotte. "You should go before it gets too late. If you have any trouble, anything you are not sure of, let me know."

"I will," she promised. "Thank you to you both for helping Marlene. She really was trying to do something good."

"I'm glad you came to us," said Monsieur Mayotte before showing her out. She refused his offer to walk her home and stepped out into the darkness alone.

Ten minutes later, and with the freezing temperature forcing her to walk faster, Adrienne arrived home. Slipping her key into the lock, she turned it, but it wouldn't budge. She tried several times, using both hands and all her strength, but it was no use. She fiddled with the door handle but stepped back in shock when the handle released and the door creaked open.

She turned and ran back across the courtyard. Her shaking hand slipped from the handle of the building's main door. She paused. There were no footsteps behind her, no commotion, no sound at all. Creeping back, she pushed her front door wide open and peered into the darkness. Nothing was out of place. There was just silence.

Scenarios played over in her mind whilst she stood on her doorstep, contemplating what to do. There could not have been a break-in, because nothing had been moved. If Marlene had run into problems, surely she would have returned to Monsieur Mayotte for help. Tomas had forever teased her about how carefully she locked doors. She couldn't imagine that she would have left the door unlocked, although she had to admit that circumstances were tense when she had left earlier. It was possible that in her desperation to get Marlene to Monsieur Mayotte's apartment safely, she might have forgotten to lock the door. They had both felt exposed on the streets, even Adrienne, and no one was looking for her.

She went in, leaving the door unlocked behind her. Clicking on the living room light, she made her way to the kitchen. Nothing was out of place there, either.

She breathed out, put her bag down on the living room chair, and removed her coat. She turned, going to hang her coat up, then froze as a figure emerged from the darkness beyond the kitchen.

He was thin and filthy and looked exhausted, but he was home. She ran to him, tossing her coat aside.

"Hello, sweetheart," Tomas said as she fell into his arms. He walked forwards, coming fully into the living room, but she refused to let him go and allowed herself to be carried along with him. "I'm sorry if I scared you."

"It's all right," she said, her head still buried in his neck. "Everything's all right now."

"I have to go again, but I'll come back."

Her head shot up and bile seared her throat. "You can't go."

He peeled away from her and looked into her eyes. "A group of us escaped. The Germans will be looking for us."

"I know. I saw Jean. He stayed the night here, and no one came."

Tomas breathed in deeply. He sank into a chair in the living room, and Adrienne sat next to him. "They were transporting us to Germany by train, but the Resistance detached the carriage. Guards were killed, and a dozen or so men escaped. They *are* looking for us."

Adrienne couldn't imagine the things Tomas had seen, nor the things he had done to get back to her. His eyes were wide and his cheekbones pronounced from all the weight he had lost.

"My cousin can help us get out of France. Will you come with me?"

"Of course I will come with you," she said without hesitation. She reached for his hand and squeezed it. It seemed unbelievable that her husband was really here.

"Good. I have to go now, in case they come looking. Do you have money in the house?" She nodded. "Good. Get it.

You'll be able to take a small bag with you, but that's it. We leave tomorrow afternoon. I'll come for you. Until then, everything is normal for you. Can you do that?"

"Yes," she said. She wasn't convinced she could, but she didn't care. "Will you eat something before you go. Or change your clothes?"

He shook his head. "I don't want anyone to suspect I've been here."

Holding her hands in his, he kissed her deeply, his warm lips pressed hard against her, reminding her of what she had missed for so long. As she watched Tomas slip away into the darkness, Adrienne knew everything was going to work out this time.

60

MARLENE STOOD IN THE TREES AROUND THE EDGE OF A farmer's soggy field. She had left the safe house where she had spent the last week early, unsure of how difficult it would be to get to the landing site alone and unnoticed. Not only were the Gestapo looking for her, but Henri would have missed her by now. She had spent one night at the address Monsieur Mayotte had arranged for her before being transported to another safe house to wait for the moon flight that would take her home.

Marlene pulled the collar of her coat up and used her hand to brush away the wet hair that clung to her face. She didn't mind. She had spent all of the previous week indoors and was grateful to get out. A mist had descended earlier in the day, and Marlene hoped it would not cause trouble for the pilot. She nervously watched all around her, waiting for the reception team she was due to meet.

The rain hammered noisily against the leaves, cascading into the woods. Moonlight penetrated the trees, allowing Marlene to see out into the field and some of what was around her. Thinking of nothing except getting on the plane, she sheltered as best she could in the trees.

Something caught her eye on the other side of the clearing. A light, maybe, but it had disappeared too quickly for Marlene to be sure. Then the outline of two vehicles came into view and three figures got out; two from the first vehicle and one from the other. She could hear voices, but the noise of the rain all around her drowned out the words. She watched them all go to the rear of one of the vehicles and offload something. Hoping it was the reception team, Marlene came out of the woods and trudged towards them.

"Good to see you are alive and well," said one of the team. It was Etienne.

Marlene smiled and nodded, unsure of what, if anything, she should tell the team. She had not seen Etienne again since leaving for Paris, and Marlene wondered if him being here didn't bode well for her. Still, she had no choice but to trust him.

The other men, as if oblivious to her presence, took lights out into the field to get ready to signal the pilot.

"Is this the end of your trip, or were there problems?" asked Etienne.

"Both," Marlene said, staring into the field.

"Almost time," Etienne said, looking at his watch. He flashed a light to signal something to the other men, then craned his neck to stare into the night sky.

As Etienne raised his arm in the air, Marlene heard the distant sound of the Lysander's humming. The other men flashed their lights in what seemed to her to be a random manner. She looked all around her, remembering the last time she had been in this situation. They had only avoided walking straight into the Germans who had appeared that night because of Etienne's sharp hearing, assisted by the silence synonymous with the dead of night. Even Etienne wouldn't hear them approaching tonight, with the rain thundering down and the wind howling in their ears.

Etienne turned to look at her. Rainwater had settled on his eyelashes, and he blinked furiously to dislodge it. Despite it being only their second meeting, she could tell by his face that something was wrong. His eyes quickly diverted to stare over her shoulder. He reached out, grabbed her arm, and pulled her back behind him. Struck by curiosity rather than fear, Marlene watched a lone figure approaching them from the darkness of the trees where she had hidden only minutes before.

"What are you doing here?" Etienne said, his words almost drowned out by a clatter of thunder from the sky above. The figure kept coming, and it took another few seconds before Marlene could make out who it was.

Henri.

She clenched her hands and glared at him. A fire raged inside of her at just the sight of him. She's been so stupid for trusting him.

"He flew over," said one of the men who had arrived with Etienne. With Henri's arrival as a distraction, Marlene hadn't noticed the Lysander pass straight over their heads.

"He'll turn and come back," said Henri as he stared into the sky. There was nothing to look at, but it no doubt served the purpose of avoiding the stares that were now fixed on him.

"How did it feel, Henri? To watch while a man was murdered. You might as well have put the knife in yourself!" Marlene spat. She could feel Etienne's eyes on her, waiting for some explanation. Henri's eyes were still to the sky.

Eventually, Henri looked at Marlene, emotionless. She raised her eyebrows, willing him to speak. He didn't.

"Here he comes," said the man from the reception team as he ran back out towards his light. Etienne looked between the two of them, then over both of his shoulders. The situation was obviously unnerving him. The plane was above them but still hadn't commenced its approach to land.

"What's he doing?" Marlene asked, now worried.

"He won't land. The weather's too bad," said Etienne.

"What? He hasn't even tried," said Marlene.

"The weather's bad down here, but it's much worse up there. It's too risky," said Etienne.

"Of course it's risky. It's the middle of the night, and we're in a landing spot probably already known to the Gestapo because of this double agent. Who knows what is waiting for us beyond this field! Just being here is risky!" Marlene yelled, her voice high pitched with exasperation and competing with an explosion of thunder above their heads.

"So it's true?" Etienne demanded of Henri. "I'd heard the rumours, but I didn't believe them. I was sure there had to be another explanation."

"My network was at risk. I had to give them something," said Henri, his eyes darting between Marlene and Etienne.

"You mean you had to give them *someone*," said Marlene.

Henri stared at her, his expression difficult to read. "I'm sorry. It wasn't my fault." He backed away from them with his hands open by his sides.

"Why did you have to kill the courier?" asked Marlene.

"I had to. They were going to kill *me*," said Henri.

"You should have let them," Etienne said before he fired.

Marlene screamed in shock as Henri's body fell to the ground. She clamped her hand to her mouth to stifle any further sounds. The bullet had struck him in the head and killed him instantly. The other two men had been collecting their lights from the field, but now they ran towards the commotion with their guns drawn.

"*Traitor*," Etienne said. "Let's get moving." His voice was stony, but Marlene detected no anger in it.

The other two men glanced at Henri's body on the ground, then turned and hurried back to the vehicles.

Marlene sat in the passenger seat of Etienne's truck, still shaken from the sight of him shooting Henri. As he drove, she thought of Henri, turning his back on his cause, endangering people he was supposed to protect, and whilst it might not have been his hands that had killed the courier, he was responsible for his death. She deplored his actions, but she couldn't help but think that she should have kept quiet. It might not have been her hands that had killed the traitor, but *she* was responsible for his death.

A wave of nausea washed over her and she wiped her clammy forehead with the back of her hand. She unbuttoned the top of her coat and leaned forwards, her head on her knees.

"This isn't your fault," Etienne said, knowing what was on her mind. "I'd already heard rumours about him. You just confirmed it."

"If I had got on that plane, London would have held him accountable for his betrayal."

"Perhaps, but you didn't get on the plane, though. That would have allowed Henri more time to work against us. We couldn't take any chances."

"Do you believe what he said? That his network was at risk?"

"Yes, but that's assuming they found him and he didn't go to them," Etienne said.

"Would he really have gone to them?" Marlene asked.

Etienne pondered this question for a long time. Marlene wasn't sure she was going to get an answer, and even if she did, it would have to be a guess. With Henri dead, no one would ever really know what had changed for him.

"It's hard out here," said Etienne. "I know I don't have to tell you, but sometimes the feeling of being on the losing side can weigh you down."

"You don't think we'll win this war?"

"We will win, but there's a lot of conflict to navigate first. It's not just conflict between countries and uniforms; it's conflict between neighbours, friends and even families. Where political views differ, there usually follows bloodshed."

"Or where what's right and what's wrong comes into conflict with the basic human need to survive," Marlene said.

"Exactly," Etienne agreed as the first shot cut straight through one of the car's tyres and propelled it to pull sharply to the left.

Etienne gripped the steering wheel and fought to keep control as another shot rang out. Marlene frantically looked around her in all directions but couldn't see where the gunfire was coming from. Another tyre blew, and Etienne was fast losing complete control.

"We're going to have to make a jump for it!" he yelled. "You ready?"

"What? No!" Marlene screamed.

"Get out and run to the trees ahead."

She pulled at the door handle and leapt out of the truck. A beam of light lit her path, and there were frantic shouts in

German. Gunfire crackled behind her. Her wrist burned as Etienne grabbed her arm and pulled her along beside him. She screamed as she tumbled to the ground and landed on her knees. Etienne's grip released as he, too, fell.

Clambering to her feet, she continued to run, but when she glanced back, Etienne still lay on the ground. Turning to go back, Etienne shook his head furiously.

"Run! I'm shot. Run! Run!" he screamed.

She looked from him to the dark uniforms fast approaching. Another gunshot. Another scream from Etienne.

She turned and ran.

Marlene hit the trees and moved diagonally, hoping her pursuers would run straight. The last time she had run through woodland, she had been guided by Henri and Etienne. Now, she was alone, and every tree looked the same as the last.

She had no plan; no clever trick. She had only her legs and the speed with which they carried her. Marlene didn't stop to listen for the enemy mobilising around her; instead, she kept running until sheer exhaustion began to blur her vision.

After several minutes of running, she struggled for breath, doubling over behind a tree. Wheezing loudly, she closed her eyes and sucked in a deep breath. She needed to calm down and get some oxygen back into her lungs.

When she opened her eyes, she took another sharp intake of breath. Niklas stood over her, directing a torch straight down to the ground. From the expression on his face, he looked wounded, as though she had stabbed him in his stomach. She stared back, not knowing what to say or do. Niklas stood before her in his uniform, sweat visible on his forehead from chasing her through the forest.

In unison, they turned their heads in the direction of a voice. Whoever the voice belonged to must have been close for them to hear it over the noise of the rainfall that still battered the foliage around them. She looked back at Niklas, his hand clasping his pistol.

"Run," he said, before he lifted the beam of his torch and ran away from her.

Marlene hauled herself to her feet and ran. Unsure of which way to go, she instinctively headed downhill. Too scared to stop this time, she kept going. Her legs burned, and she stumbled. Pain exploded through her body as she tumbled down a gorge that appeared as if from nowhere. Her body scraped its way down the side of the gorge until it eventually came to a stop on the forest floor.

Curling herself into a ball, Marlene heard only her heart thundering in her chest and the consistent pelt of rain as she closed her eyes and waited.

61

WHEN SHE FINALLY DARED TO OPEN HER EYES, MARLENE reached a hand to her head and pushed herself into a seated position. Her body ached in too many places, and she had no choice but to lie against the exposed roots of a huge tree until she could bear to think about moving. She listened, but the forest was deathly quiet.

Both eyes were tight from swelling, but there was enough light from the early dawn for her to see around her. She looked up at the gorge she'd fallen down. There was no way she could climb back up. She'd have to stick to the path she now lay on and see where it took her.

She tried to stand, but a pain shot through her left leg with such force that it made her shriek and she collapsed back to the ground. Apart from very ripped trousers and scrapes to her skin, the leg didn't appear too badly injured.

"If it's broken, you won't be able to tell by looking at it," she mumbled to herself. She looked around her for something she could use as a stick to aide her walking. Nothing. She tested the rest of her body by moving her neck, arms, hands, right leg, and right ankle.

Marlene stood again, leaning heavily on her right side. Her left ankle was the problem. It was too weak to properly support her. She hobbled around until she found a low level branch that would be long enough for her to lean on. She tried to snap it, but she didn't have the strength. Someone called her name and she froze.

The voice was too far away for her to work out who it was, but it was definitely her name. She dropped to the ground and dragged herself backwards until the bark of the tree brushed against her back.

The voice came closer. *Niklas*. She pressed herself to the tree, trying to stay out of sight. Niklas came in to view above the gorge and yelled her name again. He was alone.

As he scrambled along the top, something caught his eye. He bent down, and Marlene tracked his eyes, looking down the route she had tumbled. Even from this distance, it was fairly obvious that someone had recently come down the side of the gorge and had flattened or snapped everything that had got in the way. He descended into the gorge, gripping whatever he could on the way. No one followed him.

"Over here," she yelled, breaking Niklas's concentration and making him lose his grip. He slid the rest of the way down, but quickly sprang back to his feet.

"Marlene!" he called. "Where are you?"

"Here. Over here." She shook the low branches near her, and he came running to her. Throwing himself down beside her, he checked her over. She had never seen him look so bad. His eyes were sunken in his head, and his skin was pale. "Have you been out here all night?"

He shook his head and pawed at her body, looking for injuries.

"It's my ankle," she said.

"You're lucky. That was quite a way to fall."

"How did you know where I was?"

He looked at her and took a deep breath. "I've been looking for you for a while," he said.

"Do you know what happened to Etienne?" she asked. She was reluctant to talk to him about last night, but she would have to. She could still hear Etienne's screams of pain.

"The driver?" Niklas asked. Marlene nodded. "Dead. I'm sorry."

Niklas handed her a container of water and encouraged her to drink. She couldn't face it, but he insisted, and once she'd taken that first sip, she didn't stop until she'd finished it.

"I thought you might have been, too," Niklas said. "I wasn't sure you would have been able to make it out here on your own. My unit are sending another patrol out this morning to look for you. They say that London trains its operatives well and that you are probably still out here. I guess that's true."

She couldn't tell what he was thinking. She could not read him at all.

"I'm not an operative. I'm a journalist."

His shoulders sagged. "When you disappeared, I didn't know what to think. I waited outside the café every night, hoping to see you, but I knew you had gone. When I saw you last night, I couldn't believe it. You can tell me the truth," Niklas said, not looking directly at her.

She put her hands on his face and forced him to look at her. "I *am* telling you the truth."

He enveloped her hands in his and lowered them. His touch was warm, and the flutter in her stomach brought her new energy. He brought his hands up to her face and wiped away her tears. She hadn't even realised she had been crying.

"We should move. They'll be on their way soon." Niklas helped Marlene up and supported her left side. She let him lead her in silence.

With Marlene's injured ankle, their progress out of the forest was slow. Dawn had almost slipped away, but eventually the trees became less dense and the sound of intermittent traffic returned. Sunlight now pierced through the forest canopy, and its relative warmth helped Marlene's body to stop trembling. Niklas was patient, and if he was worried about his colleagues searching for them, he didn't show it.

They had been walking for almost half an hour before they made it to his vehicle.

"I can't go with you. I know somewhere safe, but I'm not sure where we are," said Marlene, looking around her for something familiar.

"We're east of your landing site," said Niklas, a hint of bitterness in his tone. Marlene couldn't blame him. "I'll take you. You can't exactly walk around like that."

She looked down at herself and laughed, tension momentarily releasing from her body. Her clothes were torn and covered in mud, and she could only imagine what the rest of her looked like. Niklas smoothed down her hair with his hands and gently kissed her forehead, his lips lingering for a few seconds.

"Brunette. It's different," he said, fumbling with a lock of her hair. He looked tense, like he wanted to ask her all the questions he must have but was afraid of the answers. "Did you go out with me for information?"

"No, Niklas, I didn't. I really didn't," she said. He looked a little relieved, but perhaps not convinced. "If I did, I did a pretty rubbish job, didn't I? What kind of information did you tell me?"

"Well, nothing, I don't think. You never wanted to know what I had been doing," he said.

She could tell he saw her point. He bowed his head and let out a long sigh.

"I'm glad I'm alive," she said, her voice quivering with emotion. "I shouldn't be because others are dead because of me, but still ... I'm glad I'm alive."

"No. They're not dead because of you. It was a passing patrol. They saw the lights in the field. We would have gone there whether or not you had been there. This is not your fault." Niklas gripped her by the shoulders. "This is not your fault."

Tears flowed as the enormity of what had happened to her the previous night and the death that had been all around finally caught up with her. The danger she was now in was clearer than ever. The Germans thought she was some kind of secret agent, and she had brought it all on herself. Marlene had convinced herself that she could handle it, that she could get involved in Henri's dark world, but the reality differed greatly from how she had envisioned it in her head.

"No. It *is* my fault. You should leave me here. I will only attract trouble for you." Her sobs were now quite hysterical.

Niklas pulled her towards him and held her. It was several minutes before she calmed down. With her ankle barely taking her weight and the Gestapo after her, she feared she wouldn't be able to escape from them again.

"We have to go. I have to get you to safety and return the vehicle before anyone asks questions. Which way?" said Niklas.

Marlene gave Niklas directions to the hiding place she had found on the outskirts of Paris. They travelled in silence, which she was grateful for. She had to focus on what to do next; on who she could trust without endangering them. She wouldn't allow anyone else to get hurt because of her.

"Stop here," Marlene said after a time.

"Where? Down here?" Niklas asked, pointing to the track which led to her hiding place.

"No, here on the road. I'll walk the rest of the way. I don't want to create fresh tyre tracks," she said.

"Are you sure you're not a spy?" Niklas asked, eyebrows raised and a hint of humour evident in his tone. "I'll meet you back here. I'll be as quick as I can, but I don't know what will be going on when I get back. If I bring a bicycle for you, do you think you could ride it?"

Marlene nodded and reached down to rub her ankle. She gave him a smile to reassure him, or perhaps to reassure herself. He removed his coat and helped her as she slipped her arms into it. She left the warmth and comfort of the vehicle and hobbled her way down towards the hiding place. She watched Niklas and the vehicle disappear. It didn't take long for the noise of the engine to retreat and for silence to close in around her.

Despite the earlier sun, the sky was now a dark grey, with spots of rain that threatened an imminent downpour. The wind picked up, and she snuggled into Niklas's coat as she walked. It smelled like him. The concentration it took to keep her upright meant Marlene was more or less unaware of what was going on around her. She knew she ought to listen out for any approaching cars, but she didn't have the energy. She had left some basic supplies hidden in the ruin and hoped that they were still there. She'd left a blanket, a container for water, and some canned foods. She'd also packed materials to make a fire. Now, with her face and hands numb from the intensifying wind, she realised how foolish this was. A fire was a great way to attract attention when in hiding.

As she approached the building, her eyes were immediately drawn to the three empty liquor bottles that littered the entrance. She took in the silence, satisfied that no one was there, or at least not now. She heaved open the door and her shoulders slumped. The building was already a ruin, so it was difficult to tell that the place had been turned upside down in a search.

The bullet holes gave it away.

She quickly counted the floorboards, including the ones that were already prised open, and identified the seventh plank from the back wall. It had a bullet hole right in the centre. She pulled the floorboard up, closed her eyes, then looked down. The space underneath was empty. She rubbed her face, wiping her eyes as the tears appeared.

"Damn it," she said out loud.

She positioned herself under the window at the ruin's front so she could see the track. Pulling the long coat she wore tighter around her body, she thought through her options. She didn't know how recent the search had been, but the bullet holes told her staying here wasn't an option.

Going back to Monsieur Mayotte's was too risky for Adrienne. Benjamin's old apartment seemed the only other possibility, but she did not know who or what she might find there.

As the hours ticked by and with Niklas yet to return,

Marlene made a move. Daylight had already dimmed, and she needed food, water, and a new plan.

The ruin had been grim, but it had at least sheltered her from the bitter wind that now howled around her. She had left Niklas's coat behind; a woman wearing an oversized German Army issue coat was not the way to avoid attention. Her face tightened. She knew the danger she was about to return to, but she had no other choice.

As Marlene arrived in central Paris, avoiding all streets that were close to her apartment, Adrienne's and *Place Grenat*, the dimming light had turned to near darkness. The other pedestrians in the street were loud, and her temples throbbed. There were girls chatting and giggling, and a mother yelled at her children to speed up. The various snippets of conversations she caught created a useful distraction. Sticking to the periphery of some of the groups, she walked with her back as straight as she could muster, although every muscle was contracting and all she wanted to do was curl up and lie down.

Focusing on the exchanges of those around her kept Marlene's anxiety at bay. Her face and clothes were filthy. She had used her handkerchief—or rather the handkerchief *W.B.* had given her when she'd collided with the boy and fallen off her bicycle—and her own saliva to wipe some of the dirt from her face, but there had been little she could do with her clothing. As the mud dried, it cracked, enabling her to brush some of it off., but she still looked like someone who had fallen down a hill.

It was Saturday night, and the main streets were busier and noisier than usual. Not long ago, she had been one of those people thankful for Saturday night and coffee or dinner with Adrienne. Adrienne, who would believe that Marlene was safely back in London by now. If Monsieur Mayotte knew that things had turned out like this, she doubted he would tell Adrienne. He was too protective of her, which gave Marlene some comfort. If her visit had brought trouble for Adrienne, she hoped that Monsieur Mayotte was well connected enough to fix it for her.

She had contemplated both going back to the safe house Monsieur Mayotte had organised for her previously or going directly to Monsieur Mayotte's apartment in the hope he would help her once more. She remembered the route to Monsieur Mayotte's apartment, but it was too far. Her ankle ached, and she knew it could not carry her much further. The safe house was closer, but she still needed to rest her ankle before she could continue.

Marlene arrived at the gated garden and slipped, hopefully unnoticed, through the small steel gate. When she reached the end of the shrubbery, she sucked in a deep breath. The frame of the man sitting beside the statue by the lake was familiar and reassuring.

"Thank goodness," said Niklas. He ran towards her and wrapped his arms tightly around her. "Where did you go? I came back for you, but you had gone. I was worried that ..."

She shook her head. He didn't need to finish the sentence; she shared his worry. "Was there any trouble for you when you got back?"

"No. Someone thinks I have a secret French girlfriend, but they are no more suspicious than that."

Niklas helped Marlene over to the bench and propped her ankle up on his knees. The warmth of his hands encircling her ankle brought a little relief, and she closed her eyes. He took his hands off her ankle, and she heard him rustling something. She opened her eyes, and he handed her a sandwich; cheese on thick sliced bread. He placed his refilled canister of water beside her.

"I need to rest a little, then get moving again," she said whilst chomping rather ungracefully through her sandwich. "There's a safe house near here I could go to."

"I can take you there," said Niklas, rubbing her ankle and lower leg. He pulled a roll of bandage from his pocket and wrapped it snuggly around her ankle.

"I think it's best if I go alone."

"So I don't see where your safe house is?"

"In part," said Marlene. She could see the hurt on his face. "If anyone finds out you've helped me, Niklas, the consequences for you are unthinkable. Hopefully, I'm leaving here, but you can't. You're stuck here. I don't want to put you in any more danger. The Gestapo think I'm part of the Resistance, and if they think you're helping me, they will try to get information from you."

"I would never tell them," he insisted.

"You might not have a choice. It's better for everyone if you don't know where I'm going. This is not about me not trusting you, Niklas. I do. Of course I do."

"I understand," he mumbled. His expression was once again difficult to read, but Marlene knew she had given him no comfort. "I brought the bicycles back with me. They're over there. I'll go part of the way with you to make sure you get away from here. In two streets, I'll leave you."

With a little food and a bandage tucked beneath her trouser leg, Marlene's ankle stopped throbbing.

"Try it," Niklas said, passing her a bicycle. Marlene got on and, to her relief, cycled and stayed upright, putting pressure only on her good leg.

With one hand steadying her bicycle, she reached for

him with the other. "I wanted to get a message to you. I didn't want you to think I had just disappeared," she said. "It all happened so fast."

He squeezed her hand back and nodded his understanding. There was so much more she wanted to say, but there wasn't the time.

They left the garden and cycled slowly along in the dark. The noise of the weekend revellers picked up again, only this time, Marlene blocked it out, preferring to listen to the deep breaths of Niklas. Although she wished the events of the previous night had not happened, she'd at least had the opportunity to tell Niklas she was leaving in person.

From nowhere, two hands clamped onto Marlene's shoulders and pulled her backwards off her bicycle. An involuntary scream escaped her. Niklas turned, but a fist belonging to someone she could not see collided with his jaw and he, too, came off his bicycle. Despite the impact, he bounced back to his feet and lurched forwards in retaliation.

The man who had grabbed her pinned her arms uselessly to her sides. She screamed, and he didn't bother to cover her mouth to stop her. He dragged her along, her legs flailing in all directions. She kicked at his shins, but connected with nothing but air.

Niklas was gone. Her attacker spun her around, and forced her into the dark void in front of her.

Her knees stung as they hit the solid floor of the van. The doors slammed shut, removing the little light there had been on the street in an instant. In the darkness, the van swayed and its front doors banged. She didn't hear the ignition, but she felt the clumsy movements as it sped away.

Frequent jolts sent her tumbling towards the back of the van. She fumbled in the darkness for something to hold on to, but the van seemed empty. Nothing else slid around each time she did, and she felt nothing on the floor and walls that surrounded her.

She vaguely recalled seeing the van on the road ahead of them, but she had paid no more attention to it. Whether it had been waiting specifically for her, she didn't know. She also didn't know what had happened to Niklas. She wedged her body into a corner and steeled herself for what awaited her outside of the van.

After a time, the van came to an abrupt halt. Her head slammed into the metal bodywork and everything went quiet.

62

MARLENE WOKE, GASPING FOR AIR. SHE BLINKED HARD TO steady her vision. The room was long and shadowy. It had an archway in the middle which showed that it had once been two rooms, or one room with a dual function. The archway was so cracked and chipped that it was not possible to see the smooth curves it must have once had. It would have been difficult to tell if neglect or violence had caused its damage, had Marlene not had faint memories of dirty black boots kicking the archway in anger and frustration each time she drifted back from her unconscious state.

She scratched at her wrists. The rope that had been used to bind her hands had cut into her flesh so much that her skin was raw. She had been vaguely aware of featureless faces appearing in front of her at various points since she had first woken up in the room; voices talking to her and then talking *about* her. Each time she had come round, she felt as though she were still in a dream and could not clearly recall what had happened previously.

This time when she awoke, Marlene knew she was back, properly alert now, although she wasn't sure that was a good thing. Despite the darkness, she could tell she was alone. The room had at least two windows, she guessed, seeing tiny bits of light running down two of the walls. She couldn't tell if the windows were curtained or boarded.

She couldn't see any doors, not that it mattered, given that her hands and feet were bound. Even if she could work out how to get out of the room, she would have no chance of actually getting away. A dull humming sound—a vehicle, perhaps—was all that could be heard.

She expected the room was part of a larger building, but she couldn't guess at the type of building or where it was. She didn't even know if she was still in Paris.

From the far corner of the room, metal twisted against metal; a key in a lock. Light bled into the room, bringing with it the dark outline of the man who now approached her. The door snapped shut again, as though it was linked to a tightly wound spring, and the light disappeared, leaving the room much darker than it had been only a few seconds before. The key scraped in the lock again as the room was sealed once more.

The man was now within reaching distance of her, but she couldn't yet see him clearly as her eyes battled to become accustomed again to the darkness. From what she could see, she didn't recognise him. The stranger acquired a chair from somewhere in the recesses of the room and dragged it along the bare floorboards, the resultant vibrations going straight through the wood and up into her legs. He positioned it in front of her and sat down.

"Are you feeling better?" he asked. He spoke in slow, careful French. He wasn't French, but his pronunciation gave no clue as to where he was from. She stared at him but said nothing. "Do you know why you are here?"

She didn't. Not really.

"I'm a very patient man."

"That's good, because I fear we'll be here for some time," Marlene said as quickly as she could. If French wasn't the man's first language, and she was sure that it wasn't, she hoped to confuse him. Not necessarily her best plan, but in the absence of knowing who had brought her here, she didn't dare say anything else. The only thing she knew for certain was that she might have to fight for her life. And fight, she would.

"Where were you running to?" the man asked after a long, uncomfortable silence. She wondered if he was as patient as he said or if he would soon tire and attempt to force something out of her. Although his boots were the same, she couldn't tell if he was the figure she had seen kicking the archway during one of her semi-conscious moments. She didn't recognise his voice, but this told her nothing, given that she couldn't remember which language the voices she had heard had been speaking.

"Is Paris how you remember?"

She forced her eyes to stay fixed on the floor and hardened her expression, despite the commotion going on inside her. She wanted to scream out at the man sitting before her; to find out who he was and what he wanted with her. Her mind tried to go over the various possibilities, but it was going so fast, she couldn't keep up.

"I expect it is," he said. Marlene could see in her peripheral vision that he wasn't looking at her, either. His chin was raised, and he appeared to be staring at the ceiling. "It hasn't really changed much at all. A few piles of rubble where there wasn't previously any, but much the same. Less traffic, which isn't a bad thing. An unpopular view, of course, but it's my view."

His tone was even and his French slow but good. He

hadn't missed or mispronounced a word yet. She tried to look for meaning in his words, to work out who he was and what he knew of her, but she couldn't. She wondered if it was a trick, an act, and how long he would let it continue before he finally tried to force out whatever it was he thought he needed her for. The truth was also an option. This was not her world. She didn't know the rules.

"I don't have what you want," she said.

"And *what* is it I want?"

"You tell me. I'm not part of this war. I'm living here, nothing else."

"That's not quite true."

"It is," she said half-heartedly. He obviously knew *some-thing* about her, if not everything. She wanted to tell the truth, she wanted all of this to be over, but she couldn't. For every Henri, there were tens of men or more who were doing the decent thing. She couldn't know what pieces of seemingly random information to her would trigger recognition from the man opposite her and put innocent people in danger.

"You're not very good at lying."

"I'm not lying."

"You should never have got involved. You were not sent here to become tangled up in all of this," he said, moving his arm around the room in demonstration.

Sent here.

Marlene's eyes narrowed. He smiled, and she silently cursed herself for showing a reaction, but she couldn't help herself. Images flashed through her mind as she thought of who knew what she was doing here. Henri. Etienne. Fletcher. Niklas. Nothing was making sense to her.

"Don't try too hard to figure it all out, Marlene. You'll know soon enough."

Taken aback by hearing her name, she concentrated on keeping her face neutral. Whomever had brought her here had known exactly where to find her, so it shouldn't have been a surprise that they also knew her name.

"Until then," he continued, "let's find out exactly what damage you've done."

"I have nothing to tell you."

"Come on, Marlene. I know you have problems with trust. That's understandable, given some of the things you've had to go through, but this is important. We need to know what you're involved in."

"What do you think you know about me? And who exactly is 'we'?"

"I know things about you that you probably don't even know yourself, Marlene."

Her name on his lips was too personal for her. He was trying to get her to talk by provoking her curiosity, and it was working. She pushed her shoulders back and looked away from him, keeping her breathing steady.

"Well, Marlene, as I said, I'm an extremely patient man. Why don't we sit this out together?"

63

THE DOOR TO THE MAKESHIFT PRISON CELL CREPT OPEN.
Marlene lay on the hard wooden floor, too exhausted to
move, too exhausted to even open her eyes to see who was
next tasked with extracting information from her. She
waited for the questions to begin again. She had told them
nothing so far, and she planned to keep it that way for as
long as she could.

A hand cupped her ankle, and someone fumbled with
the ropes that bound her. Thoughts of kicking out and
making a dash for freedom entered her mind momentarily,
but she doubted she would get as far as the door. She lay
still, allowing her limbs to be freed, if not herself. She had
decided some hours ago not to wonder what they had
planned for her. It would only cause her to panic more than
she already was. Instead, she emptied her mind and repeatedly told herself it was a training exercise that would soon
be over. She had to get out alive. She could not bear to think
of Fletcher blaming himself when it was she alone that had
made these decisions.

"Are you okay?" asked the man who had untied her.

Marlene sat bolt upright with her back against the wall. Her eyes snapped open, but it was still too dark to see anything more than the outline of the figure kneeling in front of her. His voice, however, was unmistakable.

Benjamin.

Feeling a fresh boost in her energy levels, Marlene launched herself at him. She screamed out in rage and pounded his chest with her fists. Benjamin tightened his grip around her and simply waited in silence.

"Let me go!" she screamed vehemently, struggling to free herself. "Let me go! How could you do this to me? How could you not tell me you were here? Haven't you heard my screams? How can you listen to the screams of your own flesh and blood and not step in to stop it?"

Benjamin ignored all of her questions and kept his grip firm. Her screaming turned to sobbing as the energy she had mustered dissipated. Her body crumpled, and she fell back against the wall, her arms by her sides.

He got up and struck a match, lighting a nearby candle. The flame flickered and she turned her head away. Her limbs ached following her violent outburst, and her throat was raw from thirst.

She waited for her brother to speak. He made for the door but turned, giving her a look that she understood meant he would be back. He left the door ajar. Her body wasn't strong enough to give in to the temptation to follow him out. He returned moments later, carrying some blankets and two mugs of steaming hot liquid.

"Vegetable soup," he said, handing a mug to her. The heat from the mug in her hands brought her a little comfort, and she sipped on the hot liquid as Benjamin fussed with the blankets. Her stomach groaned loudly as the soup made its way down her throat. Benjamin gestured for her to sit on the blanket, and he wrapped another around her shoulders. He laid the remaining blanket on the floor opposite her and sat down. Sipping his soup, he stared at her. She found it hard to read him. He didn't turn or even flinch when the door opened again.

A man she did not recognise came inside carrying a tray. He placed it down beside Benjamin, glancing only briefly at Marlene before leaving and closing the door. This time, she did not hear it being locked.

Benjamin slid the tray into the space on the floor between them. "You must be starving."

"I am," she said. Her voice was deep, not helped by her screaming at him. "What are you involved in, Benjamin?"

The irony of her words hit her. It hadn't been that long ago that her brother had been asking the same of her.

"I need to ask you the same thing."

Picking up a chunk of bread thinly spread with butter, she shrugged her shoulders. "You know what I've been doing. I already told you all about it in Paris."

"Did you, though?" Benjamin said. "I turn up in Paris, expecting to find you writing articles, and instead I find you are doing favours for a collaborator and in tow with a German. Then you and Henri disappeared. What am I supposed to think of that?"

"Do you know Henri?" she asked, feeling that it was her brother who needed to explain things to her.

"Yes. His job was to get you safely to Paris, and that was all. I didn't know what he was up to until recently. It turns out you were not the only naïve girl he has embroiled in this mess."

Her brother's comment stung, but she knew it was true. Once she had realised her mistake, she simply hadn't found the courage to back out. That was worse than being naïve.

And now she was too scared to ask what damage her actions had caused.

"He's dead, you know," she said, interjecting as Benjamin continued to berate her. "Etienne shot him. I saw it."

"Well, good job, Etienne. I would have done the same thing."

Marlene couldn't imagine a life being taken by her brother's hand. Benjamin leaned forwards and pulled something from his back pocket.

"You had this on you when we picked you up," said Benjamin, handing her the notebook she had been writing in during her time in Paris. Marlene took the notebook from his hands, but she couldn't concentrate on anything but her brother's bruised knuckles and a line of blood that trickled from a cut on his right hand.

"Where is Niklas?" she asked, unable to contain the question that had been simmering away inside her head since she had woken up.

64

ADRIENNE

ADRIENNE PACKED UP HER DESK IN THE SCHOOL OFFICE FOR the last time, meticulously putting each document in its correct file. She left the student register on a corner of her desk and placed her keys in the top drawer.

She politely knocked on the door to Monsieur Mayotte's office, even though it was open wide. He looked up from his desk and smiled warmly at her. She would miss him so much. When he had first retired, she had missed not seeing him each morning, but now they shared this great secret, and it made it even more difficult for her to say goodbye. She always knew him to be of such noble character, and his dealings with Marlene had proven to her he was everything she believed him to be.

"Going home?" he said. "I'm leaving shortly myself."

"You were wonderful with Marlene. I knew I could rely on you to help. You and Madame Mayotte."

"Where I can, I will. Your friend got herself mixed up with a terrible sort. I'm sure she's learned a lesson from it, but it shows the need to be careful, doesn't it?"

Adrienne smiled and nodded in agreement with him. He sounded like a father teaching his daughter life lessons.

"I wanted to let you know I'm leaving," she said.

Monsieur Mayotte raised his eyebrows. "Where are you going?"

"Away. I don't know where. Tomas has escaped from his work camp, and he finally made it home. He trekked for days and arrived last night."

"And is he well?"

"Oh yes. Well, he's thin, but he seems well."

"Do you have somewhere to go?"

"Yes. We have friends who are going to help us. We are leaving tonight."

Monsieur Mayotte got up from his desk and came towards her. "Is there anything I can do for you?"

"Thank you, but no, you've done quite enough. I've enjoyed having you back here, despite the circumstances."

"You come to me if you have any problems," he said, squeezing her shoulder.

He walked to the cupboard she had found the typewriter in and took a key from his pocket. "My not-so-secret hiding place, as you discovered."

"Yes," she said, a little embarrassed.

"I should have remembered your inquisitive nature." He laughed. She glanced past him as he fumbled inside. The typewriter was gone.

"Yes, you really should have." She laughed with him, surprised at how calm she was. She might have been leaving her home that night, but she didn't care because she was leaving it with Tomas. To start again.

He held out a thick bundle of notes folded in the middle. It was more money than she had ever seen at one time. She had taken all the money she and Tomas had saved last night, and it was not nearly half as thick as what Monsieur Mayotte handed her now.

"I can't take this," she said, pushing his outstretched hand away. "I didn't come to you for money."

"I know that, but you can take it," he said, handing it to her again. "I want you to be safe, Adrienne. Money can help. It can get you out of situations that otherwise would be hopeless."

She shook her head and refused to take it from him. "I can't. It's too much."

He slipped the notes into the pocket of her jacket, batting away her hand as she tried to push him back. "I'm old, Adrienne. I've been fortunate in many ways, but Madame Mayotte and I were never blessed with children. Our estate goes to no one. We will not miss this money, and we will feel happier knowing that it might keep you safe rather than sitting in a bank. Now, please take it so you and Tomas can finally enjoy being together again. Hopefully, you will not have to use it, and it can be of some use to you in setting up a new home together after the war."

He hugged her, and she sank into him, embracing him back.

"Thank you so much for everything, Monsieur Mayotte. I hope when I come back one day, you will still be here."

He laughed at this, finding it funny, although that had not been her intention.

"My dear, you will not find me here," he said, gesturing around his office. "But I will be around, God willing. Good luck and be safe."

⁓

On her way home, Adrienne stopped by Philippe's café and

ordered coffee. She couldn't tell Philippe what was going on, but she wanted to see him before she left.

"Any news of Tomas?" he asked, as usual.

"Thank you for always asking," Adrienne replied with a smile. Philippe had become a friend, and she was grateful for his company. She knew he would go looking for her when she didn't show up on Friday. She could only hope that he would not worry about her.

By the time Adrienne arrived home, Tomas was already waiting for her, ready to go. He handed her the shopping bag she had packed the previous night with clothes and other essentials.

"You will leave first," he told her. "I will wait a few minutes and leave by the rear of the building. Head to the train station, but don't go in. My cousin will meet us there. He will have transport and new identity papers for me. Do you have yours with you?"

"Of course," she said. She tapped her pocket; the same pocket that she held the money given to her by Monsieur Mayotte. Tomas was so focused on getting to his cousin that she kept quiet about the money. She would tell him once they were safely in the car and he had relaxed a bit.

"Tomorrow night, sweetheart, we will sleep peacefully in bed together," he said, cupping her face in his hands and kissing her. "See you soon."

She left her home for the last time and walked eagerly towards the future.

65

BENJAMIN IGNORED HER QUESTION ABOUT NIKLAS AND instructed Marlene to tell him everything that had happened since her arrival in France. She left nothing out, from her lucky escape from the Germans on her first night, what she had done for Henri, the Gestapo in her apartment, Etienne's death, and the truth about her relationship with Niklas and his attempts to help her.

"Well, your story matches his, at least," said Benjamin, after taking it all in.

"Matches whose?"

"The German. He's here."

"What have you done to him? I want to see him."

"No."

"He's not like the rest. Please, Benjamin. Where is he?" She knew that a person's first instinct on meeting Niklas was to see the uniform, hear the accent, and explore no further. She had done exactly the same. "Niklas didn't have to let me go in the forest, and he certainly didn't have to come back alone to find me. He could have arrested me, handed me over and accepted the praise for being the one to capture me."

Marlene watched Benjamin closely. She could see him contemplating his next move.

"I won't leave without him," she said. Marlene sat back against the wall and folded her arms, keeping her gaze locked on her brother.

"Come with me," he said, sighing. He got up and pulled Marlene to her feet. It took her a minute to straighten herself up after spending so long curled up on the floor. The pain in her ankle was more bearable, and she limped along behind Benjamin.

He led her down a corridor and unlocked the door at the end. It was dark inside the room, like it had been in hers, but Benjamin had brought the lit candle with them. Marlene took the light from him and entered.

Niklas lay on the floor, bound as she had been. Marlene placed the candle down beside him. One eye was swollen and already turning a deep purple. She noticed a spot of dried blood on his cheek but couldn't tell where it had come from. There were no cuts on his face. Her heart ached for him, and from knowing that it was probably her brother that had done this to him.

"Help me," she said to Benjamin as she pulled at the ropes tying his wrists.

When Marlene had freed his wrists, Niklas took her hands in his. His face softened and he held her gaze for a few seconds before he released her hands and untied the rope around his ankles.

"Are you okay?" Niklas asked Marlene, eyeing Benjamin cautiously. Benjamin didn't move from the door.

"I'm fine."

Niklas still stared at Benjamin. Marlene sensed the

tension in the room and knew for certain that this was not the first time that Niklas had seen her brother whilst he had been held here.

"We are safe now," she said, trying to ease the situation. "We are with the Resistance."

"Marlene!" Benjamin snapped.

"I told you before, he's a friend." She turned back to Niklas, searching his face. He must have been declared missing by now, and she wouldn't allow Benjamin to put him in any more danger. She was the reason he was here, and she wouldn't leave him until she knew he was safe.

"We can talk more in the morning. Until then, I expect you will want somewhere to wash and get some sleep," said Benjamin. "It's a car ride away."

Marlene helped Niklas to his feet, and they followed Benjamin. Before they left the house, she went into the room where she had been held and picked up the remaining slice of bread. When she returned, Benjamin and Niklas were waiting for her. Niklas stood blindfolded, his hands bound again.

"Come on, Benjamin. That's not necessary," Marlene protested.

"It is if you want him to come with us," Benjamin replied, then turned and stalked outside.

Marlene tore off a piece of the bread and put it to Niklas's lips. He took it, and she squeezed his bound hands as she helped him outside, wishing she had more to offer him. Her stomach wrenched at the bruises to his eye, and she suspected from his slow pace that there were others. She couldn't yet bring herself to ask him what had happened.

Once outside, Marlene could see they were on a farm somewhere, and the rooms that had held them were part of the main farmhouse. There were outbuildings to the side of the house, but there were no signs of activity in them. There were no signs of activity anywhere, except for a faint glow in one of the upstairs windows of the main house. It was early evening, meaning she and Niklas had been held for almost twenty-four hours.

A car was parked to the far side, half on the grass and half on a path. The door they had come out of was not the front door to the property. The front door was a large grand entrance with white paint shining in the dark. It looked neat and clean and normal, no doubt purposefully so. She wondered how many people passed this farmhouse every day and how many of those suspected what went on inside.

Benjamin opened the back door of the car for Marlene, and Niklas climbed in with her. Marlene loosened the rope tying his hands and slid her fingers between his. Benjamin paused, as if going to say something, but decided against it. He pushed the door gently, and it clicked quietly closed. He got into the driver's seat and asked Marlene and Niklas if they were okay. Marlene nodded, whilst Niklas was silent and still.

Benjamin started the engine with keys he had removed from a small shelf under the steering wheel and set off down the farm track which lead away from the house.

Lights shone up ahead as the car trundled along a narrow and uneven road. Each hole was deep enough to cause Benjamin to slow his approach and for the car to tilt in one direction, then the other, as it bounced along. The village ahead was in darkness.

Two men wandered slowly across the road in front of them, their swagger clearly affected by the volume of alcohol they must have consumed that evening. Through their slurred words, Marlene heard a song about coal miners. She was so focused on the men that it took her some time to notice where she was. When she did, however, she couldn't believe it.

"Benjamin, where are we?" she said, leaning forwards to speak over his shoulder.

"You don't recognise it?"

Niklas straightened and looked around, despite still being blindfolded. Marlene wondered if it was instinctive or if he could distinguish between light and dark.

"But, why are we here?" she asked as they drove through the village of Giverny, where she and Benjamin had grown up.

"You'll see," he said and kept driving.

They drove through the village and turned immediately left. Marlene knew the driveway so well, having spent her childhood trudging up and down it to and from her grandparents' farm. She didn't know what to think. Benjamin had told her he'd sold it.

Her mind was racing, but she ignored it. Instead, Marlene stared through the gap between the car's front seats and allowed herself to experience the full emotions of coming back. She thought about her mother and the last time they had walked together up this driveway, and how she had slept with her curtains open so that each morning she could look up the driveway to see if her mother was at last coming back for her. The treks she had made into town when her grandmother forbade her from running across the fields, the reasons for which changed frequently between it not being what little girls were supposed to do and that she didn't need any extra washing from the clothes Marlene spoiled in the mud.

The house was now only a few feet away. Benjamin stopped the car at the front door. It was grander than Marlene remembered, standing proudly in front of her as she got out of the car and helped Niklas out as well. She looked up at the window on the second floor. Her old bedroom.

Benjamin opened the front door and stood aside for Marlene and Niklas to enter. She scanned the farm, but it was too dark to see it properly, and she shivered despite the warmth coming from inside.

The lit stove inside her grandparents' kitchen immediately warmed her. She had expected it to be dreary and sparse now that her grandparents were both gone, but it was very much lived in. Warm and tidy. She looked to Benjamin for an explanation, but she followed his gaze to the stairs, where a woman descended.

Benjamin went over to her and kissed her cheek as she reached the foot of the stairs. The woman looked around her nervously before her eyes settled on Marlene. She smiled gently and tucked her shoulder length brown hair behind her ears.

"Brigitte, this is Marlene. Marlene, Brigitte is my wife."

Marlene stared, knowing she was being rude, but she couldn't help herself.

"Nice to meet you, Brigitte," Niklas said, still blindfolded and bound yet polite enough to break the uncomfortable silence that had formed. "I am Niklas."

"Nice to meet you, Niklas," Brigitte said hesitantly, glaring at Benjamin with her hands raised.

"Marlene wouldn't leave without him." Benjamin removed the blindfold from Niklas and unbound his hands.

Brigitte turned to Marlene and extended her hand. "I've heard a lot about you, Marlene." Marlene shook her hand

and allowed Brigitte to kiss her cheeks, but she still could say nothing.

"Sit down," Benjamin said to Niklas. His tone was demanding, and his eyes were narrow.

They all took a seat at the wooden table in the middle of the kitchen, except for Brigitte, who busied herself at the stove. The table had been set for three people. Either Brigitte would not be joining them or Benjamin had not expected to be bringing Niklas back with them. Marlene knew it was the latter.

Marlene rubbed her eyes with the palm of her hands. "Why did you have to snatch me from the street?" she asked.

Benjamin glanced at Niklas. There was a long stretch of silence before he answered. "My original plan was to come to Paris and bring you back here with me. But, honestly, would you have come with me then?"

She wouldn't have. Although she already had concerns, she had kept telling herself she was doing the right thing, something that mattered.

"The Paris network is imploding and communications are compromised. We think Henri tried to buy himself favour by giving details of Resistance members to the Gestapo."

"And I was an easy target," she said, finding the words hard to say.

"He *thought* you were an easy target. You proved to be anything but. When I came back to get you, I saw someone following you. Once I had ... *dealt* with that situation, you had disappeared and the Gestapo had shown up at your apartment. I tracked you to a safe house, waiting for your return flight to London."

Marlene nodded. "The flight that couldn't land." She resisted the urge to ask him *how* he had dealt with whoever had been following her. No good could come from that knowledge.

"When I found you again, I had to prove you weren't working with Henri, that you weren't a collaborator."

Benjamin reached out and ran his hand around her wrist. The physical wounds would heal soon, at least. Marlene swallowed, still feeling nauseous whenever she thought of that night; the freezing, hard floor, the pain in her head, and the terror that she wouldn't make it out alive.

"So you sold the farm," she said to lighten the mood and push away the fear rising inside her once again.

Benjamin laughed. "Not quite. It sort of turned into my office, so I thought it best if you believed it was gone. That way, you wouldn't show up and get yourself involved in all this."

"Seems like the plan didn't work."

"No. It didn't. It would have done, had you not had the great idea to come back to France. I think we're all tired, though, so we should probably eat something and retire for the night. We can discuss everything in the morning."

Brigitte placed a pan of stew in the centre of the table and ladled it into the bowls. She served Marlene first, then Niklas, and finally Benjamin, taking none herself. She poured red wine into glasses, giving each of them, including herself this time, one before finally sitting down opposite Marlene.

"When did you marry?" Niklas asked, breaking the silence once again, but avoiding the difficult subjects. Brigitte seemingly noticed his empty wine glass and refilled it and brought him a glass of water. The woman was perceptive, Marlene thought.

"Two years ago," Benjamin said. Marlene spluttered into her wine. "We were married in the village by the Reverend

Allard. He's been in the village forever. He tells us he is waiting for a replacement to be appointed, but I don't know. I'm not sure what he would do without his church. He's a nosy old fool who likes to know everyone's business."

"Quite. The gossip he gets from his Sunday service keeps him alive, I think. Do you remember him, Marlene?" Brigitte asked.

Marlene glared at her. She wanted to shout that of course she remembered him. She had spent years of her life living here, unlike Brigitte. She didn't, however. Brigitte was just trying to get Marlene involved in the conversation, and her anger was really directed towards Benjamin. Brigitte reached across the table and gave Marlene's arm a gentle squeeze. Marlene stayed silent, not trusting herself to let her emotions fly if she opened her mouth.

66

THE FARMHOUSE WAS SILENT WHEN MARLENE WOKE. SHE pushed the covers off and got out of the bed she had slept in every night as a child. Moving to the window, Marlene scrunched her toes up into the carpet and dragged her hand along the dresser. Pulling the curtains back, she stared along the farm track. For a long time, she had hoped she would see her mother walking up that track again. It was years before she accepted that she never would.

The bedroom door creaked with old age as she opened it. The hallway was dark. With no windows, the only light visible came through Marlene's bedroom window, which was not much given that the sun had yet to rise.

Downstairs was quieter still, emphasised by the rhythmic ticking of the grandfather clock by the door. Marlene ran her hand along the large kitchen table, her fingers dipping into the grooves and dents that represented her life here. The table was the one place in the house where the individuals that lived in the farmhouse became a family.

"I never asked if you resented having us around," Marlene said to the photo of her grandparents from the top of the sideboard.

"Of course they didn't." Benjamin stood at the foot of the stairs.

"I didn't hear you get up," said Marlene, startled by his unexpected presence.

"An occupational hazard these days, sleeping light. I know every sound in the house, so when I hear a new noise, I investigate." He shrugged his shoulders and brought his hand up. Marlene could now see the pistol he held. He laid it on the kitchen table and sat down. "Marlene, you really have to stop seeing the negative in everything."

"I don't."

"They didn't resent having us around."

"How do you know?" She sat down at the table with him, now holding the photograph of their grandparents. "They had raised their child and their lives had moved on. Then, all of a sudden, they had another two children to raise. It shouldn't have been."

"You're right about that. It shouldn't have been. But did you ever stop to think about what it *should* have been? Being raised by your mother is the way it should have been. But what would that have looked like?"

"What do you mean? This is about them. What they had to put up with." She cradled the photograph in her hands.

"They were glad we were with them and not her. She was my mother, too, you know, and I'm so happy she deserted us here. You were, what, five when she left you?"

Marlene nodded.

"I had just turned six. I know your first five years were the same as my first six. Maybe I remember it more clearly.

How many homes did you live in? How many schools did you go to? How many men was she with, and how many times did you see them beat her?"

"That's not fair to say these things when she is not here to speak for herself." Marlene was angry now.

"How many times did you see her crying?"

"Benjamin, stop!"

"How many times did you leave in the middle of the night? Most times, I would guess. Either because the landlord said he was coming in the morning to get the rent but she had no money or ..."

"And this was her fault?" Marlene asked, cutting him off. "She didn't ask to have that kind of life."

"Well, it wasn't *our* fault."

"Bad things happen to good people."

"Yes. I believe that. You know that better than anyone, Marlene, but you have to cope. You have to get up and move on."

"Wasn't that what she was always trying to do?"

"No. She ran away. She was unhappy with the life she had, but she did nothing to change it. If she had left me here, started again and changed her situation, maybe what you say could be true. She didn't. Within a year, she was pregnant, and so it began again. She learned nothing. She let it all happen again in exactly the same way. If you had another chance at life, would you do it all exactly the same way?"

Marlene shook her head but did not speak. She wanted so much to tell Benjamin that he was wrong, that their mother had done the best she could, but she no longer believed it. She knew that, one day, she would admit to herself that she had never believed it. The pretence was just less painful than the truth.

His words stuck in her head. *If you had another chance at life, would you do it all exactly the same way?*

67

Marlene stood in the farmyard, looking around the landscape that was her childhood home, squinting in the low sun. The single tree in the yard still stood tall, and the three outbuildings were in a better condition than they had been the last time she'd been here.

She hadn't yet come across any workers, but it was still a working farm. The herd of dairy cattle was much smaller, but they still trimmed the grass and produced milk. The same two fields were dedicated to vegetables and an orchard with mixed fruit trees. The trees were bare, waiting for spring. She had spent many hours in that field, picking fruit alongside her grandparents, a few regular workers and some seasonal workers that had been passing through.

A row of trees, a small wooded area that was a favourite place for Marlene and Benjamin to play as children, bordered the bottom of the fields. Beyond it was the village and the Seine. With nothing but fields and trees to look upon, the isolation of the countryside had worked its magic. She felt safe.

"We have to give most of our output to the Germans, but

I take the extra produce to the market in town," said Brigitte as she came out of the house and walked towards Marlene. Her long dark hair glinted in the sunshine as she headed to the fields to check the animals, and Marlene traipsed alongside her, pretending to do the same. "Have you seen the pantry? It's full of jars of jam, preserves and pickled vegetables. Visitors usually love it in there. There'll be something you like, I'm sure."

Marlene plastered on a smile, not feeling up to conversation. Brigitte continued to chat, with Marlene allowing her words to fade into the background. Her thoughts drifted to her time in Paris, what she had done and the people that had risked their own safety to get her out. She had made friends quickly in Paris, ironically, the city where she had been the most guarded. In London, she had closed herself off from people when there was no need to. Whether her future lay in London, France, or somewhere else, she would let people in.

"The Germans raided us," said Brigitte, bringing Marlene back to the present. "Only once, thankfully. When they saw the stocks we had built up, they were quite in awe. I told them it was to see us through the winter. I said they could take some, which they did. Actually, they took it all. They filled three crates. Not that I minded; it distracted them well enough that they didn't notice the false wall."

"The false wall? There isn't a false wall in there."

Brigitte nodded. "There is these days. Benjamin built it. He keeps a lot of his work there. It's also a bedroom when we have any guests we need to keep hidden for a while. Like that agent you know."

"Which agent?" Marlene asked, now giving Brigitte her full attention.

"The one that told Benjamin you were here."

"I thought Fletcher told Benjamin I was here."

Brigitte looked confused and shook her head. "He found out our name and asked if we were any relation to you. He said he flew with you. The poor man was in a right state when he arrived. He'd been with the Germans for a couple of weeks, but he got away when they tried to take him somewhere else. He stayed hidden in the room until we could move him. The Germans have never been back, so it was probably being overcautious, but you know Benjamin."

Marlene wasn't sure she did.

Marlene stood on the steps of the main house and watched Niklas mucking out the barn that housed the animals at night. Cattle had circled around him as if they were investigating the stranger who seemed at home in their midst. He moved easier than he had done the day before. The long soak in the bath he'd had on his arrival and Brigitte's help to clean and cover his cuts had made him feel so much better, or so he'd told Marlene.

"He's not bad," Benjamin said, appearing at Marlene's side.

"If this experience has taught me anything, it's that there are good people, bad people, and many people in between on both sides of this war. It's not as simple as who's good or who's bad."

"I was talking about his mucking out skills," said Benjamin.

"Oh. Yes, he's not bad. For a teacher," said Marlene. She smiled at the sight of Niklas spreading clean hay around the barn floor. He looked at peace.

"A *teacher*?" Benjamin asked.

"Surprised? He had a life before the war, you know." She turned to look at Benjamin. "I hope he has one after."

"He will. I'll take care of it," Benjamin said. Marlene raised her eyebrows. "What? I have to. I brought him into our home. That means I have to help him or I have to shoot him."

"That's not entirely reassuring," Marlene said.

Benjamin put his arm around her shoulders and gave her an affectionate squeeze. "I'm not sure I did. Have a life before the war, I mean. And I'm not sure what's going to be waiting for me on the other side."

"You'll be all right. I shouldn't say this, but it seems to have had a good impact on you. You've become a man," she said, messing up his hair playfully.

"I know." Benjamin laughed. "It allowed me to rebel at a time when that is a highly sought after skill."

Marlene nodded in agreement. She continued to watch Niklas and wondered how long it would be before he could return to teaching; how long it would be before this whole thing was over.

The sky closed in around them as the blue sky almost instantaneously turned to black.

"You know," Benjamin said, "war causes people to commit some unspeakable acts."

Marlene slipped her arm around Benjamin's waist. "Some people do it because they're evil. Most people are doing it to survive."

"I guess he'll return to teaching. It's just you and I who have to start from scratch," said Benjamin.

"All we can do is focus on ending this brutality as quickly as possible. Then look at rebuilding. Our country, our relationships *and* ourselves."

The black clouds burst and allowed their heavy loads to

spill. Marlene and Benjamin stepped back inside the door and waited for Niklas, who appeared not to have noticed yet. The loud growl of thunder soon changed this, and he came running towards the house with his jacket over his head.

The multitude of scents and waves of warmth coming from the kitchen each time the oven doors opened gave away the plans for that afternoon. Brigitte busied herself stirring the many pots on top of the stove, and Marlene sliced ham and cheese. Her forehead creased with concentration as she tried to get the slices thin and even.

Brigitte had got up early to begin cooking and had barely stopped until now. When everyone else had come to the kitchen for breakfast, she had announced that they were having a going away party. Benjamin had said that when he left, he would be gone for a couple of weeks. He didn't elaborate, and Marlene didn't press him on the matter. She hadn't really considered what impact this must have had on Brigitte, or Benjamin. Benjamin had chosen this life for now, but Brigitte had only chosen a husband and was stuck dealing with everything that went along with him. She looked forward to getting to know her sister-in-law better when the time was right.

Benjamin snuck a couple of pieces of ham from the plate Marlene had so neatly arranged. "There's plenty more where that came from, so cut good man-sized chunks," he said

"Really?" she asked.

"Well, no, not really, but it's a party."

Benjamin and Niklas would leave first thing in the morning. Marlene didn't know exactly where they were going. Benjamin had only told her he was handing Niklas over as a prisoner of war. Before Marlene had time to raise her voice at this, Niklas stopped her and explained it was the only way. Marlene had said he couldn't possibly be all right about becoming a POW, but he had reminded her that the alternative was returning to Paris, explaining his mysterious disappearance and his involvement with a woman who was believed to be a spy for the Resistance.

Brigitte would take Marlene away that evening, and she would fly out the way she had flown in. She had wanted Benjamin to go with her, but he had said transporting Niklas was the most dangerous, so he had to do that. She didn't like it, but she knew he was right.

"Are we almost ready?" Benjamin asked Brigitte, who nodded. As he transferred dishes full of food to the table, he turned to Marlene. "Go and fetch your boy."

Marlene grabbed a coat from beside the front door. Niklas sat on a trailer a little away from the house. She sat beside him, their arms touching, and looked out onto the farm. It had the illusion of ordinariness, but she now knew otherwise.

"Are you worried?" Marlene asked.

"A little. Are you?"

"Yes."

He held her hand between his palms, and they sat in silence. There was so much to say, but nothing felt quite right.

"I won't be going home yet, so I still won't see my daughter, but at least this way, I have a better chance of going home to her when this is all over." Niklas intertwined his fingers in hers, and Marlene allowed him to stay lost in his own thoughts for a minute.

"I'm so sorry I got you involved in my mess," she said. "I

should never have got myself into this, let alone anyone else."

"Don't be sorry," he said, turning to look at her. "I didn't have to get involved. That was my choice, not yours."

"I'm really going to miss you," she said, finally feeling as though she didn't have to hold back how she felt.

He smiled and squeezed her hand. "What will you do now?" he asked.

"Write my articles and see what I'm allowed to publish. Although I might not mention you," Marlene said.

Niklas laughed and shook his head. "Wise."

"I'm going to be staying in London for now. Uniting people with extraordinary stories is how I can make the biggest difference until this war ends. Then it's up to me. And I'm okay with that. Will I see you again?"

Marlene reached out and kissed him, not waiting for an answer. His hand moved up and cupped her cheek, his touch sending a tingle down her spine and a heat that spread throughout her body. She moved her hand to the back of his neck and they pulled apart. Looking into his dark brown eyes, her feelings for him were clearer than they had ever been. Her heart ached for what she had done to him, and for what he might have to go through next. She dropped her eyes to her knees.

Niklas reached up and took her hand from his neck, holding it in his. "I don't regret any of this," he said. "And I'll find you again. I'm good at it, right?"

Marlene laughed, slumped her body towards his and rested her head on his shoulder. He wrapped his arm around the back of her body and held her until Benjamin whistled from the door.

"That boy always thinks of his stomach," said Marlene.

Niklas hopped off the trailer and helped Marlene down.

She gripped his hand, not wanting to be separated from him until she had to be.

"Come on, let's eat," he said. "I can smell it from here, and it's making me hungry."

As the evening drew in, the boys got louder and louder as the wine from the cellar took its hold. Marlene was pleased that their last night spent together was a happy, relaxed one. She had expected it to be tense, with Benjamin lecturing her on what she should never have done and what she should do now. Without that, once she got on the plane, her next moves were entirely up to her, and she finally felt ready for that.

Brigitte stood and squeezed Benjamin on the shoulder; a simple gesture that told everyone their evening and their time together was at an end.

"Next time we see each other," Marlene said to Benjamin, "I promise not to bring my problems to your door."

"Ah, he's not so bad," Benjamin said, grabbing Niklas playfully by the shoulders as they all stood. "But seriously, don't regret what has happened. You can do nothing to change it. Thankfully, you are fine, more or less. What's in the past is in the past. Move on, Marlene, and concentrate on what has still to come for you."

"Whatever that is," she said.

"To London," said Niklas, raising his glass to Marlene. "And to staying out of trouble. Knowing you has been one of the best *and* worst adventures. Until the next one."

Benjamin picked up his glass also and passed Marlene's to her.

"Until the next one," Benjamin said, echoing Niklas's words.

"Oh, goodness. Please tell me you lot are not planning

more of this saga," said Brigitte on her way back down the stairs.

They all laughed as the atmosphere relaxed once again. Brigitte was wearing her coat and was tucking the hair from around her face inside the edges of the woollen hat she wore. "It's another cold one," she said to Marlene, handing her a similar hat.

"Thank you, Brigitte," said Marlene, taking the hat from her. "For looking after us so well, and for obviously doing the same for him," she said, nodding towards her brother as he looked on.

"You're welcome," Brigitte said.

Marlene hugged Benjamin, then turned to Niklas. Brigitte kept Benjamin busy with a hug and Marlene heard her whisper the words "Be safe" to him. Niklas helped Marlene put on her coat. His arms circled around her body, and she buried her face into his neck, savouring the warmth of his breath in her hair. He squeezed her tight, then pulled back, kissing her one last time.

Marlene's composure slipped as the reality of leaving finally hit her. She covered her eyes as a sob escaped. Brigitte took her by the shoulders and kept her moving towards the car.

"I do hope you'll come back to see us when this is all over," said Brigitte.

The car was hurtling along narrow roads towards some unknown destination. Marlene had recognised some of the earlier roads they had travelled upon, but now she didn't know where they were or where they were heading.

Marlene moaned and put a hand to her queasy stomach.

The roads spiralled in front of them and the car lurched in all directions as it battered across large holes in the ground. The speed with which Brigitte took the corners showed her familiarity with the roads.

"You should lower your window a little. Fresh air always helps," her sister-in-law said.

Marlene lowered the window, closed her eyes and tilted her head towards the cool draught.

When the car finally slowed, Marlene opened her eyes to another farmhouse not too dissimilar to her grandparents' ahead of her. Brigitte was leaning forwards for a better view of the narrow track they were on. The fencing on either side of the track was broken, and the occasional section of wood lay in front of them. Brigitte opted to drive straight over the wood rather than get out and move it, which made the last part of their journey the bumpiest yet.

"Are you feeling better now?" Brigitte asked.

"Yes, thanks," said Marlene.

"This is the house of a friend of Benjamin's. He has a good field for the planes to land in." She parked the car beside another two in front of the building and turned the engine off. "It's almost time," she said, checking her watch. "Are you ready to go home?"

"Definitely!" She was glad her brother had someone looking after him, and she was glad that it was Brigitte.

68

THE DOOR TO THE FARMHOUSE OPENED BEFORE THEY HAD GOT close enough to knock. An old man now stood in their path. His face was friendly, but serious. Scanning the scene behind them, he stepped aside and allowed them entry to his home.

"You are just in time," he said. "Please, come through."

He led them to a small kitchen in the building's rear. It was dishevelled, with wooden shelves on the walls almost bending in the middle under the strain. They were heaped with plates of varying sizes and a multitude of patterns. There were cans, the labels of which had long since peeled off, their contents now known only to their owner. Scraps of metal and slithers of chopped wood cluttered the others, for no apparent purpose Marlene could discern.

The old man fumbled with a row of jackets hanging on the back of the door that led outside. He eventually selected one and slipped it on.

"Make yourself at home whilst we are gone," he said to Brigitte. "You can come with me." He beckoned for Marlene to follow him.

Something was familiar about the man, but Marlene couldn't quite decide what it was. Brigitte hugged Marlene, who grinned and nodded at her new sister-in-law and then followed the old man from his house. He led her in silence to the edge of the farm. The path ahead was lit by the glistening silver of the full moon in the sky, and the air was calm. *Perfect landing conditions.*

Two other men and one woman met them in the field. Marlene kept quiet as everyone around her occupied themselves with various tasks and conversations about the time and the light. She listened instead to the sky above them for the plane arriving.

"Here she comes," said the woman standing beside her. The old man looked up and nodded in agreement. Marlene smiled to herself as she heard the rumble above her.

The Lysander landed and, once it had slowed, they all ran towards it. The two women climbed the ladder into the cramped rear cockpit, strapping themselves in. The old man stepped back and waved at them from the field. In that moment, she recognised him. He was *W.B.*, the man who had given her his handkerchief on the day she had fallen from her bicycle.

"I give up trying to figure this all out," she said.

"Figure what out?" the other woman said.

"Oh, sorry. I hadn't realised I had said that out loud."

"It can have that effect on you," the woman said, nodding to herself. "Was your trip successful?"

"I wouldn't say that."

"Well, you're still here. That, to me, is the biggest success."

Marlene had to agree. The plane's engine roared, and, moments later, she was finally on her way home. The last time she had left Paris, she was full of hope for her future with Peter. That hope had been slowly eroded, then, all at once, crushed completely. Leaving now, despite everything, she felt hopeful once again.

She also had to wonder how George would take the news of her having been aboard a plane with one of those female agents he wanted to write about.

69

HOPING TO AVOID HER COLLEAGUES FOR A WHILE YET, Marlene had asked Fletcher to meet her in a café a short distance from the office. She purposefully chose one that she didn't recall anyone at *The Post* ever mentioning. Choosing a table for two near the back, she took off her coat and sat facing the door. She ordered tea for two and poured her own when it came.

The place she had chosen was perfect. It had a stubby candle burning in the centre of each of the chunky wooden tables. It didn't have many windows, and the ones it had were high up and small. Whereas others might have thought the café dingy, to Marlene, it was warm and intimate. It was safe.

She was pouring her second cup when Fletcher arrived. He came in the door, almost at a run. Hanging his coat and his hat on the coat stand near the entrance, he caused quite a commotion by nearly knocking the thing over. Once he had steadied it, he spotted Marlene and headed towards her.

His face was flushed, and his breath was short and heavy.

"I'm so glad you're back," he said before he reached the table. "It feels like it's been such a long time. Welcome home." His arms were outstretched.

Marlene went to him and held him tightly. He ignored her first attempt to break their embrace. When he released her, she returned to her seat, and Fletcher wedged himself into the seat opposite without taking the time to pull it out at all. "Menus?" he said to no one in particular.

The waitress arrived by his side with a menu, and he quickly made his selection.

"For you?" he said, handing the menu to Marlene.

"I'll have the same, thanks," she said to the waitress. Movement caught her eye behind Fletcher, and she smiled.

Fletcher turned. "Did you follow me?"

"Hey, I'm a reporter," George said, approaching their table. "You pay me for my curiosity."

Marlene stood, and George immediately grabbed her, his powerful arms completely enclosing her frame. He lifted her off her feet and squeezed her tightly.

"I'm so happy you're alive," George said, releasing her back to the ground. "I was starting to think I might need to look for a new French tutor."

George turned a seat from the next table around and wedged it in beside Fletcher's chair, so as not to block the passageway.

"So, how did you get on?" Fletcher said.

Marlene poured Fletcher a cup of tea from the pot and added his milk while George signalled for the waitress to bring him another cup. Terrence had been right all those months ago; it had been a career-defining opportunity for her. It had also been life-defining, and she was determined to make the most of having survived it.

With her feet very much back on London soil, where she planned to keep them for quite some time, she told Fletcher and George her story.

EPILOGUE

March 1944, Scotland

As Marlene climbed down the steps of her second bus journey that day, her energy returned. She had finally arrived.

"Oakfield Farm is up there on your left," the driver said.

Marlene waved her thanks and set off towards the farm. Benjamin's letter had been brief, as usual. *If you're in Scotland, head to Oakfield Farm*. The address in Fife had been listed underneath, but there were no other details. She couldn't tell when he had written the letter, so she didn't know if he would even still be here.

Once she reached the top of the farm road, sweating from carrying her suitcase, small though it was, and the steep gradient of the track, she turned and marvelled at the view. The River Forth was calm, and the iconic Forth Rail Bridge sat majestically in her waters.

"Beautiful," she said as she lifted her head for a moment, enjoying the fresh air coming in from the water. She picked her suitcase up again and headed towards the only person she could see on the farm.

"Hello there," she said as she approached. The man had his head down, unloading something from the back of a trailer.

He stood up straight and looked up the farm road, as if checking where she had come from. His navy blue overalls were filthy from a full day of farming, and his grey hair clung to the sides of his face from sweat.

"I'm looking for Benjamin," said Marlene.

"There's no Benjamin here," he said, returning to unloading empty crates and stacking them in a pile at the back of the trailer.

"This is Oakfield Farm, is it not?"

"Aye, it is," he said, not looking up.

Marlene turned at the sound of crunching gravel behind her. A woman approached. An apron covered her clothes, and she wiped her hands on a dishtowel. She looked Marlene up and down, but the energy she gave off and the smile on her weathered face were friendly.

"The lassie's looking for Benjamin, but I told her he's not here," the man said.

"But you know Benjamin?" Marlene asked, looking between the man and woman.

"I don't know a Benjamin," he said.

"Where are you headed?" the woman asked, studying the suitcase Marlene had put down at her feet.

"Here," Marlene said. "I have a room booked at a guesthouse near here, but I wanted to come here first. My brother wrote to me and told me to come here. Benjamin Villeret. You're sure you don't know him?"

The woman shook her head. "Where have you travelled from?"

"London."

"London! Oh goodness! That's quite a journey. Come in and I'll fetch you some tea. You must be staying at Sylvia's place. I'll have one of the boys drive you over once you've had something to eat. Come on with me. I'm Annie, by the way, and that's Harry."

Exhaustion threatened to overwhelm her. Benjamin had sent her here for a reason; she just needed to figure out what that reason was. For now, she allowed herself to be led towards the house by Annie.

Once inside, Annie told Marlene to sit at the wooden kitchen table as she busied herself making tea. Harry soon joined them and scrubbed at his hands with soap and water at the sink.

"Sounds like you've come a long way for nothing," Harry said.

Marlene sat, her brows furrowed. "Not for nothing. There's a reason Benjamin sent me here. I assumed he was here, or at least he had been. What do you farm here?"

"Everything we can," Harry said. Annie had poured Marlene a very welcome cup of tea and cut her a slice of some sort of sponge cake.

"It's lambing season," Annie said. "The first ones were born this week. I'll show you them before you go, if you like."

"Benjamin ..." Harry said. He took a big gulp of tea and shook his head.

"Villeret," Marlene added.

"Is that French?" asked Annie.

Marlene nodded.

"We've never had any Frenchmen here," Harry said. "It's all Germans."

Marlene's head shot up. "*Germans*?"

"Oh, don't worry. We've had no trouble with them. They're all good workers." Harry shovelled a piece of cake into his mouth.

Marlene stood to look out of the window. "Do you mind if I have a look around?"

Harry's eyes narrowed. "What for?"

"Of course we don't mind, love," Annie said, slapping Harry with the dishtowel she had yet to put down. "You have a good look. Maybe you'll see whatever it is you're here for."

"Thank you."

"You can leave that there for now," Annie said, looking at Marlene's suitcase. "And you'll find some of the boys in the lambing shed out the back. The rest will be in the fields."

Marlene headed for the lambing shed first. *Could he really be here?*

Her insides were swirling, and her pulse pounded in her ears. She pulled the barn door towards her and went inside.

A man straightened and watched her. He leaned on the wooden handle of the shovel he'd been holding. It wasn't him.

Metal railings made up individual pens, each holding a sheep and one or two lambs. Some were sound asleep while others watched the newcomer in their midst. Then she saw him, crouched down, rubbing a lamb with a handful of straw. She sucked in a breath and her hand flew to the flutter in her chest. He looked up and their eyes met. The lamb let out a high-pitched bleat, and he placed it back beside its mother.

Marlene's feet stuck to the straw on the barn floor, and her hands trembled. *Did he want to see her?*

He rose and stepped forwards warily, not taking his eyes off her.

"Is it really you?" Niklas asked.

She nodded.

Niklas looked down at his hands and clothing, stained from his work in the barn. Marlene didn't care. She reached out and clutched his hands. The second their skin touched, he pulled her towards him and kissed her.

This time, she didn't care where they were or who might be watching. Everything felt right.

ACKNOWLEDGMENTS

I'd like to thank Helen Sedgwick at Wildland Literary Editors for your incredibly helpful developmental feedback during the writing process. Thank you also to Pete Smith at Novel Approach Manuscript Services for your work to get the final manuscript ready for publication.

Thank you to the team at MiblArt for my cover design.

Thank you to Mum and Dad. I appreciate all that you've done for me.

As always, my love and thanks to Gavin, Evie and Stuart. Gavin, for reading multiple drafts of every book and giving me the support and encouragement to keep writing, thank you.

ABOUT THE AUTHOR

Claire Anders lives in Edinburgh, Scotland, with her husband and daughter. When she's not writing, you can usually find her walking her dog in the nearby woods or with a book in one hand and chocolate in the other.

Between Moons is her first novel.